FATES OF ASTRAEUS

Fates of
Astraeus

of

The Akallian Tales: Book Three

Jeramy Goble

Noachian Books
North Carolina

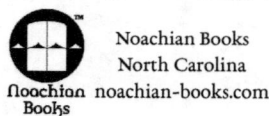

Noachian Books
North Carolina
noachian-books.com

Noachian Books and the portrayal of a flooded Martian silhouette with stone tablet insets are trademarks of Noachian Books

Edited by Jeramy Goble
Printed in the United States of America

jeramygoble.com
facebook.com/JeramyGoble
twitter.com/JeramyGoble

Publisher's Cataloging-in-Publication Data

Names: Goble, Jeramy.
Title: Fates of Astraeus / Jeramy Goble.
Description: Maggie Valley, NC : Noachian Books, 2016. | Series: The Akallian tales, bk. 3.
Identifiers: LCCN 2016909258 | ISBN 978-0-9898841-7-4 (pbk.) | ISBN 978-0-9898841-6-7 (hardcover) | ISBN 978-0-9898841-8-1 (ebook)
Subjects: LCSH: Extraterrestrial beings--Fiction. | Reincarnation--Fiction. | Cultural pluralism--Fiction. | Space warfare--Fiction. | Science fiction, American. | Adventure stories. | BISAC: FICTION / Science Fiction / General. | FICTION / Science Fiction / Action & Adventure. | FICTION / Science Fiction / Space Opera. | GSAFD: Science fiction. | Adventure fiction.
Classification: LCC PS3607.O26 F38 2016 (print) | LCC PS3607.O26 (ebook) | DDC 813/.6--dc23

First Edition

10 9 8 7 6 5 4 3 2 1

For empathy and epiphanies.

fates
of
Astraeus

The Akallian Tales: Book Three

Jeramy Goble

Chapter I

Disembarking

AZLI'S FOOTSTEPS BOUNCED and clunked the gangplank with an exaggerated violence that Lannya's mind had no choice but to entertain. Her paranoia turned Azli's steps into a dirge leading to a future that Lannya couldn't imagine at that moment. She only had an empty mental box to work with. The potential contents, were too scary to place inside. As much as Lannya wanted to keep her worries at bay, she had little say. Her fear was real, primal, and maternal. It was an instinct that she had to entertain without option, like being the torturer, and the tortured, at the same time. There was no peace. *What are they going to do with Azli?* Her mind looped neurotically.

The seconds tore away slowly as Lannya watched Azli shuffle down the gangplank to the docks. Lannya had to bite her tongue to keep from crying out of hysteria. She watched as her daughter pitifully crept downwards, still wrapped in her blanket, and with a set of ribbon restraints on her wrists. Azli asked before pulling into the docks to go out first and insisted on wearing restraints. Regardless of Lannya saying they weren't necessary, and Azli not truly wanting to wear them, they quickly and silently nodded to an agreement that having Azli exit Paige while restrained was probably the more prudent decision.

In the blurry haze of her out-of-body worry, Lannya was distracted by the faint movement of Rigella, far ahead under one of the entryways of the Harbor, stepping over to an ADF subordinate. *What was she saying? What order was she giving?* Lannya's mind raced. Her heart thrashed her nerves. She didn't have to wonder long. The throng of ADF personnel began to stir.

With each of Azli's steps growing closer to reaching the end of the gangplank, the imposing force made up of Harbor Sentinels, ADF Guardian Infantry, and ribbon infantry, matched and quickly outpaced her walking speed to anticipate her landing on the docks. The volume of their march increased rapidly as they walked faster, before quickly settling on a speed and volume. It was powerful and impressive. There hadn't really been an occasion or situation like this before that involved so many of their ground forces at once. Consequently, just as it was powerful and impressive, it also instilled in those nearby a twinge of unexpected discomfort. They were an ominous sight. A created blessing which brought with it the potential for a future curse.

They marched cleanly, and professionally. Each movement was minimized and practical. The ADF was not for show. They were for action. Nothing was done to call attention to themselves. And though their training, uniforms, weapons, and equipment minimized sound, their sheer number overcame their minimalist intentions with a sustained ostinato of power.

The ADF vehicles flanking the ground forces, and ships in the Harbor atmosphere, began to redeploy as well. Each vehicle drew in closer, and each ship slipped down in altitude. There was even less ambiguity now, on what they were poised to do, given what transpired over the next few moments.

Without realizing it, because of her paranoid mania, Lannya shuffled her way to the gangplank as well, and stepped out onto it. She had given Azli enough of a lead. There were a million hands reaching for Lannya's mental attention and she was crumbling at the thought of reaching back for them all. She wanted to shout to Azli that she hated her for killing Akal. She wanted to see her taken away and forgotten in some obscure ribbon cage Mamdod might come up with for having a part in the death of so many Astraeans. But, the maternal hands grasping at her mind were just as powerful. She wanted to shout out to Azli that she loved her. She wanted to scream that she was forgiven and that everything would be ok.

Lannya began to take another step closer to Azli when she saw her stop just short of exiting the gangplank. Azli froze into a cold stare of unexpected terror at the sight of the approaching ADF forces, but only from the realization that she was alone, and about to reap what she had sowed. There were no Einarian forces behind her. No Einarian umbrella or shield. She had a fleeting inclination to be defiant or start fighting, but it was only with her for a moment. Looking back up to Lannya, Azli remembered that wasn't who she was anymore. She had no reason to fight the Astraeans, and what made her eyes flood over at that moment, was her accompanying realization that she never had a reason to fight them.

Just a few feet from the docks now, Azli watched as the ADF forces finally arrived. They fell in around the gangplank's exit to the dock and presented their arms in a low key snap. Immediately after, every other member of each line of ADF forces stepped back, and into alternating sides, allowing for better line of sight for those behind them. Other members of other lines dropped to one knee for additional lines of sight. After those who stepped back and slid sideways completed their movement, and after the others finished dropping to one knee, each member of the ADF on the docks, some hundreds, unholstered their weapons and trained their sights on Azli.

Azli stayed exactly where she was, turning her body only slightly to face the ADF forces directly. She said nothing, made no gestures, and didn't blink. She stole quick breaths when she remembered, and waited for a command or comment. She was of no mind to antagonize anyone, and was subconsciously allocating every bit of adrenaline ripping through her veins to what was happening before her.

Lannya was as petrified as Azli was. Neither mother nor daughter knew exactly what was happening, or what would be happening over the next few minutes. All they could do was stay as collected as possible and let the events unfold. The ADF were in absolute control of the situation, which meant that Rigella was in absolute control of the situation, who had until now, disappeared into the thick concentration of ADF infantry.

The armed and poised ADF directly in front of the gangplank effortlessly parted, just enough for a person to walk through. As they did so, Rigella appeared and approached the edge of the docks. Following directly behind Rigella were her Secondary Commanders, as well as Mamdod, Elcyd, Carthal, and Heersan. Carthal and Heersan had eyes sprung open with tension and surprise at seeing Azli. Mamdod fell back slightly and took Rigella's lead while Elcyd's face was noticeably stained with hate and an impatient desire for vengeance.

Rigella moved slowly and deliberately through the ADF as she approached Azli. She had a perfectly ambiguous expression and gave no sign of her demeanor with her body language. Her arms swung freely. It was a reserved confidence, devoid of arrogance. Her mind was doing all the work that her body, face and voice didn't need to do. Rigella was calculating each and every possible scenario, as she had always done. She and the Harbor had too much experience to be anything but calculating and careful.

She started to speak, but stopped herself. She didn't want to speak yet. She didn't need to speak yet. Rigella started to pace softly over a short path, never letting her vision stray from Azli. She was sizing her up, and playing everything back in her mind as she paced. She let her mind slip back to Celeria where she first met Akal, to when Azli killed Akal, and then back to this moment.

Rigella stopped in her tracks and stared as far through Azli's eyes as she could. Her emotions and anger were starting to creep in, but she got a hold of them immediately. She flew her vision up to Lannya, still standing at the edge of Paige's top deck, and then back to Azli.

"Come on down, Lannya," Rigella suggested calmly. She rolled her fingertips backwards towards her palm, gently beckoning to Rigella.

Lannya took it as a good sign that Rigella's first words since their arrival were as friendly as they were. But everyone was still on edge. Rigella continued staring at Azli as Lannya descended.

Lannya's eyes bounced all around, down to Azli, further down to Rigella, the ships above, the vehicles on each side, and the ADF infantry. She felt almost as if she were guilty of something as well, given all of the measures taken to meet them. She expected to be met by various ADF personnel. She even requested it in the message she sent. But what had met them was frightening. Lannya made no judgment call on Rigella's precautions, nor was she angry or upset. She just hadn't fathomed this level of reaction.

Lannya caught up to Azli on the gangplank who was still a few steps from the end. Without stopping, she put her hand on Azli's shoulder and let it slide off as she passed behind her smoothly, and quietly. Azli rotated her head only enough to make eye contact with Lannya with her peripheral vision. Lannya looked back to the faces on the dock and stepped down.

Lannya started walking towards Carthal and Heersan, but not before catching Rigella's eyes. The two women looked at each other quickly before Rigella focused back on Azli. Lannya wanted to say a million things, but she had no idea where to start or if she should even try to start. Carthal and Heersan met Lannya halfway and each gave her a quick hug before returning to face Rigella's back and Azli's fate. They waited for Rigella to speak again.

Rigella gestured to Azli for to take the last step off the gangplank, similarly to how she had beckoned to Lannya.

It was a disarming gesture, and one that went a long way to lighten the palpable tension in everyone's hearts, minds, and souls. For a moment, it felt like Rigella could have been welcoming home another Astraean, or any old colleague or friend. There Azli was, recent ally to Einar, murderer of Akal, and killer of hundreds of other Astraeans, stepping down onto the docks peacefully and easily.

Azli licked her lips for no other reason but to prepare them to eventually speak, though she had no desire to be the one that initiated the conversation. Taking purposely timid and conservative steps towards Rigella, she took in a visual inventory of the expressions on the ADF forces around her, as well as the Harbor leadership. She couldn't read anyone, and she was doing her best not to be read. This was simply a scenario that up until minutes previously, no one imagined would ever happen.

Azli's walk came to a quick end as she stopped within a few feet of Rigella. Once again, she performed another scan of the expressions around her, or at least those she could see above or around the barrels of the weapons trained on her. She began to at last feel slightly uneasy. Her sight returned to Rigella.

Just when Azli's eyes had settled, Rigella wrung her upper body around as far as she could force it to go. When she couldn't twist more without breaking her spine, she savagely unraveled herself, and in doing so, brought with her momentum, the back of her closed fist into the side of Azli's head. Azli immediately fell to one knee, and almost completely to the ground, before barely breaking her fall with one hand.

Chapter II

A Cot

"What are you doing?" Lannya screamed. Her voice ripped a raw cut into the air as her body launched as far forward as it could without taking a step. Like a dog on a chain, Lannya choked herself back, in an astonishing display of willpower. The unknown, however, was how long the chain would hold.

Azli started to look up and held a hand out, silently asking her mother to stay put as she recovered from Rigella's fist. The truth was, Azli had expected this, and in fact, had expected worse. She expected much more. Her expectations had a way to go, but they were about to be addressed again.

Without acknowledging Lannya at all, Rigella jumped up a few feet and cocked her right arm back just enough to build as much kinetic energy as possible. She came back down to the ground and shoved her knuckles into Azli's forehead as hatefully as she could. Just a breath of time after, with Azli on her way to the ground, Rigella bounded back up and kicked Azli in the face.

Reality combusted to a point that those in the immediate vicinity didn't know if it could be extinguished.

Lannya broke her self-imposed leash and vaulted into a sprint at Rigella. As Azli crumbled onto the ground, Lannya reached Rigella and slammed her straightened arms into her back. Distracted by her own violence towards Azli, Rigella didn't see it coming and took the full force of Lannya's arms. She flew off her feet, into the air for what felt like hundreds of feet, before sliding into a gritty skid on the docks, scraping a bloody path into her hands and side.

It all had taken place so quickly, none of the Sentinels or ADF had a chance to react until it was all over. Elcyd, Carthal, and Heersan had reached for Lannya too late, but she was finally restrained by the infantry as Rigella's slide was coming to a stop. Azli rolled onto her back and stayed there, holding her head with one hand. Rigella, chronologically the last to be struck and the last to recover, rolled from her stomach to her back. She didn't take long to recover however, and sat up, staying where she came to a rest on the docks.

"Everyone, wait! Stop! Stop!" Elcyd echoed to the Sentinels that had begun restraining Lannya.

The Sentinels were doing nothing improper to Lannya, nor were they hurting her. They were simply restraining her, and did as Elcyd suggested. They looked to Rigella for her next command or action.

"Are you insane?" Lannya accused Rigella with

an offended shriek that slipped into a desperate falsetto. "She surrendered," Lannya continued. Her tone started to evolve into hate. "I brought her here to help us!"

Rigella continued to sit on the docks. Her chest heaved to catch her breath from the explosion of adrenaline. Her eyes were dead as they watched Lannya chastise her for the savage attack on Azli.

With the action seemingly settled, Elcyd jogged over to the Sentinels restraining Lannya and silently requested they relinquish control of Lannya over to him. They obliged and stepped back into formation.

Carthal and Heersan rushed over to Lannya as well, but she had already bent down to begin helping Azli up.

Everyone was looking over another, whispering quick checks of concern, or tending to sliced cheeks and split lips. That is, except for Rigella. No one was checking on Rigella. She remained sitting on the ground, staring out into space, with only an occasional glimpse to the others, or to her scraped hands and rib cage.

Only when Rigella finally began to stir and stand did someone address her again.

"I don't know how I ever supported your leadership of the ADF when it's so easy for you to become unhinged," Lannya admonished with a shaking malevolence. "You are unfit. Undeserving."

Rigella said nothing. She placed her hands on her hips while continuing to pant softly as if noticeably taking stock of what had just happened, especially her own actions.

As Lannya continued tending to Azli, Carthal and Heersan looked to Elcyd or Mamdod for an indication of what to do or say. Mamdod toyed with his chin as he pondered and dipped his head into a frenzy of concern over what had transpired.

"Please, everyone," Elcyd implored passionately, but softly. "No more fighting. Stop fighting. Say what you will, but please, stop fighting."

Rigella slowly walked over to reassume her position in front of the Sentinels, ADF and ribbon infantries.

"She killed Akal and helped destroy countless others," Rigella said coldly. "I will not apologize for this," she continued, as her voice grew in volume rapidly, "and I will not allow you to question my right or ability to lead the ADF!"

Heersan turned to Rigella, obviously displeased with Rigella's stubbornness.

"Ri," Heersan blurted quickly. "She knows what Azli did. We all do."

"Then what's the problem?" Rigella returned with a confused shout. "That was nothing! We could have done much worse. She would've deserved it, too." As Rigella spoke she took a few steps towards Lannya, again. "I could have done much worse."

Carthal and Elcyd stepped in front of Rigella to prevent her from getting any closer to Lannya.

"I didn't bring her here to get beat up while her hands are restrained," Lannya answered with a confident dryness. "I didn't expect her to be, anyway. I thought you were above that, Rigella. I thought we were all above that. At least plenty of us here have seen how flawed you actually are."

Rigella sniffed and wiped her bleeding hands on

her pants again. She was once more unfazed by Lannya's statements.

"I don't care what you think anymore, Lannya," Rigella snapped with contempt. "I'm tired of walking on eggshells to protect your feelings and emotions. This twisted traitor destroyed many of our people. I have to kind of question your sanity if you're able to look over all of that, including Akal's death!"

Mamdod let go of his chin and moved towards the group as Rigella continued.

"We all know that Azli deserves to be killed. She deserves to be erased. Smeared out of life. I know it, and you know it. I could have killed her and had no one to answer to. Don't you see all of that? The quicker you admit that and realize that a few hits to her face are just a fraction of what she deserves, the quicker we can all move on and get back to caring about our people, the Harbor, and stopping Einar. There is more to this multiverse than you and your sick spawn of a daughter, Lannya."

Lannya threw a jab back without wasting a second.

"I brought her here even though I haven't gotten over what she did. I brought her here to help us with information to defeat, Einar. Stop being such an emotional hypocrite."

"I understand some of you may not care about what I have to say on this," Mamdod calmly interjected, "but I need to say something. Do what you will, or won't, with my thoughts."

The Sentinels and infantry continued to stand in motionless formation while Elcyd, Rigella, Lannya, and the others, turned slightly from their various positions to face Mamdod. Lannya turned back every so often to check on Azli and blot her wounds.

Mamdod continued.

"I think we need to table these very legitimate concerns between the both of you, only to immediately continue addressing the situation with Einar. Everything else is secondary."

"Unless she has a dissertation already prepared, or maps, charts, and diagrams, I have no desire to hear anything she has to say," Rigella retorted sharply.

Carthal didn't understand Rigella's logic.

"What are you talking about?" Carthal asked with a growing confusion and impatience. "Let's bring her in, detain her, clean her up, and plan how to go about extracting information from her."

"That's out of the question," Rigella replied.

"Why?" Elcyd asked, adding to the number of those confused.

"Do none of you remember what happened the last time she was here?" Rigella posed flippantly.

"She is in no shape to put up a fight, Rigella!" Lannya shouted.

"I don't care what shape she is in," Rigella answered with a staunch authority. "None of us have any idea about what plans she may have, or ribbon tricks she may have this time around. She's not taking one step closer to the Harbor."

As she finished speaking, Rigella snapped her fingers and pointed to an empty section of the docks. The Sentinels, ADF, and ribbon infantries then repositioned to fill the empty area and blocked anyone from passing through to the Harbor without permission.

"Rigella," Lannya started again. "If you want to defeat Einar, and protect our people, then Azli is a resource you must take advantage of. You're contradicting yourself!"

"If your daughter," Rigella began, with a personal jab dripping with condescension, "hadn't already killed so many of our people, then I would entertain the possibility of detaining and questioning her. How many more times do I need to explain it to you? It doesn't matter. I'm not going to again. She is not welcome here, neither as a guest of yours, nor as a prisoner."

"Rigella," Heersan attempted softly. "We have an exponentially more secure Harbor than we did bef..."

Before Heersan could finish speaking, he was interrupted.

"No!" Rigella screamed. Her scream was accompanied by a silent threat, stabbed into Heersan's eyes, by hers.

The standoff was excruciating. All points had been expressed, and all positions had been proposed. Everyone had spoken and defended or attacked another. Everyone but Azli. She rippled her body slowly to confirm what hurt and what didn't. After slipping out from under Lannya's supportive embrace, she slowly shuffled over to Rigella. It was her only act of defiance.

"Einar used me. I won't be used again. I will tell you what I know," Azli said to Rigella, surprisingly able to look past what Rigella had just done to her. The group was collectively amazed at Azli's ability to take a higher road than Rigella had.

"Start talking," Rigella ordered.

Azli's face glistened in the reflected Harbor light. She was covered in blood and was increasingly having trouble focusing her vision.

"Einar's ship," she began, through a shaky voice brought on from shock, "is called the Dark Artery. Almost as old as he is. Focused on stealth and seclusion. It is defended by...'

Azli's voice broke as she started to faint. Her legs buckled but before she fell to the ground, Lannya broke from her friends and caught Azli.

"You don't have to do this right now, Azli," Lannya offered gently. Azli's head bobbed and swayed along Lannya's arm that supported her neck.

"She can either do it now, or leave, Lannya," Rigella crisply corrected. "I've already said she's not taking one step closer to the Harbor."

Lannya's face flushed over with a crimson that matched Azli's dried blood on her clothes. But before Lannya could verbally retaliate again, Mamdod shot from the place he had occupied since the discussion began and went to a nearby terminal.

Without saying a word, Mamdod began tapping furiously. A folding cot sprung out from the dockside terminal. As soon as he saw it, Elcyd ran to it and began wheeling it over to Azli and Lannya. Rigella's mouth opened, but she quickly checked herself. She allowed it to take place.

As Elcyd arrived at Azli's side and began helping Lannya place her on the cot, Mamdod had returned from the terminal with some healing packs. He handed them out to Elcyd and Lannya who immediately began attending to

Azli's wounds.

It had passed the point of being the humane thing to do. While Rigella's punches had also drawn blood, the blunt impact of Rigella's boot to Azli's face had caused the most damage and needed immediate attention.

Carthal and Heersan had approached the cot, offering silently any help they could provide, or at least their support. Rigella, however, did nothing. She stood in place with her arms crossed, offering no assistance of any kind. She did take the opportunity though, to step to her Secondary Commanders and give them a few instructions.

Within moments, the vehicles on the docks turned around, and began returning to the inner Harbor structure. The numerous ships of various classes began to withdraw. A large portion of Sentinels, ADF, and ribbon infantries, about-faced and began marching back to the Harbor. An adequate amount of Sentinels and ADF infantry remained behind, still blocking the group's path to the Harbor. The whole time this redeployment of forces took place, Rigella stayed, coldly waiting for her friends to finish fussing over Azli.

As Elcyd and Lannya finished tending to Azli, Mamdod stood up and looked to see if Rigella's demeanor had changed any. It didn't seem it had.

"If you won't permit her to return to the Harbor," Mamdod said, "I won't argue. I understand that. But I won't let someone stand here in pain, pouring blood."

Rigella didn't flinch. Her head however, dipped only slightly, and extremely slowly, in a most microscopic display of concession to Mamdod, and the general overall opinion of everyone else.

Chapter III

Pressing for Information

Azli had been stabilized, and while Lannya leaned over her daughter, blotting sutures and her swelling forehead, Elcyd exchanged quiet confusion with Carthal and Heersan. Mamdod retreated back to a lonely corner of the docks, sickened by the obscene sight of what had taken place, but even more so, further disgusted with himself and what his ancient game had brought upon the multiverse. None of them had time for this. The leaves on the tree at the ribbon island had been falling ever since Akal was killed. The clock was ticking.

Whether or not she realized it, Rigella had been somewhat ostracized for her behavior. Carthal and Heersan had never seen Rigella lose control like that. They were scared. Not for themselves, but for the Astraeans. Elcyd was of a similar mind, but in his occasional exchanged glances with Mamdod, he was glad that the situation had seemed to finally settle and cool down.

While waiting for Azli to recuperate a bit after her punishment, Rigella had started pacing. With each step, she grew more and more tired of having to waste her time on her, and it was evident as the minutes passed. Her steps became harder, her speed increased, and her looks over to Azli became more frequent, and were often joined with forced sighs of impatience.

Heersan heard one of Rigella's sighs and looked over at her as if she were a pouting child.

"Rigella!" He flung sharply.

She was surprisingly distracted and stopped pacing long enough to look at Lannya then quickly to Azli.

"Well? Are you ready to talk?" Rigella disgustingly inquired.

Azli rolled her head on the cot's built-in pillow before coming back to focus her slightly clearer vision on the stars of the multiverse directly overhead. She reached for her tired and sliced eyes and grimaced when she tried to feel her face in the first estimation of her wounds she had attempted since Rigella's assault. She didn't know what to expect, and was initially smothered by an excruciating wave of painful drops that trickled quickly down through her face, but she quickly bore the pain well with an interrupted grunt. She immediately pulled her hand away and instinctively closed her eyes, before letting them peel apart slowly again as she brought herself up slightly on an elbow. She looked at Lannya and took a few slow breaths before nodding at her, giving her a cue that she was all right for the moment.

Tilting her head up to Elcyd, Azli began to speak,

and paid absolutely no attention to Rigella or her question.

"Einar is diverting ribbon traffic," she started, before an involuntary spasm of pain. "I don't know how much control he has," she continued, "but I know he can do it."

Mamdod took a few steps out of the shadows, back towards the group.

"Diverting traffic?" Elcyd replied, not understanding. "To what end? What can he do?"

Having to shut one eye from the pain, Azli held a side of her face in her palm as she answered.

"He can steal souls," Azli announced. "He usually grabs them before they go to the island the first time, or, maybe at other times, I don't know. He can make them go somewhere else. Usually to his ship, I think."

Rigella blurted out in disbelief.

"Steal souls?" She echoed, before turning to Mamdod to ask her follow-up. "How can anyone do that?"

"I have no idea how that's possible," Mamdod immediately returned. "But, I would imagine if someone has had enough time, as he has, with the level of understanding of the ribbons someone could gain after so much time, that anything is possible. Look at all the technology used at the Harbor to interact with the ribbons."

Elcyd took over the line of questioning.

"What has he been doing with this diverted ribbon traffic?"

"They're the ones that have made up most of the Einarian forces as far as I know," Azli supplied, as she flattened back out slowly on the cot. "He receives them kind of like how Mamdod does on the island. He then starts lying and manipulating them immediately."

"Is that what happened to you?" Rigella asked to confirm. Her question was saturated in judgmental condescension.

"I guess so," Azli answered weakly, and with little concern for Rigella's attitude. "When mom got banished from the Habitats and died while carrying my last regular life, my first memory after that was showing up in some room on the Dark Artery."

"How is he doing this, Azli? Think!" Carthal asked out of urgent need for the information, with little concern for her.

Azli groaned and shifted restlessly from one side to the other, propping herself up, and then falling flat on the cot again. Her face stung with relentless pain from her blood pressure coursing through her face. She was trying to alleviate the pain by moving in hopes of affecting the pressure, but it was no use.

Azli was tired of the pain, but she was more tired of appearing or coming across as helpless. She wasn't angry at any of the Astraeans around her, nor was she impatient, or feeling put out. At that moment, she simply wanted to push through the line of questioning so that she could rest. She had been stitched up, her largest wounds were cauterized, and her bleeding had stopped. She was through with the cot.

"I don't know, specifically," Azli forced out as she stood. "He only ever hinted abstractly at needing to protect his ability to do it, or keep what was doing it, secret, like it was a device or process, or something. That kind of thing.

If he ever talked about it in detail with anyone, I wasn't ever involved."

Azli turned to face Rigella after standing, but quickly lowered her throbbing face into her palms. She gathered her footing and her thoughts, and struggled once more to focus away from the pain. She lifted her head back up and looked around to each of the group while thinking of what else she might have to share.

"I don't..." she started without an ending. "What else do you want to know?"

"Well, just a moment," Elcyd said. "Before we move on, can you tell us anything else at all about this technology or process he uses to intercept and modify ribbon data? Does he do it from his ship, or..."

"I don't really have any better information," she replied submissively, almost sounding as if she truly regretted being somewhat ignorant on the topic. "The only other thing I can think of is that it must take a lot of energy to do, or take a while to do."

Carthal and Heersan left Lannya's side and approached Azli. They were extremely anxious for any information they could act upon, and were hoping Azli could provide something actionable.

"Whenever we spoke about growing our forces," Azli attempted to elaborate, "or, when he would talk about trying to harness a particular type of soul, he would talk about needing to make time to do it, or, wondering if we could accomplish something in time."

"How do you know he wasn't talking about the time for the leaves to fall off the tree after Akal died, or something else?" Mamdod asked logically.

"Because this was before," Azli began, ashamed and unable to finish.

"Before you killed Akal," Rigella completed calmly, but with a continued intensity.

Azli swallowed, out of awkwardness, but possibly also as a subconscious effort to bury just a pinch of her shame.

Her head dropped slowly before finally nodding in confirmation.

Heersan cleared his throat in an effort to push through the latest wave of tension, and started considering potential scenarios.

"As I've been listening, I've been trying to remove myself from my personal investment in all of this and think of how he may be doing whatever it is he has been doing."

Heersan's eyes popped open slightly wider into an unfocused stare that concentrated on his stream of consciousness. His hands came up and danced slightly in the air as he started to explain his ideas.

"Azli says that it wasn't an easy process for him, right? That he has to make time for it, or make a special effort to undertake the process."

Everyone listened to Heersan intently, hoping to help jump on a train of thought that would lead them to an answer. Heersan continued.

"When I compare that to how we interact with the ribbons, we need a piece of technology to use or to interact with the ribbons in every way. To pull up data, modify data, create items, fabricate vessels, whatever it is, there is always an interface of some kind. The only exception is when we call a ribbon to transform into one of our previous lives."

Mamdod's face sprung up with the beginnings of an epiphany.

"He's using some kind of tool to do this," Mamdod added. "And it's probably also the reason why we can't rewind time right now, or, anymore, I don't know."

"Yeah, I think it might be a device of some kind," Heersan obliged. "Azli said she didn't know if it was that, or if it was a process, but it has to be a device of some kind. Something that can probably be stopped, or at least destroyed."

"Well, I wasn't trying to influence your thinking," Azli added quickly. "Like I said, I have no idea how he's doing it."

"I know that," Heersan acknowledged, slightly agitated at being interrupted. Azli was just a tool providing information at that moment. She was not his friend. "Regardless, it's a possibility we need to consider, investigate, and if necessary, rule out. I wonder if he does it from his ship somehow. How familiar are you with the Dark Artery, Azli?"

Azli shook her head and began a slow shrug as she was obviously trying to consider the possibility.

"I would say I know the ship pretty well," she answered with a dash of doubt.

Carthal was interested in the idea and had some follow-up questions.

"Do you remember Einar going to areas of the ship that no one else did?" Carthal asked with quick eagerness. "Ever see anything on the ship that you didn't know what was? Objects? Tools?"

"I might have, and not known it," she replied while still shrugging. "The point is though, is that I can't think of any rooms, areas, or, items that were off-limits or secret. Again, if there were, he didn't tell me about them."

Rigella, who had started pacing slowly and quietly during the conversation sighed obnoxiously and sat down on the cot, but then immediately shot back up.

"You don't have anything to help..." Rigella rambled in frustration in Azli's direction, before interrupting herself and turning to her friends. "She doesn't have anything that we can use."

"Rigella, quit whining. We're trying. She's trying," Lannya answered emphatically.

"That's it, Rigella. Lannya," Elcyd barked. "Shut your mouths for two minutes and put your people first, please. I've bitten my tongue to the point it's almost cut in two, and I'm tired of it."

An immediate silence followed. Both Rigella and Lannya froze angrily as the rest of the group's feet shuffled.

Carthal huffed softly, trying to get his mind back on topic before speaking again.

"So, even if Einar is using some kind of device on his ship, or somewhere else, I don't see how there's anywhere near enough time to look for it. What's the priority? To find how he's doing this and stop it, or just continue focusing on tracking him down, or what?"

There were no rapid suggestions or thoughts. The group was weaving in and out of priorities and variables in their own minds as they considered Carthal's concerns.

Chapter IV

A Served Purpose

The top echelon of Einar's commanders slid into a frenzied halt in front of the entrance to his command quarters. Smeche, officially Einar's next in command, but unofficially, his second after Azli, looked up to the room's privacy indicator and saw a humming bar of green light, letting the gathering at the door know it was permitted for them to disturb Einar. After Smeche pressed a button that sounded two quick and high-pitched pulses of sound into the chambers to let Einar know they were about to enter, the door slid down slowly, but smoothly, into the floor.

By the time the receding door reached the eye level of Smeche and the other senior subordinates, Einar had already turned from a wall of data displays. Catching eyes with Smeche, Einar tossed a portable command pad onto his desk. Einar's hands on his hips and elevated chin commanded Smeche to speak.

The door sunk flush with the floor and Smeche barreled into the room followed by his frantic team. They walked with an intense stomp, almost stumbling from the shock of the news they had to share, and at the thought of the possible implications.

"What is it, Smeche?" Einar prompted as the group reached him.

"We've lost, Azli, sir," Smeche answered without hesitation.

"How? Elaborate" Einar commanded.

"Her follow-up attack on the Harbor failed," Smeche began, speeding up as he spoke. "As you know, she had planned to go and deal another blow to the Harbor to set them back, distract, and delay them further, in hopes of holding them off until all the leaves fall, but, it backfired."

Einar's jaw tightened and twitched once as he remained frozen otherwise, and listened to Smeche continue.

"The Astraeans have created a formidable fleet," Smeche continued. "Far quicker and far more powerful than we had anticipated. They countered Azli's attack and pursued her and our remaining ships. As instructed, none of them that were being pursued returned here as to not be followed, but a few made it back eventually, and we have more details coming in from elsewhere in the multiverse, from others that escaped and are now in hiding."

Einar showed no emotion. He let his eyes tilt up to the ceiling of his command quarters as he assimilated Smeche's report. He began cracking his knuckles one at a time, and let his eyes fall back to Smeche.

"Our people say that Azli got separated and was pursued into Universe CG. We have no other confirmed information than that, but must assume she was captured."

Einar didn't immediately reply. He only raised his hands up to his face and began scratching his sideburns with his index fingers. His head rolled slightly as he continued to process everything he had been told.

In a startling twist of demeanor, Einar then snapped an about-face and walked around to his desk. With a few taps on his main command terminal, the displays he had been reviewing before his subordinates arrived, faded out, or slid away. A few additional taps after that, and a new bank of displays and command arrays slid up out of his desk into place, or faded into view.

"The Dark Artery must relocate," Einar stated with an almost calming dullness.

Smeche looked to his team to see if they were as curious about his lack of concern for Azli as he was.

"I am beginning a capacitor dump into the engines now," Einar explained. "We'll recharge the capacitors and dump them again and move the ship. Understood?"

"Yes, Einar," the senior navigator next to Smeche replied.

"The second capacitor load should charge fairly quickly," advised the senior engineer.

"Good," Einar acknowledged. "Our intended destination is what we discussed previously, but check in with me to confirm before that second capacitor load is ready."

"Very good, sir," replied the navigator.

Einar started gesturing at his display, moving and grouping the data to his liking. As he did so, he issued a reminder.

"We have spoken about this exact moment, more times than I can count. We knew we would be met with a fierce resistance the minute we had to tip our hands to the Astraeans. After Akal was killed, everything else is mere details. We just have to wait them out and wait for the leaves to fall. Though we still have the advantage, we must continue anticipating any possible responses. We must assume they have all information and all answers."

The group stood motionless after listening to Einar's comments, and waited to be dismissed, or waited for additional orders. Einar had already forgotten about them. He was deep into tapping and flipping through commands and data. Projections popped up of planetary and star systems, as well as ribbon path and intersection diagrams.

Smeche faked a tickle in his throat and forced out a scratchy cough for one final bit of attention.

"Yes, what else?" Einar asked as he stared through his 3-D displays.

"What would you have us do about Azli's situation?" Smeche inquired.

Einar dropped his focus from his displays and turned it back to Smeche. He held out his hands in confusion. The matter had been addressed as far as he was concerned.

"You said we must assume she was captured, correct?"

"Yes," Smeche answered immediately. "But, don't

you want us to confirm what happened to her and attempt a rescue if possible?"

Einar made no effort to entertain the notion.

"No, there is no need. Azli served her purpose," Einar provided, flatly.

Smeche couldn't help but take Einar's view on Azli somewhat personally. Not only did Smeche have secret feelings for Azli, but Einar's disregard for her was also an indication of how he or any of the other Einarians could be regarded at any given moment. This blatant apathy was a new side to Einar that Smeche hadn't quite seen before. Einar had always been cold, distanced, and driven by his mission, but there had always been at least the facade of caring about his people. There was a sense from Smeche's point of view that Einar had dropped that concern, or at least stopped pretending it ever existed. It suddenly popped into Smeche's mind that with Einar getting closer to his goal, that his need for his supporters was rapidly diminishing.

Smeche didn't realize with his next question that he had allowed a bit of edgy bite into his tone.

"What do you mean she served her purpose?" Smeche sought to clarify.

"She served, her, purpose," Einar repeated, annoyed with Smeche's attitude.

Smeche's face compressed, showing he wanted more information.

Einar had grown tired of Smeche's dash of insolence and furiously shoved his displays into their storage compartments, or made them cease projecting, by a violent thrust of his hands. With his vision locked on

Smeche, Einar came back around his desk and walked to within only a foot of Smeche. He then began to expand on his answer for Smeche's benefit.

"Why are you still in this room, Smeche? She served her purpose. We needed her anger, and her hate for her parents. We had to let her get her revenge and destroy Akal, not for her own peace of mind, but for our mission!"

"She had to get revenge?" Smeche began. "Aren't you the one that banished her mother? You were afraid you couldn't get rid of Akal on your own!"

With a furious jerk, Einar reached up to gesture at a piece of equipment similar to those that controlled the displays at his desk, and simultaneously launched and directed a thick and constant stream of ribbon energy that encompassed Smeche. He then gestured again to cause the ribbon beam to sling Smeche back into a booth of sorts, along a wall, not too far from where Einar and the rest of his command team stood.

After a few other quick gestures of wrists and fingers, the large ribbon beam that had been initiated expanded to the outer perimeter of the booth holding Smeche, essentially locking him inside. Next, thousands of much smaller and thinner beams shot out from the bottom of the booth, through Smeche, to the top of the booth. Very quickly, these numerous small beams began crackling and flickering as they shocked and tortured the bits of Smeche's soul that were tied to thousands of his past lives.

As the small beams waved and trembled around and away from Smeche's core soul, one could see the legs, arms, heads, antennae, and countless other various body parts extend out along the individual beams, with expressions of extreme pain and agony.

The sound in the room was the worst part for those looking on. It was a rarely experienced symphony of sickness. Groans, cries, and shrieks of unimaginable pitch and volume from thousands of voices caused the fear in the onlookers to multiply exponentially. Many of the command team began to shuffle backwards, or cover their ears.

"No!" Einar screamed, exhausting all the air he had at that moment. "Don't you dare leave! Watch! Listen! This is the fun you can expect if any of you want to consider questioning me. Do you understand?"

Einar's screaming was vulgar, without vulgarities. It was an obscene darkness that penetrated anything and everything his command team was made of. He looked to the flailing soul and fluctuating body segments of Smeche, and then back to the rest of the group.

"This plan has been in the works for age upon age. Just do what I have told you to do, and if you allow even a hint of the possibility of leaving, or defecting into your mind, I will know. And you, your families, friends, across your millions of lives will not escape me, and will receive treatment much worse than this! This. All of this, is all I have planned for, for almost all of time. Do you understand? Do you?"

The group stood shocked, with skin afire with fear and adrenaline. Each of the command team had a burning chest needing to gulp air in panic, but none allowed their chest to rise suddenly for fear of unwanted attention. Most couldn't help but let their sight drift back to Smeche, and watch as he pitifully continued to writhe in a thousand pains of a thousand types, across his soul's time and space.

"Stay here," Einar commanded.

The command team stayed in place as directed. Einar walked over to where Smeche was being spiritually dissected, but held together only enough to maintain integrity. Einar stared into the booth, through the thin, outer ribbon wall, and tilted his head in fascination at what Smeche was going through. His mouth hung open as his eyes and mind glazed over from the sound and sights. That only lasted for a moment, until Einar snapped out of his trance and gestured at a nearby control for the number of beams slicing through Smeche's soul's millions of existences, to increase.

Chapter V

A New Owner

"However we decide to proceed," Rigella rushed through. "I don't want Azli to hear what our decision is, or anything else we think. She will not enter the Harbor, and she can't stay any longer."

Lannya bristled and started to reply, but Rigella continued while quickly making eye contact with each member of the group.

"And if any of you have any issue with that, disagree with my decision, or can't understand why this is my position, then you can have my resignation as ADF Central Commander."

Carthal rolled his eyes at her statement and questioned the need for Rigella's melodrama silently. Rigella noticed.

"Don't look at me like that, Carthal." Rigella added, while pointing up towards the roof of the top dome. "Really. If any of you honestly, truly think her staying here is a good idea, then speak up. If any of you have anything else to say to her, say it. If you have any other questions for her, ask them!"

Heersan couldn't help but point out a very major difference between Azli's presence now, and previous times.

"She doesn't appear to be here as an enemy now, Rigella."

Rigella spun around and threw her arms up in the air in confusion at their willingness to give Azli any kind of chance.

"What?" Heersan challenged. "She has sat here with a busted body and told us..."

"Told us what?" Rigella interrupted sharply as she turned back to the group. "Einar can manipulate the ribbons. Great. That isn't news. What has she actually given us that we can act on? Einar's location? His ship? Specifics on how he manipulates the ribbons? No. None of that!"

Azli took a turn at interrupting.

"Hey!"

Rigella whipped her head around, surprised at Azli's gall. Azli had everyone's attention.

"I never said I wouldn't take you to the Dark Artery, and you never asked."

Rigella jumped all over that and practically ran over to Azli and got in her face again.

"Ok. A few things," Rigella countered sarcastically. "What makes you think I would, A. Trust you. B. Risk any of our people in a mission dependent on trusting you?

C. Trust any information you've hinted at, given us, or might give us?"

Rigella huffed in Azli's face and walked over to Elcyd and Mamdod.

"And D.," Rigella whispered only so that her friends could hear. "The Ontelbar are closing in on where they think the Dark Artery is anyway, with clean and friendly data." Her next statement was once again for the benefit of the entire group. "She's worthless!"

Without a sound or gesture, Azli was suddenly struck by a beam of ribbon energy. The group around her flinched at the unexpected ribbon and squinted from its brightness. It was fairly dark at the end of the section of docks they were on and they initially struggled to see what was happening.

Azli was tired of Rigella's stonewalling and was seemingly about to leave. She wasn't permitted to enter the Harbor, and wasn't being captured or detained, and was far from being listened to, so she felt her time had come to leave.

Lannya attempted to wave her off and persuade her to stay.

"Azli, wait. Don't go yet!"

Azli looked at her mother through the pulsing energy. Her tangled face was worn not only physically but emotionally. She pleaded silently to Lannya to be permitted to leave. Azli's chest heaved slightly, them moderately, and then finally, heavily. With each sigh of fatigue, her head dipped further and further down. Her shoulders followed.

Azli shook her head gently at herself, her situation,

and the Astraeans' quagmire. The gentle energy from the ribbon energy encompassing her was a steady metronome, consistently reminding her to make her decision to leave right then, or not. She thought about it quickly and decided against leaving, at least until she and her mother had said a proper goodbye. After a few moments, she lifted her head quickly and looked up through the ribbon. Within a second, a beam of smaller ribbon energy, inside the main one, shot through Azli, spiritually impaling her. As the internal beam struck Azli and dissipated, the group flinched once again, and involuntarily looked away from the brightness. Almost as quickly, the group looked back to Azli's position and found her still standing there. With her last summoning of the smaller beam, Azli had rewound her personal time to before she was attacked by Rigella, and then allowed time to catch back up to the current moment. She then allowed the main ribbon to recede, without using it for another purpose, and without leaving.

Her face returned to its usual beauty, though she was still flawed and diminished by her internal conflict and the past horrors she had inflicted on others. There was also no more pain from the wounds now that they had been rewound, though again, she was still haunted and sickened by those past travesties that could never be rewound or forgotten.

"It's time for me to go," Azli responded to her mother. Her voice was monotone and calm. There was no malice in it, but there was also no hope. She just knew the time had come to leave.

There was no indication from anyone in the group

that they were going to argue with her. For better or worse, they all agreed that it was time. Except for Lannya. She walked slowly over to Azli replaying everything that had transpired from Universe CG through that moment.

"Stay nearby, or stay in contact," Lannya pleaded softly. It wasn't just a mother's selfish plea, but also an Astraean plea, to see if, together, they could uncover any more information from Azli's memory.

"There must be something more we can find to tell them," Lannya suggested frantically, but softly. "Einar must have said things to you, or showed you things. You must have seen something, or discovered something on your own."

Azli shook her head doubtfully while combing her mind once again for anything that might help. Her mouth crept open in exasperation. Nothing else was coming to mind.

"Think of something!" Lannya finally shouted in desperation, not wanting to let Azli go.

"I can't!" Azli shouted back through drowning eyes. Her frustration had knotted her stomach. Her soul was consumed with inadequacy and shame.

Lannya's face twitched and crumbled from a fresh coat of uncertainty. But, just as quickly as she was overcome with worry, she was relieved. She had an idea. She turned slowly and faced her friends with a renewed hope, as if turning out of the darkness and into the streaming sunlight.

"I'll be leaving with, Azli," Lannya announced. Her face firmed up with confidence.

Rigella's forehead folded in on itself with

amazement and a surprised disapproval. She quickly tried to hide her concern and unfolded her forehead.

"No, Lannya," Heersan easily offered with a sincere dismissal. "You don't have to do that. We can come up with something." Heersan looked to Rigella in hopes she would defrost a bit of her inflexibility.

"I know I don't have to," Lannya confirmed. "But as Rigella likes to point out so frequently, you don't really need me. You all got along just fine without me for a long time. And you know what?" Lannya continued, fully secure in her decision. "It's not even really about that. Right now, at this moment, I couldn't honestly care less about how well Rigella, or the Astraeans as a whole get along without me or not. I've got my daughter back, and I'm not going to let go. If she can't stay here, and if she's going to leave, then I'm going with her."

The group, including Lannya, looked to Azli to measure her response to the conversation. Her eyes were the only thing that moved, as they flittered around, helping her determine how she felt about Lannya's plan.

"No, Heersan's right. You don't need to do that," Azli finally said. The volume of her voice was extremely measured and delicate. "I'll leave and we can easily stay in touch, meet up anywhere we want, and anytime we want."

Lannya knew keeping in contact would be an easy matter, or, meeting up. Rebuilding bonds and strengthening their relationship would happen, regardless. But she also knew that there wasn't a very good reason not to leave with Azli. There was a regret and thirst that had festered in Lannya for ages that she finally had an opportunity to legitimately remedy. Not only could she build something new with her daughter, but in the dusty recess of her thoughts, something tapped on her mind's glass, suggesting to her that through a new relationship with Azli, she may even be able to make up a bit, for her part in the failure between her and Akal, however big her part might have been.

"If you're ok with it," Lannya began. "I want to go with you."

Azli looked over her mother's shoulder, to Rigella, Mamdod, Elcyd, Carthal and Heersan. The only face of apparent indifference was Rigella's. The rest of the group emitted a concern for the future that was nurtured by the unfortunate path all of the most recent events and conversations had taken since Lannya and Azli returned to the Harbor. They felt as though that whatever took place was a lose-lose for everyone. Someone would be hurt. Someone would feel rejected. Someone would feel forced into something. Lose-lose.

Azli eventually permitted a nod. She was conflicted, but due to a slight amount of selfishness at wanting her mother to be with her, but also mostly from a genuine need and appreciation, Azli gladly nodded.

Lannya reciprocated a small nod in excitement and as a bonus, even found a surprise grin in the corners of her mouth. She quickly forgot it again, however, and turned to face the rest of the group.

Carthal let his head fall from disappointment, and began an angry staring contest with the ground of the docks. He didn't want to look anyone in the eye, out of disbelief at how they had arrived at not only a place where Rigella would refuse to detain a potentially powerful source of information, but also a place that forced one of their friends to feel like she had to leave.

Heersan, Mamdod, and Elcyd all shared similar thoughts as Elcyd picked at his lip and shook his head. Heersan's mouth was somewhat agape while looking to Rigella, Mamdod, Elcyd, and back to Rigella with a silent demand that someone not actually allow Lannya to leave, or at least not leave the situation as it was.

No one said anything. There was nothing else that could be quickly said or done. Lose-lose.

Lannya did a final survey of expressions and body language and nodded at them though none of them noticed.

Heersan looked back to Lannya when he heard her begin to move next to Azli and whisper something to her. He couldn't make out what was said. A destination for them to head for, he assumed.

"Please, all of you, take care of yourselves," Lannya offered sincerely, making an obvious effort to wish Rigella the same good will. "I'm sure I'll see you all again, and talk with some of you sooner than that, or at least I hope I do."

Some of the group had already returned to looking at Lannya, but those who hadn't, did so then, including Rigella.

Lannya turned to Azli and looked up, signaling that it was time to leave. Two huge ribbons then erupted from high in the dark abyss of multispace high above. Just as they were struck, Carthal hopped a few steps towards them.

"Wait! At least take Paige," Carthal shouted into

the ribbons.

"Carthal," Rigella blurted. "You can't give them Paige."

Heersan put his hand on Carthal's shoulder as he addressed him.

"We'll need Paige," Heersan said, each word dragging with emphasis. "It's not really your place to give her up like that."

Carthal allowed everyone to hear his replies to their objections.

"If we're effectively banishing Azli," Carthal declared to Heersan, before looking to the rest of the group, "and not giving Lannya much of a choice on how to react, then I don't see why we can't let Lannya have Paige to give them a good base of operations as they travel. We all will still be here and can have the fabrication facilities come up with anything that we need. You sure don't need it Rigella. For any of us to deny Paige to Lannya, or to refuse to allow her to have it for any other contrived excuse is petty. Let her have the ship and let them go."

Heersan stepped back to soak in the clarity of Carthal's truth. They both then turned to Rigella to judge her disposition on the matter.

Rigella made no sound as she stared as rigidly into Carthal's eyes as she could, begging her mind to come up with an excuse to deny Carthal's suggestion. But she couldn't. She strained so hard to think of something, but with each second that passed, her desire to hold out waned.

She finally stomped over to a command terminal and issued the necessary command to relinquish control over Paige's navigation systems that the Harbor had overtaken when they returned. And though Rigella had given command permissions of Paige to Lannya a while back, this time, she also tapped in a command to transfer over official ownership of Paige to Lannya.

With Rigella's last tap on the screen, she closed out her command terminal window and turned back towards the Harbor without another sound, word, objection, or action. As she made her way back up the docks to the main Harbor complex, the remaining Sentinels and ADF personnel fell in behind her.

Elcyd's head dropped. His heart beat a little less vibrantly, and his soul had been coated with a moldy disappointment. He and the others felt a rare sting not often experienced by Astraeans. It was a sting of discordance, and the inability to compromise. One failure, of an increasing amount, among Astraeans. More and more Astraeans, including the group of friends standing at the end of the docks, found their fear growing that the Astraeans would not be able to weather the sustained barrage on their ideologies, and their future. There was still hope however, and the largest hunk of that hope, ironically, was based on the awareness that they were indeed flawed as a people, and as with any flaw, it could potentially be overcome or at least compensated for...

"What are you going to do? Where are you going to go?" Elcyd asked of Lannya.

She looked at Azli before answering. No immediate reply came to mind.

"Uh," Lannya grunted, which was followed by a clueless sigh, while still looking at Azli. Quickly after, she let her shoulders drop.

Lannya spun her eyes and head in a circle, overwhelmed by the notion.

"I don't know," she said. "It's just best we get out of here for a while. I'd like to stay in touch with all of you and do what we can to keep helping."

Azli quickly added on.

"Yeah. I want to do whatever I can, too."

No one acknowledged Azli except for Lannya.

"Well, I'm not going to try and hide that we're keeping in touch or anything," Heersan said to Lannya. "Definitely stay in touch, and we will, too. Let us know what we can do for you here if you need anything, and maybe we can have you look into some things while you're gone."

"Ok," Lannya confirmed. She then forced a swallow that the prospect of missing her friends forced her to take. Her eyes glazed over and grew wide.

"We'll get through this," Heersan whispered, attempting to reassure her. "Whether you're here or out there, we'll all get through this."

Lannya didn't ask Heersan to clarify whether he was referring to her and Rigella's argument, or the Astraean situation as a whole, but she had to believe he meant both. After a few hugs from Carthal and Elcyd, with Mamdod watching from the shadowed rail a ways back up the docks, Lannya turned to Azli and flicked her head in Paige's direction.

Chapter VI

Gravitational Lensing

Rigella seethed with anger as she walked back to the Harbor. *How dare they give Azli any quarter*, she thought. *How could they possibly have a problem with me smacking her around some?* She reassured herself of her actions by reminding herself once again, how much more she could have made Azli bleed. She strolled through her mental index of ways she could have caused Azli pain. She smiled as her mind paused on particular gruesome ways she could have killed her.

It was a smile of not only the thought of revenge, but the thought of justice. *The multiverse just can't allow Azli's actions to go unpunished*, Rigella thought. *It just can't. There was no justification at all for showing someone that level of mercy. What purpose would that level of consideration serve anyone or anything? How could that person ever be trusted or thought of as a benefit to*

45

existence? Rigella considered. *Oh, yeah*, Rigella imagined sarcastically. *Let me introduce you to Azli. She's the one that killed Akal and helped murder a few thousand Astraeans a while back, but gosh darn it, she helped us learn what kind of drink Einar liked, or some other absurd situation*, Rigella pondered.

Rigella stomped up the stairs in the Harbor lobby as she continued thinking, and received a notification along the way. After reaching the landing, she walked over to one of the upper landings that looked over the outer docks she had just left. She could see Lannya, Azli, and the others where she had left them. But Rigella quickly shifted her sight to the subject of the notification she had received. The victorious portion of the fleet she had dispatched to pursue Azli and her group was returning. The majority of Einarian ships that had engaged the Harbor were destroyed. Only a few successfully evaded the ADF.

Gallons of relief poured into Rigella's blood. Her mind raced a little less, and her heartbeat thumped a little softer. Her bloodlust for Azli was replaced by gratitude for the relative safety of the fleet. Most of what she considered *her* forces, as a mother regards her children, had returned to the Harbor in victory. But it went beyond that for Rigella. She *was* their mother, but also their father, protector, trainer, guardian. She considered herself something far beyond responsible for them, and she felt a similar sense of duty towards the Astraeans as a whole. Their collective fates were on her shoulders, she felt.

Without expecting it, a subconscious flag of doubt suddenly unfurled itself in front of her mind's eye. She was losing touch, and progressing beyond obsession, the flag's warning suggested. Her intentions were no longer noble or properly estimated, the flag hinted as it rippled. With another flip from the wind from her mind's gales, the flag finally insisted that she had lost control. She had turned her mission into a personal vendetta that could be waged by increasingly immoral and Pyrrhic means. She would win at all costs. All who oppose her would be extinguished. *How dare someone question my methods?*

As some of the returning ADF ships slipped back behind the security curtain and were once again hidden, the energy Rigella gave to entertaining her conscience's notion that she had lost control, dissipated just as quickly. *I'm doing what's best for our people*, she confidently thought, in what she convinced herself was unconditional confirmation, more than reassurance or an answer to doubt.

Her mind settled. Her thoughts cleared.

"Have the returning captains report to me for a debriefing," Rigella ordered. A newly developed local communications pin on her collar transmitted her message in real time. She continued with her instructions to an ADF officer on the other end. "We'll need to settle on a permanent location for the fleet to stay when not deployed, but keeping them behind the curtain for now is fine." As she spoke, her vision shot back over to the end of the section of docks where Azli and Lannya were about to depart from. Her mind was still settled, and still clear. She was done with Azli, and for all she knew at that moment, Lannya, too. She had an enemy to destroy and a people to protect. Lannya and Azli weren't even details.

She slapped the nearby banister as if checking something off a list and turned to check in with Harbor intelligence and the returning ADF captains. As she walked, the crowds of people around her dodged and swayed to avoid her. They were blurry filler in her peripheral vision that were of no consequence to her planning. She looked mostly at the floor as she made her way across the Harbor. It wasn't a matter of having contempt for the crowds, especially considering the crowds were who she was trying to save, but it was more that she was becoming more and more removed from her fellow Astraeans. They weren't a part of the immediate strategy or goal. They were just blurry background.

Rigella continued making her way through the Harbor and eventually made her way to a repurposed area of engineering, dedicated strictly to intelligence. She walked under the archway and immediately walked to a bank of screens processing numerous algorithms, which were in turn evaluating astronomical data coming in from Ontelbar.

"Central Commander," an analyst addressed nearby. "I have a sizable bit of data to show you. Just one moment while we complete these positioning models."

"Good," Rigella acknowledged efficiently. "When you're ready."

While waiting for the analyst to present his data, Rigella watched as Elcyd entered the room. He greeted some of the intelligence analysts nearby and spoke with them for a moment before catching sight of Rigella. He hadn't been looking for her, and didn't expect her to be there. It almost appeared to Rigella as if he had considered leaving, but he not only stayed, but immediately began walking towards her. At the same time, the intelligence analyst started to approach.

Rigella spoke to Elcyd first.

"Have they..." Rigella started, wondering if Lannya and Azli had left. Elcyd anticipated her question and then locked a look on her, not one of fear, but of careful consideration.

"Yeah," he said.

With no pause, comment or nod, Rigella then instantly turned her attention to the intelligence analyst.

"What do you have for me?" Rigella asked. She was ready to get back to work.

"We think we might have dialed in on a method to track Einar," the analyst said, barely able to contain his excitement.

"What?" Elcyd shot out in surprised shock.

Rigella couldn't help but swing her head towards Elcyd with a reactive reflex to his question before looking back to the analyst.

"Talk to me. What have you found?" Rigella pressed.

"Well, let me tell you the one weakness to all this first," began the analyst. Rigella stepped back and let a little wind out of her own sails of anticipation. Elcyd didn't twitch or flinch.

"We think our method is solid," continued the analyst. "And we think the information from the method is accurate, but as it is right now, there is about a three to four-day delay between updates on the latest information."

"And just to confirm," Elcyd started to ask. "The

reason for the delay is?"

"The size of the multiverse," the analyst answered with a helpless shrug. "Despite the ribbons, our technologies to interact with them, knowledge of the multiverse, our souls, and everything in between, we simply can't overcome the staggering size of the multiverse. Again, regardless of our technologies, relays, repeaters, ribbon data accelerators, allies that help with our data collection, you name it... It's just not comprehensive enough to eliminate the delay in gathering real-time data on any particular point in the multiverse."

"Ok," Rigella acknowledged, wanting to get to the main point. "So, you're telling me that we can't gather this data in real-time, right?"

"Correct," the analyst quickly confirmed.

"Understood," Rigella said while tilting her neck as if mentally tabling the topic. "So tell me about the good part of your news."

"Right, ok," the analyst obliged enthusiastically. Before continuing, he reached over and activated a nearby display, and then tapped a few commands to bring up some of his team's work. "So, here you see some of the methods we and the Ontelbar have used," he continued. "Or currently use, to observe and monitor various phenomena in the multiverse. We've had teams and teams of Harbor personnel, in conjunction with Ontelbar gazers, going through and evaluating the hundreds of methods and tools we know of, and determining which of those would be the most feasible in helping narrow down Einar's location. No one was getting anywhere fast. None of us were able to quickly evaluate and do a preliminary application of each method that yielded any significant hope of tracking Einar down. A lot of time was being spent trying to find the right tools, before we could even get to using any of the tools. That is, until we came across a very old human concept from before they were able to prove the existence of dark matter, as they called it, for themselves. The concept, as it was known then, was called gravitational lensing."

"I remember that term," Elcyd interrupted softly, turning to Rigella. "Something about how light is bent around a collection of matter that passes between the source of the light and an observer."

"Precisely!" The analyst happily affirmed. "It was exactly that phenomena that we decided to pursue with the Ontelbar, and had them begin looking for from their observational spires. But we had them modify the criteria and method. They shifted from looking for known, natural occurrences of gravitational lensing, to searching for possible variations on these events by evaluating how these occur naturally as a control, and then evaluating the data as a whole to identify possible abnormalities, or gravitational lensing that could be happening by artificial or engineered means. By shifting our focus on how we view these events, and modifying our algorithms, we believe we can now identify these types of events that are not happening naturally. The bending of light caused by artificial means does not exhibit the same behavior as the bending of light caused by natural matter, or dark matter..."

Elcyd had quickly gotten lost in the last few seconds of the analyst's explanation and was doing a poor job of hiding that fact. The analyst caught Elcyd's understandable lack of understanding and attempted to summarize.

"We think Einar is attempting to harness ambient energy in the universe for his ship, and cloak that process by a means that, without deeper inspection, would appear as natural gravitational lensing."

Rigella quickly looked away without direction to process the information. While still chewing on what the analyst had told her, she posed a question.

"Wow, that is an impressive leap and hypothesis," Rigella said, with reserved enthusiasm. "What was it about this one idea that made you pursue it? What made it more feasible than any of the other ideas your teams had already abandoned?"

Rigella was legitimately curious and wanted to ask her fair questions to ensure little time was wasted. The analyst nodded quickly before Rigella was finished speaking with a respectful understanding of her need to be skeptical.

"Right," the analyst returned, already prepared to answer. "Combined with what we had learned about Einar's ship, and what we had already learned in our initial searches for his ship, some of the methods we knew we could rule out quickly. Between the likelihood of gravitational lensing being a worthwhile route to pursue, and the speed in which we could confirm or dismiss it, we decided it was a good possibility to check. It was worth it, obviously. The idea to look into it came from Lannya, actually."

Without moving his head, Elcyd looked at Rigella.

She was expressionless, but silent for a moment. Showing no indication of appreciation for Lannya, Rigella responded.

"Ah. I'm glad it seems to be turning into a fruitful endeavor," she said. "What's the next step?"

"Well, as I said," the analyst began to remind her. "There is a delay of a few days before we can get data back on a particular position in multispace, or a universe's local space, but as soon as that comes in, we'll be able to compare and should be able to quickly narrow down areas to search."

"Do you think Einar is aware we can potentially track him?" Rigella asked as she leaned in and raised an eyebrow.

"None of us here think he's aware," the analyst said just above a prudent whisper. "He may have considered it at some point, if it's accurate, but I doubt he'll know if and when we confirm it. If this method of potentially tracking him is accurate, then our assumption about him disguising his ship's collection of ambient energy as gravitational lensing is also accurate. And that suggests he is probably very confident we wouldn't notice the difference between the naturally occurring events, and the ones his ship is creating."

Rigella sucked in a huge breath to give her mind and body a minuscule respite as she looked at Elcyd and back to the analyst.

"Ok," Rigella said with a nod at the analyst. "Let me know, or have someone from your teams let me know the moment you get the next data set back and begin to process it. How will you know which spots in the multiverse to compare your current data and new data with, in order to narrow down?"

The analyst couldn't help but let an impish grin slide into place on one side of his mouth.

"What? What's that for?" Rigella asked playfully.

"Before we started applying our modified calculations to look for artificial gravitational lensing, we started out with trillions of trillions of the occurrences."

The analyst returned to another grin, soaking in the joy of being in control of the anticipation.

"And now how many?" Elcyd asked, unable to contain his own grin.

The analyst let his eyes dart back and forth between Elcyd and Rigella, in a final jolt of anticipation.

"Twelve," the analyst answered.

Rigella's eyebrows practically flew off her forehead. "Twelve?" She let her mouth fall open slightly as she slapped her hands down on the analyst's shoulders in affectionate recognition. An astonished smile attempted to overtake her dropped jaw.

While still holding onto the analyst's shoulders with pride, she turned to Elcyd. Her face rapidly shifted from one of innocent excitement, back to one of mortal calculation.

"We're going to find him."

Chapter VII

Gimpan

The news of the conflict between the Einarians and Astraeans had spread rapidly. The news, and how it was slanted, was initially an advantage enjoyed only by Einar, but after Lannya's, Heersan's, and Carthal's visit to Caecus, and learning of Einar's propaganda, the Astraeans had successfully answered much of the damage that had been done. The Astraeans had old relationships and trust on their side, which it turns out, are far more powerful than new lies and hints of manipulation.

The Astraeans had quickly used their connections and friendships to spread the word of what was happening. Ribbon traffic flooded with messages, old allies corrected the misinformation by word of mouth, Astraeans traveled out from the Harbor, or from wherever they were in the multiverse, and quickly put a healthy dent in Einar's plan to ruin their credibility, and to add to the distractions and enemies the Astraeans had to face.

It didn't completely undo the damage, however. Their efforts to battle the propaganda gave them a solid chance to overcome it, but it already settled in too deeply in certain portions of the multiverse. Rigella and the ADF worked tirelessly to deploy forces to those areas giving them trouble, in an effort that they hoped would contain those conflicts, in both location, and scale.

The fabrication facilities were in constant production. The processes and speed seemed to improve every few minutes due to the amount of knowledge those working in the facilities gained from the volume of work they were doing. It was a stunning environment to witness. Each engineer and fabricator working in the facilities were keenly aware of what was at stake. With each piece processed, part generated, and unit assembled, they were inspired to do that much more, that much quicker. They were working not only towards the strength of the ADF, the security of the Harbor, or the future of the Astraeans, but for the lives and peace of the multiverse.

Rigella and Elcyd finished speaking with the intelligence analyst, and had started making their way out of the room towards general engineering when they heard a commotion from a far back corner of the intelligence section. It was uncharacteristically boisterous and bordered on being unprofessional. Both Rigella's and Elcyd's attention were stolen by an elusive inquisitiveness. They had to investigate. Elcyd first tapped a nearby analyst on the shoulder in hopes of getting an idea of what was causing their wild behavior.

"What's going on back there?" Elcyd chuckled at

the analyst.

The analyst, who had turned his attention away from the nearby display on the wall showing some of his work, had also begun to peer over his fellow analysts' heads to look at the group in the back.

"Heh! I'm not sure," the analyst replied, also with a chuckle. "But, that group supports our undercover planetary operatives on conflict planets. If they're cheering, then it has to be a good thing."

With that, Rigella and Elcyd made their way towards the back of the room. As they grew closer, other analysts from other areas also began to congregate around the rowdy bunch to see what the fuss was.

The back corner of the room was blatantly more disheveled than any other section of the intelligence section. This area was staffed and worked by analysts that were extremely proud of their work, and even more protective of the operatives they supported. They were one of the more obsessive groups, and Rigella empathized with them tremendously.

The conflict planets the operatives were on were often-times full scale war zones. The spectrum of conflict encompassed all manners of combat, but more often than not, they were conflicts involving entire civilizations and species on whole planets. Whole cultures were usually at risk in these conflicts, and the Astraeans were intensely interested in ending these conflicts that Einar's propaganda stirred up, as quickly as possible.

Rigella and Elcyd stood quietly for a moment, allowing their colleagues their moment of celebration. Elcyd skimmed the sight before him with a conservative smile that was fueled by his own personal pride in his fellow Astraeans. While he took in the moment, enjoying the revelry, Rigella rubbed her hands together in a symptom of sorts, of her withdrawal for information on their combat and intelligence advances. The waving grasses of analysts parted a particular way for a moment, and Rigella caught sight of a senior operative analyst, and called him over.

"Tapton!" Rigella slightly shouted. She waved her hand and beckoned him over. He looked up and waved back and started to weave through his teammates towards Rigella.

"Rigella! Elcyd!" Tapton belted as he approached. "Please pardon the noise. We just got some amazing news!"

"It looks that way!" Rigella returned, shouting again just above the surrounding noise. "What's happened?"

Tapton cuffed a hand around his mouth to help direct his shouted reply.

"We've just received word that the Einarians have fled from Gimgan. We ran them out!"

"Fantastic!" Rigella roared in a rare display of genuine excitement, reminiscent of how she had acted in the past.

"Yes!" Tapton reciprocated. "Luckily, the native Gimgans are simply too connected with information, and fortunately, with us as well. The planet never really got anywhere near accepting Einar's propaganda. They knew better. We did have to put up a good fight in their local space and atmosphere however, and while we did sustain some losses, it was a decisive victory for us. We weren't sure what to expect given Gimgan's importance and influence, so we are very glad to have this news. The reaction from the team here is actually a little delayed. We heard we ran the Einarians off, but being Gimgan, there were of course some symbolic games some of our people had to take part in with a few Einarians on the ground. We just heard that we won those as well."

An intelligence analyst from a different discipline, that had come to find out what the celebration was for, leaned over to Elcyd after hearing Tapton's comments.

"I'm not familiar with Gimgan," the eavesdropping analyst said to Elcyd. "What did he mean by our people having to take part in some games?"

***

Gimgan is a colossal planet. It is just slightly bigger than WASP-17b from Earth's universe, which is in turn, about twice the radius of Jupiter, also from Earth's universe. Gimgan was originally too large and gaseous to be considered a planet, but as the indigenous organisms evolved, they began to naturally secrete a material that solidified large areas into solid ground over time. This natural process of secreting materials that hardened the ground, similar to a tree and its resin, provided energy to other native organisms and again, via evolution, was adopted by other species and flora. All native Gimgan life, portions of which evolved long ago into highly intelligent creatures, is sustained by this symbiotic relationship between themselves and the planet. The native Gimgan races secrete their resin-like material which build up the land and structures naturally, that over time, break back down, and provide the Gimgans with energy.

The result of eons of this cyclic process is a singularly rare landscape that enchants and seduces millions of lifeforms and beckons billions of visitors. The ground, and most of Gimgan's natural formations, resemble the translucent caramel of fossilized amber. As a visitor walks around and looks down, or looks into the structures and features made of this material, it appears either boundless or adrift. Restless. Depending on how thick the material is at a given point, or the amount of light striking it, an onlooker has no choice but to be swept up in the simultaneous seduction and ambiguity of the beautiful material. The shape of the landscape changes somewhat quickly however, when compared to conventional landmasses, given the material's propensity to break down after three or four hundred years.

As a result, things are very fluid on Gimgan. Citizen populations are frequently migrating, as they have adapted to doing for centuries, and cities are often under a very complimentary construction. The Gimgans have mastered moving facilities from one location to another. The frequent change of the landscape is something looked upon affectionately by native Gimgans, and not only respected, but appreciated and enjoyed by visitors for the excitement of discovering what's changed since their last visit. As the land breaks down, changes shape, and then forms new continents, large seas of Gimgan's original gases move and change shape as well.

Native Gimgans are thin and limber, but don't move often so they can stay connected with the ground. They are usually found throughout the planet holding political or business positions, and remain in their positions of employment for the majority of the day. And while Gimgans do have to spend large amounts of their day tethered biologically to their planet's surface, or to biological structures connected with the surface, they are able to break that connection for a few hours at a time, which they refer to as their "fasting time," and is usually spent managing or engaging in high stakes competition and games, whether a physical contact sport, or game of the mind.

Games. The primary and only concern on planet Gimgan. It is each Gimgan's sole purpose in life, to either develop games, compete professionally in games, modify or expand games, or work in the gaming tourism industry. Gimgan is known throughout its own universe, and many others, as being the prevailing destination for gaming, gambling, and strategy.

The almost incalculable size of the planet allowed for the creation of entire states devoted to different kinds of games. Numerous artificial microclimates and atmospheres allowed practically any race to visit and enjoy a game of their choosing. Games ranged from contact sports, team sports, combat sports, (both small, and simulated battles between tens of thousands of life-size armies), as well as almost as many card games, table-top games, and board games, as there are different species in the multiverse. The games available were wildly varied in regards to being suitable for particular species, and their features or weaknesses, age, cultural and historical sensitivities, as well as well-separated zones for lethal and non-lethal games. The lethal portion of the planet was only a fraction of the total available landmass, but was still substantial due to the overall size of Gimgan.

Not one person's or creature's eye could look anywhere while on Gimgan without seeing a scoreboard, game board, statistics ticker, playing surface, or people and creatures without a costume or outfit needed to participate in a particular game. Structures, cities, and buildings were architecturally and aesthetically whimsical, but at the same time, blended in perfectly with the landscape.

Many buildings had seemingly random arms, branches and sprouts that stuck out into the many open-air causeways and walkways, which were made of a rubber-like material in bright primary colors. Some buildings were tall skyscrapers, and others were expansive, single-floor structures serving different purposes. Bobbing and floating in the air at all heights using various thrusters or manipulations of electromagnetism, were other towers and buildings that could frequently be seen to have creatures jumping from one to another, through tunnels, into pits, or vehicles darting back and forth between them.

The environment was a perfect example of stimulation. The entire planet was safe, clean, and welcoming. It was an amusement planet for all ages, all interests, dreams and imaginations. Nowhere was there an alarming sight or harsh sound. No activity, competition, or game, no matter how complex, physical, or cerebral, was ever too innocent, or at the other extreme, too obscene. Anything and everything on Gimgan was meant to stimulate the mind and imagination for maximum entertainment. Even the skies were often lit up, miles overhead, with projected games, made possible by massive and synchronized laser emitters, depicting massive games of all types, by those willing to pay for them.

The popularity of Gimgan, and its influence on other planets, cultures, and universes, was why it was such an important victory to whoever won the conflict there. The military portion of the conflict was decided in the near space surrounding the planet, but there was a very Gimgan representation of the Einarian & Astraean war, that had to predictably take place on the surface.

***

In the first days following the formation of the ADF, and establishment of its initial priorities and missions, the Harbor decided it would be of great benefit to send groups of operatives to scout and see just how entrenched the Einar propaganda machine was on some of the more socially influential planets. Gimgan was at the top of that list. Shortly after the operatives assigned to Gimgan arrived, they found that not only had the Einarians established a solid presence on the planet, but had spread their propaganda to a degree the Astraeans thought could not be overcome.

The majority of the Astraean operations on the Gimgan surface were purposely restricted to clandestine intelligence gathering, surveillance, and efforts to counter Einarian falsehoods. There were a few acts of physical subterfuge upon the Einarians, but the Astraeans had no desire to initiate, or otherwise take part in, a war on the surface of Gimgan. Gimgan was too large, too public, and too popular, and both the Astraeans and the Einarians seemed to be keenly aware that any attempt to bring the fight to the streets of Gimgan, by either starting it, or failing to frame the other side for starting a war, was not at all in their interests. So, while the forces of each side fought their battles in local Gimgan space, each side was also doing their part on the ground, in a proxy war of information, image, and ideology.

The native Gimgans knew what was taking place between the Einarians and Astraeans, above their skies, on the ground, and far away from their world. And while many races might resent the possibility of being treated as pawns, or remain neutral and as unbiased as possible in such a conflict, they found joy in actively picking a side and taking part in yet another display of strategy. Almost as old as their earliest beginnings as a race, was the almost spiritual purpose they found in considering all possible options in every scenario, which helped them not only empathize with others and other ways of thinking, but helped form a moral compass in a way. Going hand in hand with their love for cunning, was their love for reaching a victorious end for the most noble cause. Though the Gimgans had publicly chosen sides for various conflicts in the past between countless other cultures, the Gimgans this time decided to publicly remain uncommitted to either side in the Einarian and Astraean conflict.

Privately, however, the Gimgans were unconditionally on the side of the Astraeans. They withheld their support for the Astraeans, not out of fear of the Einarians, especially considering they were a formidable military power in their own right, but chose to lie about being neutral, because they believed it to be the most sound, strategically. Behind the scenes, the

Gimgans were supplying the Astraeans with information as to the Einarians' movements, communications they intercepted, and even had hidden ports on desolate areas of their planet where they allowed the Astraeans to land, and repair their ships, or provide the Astraean forces with other arms or tools. While the Astraeans, and secretly, the Gimgans, were decisively handling the Einarians in the skies, the feigned Gimgan neutrality allowed them to assist the Astraeans with their efforts on the ground.

The leader of the group of Astraean operatives on Gimgan went by the name of Mohio, who had taken the form of a Gimgan while there. Being an Astraean, he didn't need to root himself as often as native Gimgans do to gain nourishment, so as far as anyone knew, at any given time, Mohio was just out and about during some of his fasting time. Together with his covert subordinates, they did all they could to quietly begin tipping the balance of public opinion that had been swayed heavily by the Einarians. They did so quietly at first, but quickly increased their efforts. First it began with anti-Astraean posters being ripped, and pro-Astraean posters being placed on walls and light poles, then quickly to mass communications and advertisements on various media or in-between games, especially those taking place on the huge displays in the sky, and towards the end of the battle in Gimgan local space, Mohio, and his closest friends began openly challenging Einarian supporters, or Einarian operatives directly, to "friendly" games of various types on the ground. The fights in the skies may have mattered more to the overall power of the two combatants throughout the multiverse, but everyone knew a war of public opinion was very often times just as important.

A day or two before the Einarian ships were forced to flee Gimgan space, Mohio and his team entered one of the more prominent and large gaming facilities known as the Vavalaga. The need to hide their identities, or conduct their activities in secrecy, had mostly evaporated. It was a suggestion from a Gimgan ally that they come out of hiding, and essentially challenge the Einarians to a Gimgan variation on a duel. Mohio could think of no better place to do that, than the Vavalaga.

The Vavalaga was an enormously expansive building that housed countless single-person games, booths, virtual and augmented reality spheres, exploration tunnels and tubes for younger visitors that twisted around and vaulted up into the ceilings. Similar but more complex tunnels and paths, suspended from the ceiling, also curled intricate paths throughout the facility. They vaulted up, out, and through the ceiling and walls, and back inside, allowing adults of various species to play a myriad of combat games. The whole complex would remind most humans of everything an arcade could ever possibly be.

This was also one of the primary locations in the region that, in addition to providing countless games, one could place bets on anything and everything that could be wagered on. In that context, it was a humorous idea of the Gimgans, to suggest Mohio make an obscenely expensive wager in favor of the Astraeans against the Einarians. It was the Gimgans thinking that not only would such a ploy garner the wrath of the hidden Einarian operatives, but also, especially considering their forces had taken such a beating out in Gimgan space, give them no choice but to answer whatever challenge the Astraeans made.

Mohio walked into the Vavalaga, still sheltered by a hooded cloak of brilliant blue which was adorned with hundreds of geometric metal shapes made of tough golden strands. Each symbol was only attached to the jacket at one point for each symbol. The coat clinked and rattled as Mohio approached the main counter inside the Vavalaga. It was next to impossible to hear the noise from the coat however, given the myriad of sounds filling the expansive complex.

Mohio's team flanked him in support on each side of the counter, with some stragglers remaining on the surrounding steps, and the main floor below that. Over the crunchy sounds of the games, screams of winners, shouts from players of team games, laughs, burps, and mechanical hullabaloo, Mohio waved over one of the attendants behind the counter. After the attendant came over, Mohio leaned over the counter a bit. He could feel the light from the counter below warm his neck and chin.

The attendant leaned in as well so he could hear what Mohio was shouting over the ambient noise. The conversation only took a moment, but the attendant leaned back quickly to look in the eyes of the hooded guest to confirm he heard correctly. Mohio nodded slowly with an accompanying slow blink. Mohio's lips flattened and spread to the sides of his cheeks. He was enjoying this.

The attendant continued looking at Mohio for a few extra seconds after Mohio confirmed his doubtful expression, but then shrugged in astonished reluctance and walked over to what seemed to be a superior. The attendant tapped the man's shoulder to get his attention and relayed to him whatever had been agreed to between Mohio and the attendant. The apparent superior jerked back from the attendant in an effort to confirm he heard correctly, just as the attendant had done to Mohio. Mohio watched as the attendant looked back at him, and pointed at him while wearing a huge smile.

The superior continued talking to the attendant and also began typing commands into a nearby terminal. When the conversation between the attendant and his superior ended, the main scoring display and wager ticker at the center of the main counter pylon cleared. A final quick visit from the attendant let Mohio know that his superior had agreed to his request. The attendant shook his head in disbelief and wished Mohio good luck as best as he could with only his eyebrows. After that, the attendant approached a bank of various microphones and transmission units to announce what had just been settled.

"Pause your games, or hold your die," the attendant belted into the microphones. "Lower your weapons, and try this on for size! We've got a major announcement here for you. This may be your best chance at astronomical stakes while you're here with us on Gimgan! There aren't many in this universe, or anywhere else I dare say, that aren't aware of the Einarian and Astraean war. And while the battle they've been fighting in Gimgan space is about over, it looks like there is one point of business still left to be decided!"

The music, sounds, and noise across the cavernous room had mostly ceased. The crowd was hanging on every word of the attendant's building anticipation.

"It seems that we have a group of Astraeans here

that are not only pleased with their latest victory in Gimgan space, but have a grudge to settle down here as well!"

The room erupted. Thousands of creatures and people that found more pleasure in gaming, theory, and strategy, than war, could appreciate very few things more, than someone wanting to settle a grudge via a game. As the announcement was made, and the room continuously overflowed with renewed cheers and enthusiasm, Mohio stepped forward to own the moment. First, he slowly peeled back his hood, revealing his face, and then removed his cloak, revealing his entire form, and clothes.

Mohio had recently changed from the Gimgan form he used as cover, to his usual male form, now that his cover was no longer needed. He was an incredibly fit and cunning black human. His mind and physique were always poised to act. Each crease in his skin was caused not by age or neglect, but by the peaks and valleys created by his muscles. His bulk and build were not to intimidate, or to show off, but were practical and efficient. He trained regularly for his own enjoyment, health, and physical ability. He was also adorned with numerous tattoos, all of a bright chalky color that stood out perfectly on his ebony skin.

The most prominent tattoo that stood out first to most onlookers, was the set of white squares that wrapped around his left forearm which alternated between the black squares made of the negative space of his skin. It was a simple chessboard. But it was more than a chessboard. It was a representation of gaming recognizable by many across the multiverse. His informed respect for games and strategy was known to Gimgans, and those in the room had their cheers and excitement injected with that much more titillation than before. In addition to his chessboard tattoo were dozens and dozens of other imagery related to gaming, strategy, warfare, and the tools to take part in gaming, or measure various activities in gaming.

"Dial in your discs, carry up your credits, cough up your cash. Prepare to wager, prepare to bet. A better match, you're never going to get! The Astraean operations team have challenged their Einarian counterparts to an event for the ages! A match for the millennia! A game for the galaxy, worthy of the Gimgans! The Astraeans have challenged the Einarians to a best, two out of three contest, playing, Star Slaughter!"

The crowd throbbed and waved fiercely trying to get to the booking counter, as handfuls of credits, discs, cash, coins, gems, and other forms of physical currency started sprouting up in the fists of the crowd, ready to be wagered. The previously empty screen on the giant pillar behind the counter started filling with wagers being placed on a variety of side bets. They were being taken on the win-loss ratio of the contest, length of each round, moves and strategies the two sides would use, and hundreds of other possible topics. This was before the Einarians even answered the challenge.

The audacious Astraean challenge wasn't a simple diversion that some might seem as a waste of time, or something that would diminish their greater conflict with the Einarians. There was no intention to belittle the memory of those they had lost. It was not only an effort to help influence popular opinion of the conflict, but also a matter of pride and a symbolic gesture by the humbled Astraeans that their cause was right.

The floor of the Vavalaga couldn't be seen. What little empty space there was between games, tables, machines, droids, and concession stands, had been taken up by hundreds of additional Gimgans and visitors from across the multiverse. Everyone wanted a piece of the action. Additional Gimgans had come over to the Vavalaga to assist in taking bets and placing them into the system. Just minutes after the announcement, thousands and thousands of bets had started pouring in from across the entire planet, with some remote bets coming in as well from across the multiverse. This was *the* event.

Mohio and his fellow Astraeans stood fiercely proud with crossed arms around the perimeter of the main betting counter, waiting for the Einarians to respond or to arrive. While the Astraeans and the thousands of gamers inside the Vavalaga waited, the Gimgans in charge began piping in an intoxicating wash of what could be best described as a seductive music made of steady electronic beats and thick synthesizer pulses. The hype had organically swelled on its own to a point that threatened to rupture the seams of the building if it were possible. The ultimate war between the nebulous concepts of good and evil was far from over, but this would be one battle that no one wanted to miss.

Impatience didn't have time to take root in the room. The arrival of the Einarian operatives came quickly in the form of an obnoxious strafing of flickering laser lights on and around the entrance to the Vavalaga. What was night in this region of Gimgan became temporarily lit up by the Einarians' arrival as they bathed the immediate area in wild patterns of light, emitted from the bottom of their transport. Many transports and ships in and around Gimgan had similar light displays for show, or to assist in advertising, and were a sign of pride for Gimgans, but no one had ever seen such an elaborate and impressive display like the one coming from the Einarian transport.

The massive group trying to make their way inside the Vavalaga stopped as they were distracted by the approaching lights. When they saw it was the Einarians arriving to answer the challenge, they forgot about trying to get in for a moment and cheered ecstatically, knowing the contest would indeed take place. Many that were in the Vavalaga already, struggled to push their way back out, to watch the Einarians make their landing at the nearby platform outside the entrance.

The streets and skies adjacent to the Vavalaga were congested by those being beckoned to the spectacle. Masses of beings and people spilled out for blocks, and ships and transports littered the skies of all elevations. The viewing area for a game of Star Slaughter was massive, and if a spectator was within a few miles of the Vavalaga, where this particular match of Star Slaughter was going to take place, they would have no trouble watching the contest unfold.

After the Einarian transport settled on the nearby platform, a ramp popped out from underneath. Almost immediately, as the sound from the crowds grew to an immeasurable level, feet appeared at the top of the ramp and began to walk down. The feet belonged to an instantly recognizable Einarian.

Her name was Nemilos. She was in the form she

usually adopted, which was that of a female Pulma, a mostly humanoid-looking race with olive skin. The most noticeable feature of the Pulma race is that instead of breathing with lungs, they breathed through their hair. The equivalent of their inhale was exhibited by their long hair extending out to a sharp corona around their head. Their hair falling back down to a limp state was the equivalent of their exhale. Watching a Pulma breathe was intriguing, but intimidating.

Nemilos marched off the ramp, followed by her own team of fellow operatives. The crowd around their transport parted slightly, but quickly, as they made their way to the Vavalaga. The Astraeans looked over the heads of the crowd, and out through the doors to the approaching Einarians. Mohio smiled and nodded at his team to follow him to the entrance. They were off to welcome their opponents.

"And here we are!" The Gimgan attendant announced to the vicinity. "The two sides are here and ready to light the sky with a legendary contest of Star Slaughter, the likes of which we surely have never seen before, and will never see again! Get your wagers in now! Stay tuned for additional announcements. The contest will begin shortly!"

The equally ancient, powerful, and experienced groups of highly-trained operatives marched towards each other. The crowd, similar to how it cheered outside at just the arrival of the Einarians, collectively screamed and swooned even more insanely at the sheer spectacle of these two sides meeting like this since the relatively new war between them had begun. This is exactly what the Astraeans wanted, and what they had anticipated. This fight, this game on Gimgan was just as important an element of their fight against Einar as was a gargantuan battle of thousands to the death.

Nemilos smiled at Mohio. It was a frightening smile that was further bent by a demented tilt of her head and drop of her eyebrows. If there hadn't been a clear understanding of what this meeting and game were all about, and if it weren't taking place on Gimgan, or if absolutely any circumstance of this meeting were any different, there would have been no civil march towards the other. There wouldn't have been any smiles or peaceful cohabitation of the room. There would have been immediate lurches at the other for first blood, complete blood, and all blood. Nemilos' hate for the Astraeans rivaled Einar's. She had been a close friend to Azli and was a trusted confidant to Einar. Mohio, for his part, was extremely close to Rigella, and thought similarly in regards to priorities and obsession. Nemilos and Mohio were exemplary champions for their respective side.

The two finally reached each other, still flanked by each of their teams. The crowds around them drew in closer and closed the paths behind the two champions so that they and their teams faced each other, but were otherwise completely surrounded.

Nemilos maintained her smile, but slowly tilted her head to the other side of her shoulders while her hair extended and dropped repeatedly. Many in the crowd looking at Nemilos were legitimately scared of her, and if not for the surrounding thousands, would have been sent fleeing out into the dark streets from terror. Between the movement of her hair that allowed her to breathe, which was a disgusting sight to some, the odd movements of her head, and her perpetual smile, she made most of the room feel uncomfortable and as if they were in danger.

Mohio on the other hand, a staunch statue of strength, stood in front of Nemilos, with his arms by his side, as his hands formed fists. In his silence and pose, he let the people around him know that he was there to defeat Nemilos in this contest, just as the Astraeans had won the battle in their skies, and just as the Astraeans hoped to defeat Einar in the overall war. Not only this, but he would protect them. He and his team of Astraean operatives would defeat Nemilos and send them fleeing along with the fleeing portion of their fleet that had recently been beaten. Mohio involuntarily flexed various leg and arm muscles from the adrenaline and anticipation of beginning their game. Each tattoo, symbols of respect for countless cultures and their various forms of strategy and combat, seemed to ripple and flex along with his muscles. The match-up was extraordinary.

Nemilos let her smile fade slowly into an open mouth, while being in no hurry to speak.

"How's Akal?" Nemilos asked with a false concern, knowing that Akal had been killed by the Einarians.

Mohio was ready with a reply.

"How's Azli?" Mohio wondered, rubbing in that she had defected. "I'm surprised you're still here," Mohio continued as he pointed quickly to the skies. "Seeing how your ships got scared off and everything."

Nemilos conjured another wicked grin and said nothing else.

"Gimgans and all gaming fans," the attendant yelled over the intercom. "The Astraean and Einarian teams have met. We have ourselves a contest! Please begin filing into the appropriate queues to be seated for the contest, and we will begin in ten minutes!"

As the attendant finished speaking, he leaned over to a bank of controls under a portion of the center counter and flipped numerous old switches. It was obvious the switches and this particular facility had been there for some time. After flipping the switches, numerous things began to happen. The previously covered fabric top of the Vavalaga began rolling back from the center, to the outer edge of the building, revealing a massive expanse of nighttime Gimgan sky. When the fabric finished coiling up to the edges of the walls, extremely tall lengths of canvas-like material shot up into the sky to temporarily block the light pollution from the surrounding buildings. As the shades slid up for miles into place, the scene high above become brilliantly clear and detailed. When the shades reached their final height far above in the lower atmosphere of Gimgan, a quick flash of light seemed to take a snapshot of the sky. Then, using an amazingly powerful lighting and laser system, the image of the night sky was superimposed upon itself, digitized and recreated high above in an extremely vibrant three dimensions that appeared much closer to the Astraeans, Einarians and onlookers. This was the playspace for Star Slaughter.

Another set of switches the attendant had flipped opened recesses in the floor and temporarily swallowed up all the remaining games, booths, spheres, stands, and all other extraneous objects. All that was left was a bank of seats that would be inhabited by Mohio, Nemilos, and their respective teams of operatives while they played the game. The seats automatically leaned back comfortably to allow the players a perfect position to view the playing space, high above.

The majority of the onlookers had taken seats along the walls at the outer perimeter of the building, leaving the bulk of the floor empty. Whoever wasn't able to find a seat to watch the game inside, trickled outside, boarded their ships or friends' ships and transports. Anyone within miles that wanted to watch the game unfold, had a place to watch it from. And while games of Star Slaughter took place all the time at the Vavalaga, or many other similar arcades across the planet, everyone knew there would never be another game of Star Slaughter like this, again.

Star Slaughter was thought by many to be the most challenging, complex, and beautiful game to ever exist. The mechanics and systems of the game were very straightforward, but simultaneously allowed for an almost exponential variety of strategies. At a minimum, there had to be two opposing players, each controlling a paddle of sorts that could be moved around a confined area of the outer space within the simulated night sky above them. Each side used their paddle, which resembled a large space station, to deflect a comet that was in constant motion. As the comet flew through space, being bounced back and forth between the two sides, the comet could either be missed by a player's paddle and enter a simulated black hole behind their paddle and award the opponent points, or, the comet could strike another object in the space between the two opponents. Depending on the amount of additional players, there were many obstacles, devices, and special items that could intercept or influence the path of the comet. Each of these additional interactions with the comet awarded or deducted various amounts of points.

The most common event during a round of Star Slaughter, is that the comet would come in contact with, or come in close proximity to a star. Each time that happened, the star involved in the contact would advance in its life cycle stage. If a star was struck enough times and reached the end of its life cycle, going nova and becoming a black hole, any subsequent interactions with the comet would cause that comet to be lost. Depending on such factors such as which player last interacted with the comet, how many comets were left to a player and so on, when a player ran out of comets, they lost the match. Each side began the match with three comets, and there was a maximum of five players per side. Given that both the Einarian and Astraean operatives had fairly large teams, both sides were able to play with a full complement of players.

The teams were ready. The spectators inside the Vavalaga and in the surrounding skies and streets were uncommonly quiet. If someone had wandered into the area with their eyes closed, they would have been hard-pressed to realize there were thousands of people all around, doing all they could to contain their composure. It was time. The Astraean and Einarian teams were comfortable in their place in the Star Slaughter command chairs. Across the empty and dark floor at the edge of the walls, the spectators inside the Vavalaga waited for the first comet to be launched. Outside, in a similar anticipation, countless Gimgans and visitors stood frozen. Their heads bent back as they waited for the sky to be set afire with the launch of the first comet.

With a concussive rip, the first comet, or ball, was shot up into the atmosphere with an explosion from a facility a few blocks from the Vavalaga. Before the report of the firing mechanism settled into the streets and nearby valleys, the crowds were already screaming and rooting for the action that had already begun high in the skies above them. The crisp flashes of light, from objects being struck in the reproduced night sky, slapped the ground below with occasional interruptions of dancing streams of shadows. The entire sky seemed to be moving. Nothing was still. Stars grew in size and color as they were struck, while the tail of the comet appeared to play connect the dot with the heavens.

Mohio and Nemilos controlled their respective teams' paddles. Depending on the bonuses their team had received during game-play, or temporary rewards they had uncovered as the comet flew through space, the team captains were responsible for a wide variety of paddle options. It could be a single paddle, up to a possible three paddles. The length, physics and shape of each possible paddle could also be modified at any given time. The amount of coordination necessary was extreme, as was the need to communicate with their teammates on how to properly defend their side of the playing field, and attack the other side.

The playing field high above was so gargantuan, it was often easy for any given team member to lose track of what the other team was doing. Their paddle, offensive and defensive movements could easily blend in with the rest of the game area. It was very common for a team to seek out dense planetary and star systems, or asteroid belts, to stealthily approach their opponent, or use such areas to hide some of their traps and offensive structures.

Mohio hated being predictable, and found much success by incorporating some degree of randomness into many of his previous operations. While he usually allowed sound strategy and tactics to drive his actions, he sometimes gave them a backseat to spontaneity and chance. He also enjoyed gambits and seemingly worthless sacrifices to gain an advantage later in a confrontation. He quickly evaluated information and looked ahead to the possible results of many scenarios before acting. He was quite brilliant.

Very early in the match, the Astraeans gained an additional defensive paddle that Mohio appeared to leave largely stagnant, which is something that caught the attention of Nemilos quite quickly. It was simply a distraction, which allowed some of the other Astraean team to sneak out from their origin point and establish some temporary defenses on their flank. By the time Nemilos saw the stagnant paddle and registered that something was up, the Astraeans had already deployed some defensive gates and left the area.

The Einarian team was already well on their way to carrying out some of Nemilos' initial orders as well. Using a temporary skill modification, their offensive paddles activated a momentary cloak that allowed them to travel unseen for a time. While the Astraeans couldn't see them, they shot straight out for the Astraean side of the sky as quickly as they could. Nemilos knew Mohio probably expected an aggressive move from them right out of the gate, and she didn't care about that. She wanted to be a fly in their ointment as quickly as possible. The more time anyone had in any conflict allowed them to possibly gain an advantage, and Nemilos believed one advantage was too many.

The Astraean offense was proceeding towards the Einarian side slowly and deliberately. They were sure the Einarians would strike first, and planned to take advantage of their focus on that, to make their move. Closer and closer, the Astraeans grew to the Einarian origin. Mohio waited patiently for the Einarians to launch a strike while setting up more traps and defenses near their own base. The comet, almost an afterthought, was being batted around constellations and star systems. Each side was dedicating only a single offensive paddle to the struggle with the comet, while the remaining elements of each team were working towards the larger picture.

As expected, the activity in a whole quadrant of the play space near the Astraean origin became noticeably still and quiet. The flashes of light from various stars, nebula ripples and other phenomena ceased. But just as the quadrant grew silent, it lit back up almost immediately in a relentless fury of laser fire from the uncloaked Einarians. Mohio was ready however, and rapidly captured or weathered much of the first round of fire, and deflected with his team's defensive paddles.

Nemilos was focused intently on her offensive, but reminded her team to keep an eye out for the Astraeans as she spared a second every so often to scan the sky herself. They didn't know where the Astraeans were. As a precaution, some of the Einarian offensive began to backtrack, with plans to defend their origin once the Astraeans showed themselves.

Mohio continued using the defensive systems deployed near their origin to his advantage and with a good amount of concentration, and a wealth of skill, was able to keep the remaining Einarian offense at bay. The portion of Einarians that had left to defend their origin mostly nullified their early offensive advantage.

When the returning Einarian forces arrived back at their origin, much to the surprise of Nemilos, the large majority of the Astraean team, whose location was previously unknown emerged from a dense asteroid belt near their own base and flanked the Einarians that had remained. They were easily dispatched, which allowed the Astraeans to escort a virtually unchallenged comet into the scoring black hole of the Einarian side.

Match 1-0, Astraeans.

After only a ten second break between rounds, the area surrounding the Vavalaga was rocked again by a fresh explosion of a new comet into the Gimgan atmosphere. This time, both sides had new strategies. Rather than each side concentrating on the attack or defense of an origin, both sides fought for control of the comet as soon as it reached the plain of combat.

Each team exchanged volleys of fire, while others weaved in and out of each other, batting the comet back and forth between themselves. The faces of the spectators below reflected the constant crimsons and brilliant blues from the fight high above them. There was little to no progress made towards either team's scoring zone. It was a stalemate and an all-out battle.

The comet would get struck by one team's paddle and slammed into a star which then grew in size and danger. One team member would get killed, respawn at their origin and return to even the odds just as one side seemed to make some progress. There was no progress. They had changed their strategies, but both teams had ironically chosen the same strategy. An all-out offensive control of the comet, and disregard for the origin. If the comet reached the scoring zone, or an origin was destroyed, that would be a win, and no team could afford to abandon control of the comet to launch an attack on the origin. Whoever won this round would win it with the comet.

Just when it seemed there would never be a resolution to the current round, an Einarian player missed a team member's pass of the comet. The comet shot out into an empty area of space in the playing area which was pounced upon by the Astraeans. An Astraean which was already headed to cover the Einarian that missed the pass saw the blunder and changed course slightly and slung all of his momentum in the direction of the comet.

"Go, go, go!" Mohio screamed at his teammates in the command chairs around him. "Cover him!"

They had anticipated Mohio's command. Before the Einarians could establish a worthy reaction to their mistake, the bulk of the Astraean group fell in behind the player with the comet and raced for the Einarian scoring zone.

The night seemed to turn to day from all of the laser

fire coming from the Einarians who were in an increasingly futile pursuit. There was no lack of skill between either team. The level of knowledge and experience and warfare were almost equal between the teams as well. This type of gaming can only reach a conclusion when one person or group makes a mistake like the Einarian player did. The Astraeans were taking advantage.

The constant blanket of fire from the Einarians was relentless and punitive, but the Astraeans had enough of a lead to use the space to their advantage. They were able to dodge most of it, while only losing a few players that had to spawn far back at their origin. The blunder was too large, and the Astraeans took too much advantage. After a well-fought pursuit, the Einarians lost when the Astraeans reached their scoring zone with the comet.

The region of Gimgan surrounding the Vavalaga popped and shimmered like icecaps on an ocean. The people and creatures erupted in elated excitement from the contest. The Astraeans had won, 2-0.

The Astraeans shot out of their command chairs, leaving the units they were in control of, high above, lifeless and still. They wrapped each other up in embrace, shouting in victory at the sky as they pointed and gestured triumphantly at the 2-0 score displayed in the play space. The Astraeans had no thought of the Einarians, or concern for their feelings, nor did they even think to consider acknowledging them or speaking to them after the match. There was no need for that. In their minds, a gesture of respect and acknowledgment of honorable battle was only deserved by those who were respectful or honorable to begin with. The Astraeans found no respect or honor in the Einarians. Instead, they directed their appreciation to the Gimgans.

Mohio, after celebrating for only a moment while his team continued to cheer their victory, turned to the attendant and shouted loud enough for him to hear.

"That was an exhilarating fight, my friend" Mohio hollered at the attendant. "Thank you for..."

Before Mohio could finish thanking the Gimgan attendant, they were stunned by numerous heavy thuds that Mohio instantly recognized as Gimgan rifles that the Einarians had smuggled into the Vavalaga.

In the second it took for Mohio to turn around, a few of his team were already on the ground. The rest of his team were rushing the Einarians to engage them. This lethal attack on the Astraeans after their victories in both the Space Slaughter contest, and the battle in Gimgan space, were a larger betrayal of Gimgan custom and hospitality that most could possibly imagine. Not only was this attack cowardly, unethical, and evil, but most egregiously, it was an attack that was not earned. Most strategists would acknowledge the strength and advantage and skill in a pre-emptive attack, but not in this situation. The circumstances surrounding the Space Slaughter contest were agreed upon before-hand. It was understood that it would be a respite from the true carnage. It was a contest of honor, respect, and goodwill. The fact that the Einarians didn't have any of those virtues, was an unfortunate oversight by not only the Astraeans, but the Gimgans as well.

The Einarians didn't stick around to continue the fight. They only wanted a last word in the form of their surprise attack and began to flee once Mohio and the others began to chase. The shock of the attack, the insult upon the Gimgan culture and philosophy shocked everyone. Native Gimgans, spectators and visitors alike stood motionless in not understanding how this could happen. The Einarians had too great a lead on Mohio and the remaining Astraeans. By the time Mohio and his group had started chasing in earnest, the Einarians had already boarded their transport and escaped.

Mohio didn't linger and raced back inside to his friends, lifeless, and spread out on the floor near the Space Slaughter command chairs. The attendant slid up next to Mohio after a sprint, frantically concerned for the Astraeans.

"Rewind time. Do it! Hurry!" The attendant pleaded.

Mohio said nothing in response, and only held the head of one of his teammates in his hands. He couldn't speak. He didn't want to.

One of the Astraean survivors answered on Mohio's behalf.

"We can't right now," the Astraean said solemnly, staring at the friend's head in Mohio's hands. "Einar's done something."

The attendant's eyes had begun to drown, hating the helplessness of the situation. The Gimgans were not unaware of, or naive to the evils in the multiverse, but this senseless scorn stirred the sadness in their souls, regardless.

"Though your victories above and down here should be enough to spread the word," the attendant began to Mohio, through a broken throat of anguish. "We will do all we can to fan the flames of your cause."

Chapter VIII
Shifting

Similar fights of various sizes over various degrees of public opinion took place almost daily across the multiverse, and didn't always have results that mirrored those on Gimgan. The Einarians had made exceptional use of their wealth of time and executed an incredibly efficient plan that not only saturated great portions of the multiverse with their propaganda, but had done it quickly. To some, it would appear obvious that the Einarians should have easily smeared their stain of lies across the multiverse, but it in fact wasn't so feasible a plan.

Einar took great care and an initially large hunk of time to coordinate and consider what areas to target. Just as the Astraeans were rushing to figure out how to target their reaction, Einar had to figure out what to target. By the time the Astraeans had developed an idea on how to combat Einar in earnest, most Astraeans felt that it was too mountainous an effort; the summit of which could never be ascended.

It wasn't just a simple matter of Einar whispering lies into the ears of the influential, or slathering posters on the walls of major cities, or writing strongly-worded letters. It was a grotesque raping of the natural evolution of time, species, and cultures. Einar trained countless followers, and worked tirelessly himself, to fabricate illegitimate religions to conflict with those that came to be organically, influence leaders, establish various forms of government, philosophy, and ideology, that would most times blatantly, or at least subtly, encourage species to eventually support his view of the multiverse. He needed his motives to be empathized with, and understood. He did it on Gimgan, on Earth during the American Civil War, and other occasions across millions of other worlds. The scope of his actions was astounding. Not until the Einarians had revealed themselves to the Astraeans did anyone think such manipulation of the multiverse, on the scale they had done it, was possible.

But again, there is a reaction to every action, and that reaction can sometimes counteract the originating action. The Astraeans hoped the pendulum of fate would swing in their favor. They knew they didn't have the time to reverse Einar's propaganda by countering locations one for one. Elcyd and Mamdod, primarily, along with Rigella, decided that given their extremely finite window, they must carefully select where to counter Einar's lies. With a bit of luck and deliberate consideration, they hoped their efforts would ripple exponentially throughout the multiverse.

Their victory at Gimgan was a prime example of a successful execution of their strategy. Slowly but surely, the Astraeans pressed on through defeats in the arena of public opinion. Soon after, they began trading some defeats for wins. Eventually, with few leaves left on the ribbon island tree, the Astraeans began winning more and more wars of words. Their efforts were cumulative and multiplied rapidly, which translated into more assistance from others, in not only their fights of opinion, but also in ground and space battles across multiple galaxies, star systems, and planets. The response to Einar from the Astraeans was nothing short of exemplary and impressive, but the final cost of this rapid evolution in focus was still yet to be determined.

Collectively though, the Astraeans knew whatever sacrifices they were making were worth it. Most of the multiverse was aware of the conflicting sides now, and those who hadn't yet seen through the Einarian lies at least knew to be skeptical of whatever they were being told. There was a growing doubt in the Einarian cause, which was the least the Astraeans could hope for.

The ADF grew up quickly, both in terms of experience, ability, and size. Ships were being churned out at the rate of hundreds a day. Infantry, both ribbon and physical, were being trained up at a rate of thousands a week. The Astraean effort had not only trained up their own Astraean personnel, but had also caused thousands of residents from across the multiverse to volunteer for the Astraean cause. The ADF quickly eclipsed the Einarians in numbers and raw power, but at this stage of the conflict, Einar had no intention of meeting the Astraeans on every possible battlefield or to defeat them militarily. He only had to evade them, and wait for the last leaf to fall.

There were now 24 total Markarian-Class Capital Stations deployed across the same number of different universes. The number of Carina-class Capital Carriers had grown to 823, while the number of Scuti-Class Battleships had reached 1409. The Cephei-Class Heavy Cruisers totaled 1580, and the Centauri-Class Cruisers totaled 1733. Persei-Class Frigates had also swelled in number to 2004. The total number of Astraean and volunteer combat personnel had climbed to a staggering 90,000, with twice that in ribbon infantry.

Production of the fleet was constant and fast for the longest time and had only recently begun slowing down. It was obvious to the Astraeans that the need for them to focus on military production had lessened, given Einar's recent silence and slightly revealed plan. The fabrication facilities began to shift attention to maintaining the ships and equipment they had produced already, upgrading them, and tending to Harbor structures and defenses.

The Harbor had been reinforced to an imposing degree. It was an impressive bolstering effort, and not one that detracted from its original beauty or minimized the Astraeans and their cause. It was simply, as many Astraeans thought, how the Harbor should have been defended and protected for a long time. Additional security curtains, defensive turrets, ribbon devices and systems, security and encryption measures, docking and mooring safety protocols, and outer perimeter beacons had been deployed.

There of course was a lingering uncertainty about

their fate among Astraeans, of all rank and position. But, that was moot. They had successfully jumped the hurdle of necessary reaction and answered the challenge as best as any culture unprepared for such malice could. The Astraeans were doing what they needed to do. No one had given up, nor was anyone overly confident. The entire culture simply got to work, and focused on the fight. The result of the entire conflict would come, whenever it came. They were fully aware from the initial attack that they had no control over anything but how they reacted, and they reacted with determination and resolve.

As expected, the happy-go-lucky mood, that had been so prevalent in Astraean culture for millions of years, stiffened and dried up significantly. Once, people would linger along the docks, or next to vendor booths, relaxedly talking about the news of the multiverse, or simple pleasures such as recipes or entertainment. Now, conversations were cut short. Someone was invariably on their way to deliver something to the fabrication facilities in support of something having to do with the ADF, or someone was getting ready to be deployed on a mission of some kind. Time was no longer an abundant luxury for the almost-timeless Astraeans.

Smiles weren't completely foreign, however, and humor wasn't completely lost, but the focus on the war and constant feeling of playing catch-up up to Einar's ages-old deception were noticeably wearing on everyone from Rigella, to the newest ADF recruit. From Elcyd, to the staff at the Helper Desk. Even Mamdod hadn't been able to escape the decline in mood, though his personal disposition was often at odds with peace anyway, from his sense of regret over starting his game.

Mamdod sat along the edge of a bridge connecting the main Harbor complex to one of the many smaller sections around it. He would occasionally catch the eye of someone making their way to something that was more pressing than it previously might have been, and despite the added urgency, some fellow Astraeans still managed to offer a smile or nod. Mamdod was grateful for each one. They helped distract him, if only for a moment, from how alone he felt, even during the busiest flows of foot traffic. As the days ticked by after being freed from rules of his own making, he felt the curtain being pulled further and further back on the illusion of his acceptance.

The Astraeans never really had any other option than to try and get past the fact that he had brought all of this upon them. It wasn't a question of forgiving and forgetting, but logic and practicality. They had to not only suspend whatever grudges they may have or animosity towards Mamdod, but then welcome him in, bring him up to speed, and use whatever knowledge he might be able to impart to give them even a hint of an advantage.

The few smiles he received from strangers weren't just smiles. They were polite facades. Acknowledgment of being locked into this sick game that completely backfired in his face. They weren't glad to see him. They weren't wishing him well or respecting him when they saw him. Many empathized with Mamdod, or sincerely looked past what had happened and saw the innocence in his original intentions, as Elcyd and others had, but most Astraeans only tolerated him, and hoped he would leave after they were done with Einar, if they were in a position at that time, to be done with Einar.

Mamdod fully realized this and understood the general opinion of him. He didn't blame them, and found no fault in the distance many Astraeans kept between themselves and him. He routinely told himself that he would more than likely feel the same way if roles were reversed. He was sure that he would cross to the other side of a bridge if he were approaching himself, or gather in groups to voice his disgust or anger. He knew how they felt and didn't try to ignore it. All he could do was try to help where he could.

He had been alone for eons on the island, directing souls, but he wasn't lonely then. His memory, clouded by its own master, made his ignorance truly blissful, though hate and manipulation took root in the shadow of his game. This new loneliness was not obscured in any way. It was potent and alive. He was being avoided while being disliked, and despite all awareness and understanding of why it had to be so, Mamdod often found the isolation terrifying, and endless.

There was no other alternative but to push through it. He considered countless times the various actions someone could possibly take, to include leaving and abandoning the Astraeans, but those were involuntary thoughts that came and went from his mind. He never gave any meaningful thought to doing anything but staying and trying to help, trying to help defeat Einar, and trying to overcome what his own game had spawned.

Mamdod's days at the Harbor were mostly taken up by visiting the engineering and intelligence sections, to check on the progress of tracking Einar and collaborate with engineers and intelligence operators, or were spent in lengthy and dense meetings with Elcyd and Rigella. The few lulls in activity were mostly used to get back to the ribbon island to guide souls to their available paths. Sometimes, he would pick up a newly-fallen leaf from the tree, hold it, and trace its veins with his fingertips. Or other days, his time was spent keeping the shadows of the Harbor company, waiting for time to pass.

He had just recently returned from the ribbon island and begun a bit of people watching and soul searching when Thyra started to approach in a brisk walk. Her eyes were buried in a tablet in one hand. Her other hand held two others. The world outside her tablets didn't exist at that moment. She was completely sucked in by whatever data or history she was no doubt assimilating for use by the Harbor against Einar, and almost passed Mamdod without ever knowing he was there. Thyra was one of the Astraeans who held no grudges towards Mamdod.

"Hey, Thyra," Mamdod gently offered in her direction.

She continued walking for a few steps while looking around for the caller. She saw him fairly quickly and smiled. A real smile.

"Hi! Mamdod! She returned pleasantly, waving at him with her tablets. "What are you doing over there?" She started to approach him as she slung her data tablets under her arm.

"Just taking a moment," Mamdod replied, turning his focus into the ribbon streams under the bridge. "Aren't they beautiful? I'm still in awe of them."

"Yeah, there's nothing else like them," Thyra

replied. "How could you not still be in awe of them, right?"

Mamdod smirked playfully at himself while continuing to stare into the sea of blue ribbons. His smirk quickly sagged away, however, and Thyra noticed. She let her head tilt and fall forward a bit to get a better angle on Mamdod's eyes. She said nothing while waiting to see if he wanted to continue the conversation.

"Do you ever wish you hadn't become an Astraean?" He asked. His vision was still focused down below.

Thyra wasn't quite sure what he was implying and stumbled for an answer, only managing to blurt out a few incoherent syllables.

"I just mean," Mamdod began to clarify, "do you ever think it's too much, being an Astraean? Isn't it too much power? Too much knowledge and too many lives? Have you ever thought that one life should be enough? One life's loves and hates, failures and accomplishments, joys and heartaches?"

Thyra wasn't fazed at all by his questions, because they weren't foreign to her. She had indeed thought them before, but didn't immediately answer. She leaned over the rail of the bridge, next to Mamdod, and stared into the ribbons below as she considered her previous thoughts on such topics.

"Yes, I've definitely asked myself those questions before," she replied with a soft empathy. "I've scraped my soul raw, trying to understand why I've lived the lives I've had, made the choices I did, had the experiences they've had, and why I have access to them all as an Astraean. Having to live pretty much eternally, having a massive collection of pain seep into my brain every now and then?

It's too much, sometimes."

Mamdod nodded quickly, recognizing all of Thyra's thoughts as his own.

"But, I haven't worried about the whys and hows, in a long time," Thyra continued. "Even now, with our fight against Einar, I've actually surprised myself by how well I've been able to stay focused."

Mamdod turned to Thyra with a surprised curiosity, prompting Thyra silently for an explanation. She looked at him quickly before looking back to the ribbons below.

"Control," she said. "I never had it." She smiled widely. They looked at each other as she elaborated.

"Oh, it's not a profound epiphany or anything. It's a realization we all know and are aware of. It just takes enough quiet moments to remember. But, I had to learn to remind myself of it during the not-so-quiet moments. As soon as I started reminding myself how pointless it was to question things I had no control over, or may not have had as much influence on as I would like to think, then my ability to get the most out of existence, increased greatly. Because like you said, we have a lot of lives, and a lot of time, but even many Astraeans find ways to spend all that time miserable."

Mamdod looked at Thyra through eyes of wonder, humorously humbled by being taught such a beautiful lesson. For a few moments, Mamdod was speechless, but as the brain often does, his couldn't allow for peace or simplicity, and had to ask another question.

"But what about my game?" Mamdod asked, frustrated with himself. "I developed that. I chose to handle it that way. I came up with the rules."

"Did you?" Thyra immediately challenged. Mamdod flinched with an expression of surprise at how she could doubt his blatant role in his game. Thyra laughed playfully at the fun she was having with their philosophical discussion.

"Seriously, though," she implored. "What if everything we know about choice, and luck, and fate, and improbability is as rudimentary and undeveloped as say, how time is misunderstood on Earth? If there are ever potential unknowns, we have to be conscious of that fact."

Mamdod let Thyra's comments pour into his mind and mix with the river of contemplation already overflowing the banks of his conscience. It was a needed flood of possibility on the dry soil of his mood which provided many nutrients to his struggling sprouts of hope. Thyra's words were not just platitudes to help him cheer and chin up. He found true relief in the simple consideration that he may not have had as much say in how things had transpired as he previously thought. But he may have. That was Thyra's point. He didn't have enough information to definitively say whether or not he was in complete control of his game, his rules, or anything else that had occurred up to that point. All he could do, was press on and deal with the situation at hand. Whether or not it was by his own making, was irrelevant.

His moment of clarity, that Thyra had helped him realize, soon began to make the river of emotion and thought recede in his mind. Not only had he come to a moment of clarity for that particular moment, but as Thyra had alluded to previously, it was a relic of clarity that he could carry with him at all times, in his heart and mind, that he could refer to at any future point. And whether he realized it or not, his subconscious, now less encumbered, began to wander back to ideas on how to defeat Einar.

"Earth!" Mamdod shouted at Thyra. A spark of an idea's suspicion scraped the inside of Mamdod's mind.

Thyra jumped at Mamdod's seemingly random exclamation and could see him working to ignite the idea's spark.

"You said something about Earth a minute ago," Mamdod began to rapidly ramble while looking at the ground to organize his thoughts. "Elcyd has mentioned before that the last Astraeans to arrive here lived their last regular lives on Earth, right?"

He gave no real time for Thyra to reply as her eyes widened to endearingly take in Mamdod's excitement. He slowly raised his clenched fists from his side as he continued racing through his idea.

"All of the people that I've helped at the ribbon island since my game started, also came from a life on Earth!"

The adrenaline surged through Mamdod as the excitement over a possible clue made his eyes jump up to Thyra.

"That has to be worth bringing up to somebody!" He shouted through a euphoric smirk, anxious to discover whether or not his idea would be actionable.

Chapter IX

Correlation

Thyra didn't need to say anything in response to Mamdod. He had already begun taking steps backward in the direction of the main Harbor complex to look for Elcyd and Rigella. Thyra immediately began following him close behind, with a wild grin. By the time Mamdod had turned around to face the Harbor, they were both sprinting across the open walking areas, dodging curious and confused Astraeans.

They weaved in and out of fellow Astraeans, transports, ribbon cargo pods, and other obstacles strewn about. After a few minutes of all out sprinting, they zipped in through one of the open, main Harbor entryways and flung themselves into the Helper Desk.

"Where is Elcyd?" Mamdod asked in a quick huff of depleted breath. The confused Helper tapped a screen quickly and looked back to Mamdod.

"He's in his office, but," the Helper attempted with concern.

"Thank you!" Mamdod interrupted as he and Thyra took off again. Up the stairs they went. As fast as the elevators were, the crowds around them were thick and there seemed to be a wait. Mamdod figured expending the extra energy was worth it, anyway.

Up a few flights of stairs, while huffing and clawing through the corridors as quickly as they could, they finally reached Elcyd's office. His door was open and the sound that accompanied Elcyd's and Thyra's scrambled sprint to find him, startled him, causing him to jump and eject a stack of data terminal pads into the air as he almost fell off of his stool. Before Elcyd could even fully register who had come tearing into his office, he started shouting at whatever, or whoever, it was.

"What in the Kestrellian sky is..." Elcyd shouted as he began to collect himself after almost hitting the floor. He quickly looked up and identified the obnoxious interruption. "Mamdod? Thyra? What's the matter? What has gotten into you both?"

Mamdod couldn't speak immediately. He bent over and grabbed one of his knees and pointed at Thyra, hoping she would be able to start explaining while he caught his very labored breath. Thyra wasn't doing much better, but flung a finger up at Elcyd, letting him know she'd be ready to speak in just a moment. Elcyd took the opportunity to scoop up the data terminals from the few hunks of bare carpet.

"I'm glad I wasn't holding an arm full of knives," Elcyd began to gripe while bending and stooping, "or, trying to input time-sensitive calculations to stop a bomb from blowing up or something!"

"Elcyd" Thyra finally was able to force out. "Mamdod has an idea that might help us with Einar."

Elcyd snapped up in excitement and completely forgot about being startled or inconvenienced. As he started to stomp over the piles of artifacts, papers, and broken chunks of technology, he plopped down the few pads he had picked up onto his desk. Upon reaching Mamdod, Elcyd bent over and met Mamdod's eye and began helping him up.

"What have you found out?" Elcyd pleaded eagerly. "What have you learned?"

Mamdod looked up to Elcyd to signal he was about recovered, and smiled over at Thyra in appreciation for her assistance in beginning the conversation.

"I'm sorry," Mamdod said quickly, through a chuckle and a cough. "I guess we could've come in a bit more calmly, but, I think I may have an idea on where Einar is manipulating and directing ribbon traffic from!"

"What?" Elcyd gasped, not expecting such a proposition at all. "Where? How?"

"I think it has something to do with Earth," Mamdod began. "You've told me before about how all Astraeans that make it to the Harbor lived their last regular life on Earth, right?"

Elcyd nodded quickly. His eyes were open intently as Mamdod continued.

"Well, since my game began and my memory was released, the souls I've helped at the island have also come from there, Astraean or not."

Elcyd's head tilted from having no explanation or understanding of the building oddities. He held up his hand at Mamdod, prompting him to pause, which allowed Mamdod to catch up on a few more breaths. Elcyd spun around and darted over to his desk terminal. After tapping a quick command, a connection with Rigella's office was established.

"Rigella," Elcyd blurted at the screen. "Apologies for the interruption. Do you have a moment? Mamdod and Thyra are here with some possible news on Einar."

Rigella didn't hesitate as she gestured for a few nearby subordinates to wait.

"Yes. I'll be right there."

Elcyd tapped a button and ended the connection. He began to rub his chin roughly as he came back out from behind his desk, and considered any and all possibilities that had come to mind. Mamdod's breath had returned, and allowed him to pick back up on his line of thinking.

"I probably never would have thought anything about it," Mamdod added as Rigella jogged calmly into the room, "but when Thyra mentioned something about Earth, I considered that there were too many very specific issues lately, involving Earth." Rigella placed her hand lightly on Mamdod's shoulder and quickly jumped into the conversation.

"Hey, I came right over. Will you ask a few senior engineers to join us, Elcyd, just in case we need them? I'm sorry, Mamdod, please continue." Elcyd immediately returned to his terminal and silently began reaching out to engineering.

"Yes, ok," Mamdod resumed, hoping silently that

this would be the last time he would have to start the conversation. "There are just a few coincidences that I think we need to investigate. Elcyd recently told me what I think all of us know, and that is that all Astraeans that come to the Harbor have lived their last regular lives on Earth, right?"

Rigella nodded in agreement. "Mmm hmm. Right."

"Well, all of the souls I've helped at the ribbon island, since my game began, have also come there from Earth. Why would all souls, Astraean and non-Astraean alike, be routed to the ribbon island through Earth?" Mamdod's eyes jumped around for a second as he recollected the other coincidence he wanted to bring up. "And wasn't it Einar, previously known as Daebaugh, that personally expelled Lannya from the Habitats?"

Elcyd's office was overcome with bewildered silence as the inhabitants tried to piece everything together. To make sure everyone was on the same page, Mamdod quickly followed up with a few rhetorical questions that none of them knew the answer to.

"Why was Einar on Earth? Why did he personally have a hand in ending Lannya's last regular life? Why does everyone's last regular life come from Earth?"

By that time, a few engineers had entered Elcyd's office, with the others spilling out of the door due to the cramped size of the room. A lead engineer spoke up having heard the questions.

"So, you're suggesting that Einar is based on Earth?"

"Well, no, not necessarily" Mamdod replied,

being careful to make sure no one misunderstood. "I'm only saying that I think those coincidences are worth investigating."

"I agree," Elcyd said in support. "There has to be a reason Earth is coming up so frequently during some fairly eventful circumstances."

"I don't disagree that we need to look into to this," Thyra offered, "but I can't think of a reason why Earth would be so important. Why would he have picked Earth?"

"I don't think that's a question we need to answer just yet," Rigella said, noticeably outlining priorities in her mind. "We may never discover his motive for selecting Earth, if there is indeed something going on there, but for now, we should definitely go and check it out."

Seeing silent expressions of agreement on everyone's faces, Rigella turned to Elcyd.

"Can I use your terminal, quickly?"

"Of course," Elcyd swiftly replied.

Rigella shimmied and danced between Elcyd's piles until she was within an arm's reach of the terminal, which she then grabbed and spun around to face her. With a few quick taps, she had opened a line to the ADF Readiness Officers.

"Central Commander!" A Readiness Officer quickly spit out in recognition.

"Yes, hello," Rigella acknowledged. "I need an overview of what forces we currently have in the 9th universe, and what we currently have available for deployment. When you have it, just send it to me by encrypted message. Put this at the top of your department's priority list. Understood?"

"Yes, Central Commander," the officer replied professionally. "It should only take a few minutes to gather that for you."

"Great, thank you. Rigella out." She tapped the console and ended the discussion with the Readiness Office, and turned her attention back to the room.

"I'm still considering whether or not we should send any of the ADF, but I wanted to know what we had at our disposal, just in case. We don't know if this may be something Einar had considered we would discover and investigate, to draw out our forces, or if it was an oversight, a trap, or anything in-between."

"I know it's not the most important question to answer," Thyra began to reiterate, "but I'm still hung up on why he would have chosen Earth over any other planet in any other universe."

"Yes, I agree the answer to that question doesn't trump needing to investigate this," Mamdod added, "but, it's a good question that might provide some context to information we haven't uncovered yet."

"If there is something there," Rigella continued to speculate, "I would imagine it plays some part in what he's doing to interfere with ribbon activity?"

"Yes, that's what Thyra and I were thinking," Mamdod confirmed.

"Do you think it's a device," Rigella started to suggest, while glazing over and searching the blurry room for other possible ideas. "Or maybe a structure, or..." She began to trail off before thinking of another possibility. "Or, maybe something unique to the planet itself?"

The room had no immediate answers and had

nothing to suggest.

Mamdod flicked his head up at the engineers with an idea.

"Could your team look into the 9th universe for any recent anomalies, and maybe check in with the Ontelbar as well, just to see if there may be something we can use?"

The lead engineer did a quick scan of the room in an abbreviated agreement check and agreed.

"Yes. We'll look into that right away," the engineer provided.

Rigella moved on to her next question.

"Regardless of whether or not I send any ADF to Earth, did any of you want to go, or have any suggestions on how we should go about looking into this, dirt-side?"

In the past, small operations such as this, were carried out by Rigella, Carthal, Heersan, and Akal. With Akal being dead, and his proxy, Lannya, being practically expelled along with Azli, and with Rigella more than likely staying behind at the Harbor, the room grew uncomfortable quickly with no ideas coming forth on how to proceed. Rigella picked up on it immediately and tried to brush past it.

"I think Carthal and Heersan could handle this," Rigella suggested somewhat warmly, hoping they could get back on course with their planning. "It would need to only be an intelligence gathering mission. If something else needed to happen, we could quickly reinforce them and take action with the ADF."

Mamdod looked down to ponder for a moment and came back up quickly with a comment.

"I would like to go as well," he said with a strong voice.

"You?" Elcyd asked only from surprise.

"Yes," Mamdod replied while nodding to himself. "If there's something going on there with the ribbons, I'd like to be there."

The room understood.

"I want to go, too," Thyra quickly and confidently appended.

"Ok," Rigella began to summarize, not wanting to waste any time. "We have a plan. Mamdod and Thyra, if you two want bring Carthal and Heersan up to speed, you can let me know if they agree to go and if you need anything. I'll let you know what my ADF readiness report looks like and we can finalize the details then."

There were a few softly spoken signals of confirmation as everyone started to shuffle out of the room.

Chapter X

From Scratch

Azli sat on one of Paige's top deck benches and stared hazily at nothing while massaging her eye socket with the top of her index finger. After she rewound time, it was as if her face had never been sliced, and her bones had never broken, but, her memory of the pain was intact. Her memory of thinking how she deserved the attack as Rigella kicked her, was intact. Her mind was cluttered with other confusion, and lost without any plan or purpose. Despite all she had done and all she had been, her mother still loved her. But, even so, Azli felt unworthy of kindness and love. She had been spared, and protected, and it felt like a dream. It wasn't a happy dream necessarily, but only a feeling of detached from reality. Her mother had virtually turned her back on those that had sustained so many deaths by her own hand, all for the cause of family and hopes of creating the bond between a mother and daughter that never had a chance to grow. But, she couldn't ever recall being more aimless or empty than she was at that moment. *Empty.*

Empty, empty, she kept saying in her mind.

She still couldn't conjure any anger for how Rigella treated her. She couldn't conjure feelings of any kind on any topic. She was done with caring. She felt that she didn't deserve to care. The only particulate floating above the emptiness in her mind was a reminder of remorse that she owed to her mother. Once she felt she had repaid that debt, she would be out of the Astraeans' hair. She didn't know in what form her departure would take, she just knew that she had to leave once she felt she had done right by her mother, whenever that might occur.

It wasn't a matter of her not wanting to help the Astraeans, or the Einarians, or a matter of picking any kind of side. It was a matter of her feeling worthless, hated, and evil. She knew, just as everyone else did, that she had done more than enough to quantify her feelings. She couldn't stand the thought of herself, or others having to put up with her anymore. She made herself sick.

Lannya sat across from her on a similar bench, with a similar blank expression. Her mood and hope had careened onto the rocky shores of the same island Azli was stranded on. Despite having her daughter with her, and having started the long process of bridging a million gaps of varying lengths and depth, she wasn't happy. The joy Lannya felt following her and Azli's fight in Universe CG after they reunited, quickly dissipated. She was afraid the illusion of a functional mother-daughter relationship would forever remain an illusion.

The worn cushion of Lannya's bench creaked and rubbed roughly as Lannya repositioned, possibly as a means of subconsciously hoping the adjustment would improve her mood. It of course didn't help, and she allowed her head to fall into the palm of a hand and bent arm which was propped on one of the upper deck railings.

Paige slipped along to a destination Lannya had quickly selected in their rush to leave the Harbor. The destination had long left Lannya's mind, and as she was momentarily distracted by the flashes of ribbons shooting along beneath Paige, she realized she had forgotten where they were going, and couldn't rustle up any hint of caring.

Lannya strained her mind in hopes of forcing an idea of what to do next, or as she looked at Azli, struggled for something to say. Nothing immediately climbed up from the basement of her mind. With Paige randomly traversing to a pointless place in the multiverse, neither she nor Azli were serving any purpose to anyone, good or bad, pro-Astraean or pro-Einarian. She didn't regret being so vehement about her dedication to her daughter, or the effort she put into winning her back, she only regretted the hollowness of the aftermath.

Lannya looked up at Paige's main sail. She couldn't think of anything else to do. She then huffed in frustration, stood up and kicked a nearby stack of cargo pods, sending some of them flying or rolling into the shadow of an open storage pantry.

"I hate this," Lannya finally directed at Azli with a furious density. "I hate everything you did. I hate Einar for using you."

Lannya stomped a random pattern into the top

deck as she walked around it, trying to clear her mind.

"I hate Rigella for attacking you. I hate them all for rejecting you, and I hate being out here doing nothing with nowhere to go."

Azli rolled her head and looked at Lannya to see if she wanted her to say anything. It didn't seem like it. Lannya was still stomping around the deck in muddled contemplation and only looking at the ground in front of her. Azli was relieved, because she didn't know what to say anyway.

Just as she thought nothing would come to mind, her thoughts surprised her.

"We could go to the Dark Artery," Azli threw out flatly. Her head was drooped, but her eyes shot up to judge Lannya's reaction.

"What kind of idea is that?" Lannya asked with a crisp disgust. "After all of this, that's the first thing out of your mouth?"

"I don't know what you want, or what you want me to say!" Azli shouted back. "That's what you wanted me here for, right? To help you all get Einar?"

"No, Azli!" Lannya returned quickly as she approached her. "I wanted you back because you're my daughter!"

"Yeah, I know," Azli shouted as she rolled her eyes from her frustration with the argument. "I mean, you still need my help, right? At this moment, you want me to help you all find Einar, right?"

Lannya spun around and resumed her pacing on the deck in an effort to bring the frustration between them down.

"Yes, we need your help," Lannya confirmed.

"Well, let's just go. I'll show you where his ship is," Azli offered. "We can worry about everything else later. Let's just do something. Focus on... something."

Lannya stopped and looked up to draw a few large breaths before shoving them out. She turned back towards Azli.

"My frustration isn't all because of you, Azli," Lannya said, wanting to put some clarity in their tense conversation, and hoping to address her suggestion. "I agree we need to do something, and I want to do something. But, going straight for the Dark Artery might be biting off a bit too much right now."

"No, there are a million ways to confirm it's there. Disguise Paige, and ourselves," Azli said confidently. "We can do this."

"Azli," Lannya started while rubbing her closed eyes. "I was thinking of something a little more..."

"Safe?" Azli correctly predicted.

"It's just us, Azli!" Lannya shouted as she threw her arms up. "How do you expect..." Lannya cut herself off and changed topics, needing to have something else answered first. "You know, I haven't asked you this yet, but I need to."

Lannya's voice stepped down in intensity a few notches. "Why did you stop fighting? What made you give up? What made you turn?"

"I don't know!" Azli shouted. She surprised herself with her honesty and also ratcheted her attitude back some. She reiterated her exposed honesty.

"I don't know."

Mother and daughter maintained their focus on each other, but took a break in the argument to internally evaluate any progress they may have made.

"Look," Azli continued. "I know what I've done, but I also know Einar, what he's doing, how he works, and where he's at. If you all are serious about getting to him with the little bit of time you have left, then let me help. That's what your issue with Rigella was about. I don't understand. Did you just want to put me up on a shelf somewhere with a plaque under my name that says 'daughter?'"

Lannya slid her hands down her cheeks and pressed in as she did for as much friction as she could generate. She stared a dark and ancient hole into Azli as she responded. Her voice resonated with an understated power that can only come from a confident Astraean and wronged mother.

"If that's what you think, then you can throw yourself overboard and go back to Einar for all I care. If what you've done really registered, to include murdering my husband, your own father, and how I still held out hope for you despite all of that, you wouldn't say something so ridiculous. How dare you."

"No," Azli grunted with a raw realization of her poor word choice. "That's not what I meant..."

The frustration at the entire situation, as well as their shared emptiness and loneliness boiled up and over once again. Azli threw her hands up and flung herself back onto her bench as Lannya kept her eyes trained on her. She didn't let Azli know right away, but she was considering her suggestion. *Like she said*, Lannya thought. *Everything else needs to take a backseat to taking Einar out.*

Lannya finally took her eyes off of Azli and glanced over at a nearby terminal. Only now did Lannya see the destination she had randomly selected when they left the Harbor. She ran her hand down the back of her head and neck as she let the destination escape her lips.

"Trigitag," Lannya said softly. She looked over to Azli to see if she had heard. Azli's eyes were trained on her, so she assumed she had. Lannya looked back to the display and further considered the prospect of searching out the Dark Artery as her outlook started to sway. Their exile from the Harbor may have afforded them the autonomy they would need to venture to the Dark Artery. Lannya wasn't the strategic thinker that Rigella was, but she did know that the fewer elements to a scenario there were, the easier it may be to accomplish a task. Beyond that, Lannya felt no allegiance at the moment to the Astraeans, or at least, to Rigella.

Lannya turned to Azli, ready to give in to her proposal.

"Ok. Where do we go?" She asked calmly.

Azli showed no sign of excitement or dread, but merely provided flat instructions.

"We're headed to Trigitag, you said? Meet up with the Trigitag ribbon then take that to universal intersection seventy-two-B."

Lannya listened to Azli give the last few instructions on how to locate the Dark Artery and found herself in a foggy mix of purpose and disbelief. She couldn't believe after all that had happened to the Astraeans, and how little hope there was in finding Einar before the last leaf fell, that she was actually hearing someone tell her how to find Einar. After Azli finished with the details on how to reach the Dark Artery, she plotted the course into the nearby terminal and turned back to Azli.

She felt a surge of adrenaline tingle to the top of her skin, followed by paranoia. She smacked herself around mentally with a hundred doubts and questions. She couldn't decide if she truly trusted Azli, and she considered also that Azli might be leading her to a trap. The only thing that swung Lannya's internal pendulum to the trusting side was what she saw in Azli after their fight in Universe CG. Lannya knew all too well that Azli could have been deceiving her then, or could be now, but there was just a small splinter of something that kept her from kicking Azli off Paige and leaving her in her ribbon wake.

"Ok," Lannya said with a dry uncertainty. "Here we go." She then looked around the boat and directed her next comment to Paige's various audio receptors.

"Paige? Increase flow factor to maximum after we go below deck," Lannya directed. "Come on," she then said to Azli, and started down the stairs below deck.

***

After descending into Paige's interior while submerged in the ribbons, a shallow conversation continued, but then quickly dwindled back to nothing. After Azli explained to Lannya that their destination was a secluded area of universe seventy-two-B, just outside the Dark Artery's monitoring radius, they quickly discussed their final approach for when they arrived. Following that, Lannya rushed Azli through a few of Paige's features in case she needed them. The remaining portion of the trip was swallowed by silence, except for a few sighs from the two passengers. Or, the clanging, beeping, and whirring of various ship mechanisms and systems would occasionally break the monotony. They both had lifetimes worth of additional thoughts and arguments in their minds, but neither of them had the will or energy to keep the fire fueled.

Azli occasionally stood up without saying a word, and would stretch, or shuffle to various parts of Paige's common areas. She browsed through shallow drawers, and pressed buttons on and off to see what happened. Lannya watched her explore with just enough concern to power her eyes so that she could follow her around the room. Slowly but surely, emboldened only by her accumulating boredom, Azli strolled and wandered out into Paige's other areas. Each time she did, Lannya would toggle on Paige's various security feeds to keep an eye on things. There was still a degree of distrust that prompted her to turn on the feeds, and a portion of prudence to do so, given the volatility of their newly sprouted relationship, but also, Lannya was mostly only curious. She just wanted to watch her daughter explore. She wanted to watch her daughter walk, and see what drew her curiosity. How she strolled and how she turned her head. How Azli carried herself, and how she behaved were things Lannya as a mother had missed out completely on, and she was trying to catch up.

After what felt like hours of Paige traveling at her fastest ribbon speed, the boat's voice came over the sound system and splintered the stagnant silence. Azli heard

Paige begin to speak and started to return to the common room. Seeing that Azli was making her way back, Lannya switched off the video feeds.

"At current flow factor: Maximum, we will reach our destination of the Rhombex System in ten minutes," Paige announced.

Azli's steady stomps could be heard approaching the common room. Lannya stood up and began a standard systems diagnostic, and a scan of local Rhombex space for contacts, spacial phenomena and conditions.

"There seems to be a large solar storm on the far side of Rhom," Lannya announced as Azli entered the room, "but nothing that affects our arrival."

"The Dark Artery is adjacent to Rhom over there," Azli explained, as she pointed to an area of the system's projection coming from one of Paige's terminals.

Lannya turned slowly to Azli with a curious brow, still somewhat in disbelief that the Dark Artery was so close after so little effort. Azli continued.

"That star is incredibly active, and has only become more so over the millennia. In addition to its storms, he's used his own technologies to disguise and hide his ship. But there it is," Azli said as she pointed to a location on the projection once again. "That's where it is."

The two of them stared in silence at the projection, contemplating and wondering.

"Ok. Let's go back over our approach and plan of attack," Azli suggested. Her voice was soft, but edgy from the prospect of any potential mission.

"Well, the arc and length of those solar ejections are extending way out to here," Lannya observed, tracing areas of the projection with her finger. We could stay below deck, put up Paige's shields and use one of the ejections to camouflage us as we approach. We'd just have to time it carefully."

Azli waited a moment to see if Lannya was going to address the second half of their trip. An answer didn't come quickly.

"And once we're close enough to it?"

Lannya shot a look at Azli in frustration and turned back to the projection.

"We could've spent more of our travel time talking about that," she spat out sharply.

"But we didn't," Azli returned, not willing to take all of the blame for the silence between them during the trip.

"No, we didn't," Lannya echoed more calmly, conceding some of the responsibility.

Turning back towards the display, Lannya continued.

"I don't really know what's practical, or what's worth considering. Should we try to focus only on gathering information, and relaying the location back to the Harbor, or are we talking about boarding the ship, and if so, what do we do once we're on board?"

"Honestly, if we're here," Azli started to offer with a courageous vigor, "we should take advantage of the opportunity. "I know Einar, the ship, the systems, and the protocols."

"Ok, I'm listening," Lannya replied sincerely. "So you're saying that we should board the ship. And then what?"

"Go for the kill," Azli answered coldly. Lannya searched Azli's eyes for any hidden or sheltered emotion.

"I'm tired of all of this," Azli added. "And it's all his fault."

"How?" Lannya wondered. "I mean, between having past lives, and being on his ship with whatever he's come up with over the years. How do we kill him?"

"We can use the same weapons we used…" Azli attempted to finish her sentence, but when it came to explicitly mentioning killing Astraeans and her father, she choked up for the first, extremely noticeable time.

"Right," Lannya said. Her lips moved only slightly as she spoke, and her meek speech matched her amazing restraint. They both knew what Azli couldn't finish saying, and Lannya just didn't have it in her this time, to make Azli finish her thought, or to finish it for her. The tears in Azli's eyes were the only thing keeping Lannya from forcing the moment.

Azli swallowed and wiped her eyes. As she continued detailing her plan, one would have been hard pressed to miss how much pain she had just consumed.

"We have plenty of lives and power between us, and given my experience with Einar and the Dark Artery, I have no doubt we can get to Einar fairly easily, and fairly quickly, and then kill him."

Lannya ran her hands through her hair and began pacing through multiple forced exhales, trying to soak in the plan, and imagine accomplishing such a herculean task. *This is what it all comes down to*, Lannya thought. *We could kill Einar and be done with the whole nightmare.* But the shadow of reality loomed over every consideration.

It can't be this easy, she thought as the doubt crept in. *He's had millions of years to plan for any contingency.*

Lannya spun back to Azli.

"Don't you think he thought of losing you and prepared for that?" Lannya pondered out loud. "Either by death, or defection, or whatever, don't you think he would have adapted to protect himself from something like this?"

"Entering the Rhombex System. Flow factor decreasing to zero," Paige softly interrupted.

"Sure, he may have adapted and considered all contingencies," Azli affirmed, "but he's only had a fraction of the time to change all the procedures and behaviors I'm familiar with."

Lannya crossed her arms to help formalize her final thoughts.

"If we go, I'll follow your lead. I'll use Rhom's solar ejections to hide Paige and get us there, but once we're on the ship, it'll be your show," Lannya clarified.

Azli nodded slowly in understanding.

"You know, that I know," Lannya began to conclude, "that I could pretty much be committing suicide by trusting you like this, right?"

Azli nodded again slowly.

"I'm not asking you to trust me," Azli said. "I can't ask you to do that, yet. But if you do decide to, I think we can do this."

Lannya rocked her head around slowly to stretch her neck before centering it back and asking Azli her final question.

"So what's the plan once we're on board?"

"I think we should board and hide in plain sight," Azli started. "We can hide Paige somewhere nearby, but then hop off and ride a ribbon and ride the rest of the way in. Do you have any Rhombexian past lives?"

Lannya nodded.

"There are a lot of Rhombexians on the Dark Artery that do a lot of the menial security and utility work," Azli continued. "We could go with a story about how I was captured, but then escaped. You could be a Rhombexian escorting me to see Einar. No one goes anywhere without an escort on the Dark Artery. It's part of Einar's paranoid security measures."

"And," Lannya started, leaning in due to the weight of her impending question. "What do we do once we're with him?"

"The ribbon guns, he calls them. They're all over the place on the ship. Most of them are in huge storage vaults, but there are a bunch more in the research and science section, with a few in Einar's personal rooms. He works on them constantly to improve them or configure them for different uses. The point is, they're everywhere. We just need to get one of us near one of them, and him in front of it."

Lannya thought for a moment and looked around to draw a bit of confidence from the warmth and familiarity of Paige's surroundings. There were only a few follow-ups Lannya could think of.

"What's the likelihood of anyone identifying me as anything other than a Rhombexian? Would I be able to stay with you the whole time, or would that be odd to anyone?"

"There are plenty of security scanners and measure in place to detect trespassers, but I know my way around those. And as far as staying with me, like I said, it's the rule, not the exception, to see escorts all over the place. You as a Rhombexian escort, and even I, would be a fairly common sight around the Dark Artery. The biggest hurdle is selling the story of being captured and escaping, but I can sell it. After that, it's getting Einar in front of a ribbon gun."

Lannya puffed out her chest to conjure an extra dose of confidence, and didn't take long to respond.

"Ok. Let's do it."

Azli blinked slowly and couldn't help but smile, though very reservedly.

"It's a good plan. We can do this," Azli said to Lannya, bolstering the mood between them.

Lannya said nothing, but felt a crumb of fresh hope roll into the pit of her empty and worried stomach. If Azli had intended to deceive her, Lannya thought, she doubted that she would have thought to reassure her after she had agreed to go.

Chapter XI

Almost for Naught

Lannya refreshed the projection of the Rhombex System and watched the display populate with the latest contacts and current solar storm extensions coming from Rhom. They had come up with a plan and agreed to it, and was now just a matter of effectively riding a solar mass ejection from Rhom, to a place they could stash Paige. After that, they would take a ribbon to the Dark Artery, and hunt down Einar.

While Lannya calculated how to take advantage of a feasible solar mass ejection, and what precautions would be needed to protect Paige, Azli used one of Paige's fabrication modules to create a convincing uniform for Lannya to wear while she assumed a Rhombexian form on the Dark Artery. The reference uniform in Paige's database were somewhat dated, but Azli knew exactly what types of tweaks to make to bring the uniform up to current standards.

"Didn't you say Paige got frequent database refreshes from the Harbor?" Azli projected back through Paige's interior to Lannya.

"Yeah, why?" Lannya shouted back.

"These reference uniforms she has are decades old," Azli advised. After initiating a synchronization between Azli's changes and the Harbor's database, Lannya stepped through the hatch carrying a tablet. With her eyes on the data in front of her, she brought Azli up to speed.

"Ok, I have the latest information on Rhombexian space and the solar storm. I think we're good to go." Lannya looked up from her tablet and reviewed the uniform Azli had just generated.

"Ah, that is different." Lannya was surprised but mostly grateful for Azli's updates so she wouldn't show up on the Dark Artery looking noticeably out of place.

"Well," Lannya continued. "The Harbor's only known about the Dark Artery and the extent of the Einarian forces for a short time, so I'm kind of impressed that we have any kind of uniform information to go off of at all."

"That's a good point," conceded Azli. "Ok, so what's next?"

"Right, ok. So, we need to swing Paige over to this quadrant of the Rhombexian System. That's the area getting bombarded with most of these flares and ejections. Once we're in place, we'll have to use Paige's shields to protect us, but we'll use the ribbon emitters on the ribbon masts since they won't be in use, to effectively cloak us inside the ejections. The key is to jump into a coronal mass ejection just at the right time so that we don't give our position away, and then quickly fly through the wake of the ejection. We'll then take her and leave her in asynchronous orbit behind this moon here, and then catch this ribbon over to the Dark Artery."

"Yeah, let's do it," Azli agreed quickly.

"Ok," Lannya returned. "Throw me the uniform. I'll meet you back at control in a minute and we'll head in."

Azli tossed the uniform to Lannya and cleaned up quickly around the fabrication module. As she cleaned, she couldn't help but imagine how many different ways the plan could fail, but deep down, she felt it was a fairly solid plan. She was just slightly on the excited side of anxious, and was ready to help put an end to Einar. *Mamdod may have come up with the game that started all of this*, Azli thought, *but Einar is the one playing games.*

She finished cleaning and quickly marched through Paige's metallic halls and floors to meet Lannya back in the control room. Lannya had already changed skins into that of a Rhombexian, and put on the uniform worn by security on the Dark Artery.

"You look absolutely perfect," Azli said with slight astonishment. "You should blend in immediately."

Lannya responded with the native sounds of a Rhombexian, which resembled low thuds of vacuumed air that varied in pitch only occasionally. Words were formed in their language by making sounds of different lengths. Lannya thanked Azli for updating the uniform and asked if she was ready to hop into one of the solar mass ejections.

"I think so," Azli answered. Lannya started to turn back to the controls, but before she could, Azli had something else to say.

"Hey," she said, just above a whisper.

Lannya turned back to her. Azli swallowed and licked her lips.

"Thanks," Azli added.

Lannya looked at Azli through her Rhombexian eyes but only nodded. The enigmatic topic was trust, and the amount shared between them was growing.

Lannya turned back to the controls.

"Belt up," Lannya began, in her Rhombexian language. "This will be a rough ride, but it shouldn't take all that long. When we stop, we should be sheltered and hidden behind Rhombex's moon."

Azli sat down into a nearby command seat and belted herself in. After Lannya confirmed Azli was good to go, Lannya also looped a belt bolted into a nearby support column, around her torso. She also slid her feet into built-in cups in the deck plate, for additional stability. Lastly, Lannya pressed a button on her command terminal that stowed away any medium to large objects, as well as made protective covers slide into place over bins, doors, and cabinets, so that nothing could potentially become dangerous projectiles. All that was left, was to try and anticipate a solar ejection, from Rhom's surface, for Lannya to thrust Paige into.

Lannya's Rhombexian, stone slab of an arm hovered over Paige's thruster controls. The moment Lannya saw an approaching solar ejection, she would initiate the thrusters and slingshot the ship into the massive wave of energy. They didn't have long to wait. After a few seconds, Rhom blasted out another burp of plasma and radiation. Lannya was on top of it and punched the thruster ignition control.

Paige immediately started shaking violently, and from Lannya's and Azli's standpoint, it felt as if the shaking would turn catastrophic. The degree and speed of the dangerous tremors were above and beyond what Paige endured when she was thrown from the ribbons during the initial attack on the Harbor. It was frightening to the point that both Azli and Lannya were sure the ship wouldn't survive it.

System stability warnings immediately began to clash with the harsh dissonance of hull integrity alerts. Paige's declarations of weakening shields and various ship malfunctions were being announced back to back with no apparent end in sight. The sound coming from the solar and mechanical chaos was deafening, and poked splinters of pain into the mother's and daughter's ears. The entire plan seemed to be failing, and any hope to complete it was being extinguished rapidly.

There was barely any opportunity to focus. The ship was shaking to pieces, the sounds were hateful and hurtful, and neither Lannya nor Azli could hardly keep their eyes open from the constant flickering of blinding light coming from the solar ejection into various points of the ship. But, Lannya put all focus into everything she had to stare straight onto one of her stone extremities as she slowly guided it up through the G-forces and confusion, to one of her command screens slightly above her. Her intention was to pulse Paige's thrusters again, to knock the ship out of the solar ejection's wake.

"Don't! They'll see us!" Azli screamed out, with an

involuntary vibrato.

"We can't survive thi..." Lannya started, shouting in return, but quickly cut herself off.

The sounds, shaking, and lights quickly began to subside. Alarms started to flash less frequently. Red lights turned to green. Paige began to announce statuses of various systems being restored. The chaos was being replaced slowly by order.

Azli and Lannya embraced an increasing silence and attempted to regain control of not only Paige, but their fear, and adrenaline. They said nothing, and listened to the ship as it self-diagnosed and self-corrected. A few minor issues seemed to linger on, but most had been resolved. Still, silence between Lannya and Azli remained as they finished returning their own bodies and minds to a lessened state of excitement. Azli unbelted herself and let her head collapse into her arms on the table in front of her. Lannya slipped her feet out from the deck cups and hugged the support column her torso strap was still connected to. Mixed in with the sound of the few remaining minor alerts, were the long and hard breaths of Paige's two exhausted passengers.

After Lannya finished running through each of the worries, fears and pains that had overwhelmed her moments before, and realized they had truly been resolved, she forced a few huge deep breaths, and allowed herself to turn slightly to review a ship's status monitor. She shook her head in amazement, and pressed a button to be struck by a beam of ribbon energy which was directed from outside the ship to the inside of the common room. She was her normal form once again.

"I knew the ride would be rough," she said to Azli. "But I couldn't have imagined that."

Azli lifted her head up from the table.

"How did we get out of that? What made it subside?"

"The best I can tell," Lannya began to surmise, as she reviewed their flight data on the monitor, "was that since the wake of the solar ejection got smaller the deeper we flew into it, the less plasma and resistance we had to fly against after we initially jumped into it."

Azli stood up and confirmed her footing as she wobbled weakly and caught herself with a hand on the table.

"If we ever get back to the Harbor," Azli said while rubbing her head, "remind me to thank Hergie for building one hell of a ship."

Lannya nodded in agreement and chuckled silently to herself.

"Did we end up where we wanted to be?" Azli asked, wanting to confirm their status.

"Yeah, right behind the moon here," Lannya confirmed.

Azli shuffled slowly over to Lannya to take a look of her own at the monitor.

"Wait a second," Lannya said as she began tapping the screen furiously. She twisted and turned the monitor's point of view of the space around them.

"Where is it?!" Azli shouted at the monitor. "Where's the Dark Artery?!"

Lannya grabbed the lower ledge of the command control console and squeezed it to the point her knuckles turned white. Either her fingers were going to dislocate, or the ledge was going to snap off. Her head dropped down below her shoulders as she felt her nerves being shocked with a combination of ferocious helplessness. She couldn't take it and had to erupt at Azli.

"Where is the ship, Azli?" Lannya screamed at a volume that, combined with her gasps for air, made her voice crack with desperation and disgust. "You're the Einar expert that just wanted to help end the war, right? The ship's been here for millennia! Blah blah blah. Where is it?"

As Lannya repeated her question, she slammed her hands into Azli's shoulders, pushing her, maliciously, into a nearby panel.

"I don't know! It was here just days ago! Stop!" Azli screamed back, poised and ready to fight back this time, in case Lannya tried to push her again.

Lannya shook with anger, at a loss on what to do or say next to Azli.

"If this is a trap...," Lannya said with a fiery and coarse breath. Her stance seethed with anger.

"It isn't!" Azli shouted, with an accompanying fist that slammed into the nearby panel. "It isn't! I don't know where it's at! He must have moved it!"

Lannya stood motionless for a few moments. Her chest heaved up and caved in rapidly. She was almost nauseous from virtually being right back where they, and the Harbor, started, with no idea where the ship was.

After a few more seething seconds, Lannya gave in to her frustration and did an about face to return to the support column and proceeded to kick it a dozen times. She then let loose a gritty howl that sounded as if it came from twenty lungs, fueled by ten diaphragms, powered by as many people. Neither of them wanted to start from scratch with looking for Einar, and their frustration was exacerbated by having no other leads, and nowhere to go.

Chapter XII

Lighting the Fire

Azli and Lannya collapsed onto adjacent seats and returned to the irritated silence that so far, had overwhelmingly monopolized their relationship. The gap of silence didn't last as long as it had previously, however. Lannya sighed and asked a disappointed question of Azli.

"Well, what now?" Lannya was careful to direct her tone at the situation, and not at Azli.

Azli glanced at Lannya as she was asked the question, rubbed her eyes quickly, and then spun in her seat to begin reviewing a nearby terminal.

"I guess it's a safe bet that Einar thinks I've been captured or something," Azli started, speaking in the direction of the terminal. "It makes sense that he would have moved the ship, and I can guess at some possible destinations, but even if we were in good standing with the Harbor, the tree wouldn't have enough time for the Astraeans to investigate them all."

Lannya picked up a wrench and haphazardly flung it across the room, which still found the toolbox she had roughly aimed for.

"We might want to consider going down to Rhombex," Azli suggested strongly. Lannya could tell she had plenty of motive behind her idea, and turned towards her as she elaborated.

"The Dark Artery had been parked here for ages. Einar moved it into this area, however long ago, because he could find and mold powerful allies, in the Rhombexians. He built relationships down there, over countless generations. Like I said before, he staffed a good portion of the ship with Rhombexians, and there was a fairly busy trade network between the ship and Rhombex. I bet we can find out where he went from somebody down there."

Lannya stood up and inhaled deeply while staring aimlessly at the room's ceiling.

"I think we're just going to end up wasting time, Azli."

"Huh?" Azli asked. Her face bent with confusion. "There's a real good chance we'll be able to get some solid info down there."

"But even if we do, we still have to travel to wherever this new place is," Lannya explained with animated gestures, "get there safely, come up with a new plan to board the ship, and then hopefully live long enough to do something."

"Ok, well, that's my suggestion," Azli said prickly, through a growing impatience. "What do you suggest we do, then?"

Lannya's chin dropped as her eyebrows jumped. There was obviously no other option in her mind.

"I didn't want to, but I think we should go back to the Harbor, or at least contact them. We had a good plan and a bit of an advantage with you being off the farm for so little time, but he's gone. The ship's gone. There's no point in trying to do all this new surveillance and research by ourselves. For all we know, the Harbor already knows where he's at now."

Azli squeezed her eyes shut and scratched her head. Her idea was all that made sense in her mind.

"Look, Rhombex is right there," Azli attempted to explain while trying to remain calm. Her arms stretched out at the display monitor with Rhombex showing. "You're not in a hurry to reconnect with the Harbor, and I know I'm not. I think this is worth the time. Let's go down. We'll ask around some, and find out what we can, and then decide what to do after that."

Lannya took the least amount of time to consider Azli's latest plea, when compared with any other of her ideas. She was beginning to realize she was taking issue with Azli's ideas, in part, just for the sake of taking issue with them. She needed to be more objective about Azli's suggestions, she decided, and huffed loudly to clear her mind.

"Ok. We're already here, and we can't afford to waste more time by arguing," Lannya conceded. "What's the story down there right now? The last life I lived here was before the Dark Artery was around. It's been a while."

"Alright," Azli said as she zoomed in on Rhombex. She tapped a few times and brought up some of the statistics for the planet. "The most important thing for us right now is getting to the right people. Most of the planet is made up of Einarian sympathizers, because again, Einar and the ship were here for so long. Why they're sympathizers, or finding out what lies and tales Einar has told the planet over the years isn't a priority right now. Any friendlies are surely aware of the Einarians' fight with the Astraeans, and have probably been warned about people trying to flush Einar out. If I go down there in disguise and get discovered by the sympathizers, then that would probably be bad for us. Where we need to focus, is this face of the planet, here, where the majority of the Rhombexians that don't support Einar live. They're Rhombexian fundamentalists. I'm very familiar with them because I used to help plan and carry out operations against them. They hate Einar, the Dark Artery, and me. They've always felt, and rightly so, that Einar has just been exploiting their people and resources. Needless to say, we don't want them finding out that I'm who I am, either, or they'll probably just capture me, or kill me somehow, out of revenge. But I think if we can get in front of the right people, in front of the fundamentalists, and just pose as average Astraeans trying to locate Einar, then we'll be able to get some good intel."

"Well, I'll follow your lead," Lannya said, gesturing at Azli. "I'll wait until we get to the fundamentalists, and then I'll reveal myself to them and see if we can get some help."

"Sure, that's fine," Azli confirmed quickly. "We'll assume some Rhombexian forms and hop down here." Azli pointed to an open area on a map of one of the faces of Rhombex. "It's a huge market that is constantly packed with Rhombexians, vendors, carts, and banners hanging all over the place. We can slip in easily without drawing attention. If memory serves, there are a number of fundamentalists that operate out of there. We can start there."

Lannya nodded.

"Ok," Azli wrapped up. "Let's go."

***

Rhombex was a large planet known throughout universe seventy-two-B, and to many in other universes, for being home to the Rhombexians, masters of metallurgy, metalsmithing, and all related engineering. For countless generations, Rhombexians trained their children, male and female alike, the skills needed to be masters of metal. There was a true passion and pride for artisanship instilled in their children from an early age. They were not only being trained in a vocation and skill, but were taught to be stewards of their art. And where many similar cultures around the multiverse practiced similar skills with disregard, and almost a disdain for conservation and nature, the Rhombexians had the utmost respect for the natural world by recycling their materials, and guarding against needless waste.

The planet itself had been shaped long ago by Rhombex's earliest craftspeople from a sphere, into a twenty-sided geometric masterpiece. Over thousands of years, using all manners of tools and machinery, the Rhombexians worked, shaped, cut and dug the planet, made mostly of galena and pyrite, into an awe-inspiring shape like no other planet in the multiverse. Depending on how the planet was viewed from space, one could see what appeared to be many different shades of metallic gray reflecting brightly back at them, though the whole planet was made from predominantly, the same materials.

Down at ground level, Rhombex's metallic, lead surface meandered to every horizon, and flowed seamlessly into all buildings and structures that were chiseled out of, or adorned by, the same minerals and refined metals. Though some visitors found traversing the purposely tight streets annoying, further confined by claustrophobic, tall walls, they couldn't help but be enchanted by the dull shine reflecting from the surface of everything they looked at.

The Rhombexians were fascinated by edges, lines, faces and any other geometrical features. They combined their excitement for such things with their love for mazes and logic. Most of their architecture and infrastructure reflected this, but did occasionally allow for wide open areas when necessary, such as the market that Azli and Lannya were headed to.

As planned, Lannya and Azli jumped down into the market located in the city of Ingon, located on Rhombex's Mercantile Face. Though their arrival had gone unnoticed, the noticeably thin crowds and few vendors struck Azli as odd. While Lannya remained still and quiet in an ancient Rhombexian form she had assumed, Azli, in a Rhombexian form of her own, glanced around slowly, pivoting up and around in an attempt to identify anything out of the ordinary. Without consulting with Lannya, Azli approached one of the passing market patrons. Rather than speaking a greeting to a stranger, Azli met the fellow patron with a clinking thud of their

Rhombexian extremities. Azli swung out a heavy mineral shaft from the middle of her torso, which then telescoped out and grew by a foot or so to a dull point. The arm seemed to build steps out from itself, each layer smaller than the next. The stranger Azli approached did the same. In less than a second, Azli and the stranger had extended the arms and smacked them together modestly, which resulted in a heavy pop with the slightest of metallic brilliance on the edge of the sound. Once they had greeted each other, the conversation began.

"Do you know where the recycled lead merchant is today?" Azli asked with the confidence of knowing such a question would be common and expected. "My friend and I have a huge battery order that needs filling."

The stranger initially seemed receptive to Azli's question but quickly started acting afraid and skittish as he rotated around nervously to check his surroundings. Like dry marble, the stranger's body simultaneously slid and scraped as his body twisted to and fro. As Azli finished speaking, he had already shaken his head rapidly and walked away without answering.

Azli looked back to Lannya. Lannya's square Rhombexian face and upright rectangular head hadn't moved. She had even less of an idea than Azli did, as to why the stranger reacted that way.

Next, hoping for a different outcome, and seeing no need yet to change her line of questioning, Azli approached one of the few vendors nearby. Lannya followed closely behind.

Azli stepped up to the vendor's metal stall with high walls and counters, and once again extended her arm appendage out to the vendor. They then exchanged their own stone smacks and started their conversation.

"There is usually a recycled lead vendor at the market," Azli began casually. "Do you know where she's at? And actually, do you know where everyone else is? I've never seen the market so empty."

The vendor said nothing and returned to the rear of his stall after greeting Azli's Rhombexian body. He pumped a bellows to stoke his forge, picked up his hammer, and started to tap away at something on the horn of his anvil. Some embers from the forge escaped into a slight breeze that blew past the vendor. His slowly growing smile was partially obstructed by the flying bits of fire.

"Who are you?" The vendor asked with a dense suspicion.

"My friend here," Azli replied calmly as she gestured back towards Lannya, "is named Borona. I am Vanadia."

The flickering flames and floating embers continued to highlight the vendor's grin, soaked in an eerie perception that remained unchanged as Azli obliged him with their Rhombexian aliases. The walls of the vendor's stall appeared to grow and then recede from the reflected flames shining shots of light ranging from flat and dull, to sharp and bright.

The vendor tossed his hammer onto his anvil and let go of his grin.

"Every Rhombexian on this planet knows why the market is quiet today," the vendor said, displeased with what he registered as attempted deception. "So, what I want to know," he continued as he quickly flipped a lever that rotated a crucible, dropping molten metal into a device that looked threatening, "is why you two don't know!"

"Wait, wait!" Azli shouted out quickly. "We just got back to the planet after doing business in the Blokkioid System. Does it have something to do with the Dark Artery? We noticed it was gone."

The vendor stopped in the middle of whatever process he had begun with the molten metal. He apparently wasn't willing to harm or kill fellow Rhombexians that seemed innocently ignorant of the situation, and at the same time, were convincing in their honesty by bringing up the Dark Artery.

"Yeah, it has to do with the Dark Artery!" The vendor belched out, frustrated from having to explain it. "Einar and his people came down here a few days ago and gave us this huge production about their fight with the Astraeans and how they're relocating the ship. Warned us that we may run into Astraeans posing as Rhombexians to get information, or a whole lot of other possibilities. They suggested we close up shop and stay close to home for a bit until the war is over, to avoid any confrontations."

Lannya still hadn't said anything, but slouched down and dropped her head in a feigned sense of reciprocated frustration with how their people were being treated. The vendor continued spouting off in anger as he started working the metal on his anvil again.

"They warned us that they would be leaving some of their people behind in Rhombexian form to keep an eye out for Astraean allies or operatives. Most of the market vendors just didn't want to mess with it, so they're staying home till it's all over. Same with the citizens. The streets are empty."

Azli backed away from the stall to stomp her foot and shake her head in her own display of disgust. Lannya took the opportunity to speak up for the first time since their arrival.

"We don't want to get into any of that," she said. "We just wanted some lead for our own business."

"Well," the vendor replied while hammering, and spitting while speaking. His attitude had an added bite from the planet's disrupted commerce. "It's going to be a while till things get back to normal. Better settle in and stay out of trouble!"

Azli tapped the counter and nodded at the vendor, thanking him for his time and information with her gesture. She and Lannya then turned and began to wander their way out of the market area, while making up chit-chat about how they were going to find the lead they needed and survive the coming lull in business. When they were noticeably out of range from being overheard, the conversation shifted abruptly to what they really needed to discuss.

"I have no idea how to locate the lead vendor outside of the market," Azli whispered. "She's one of the primary fundamentalists we used to work against from the Dark Artery. She's the only one I know of by name or face, and if we try to find her, there's no telling who we'll be talking to, or who they're loyal to."

Lannya thought on Azli's comments silently while trying to keep an eye on their surroundings, and without calling attention to themselves.

"Azli, I don't like this. Everything feels wrong," Lannya said as softly yet firmly as she could. "We are at a complete disadvantage. We don't know who's watching us, who's listening to us, and we pretty much have no one to help us if something happens."

"I know, I know, shhh," Azli answered quickly, trying to maintain a guise of calm. "Look, if something happens, or if we get split up, let's meet back on Paige. She's hidden and shouldn't show up on any of their instruments. But until something goes wrong, I really think we need to try to get to the fundamentalists. Einar's allies are obviously way too paranoid from all the warnings and threats to try and use them for information."

Lannya slowly shuffled closer to Azli and rushed out a reply born in a growing urgency and concern for their safety.

"Fine, ok," Lannya rushed. "Just get moving. We need to get out of this area and off the main streets."

"Right," Azli obliged swiftly. "Come on. I think I remember the way to the main concentration of fundamentalists."

Chapter XIII

The Forge Forum

Lannya and Azli kept to themselves as they weaved in and out of the tight streets of Ingon. The dust from the many metals and minerals being worked by smiths of various disciplines coated the ground. The close quarters created by the high walls of the streets and buildings gave the impression of being trapped by increasingly encroaching mirrors of a foggy gray, but they pressed on with Lannya following close behind Azli. Lannya's paranoia and concern grew with each step, but she swallowed it and dismissed it as best she could. Azli knew this planet, knew these people and knew what they needed. Lannya was completely at Azli's mercy and judgment, and for the moment, she felt somewhat relieved by that.

The Rhombexians were a good-natured species that had done good things on a small scale, with love and compassion, but as far as the Astraeans were concerned, they were no better than the Einarians. Despite being lied to and manipulated for thousands of years, the Astraeans equated the Rhombexians with the Einarians. They had assisted Einar, given him and his people multitudes of resources and assisted him for years with thousands of laborers. They might as well have been Einarians themselves, the Astraeans believed.

However, as Lannya and Azli slipped through the shadowy streets, Lannya couldn't help but turn her head often, a few millimeters at a time to one side, and then another. With each step, she looked through a passing window or hole and saw the warmth of family, smelled the fires of home, and heard the sounds of laughter and love. She didn't initially know how to process the alien feelings trespassing through her soul, but as they passed home after home and family after family, a new truth began to reveal itself to Lannya. When she took a break from looking at all the homes as they walked, and settled her vision in front of her, she watched Azli lead her to something that may help them locate Einar. The new truth broke through an ancient membrane of Astraean denial. The Astraeans weren't perfect, and never would be. Nor should they turn their backs on an entire species because of guilt by association. Lannya didn't question the huge disparity between Einarian and Astraean morality, but she did start to see that perspective and context are perhaps more powerful than morality. As she continued to follow Azli's lead, she made a mental note to bring it up to her at some point.

Their pace began to slow as Azli looked over her shoulder to get Lannya's attention. Azli took a few additional steps towards a tall median in the city streets, and beckoned Lannya over to join her in a bit of shadowed cover.

Azli looked up to the darkening sky above the tall buildings, a few miles in the distance.

"See the light on the horizon over there?"

Lannya nodded and looked around to evaluate their surroundings.

"That's in the same direction as the Archean village," Azli explained. "It's where we were pretty sure the majority of the fundamentalists were from. That light is probably coming from a Forge Forum. It's a huge celebration of fire, and what it's given to the Rhombexians. It's an ancient tradition that only the fundamentalists do now."

Azli turned back to Lannya as she finished speaking.

"Let's go check it out," Lannya suggested. "It's probably our best chance at finding some of these fundamentalists by far"

"Exactly," Azli agreed.

The two of them stepped out from the median and rejoined the dusty trail of stone at the base of Ingon's main line of buildings. The streets that had previously given Azli and Lannya some company had mostly emptied now that they were at the outskirts of Ingon and about to enter the Archean village. There was less light in windows. Less sounds of family, and fewer inviting smells. While the rest of the planet had maintained their ancient ways, they had still adapted and evolved to include new technologies and iterations of metallurgy. The Archean village however, did not. They held defiantly and proudly to their ancient lifestyle, and only that lifestyle. They were incredibly intelligent however, and just as bright as the most intellectual Rhombexians on the other faces of the planet, but inside their village, the old ways were cherished and respected, religiously.

The height of the buildings and opulence of the homes became shorter and less refined as Lannya and Azli grew closer to the Archean village. The homes and buildings, while still metallic and shiny from the abundance of galena, were one level, square, and practical. There wasn't the height or extremes in decorative carving like there was in Ingon. The village was humble and inviting.

The paths and alleys in the village showed more life than the outskirts of Ingon did, though it seemed to Azli and Lannya that those in the streets were making their way to the village center. As they walked closer to the village center, the temperature began to rise, the light increased, and the sound started to build. After a few twists and turns through more streets and courtyards, they reached the village center. And though they knew what to expect, they were still overwhelmed by the sight before them.

Taking up the bulk of the sizable village square was a monument of fire. Along the outer perimeter of the square was a towering wall of stone, glowing various shades of red and orange. The huge wall had been channeled out in the middle to allow fires to be built inside. Rotating shifts of Rhombexian fundamentalists kept the fires burning, so that the walls would perpetually glow during the Forge Forum. These ominous and mystical walls on the perimeter, the fundamentalists believed, would protect the center of the square, where they gathered to meet, speak, and celebrate fire. There was a break in the middle of each of the four sides of the perimeter wall to allow villagers to enter and exit at their leisure.

The largest portion of the Forum was in the center of the square. Over many weeks, the villagers would construct a soaring pyramid made of coke and tungsten which was then ignited as well during the Forge Forum. Again, teams of villagers would rotate in and out from deep within the pyramid to keep it lit, so that all could have a chance to take part in the Forum. The only portion of the pyramid not lit, was a series of wide steps leading up to a podium of metal. There, the Rhombexian fundamentalists could ascend and address their fellow villagers about any issues they wished to have discussed or voted on. Because of the proximity of the majority of the pyramid's fire, it would cause the Rhombexian climbing the steps to glow softly red from the heat, demonstrating symbolically, the strength they receive from fire.

Azli and Lannya approached a break in the wall, and while Azli explained the most important aspects of the Forge Forum to Lannya, they crossed the threshold of one of the wall gaps. Once they had passed through, they saw thousands of villagers gathered. There was very little movement, and whatever amount of conversation there was, was hard to distinguish over the roar of the blazing pyramid of fire. Though Azli was still cognizant of their need to tread lightly, she felt safe enough to lean to Lannya and speak to her in a more normal voice.

"I don't understand," Azli said to her. "From

everything we learned about the fundamentalists and these Forums, there are usually always people talking up at the podium. We heard about fights breaking out from someone not getting a turn."

Lannya leaned in a bit to further close the gap between her and Azli.

"I'm sure it's because of what that vendor was talking about. Everyone's too scared to be in the spotlight, I guess."

Azli nodded while being somewhat hypnotized by the pyramid's power.

"Let's go over there and belly up to that group," Azli suggested. "Maybe chat them up a bit?"

Lannya swung her jaw out and sprung open her eyes. She was nervous.

"We'll just play dumb and innocent," Azli said smoothly, trying to reassure Lannya. "Let's just ask a few questions."

Azli then started to make her way to the group of nearby villagers. Lannya was right by her side.

"He...," Azli started to say, before remembering Rhombexians don't greet each other verbally. She extended her arm-like appendage and gently thudded one of the villagers on their shoulder.

The villager turned to Azli and dipped their head.

"Is everyone afraid of speaking?" Azli wondered calmly, and legitimately. "I've never seen the podium empty at a Forum before."

The villager chuckled before replying.

"You're more than free to climb up there, if you like!"

"Ha! Well, I don't really have anything that needs to be addressed. But, my friend here, she might!"

Lannya turned sharply to Azli, and before she could react in a way that would seem odd to the villager, she started thinking of a possible topic. *Something worthwhile, but nothing too dramatic*, she thought.

"There are a few things," Lannya obliged confidently. "I'd like to see Ingon incorporate more of our ancient ways into the city's day-to-day, or maybe have the Forge Forums held on different faces around Rhombex, things like that... But, nothing too urgent. I'm mostly satisfied with just living in peace."

The villager turned to Lannya and then back to the fire. A slight hint of approval came across his face in the ebb and flow of the firelight.

"Well, enjoy it while you can, friend," the villager said as his voice sunk. "As usual, it looks like outsiders, or those in the cities dealing with outsiders, are going to be bringing us something that isn't good for our village. I just wish we could be completely done, once and for all with..."

The villager stopped himself. A face of fear and panic overtook him in the realization of what he was saying and what it could mean.

Neither Azli nor Lannya wanted to press him, but they didn't want to discourage him from speaking either. They said nothing and kept their eyes locked on the pyramid.

"Never mind," the villager wrapped up quickly. "I didn't intend to go off like that."

"Don't worry," Lannya provided with masterful

skill and speed. "I think I know what you were getting at, and if so, you're among friends, at least while you're speaking with us."

The villager turned to Lannya and sized up her demeanor as she spoke, and once again, turned back to the fire. Azli saw an opportunity and felt a rush of adrenaline shove her into taking advantage. She didn't know if the villager was referring to Einar or the Astraeans. She had a fifty-fifty shot.

"At least with Einar's ship out of our space," Azli started casually, "that's one less thing to bring trouble to our village."

After Azli finished speaking, she capped it with a sigh for dramatic effect, and returned to staring at the fire. Lannya stood silently and dumped every ounce of energy she could muster into her hearing, hoping the villager would mention where the Dark Artery had relocated to.

"Be careful what you say and who you say it to," the villager warned. He leaned in closely to Azli and Lannya before continuing. "And you're right," he said with a slow rasp. "Let the Salacians deal with him!"

Azli and Lannya managed to control their excitement long enough to chuckle as the villager did so. They couldn't believe they had just heard where the Dark Artery was. *The Salacians!* Lannya screamed in her head. *The planet of Salacia!* Before they had finished laughing with the villager, both Azli and Lannya had run dozens of ideas on how to get off Rhombex as safely and quietly as possible to get the information back to the Harbor.

Lannya tried to think of a reason to get out of the conversation but only tripped and stumbled over every thought. Her two Rhombexian hearts pounded and beat out any hope of concentration. Azli looked at her and exchanged looks of poorly restrained distraction. Luckily, before either of them came out with something stupid to tip off anyone nearby, the villager who had been distracted by his own inspiration turned away from the fire once again and spoke.

"You know," he began, "The moment we're afraid to speak at our own Forge Forum, is the day the reason for our village's existence gets lost."

While the villager spoke, Azli and Lannya shared a silent relief that they might be saved from having to break the conversation.

"I don't know what I'm going to say yet, but by the Fire, I'm going to say something!"

The villager knocked both Azli and Lannya on the back with his rocky appendage, scraping a dense crack to say his goodbyes. He then turned and disappeared into the crowd while making his way towards the base of the pyramid's stairs. Azli and Lannya started to walk backwards deliberately while looking around in paranoia, hoping they could make a clean escape.

"I can't believe it!" Lannya whispered in astonishment.

"He could have been giving us bad info," Azli returned, while still walking backwards casually.

"I don't think so. Not from the way he sounded," Lannya offered.

They had almost gotten back to the perimeter wall. As they neared it, Lannya began to turn around. Azli turned as well. Just when their backs were to the majority of the crowd and the pyramid, they heard thundering and amplified crunches, booming throughout the square. Their newest village friend had ascended the pyramid's steps and approached the podium. After greeting the crowd by pounding on the massive slab of metal in front of him, he began to speak.

"What a spectacular evening for a Forge Forum!"

In appreciation and applause, the crowd of villagers clapped and stomped their formidable appendages of mighty minerals together, and on the ground. Lannya and Azli were compelled to turn back around as he continued to speak.

"I have been reminded tonight of how lucky we as a people are. We traditionalists, and even the modernists outside our walls, we Rhombexians with a shared blood, are a fortunate people. Fortunate in family. Fortunate in fortune, and fortunate... in fire!"

The ground rumbled again in noisy thumps, smacks and pounding of stone, metal, and mineral. While the villager waited for the applause to subside, he began to glow, as expected, from the cumulative, intense heat of the surrounding pyramid. It was a powerfully primal moment to witness and for a few seconds, Azli and Lannya were enjoying themselves. The applause finally silenced.

"I didn't want to take too much time," the villager continued, growing brighter and brighter. "I only wanted to express my appreciation for you, and our village, and say that I hope to encourage our Forge Forum to spring to life with the lively discussion and exchanging of ideas which has traditionally taken place for centuries."

Azli and Lannya sensed the villager was about to

wrap up his comments and started walking backwards again, preparing once more, to turn around and leave.

"I want to thank my new friends as well," the villager said, reaching his arm out in the direction of where they had previously been standing. He glanced quickly in the same direction, but couldn't confirm whether or not they were still there.

"I want to thank them for helping stoke my passion for our culture enough, to come up and speak to you tonight," he continued. "And before I leave the podium, let me say to you all, that no one should ever make us feel ashamed of who we are, what we are, and what we believe! Don't let anyone make you shrink away from your culture and history! No one will make us fear being in our homes, and no one will make us regret being Rhombexians! No one will ever use us again! No one! Not any Astraean, and definitely not any Einarian!"

The provocative and inflammatory stab at the dangerous situation forcibly ripped Azli and Lannya away from the spell of fascination they had been under. What the villager had said was exactly the type of thing the vendor back at the market had said the Einarians warned against. Without wasting another second, both Lannya and Azli began to turn to leave, once and for all.

But before they could finish turning around, an explosion of grotesque and terrifying proportions tore apart the pyramid. Originating from the gargantuan slab that made up the top of the podium, the detonation crumbled the pyramid up into countless chunks of molten-hot metal, sending them far into the sky, and ripping through the majority of the villagers around the base of the pyramid. Those who weren't killed immediately were slung to the ground from the concussion wave, wounded, mutilated, or in Lannya's case, stunned and shocked.

The few, hazy seconds immediately after being slammed to the ground found Lannya racing through a mental checklist of priorities. *Alive? Yes. Is she alive, too? I can't tell. Any noticeable wounds? No.* The checklist then became verbal.

"Azli? Azli!"

Lannya tapped and slapped her, and grasped at her Rhombexian jaw to examine her eyes.

Lannya was afraid Azli had lost that life, and started to think of catching a ribbon to meet her back on Paige, but Azli twitched and started to flail with life.

"Can you walk?" Lannya shouted at Azli.

"Yeah!" Azli screamed, though holding and grunting at her sore torso.

Lannya got up first, leaned over and started to help Azli up. "Come on. We've gotta get back to Paige!"

"Wait!" Lannya bellowed at herself before turning to Azli. "Can you rewind any of this?"

"No, I can't," Azli grimaced while grabbing at her side again. "I got knocked unconscious."

Lannya's heart sank as she ducked under Azli's arm and scooped her up to support her. Azli gathered her footing and stood slowly, looking over her body and assessing her pain levels. As she did, Lannya watched as the remaining last chunks of flaming pyramid fell back to the village square, and rolled through the littered and smoldering corpses.

While Lannya's heart became drenched in sadness

from the obscene view before her, she noticed movement among the corpses. Shadowy figures began to creep from behind the pile of pyramid rubble.

"Azli, do you see that?" Lannya asked. Before she gave Azli a chance to respond, she shouted out, "Get to Pai..."

But Lannya wasn't able to finish. Before they could summon any ribbons, a beam of dark energy that prevented that ability struck them both.

"Run!" Azli screamed.

They turned and stumbled on their own feet in their panic to get away from whoever was targeting them. The creatures that shot them with the beam looked like Rhombexians, but they were mostly likely Einarians assuming Rhombexian form which the vendor at the market had warned them about. This weapon they used to suppress their ribbon summoning abilities was new to them, however.

Azli and Lannya secured their feet under them and dug in with torquey traction. Though they could still feel the tingling and fuzzy sting from whatever they were struck with, it didn't prevent them from running away from the square as fast as they could. A few quick whips of their heads revealed that they were being pursued by the Einarian Rhombexians, and just when they began to feel the tingling dissipate, they would be struck with a beam again, renewing whatever hold on them it had that prevented them from calling a ribbon. It was obvious that someone wanted them captured rather than killed, because those chasing them struck them repeatedly with the beam.

Still running at an all-out sprint, Azli and Lannya were doing everything they could to dodge the repeated beam strikes, but it was no use. The more they ran, back to the center of Ingon, more and more of the Einarian Rhombexians emerged from homes and buildings to fire even more beams of the ribbon-restricting energy at them. There were less and less possible places for Azli and Lannya to try and get to, with more and more Einarian sympathizers emerging from the darkness with these new weapons.

With little choice, Lannya decided to split up and cut a hard right into one of the few routes that seemed to be free of Rhombexians. She sprinted with every ounce of energy she could summon, weaving, dodging and zigzagging through all sorts of crevasses in the city. She had no other goal but to keep going as long as she could, to try and put as much distance between her and the Rhombexians preventing their escape. She ran harder and dug into the ground deeper. She still felt the effects of the last beam strike, but she told her mind and soul that continuing on until she no longer felt the restrictive beam was her only option. She pressed on and forced the pain out of her mind. *Keep going, keep running.* Go, go, go. Keep going, she told herself.

With no warning and to her rapturous surprise, Lannya finally felt it. The last residue of the beam that suppressed her ability to call a ribbon left her. She was free of it, and out of energy. A millisecond later, a summoned ribbon shot down from high above the surface of Rhombex and swallowed Lannya into her escape.

Back near the center of Ingon, Azli continued

sprinting around medians, in and out of covered walkways, through archways, and darting diagonally across open streets, and anything else she hoped would give her most recent beam blast time to fully dissipate. She was desperate for a free and clear path to follow like Lannya had found, but was coming up empty. At a full on sprint as well, she was quickly running out of energy and hope. She knew, more than anyone, that if the Einarians captured her, her fate at the hands of Einar would be as bleak and black as imaginable. Her soul began to fill with despair, and started to flirt with giving in to her exhaustion.

With a jolt under her feet, her desperation was replaced with surprise and fear. The ground beneath her gave way, causing her to drop down into a carved-out slide of sorts. For hundreds and hundreds of meters she slid, gradually sliding faster by the second. Every so often, a door would open and a rubber bumper would quickly but gently nudge her in the direction someone was steering her in. Once she had changed directions, the door that had opened to reveal the path she had gone would close, and a different path's door would open, to misdirect anyone following.

Azli slid and slid with no indication of what her destination was, but had been sliding long enough to calm down slightly, at least in the relief of being out of danger from the Einarian Rhombexians for the moment. She still felt the tingling from her last beam blast however, and before she could wish silently that it would dissipate soon in order to summon a ribbon, she vaulted out of the tube, and into a wall of one room of many, dug out deep below Rhombex's surface.

Azli rolled over to quickly assess her surroundings and was immediately met by a smiling Rhombexian.

"The Astraeans have friends here," he whispered through a mischievous grin. "And we have tricks, too!"

He then leaned over and opened up a valve that built up pressure inside a directed crucible with an exit point sealed by a lead cover.

"Go!"

As the mysterious Rhombexian shouted, he swung a wheel that quickly flipped the lead cover away from the crucible opening. As it flipped up and away, a huge jet of hot material shot out and struck Azli, completely covering her Rhombexian body. As soon as it hit and encompassed her, she felt the restrictive feeling from the energy beam leave her. Not wanting to risk another second, she immediately called a ribbon and vaulted up and away from Rhombex's surface.

Chapter XIV

The Grand Table

Thyra couldn't recall a time that the Grand Table in the Harbor library had ever been so popular. Massive and rectangular, the Grand Table, the largest in the library by far, rested prominently in front of the reserve and reference sections. As Harbor and ADF leadership finalized plans for a potential visit to Earth, they took advantage of its size and significance to exchange ideas and sift through research.

The Grand Table was tastefully ornate in rich wooden tones with elaborate grains, and had various shelves cut into the sides to accommodate books and other materials used by a library visitor. On top of the table were small ribbon transport systems, similar to the ones in the library floor, as well as rotating platforms that allowed massive teams performing research to quickly share materials, or shoot them rapidly to other areas of the table. The congested table was littered with copious materials being passed back and forth for others to review, which was accompanied by a flurry of loud conversations and their hectic, but determined chaos.

The special reference and reserve items in the Harbor library were particularly delicate and rare, and thus, heavily protected. After the formation of the ADF and establishment of the Sentinels, a few Sentinels were placed at periodic locations throughout these sections. The knowledge contained inside them was beyond priceless, and absolutely irreplaceable. There were numerous texts from indigenous cultures from all over the multiverse, many of which had been extinct for millennia. It was these texts, with a priority placed on those ranging from philosophy to mathematics and physics, that were of interest for the huge mob gathered around the table.

Along with Elcyd, Siguren, and Thyra, Mamdod was leading this massive, albeit rushed, effort to try to determine what might happen to the ribbons, and possibly time and space, once the leaves fell off the island tree and their stewardship was transferred from Mamdod to Einar. There was also research being performed to predict possible scenarios as to what might happen if Einar is killed prior to the ribbon island tree losing all of its leaves.

They all knew Mamdod's game, and the rules he had established for it, but they also knew how many different scenarios there were that he had no information on. It was these unknowns that the bulk of the effort was being focused on. Teams of Astraeans took turns sitting at the table, skimming through volumes of texts, or ran back and forth to colleagues around the table or over to another obscure portion of the reference section. Ironically, many of the Astraeans doing the research had lived lives at the time and place many of the texts were contributed to, but as with so many other curses of semi-immortality, most Astraeans had forgotten far more knowledge from the past ages than they had retained. Regardless, they were hoping to skim, check and correlate any information they could find that may shed some light on any unknowns they could possibly exploit to even the odds against Einar.

Elcyd was overseeing a subset of the group that was looking into the physics of how the possible shift of ribbon stewardship might affect the multiverse, but the effort was slow-going. The majority of minds from individual universes seemed to have no data, physics-based or otherwise, theoretical or otherwise. Those universes that did have relevant data or feasible cosmological models didn't seem to share anything between them that could assist in the Astraeans' research, but there was plenty of data from multiple individual universes to continue sifting through.

Thyra and Siguren were leading another subset of the group focused on examining the folklore of countless cultures across the multiverse, as well as their histories and philosophies, in hopes of uncovering something that could help. Those in this group surmised that the answer to their *what-ifs*, might come in the form of stories or legends passed down through a culture. They thought it possible that something, somewhere in the early dawn of existence, might have interacted with Mamdod, Einar or Akal before the game began. There were no applicable stories known to the researchers off the top of their heads, but they knew there was an almost incalculable amount of history to review.

The respectable remainder of the group was broken down into dozens of even smaller subsets looking into topics less likely to yield any information related to what they needed. Numerous groups of two or three Astraeans each, reviewed data involving government, transportation, the arts, industry, popular culture, symbology, architecture, and an almost unending list of other subjects. Coordinating communications between the groups, and trying to expedite and prioritize findings, was Mamdod.

In addition to being the liaison between the groups and working to keep the task organized, Mamdod also spent time fighting with himself over what scenarios he should pass along to the groups to look into. It was a lot of pressure, determining what to look into, and then helping keep the teams focused on doing that research, but Mamdod wore the stress well. He didn't think of it as stress however, and didn't feel stressed. He was focused and decisive in his direction of the effort. He quickly evaluated the likelihood of a scenario and dismissed it or assigned it out. When a group hit a wall on a particular line of inquiry, or became stumped, more often than not he would provide a comment, bit of info, or a quick jolt of encouragement to keep the teams moving.

What would happen if Einar did gain stewardship of the island? What could he do with the ribbons? What would he want to do with them? What might be possible to do with the ribbons that hadn't been tried yet? How could the ribbons be used to harm species, planets or universes as a whole? If Einar is killed and the leaves fall, would the

*need for stewardship of the island be obliterated? Would
the function of the ribbons and how souls traverse them in
life and in death, remain?*

The questions and scenarios flew around the table.
Ideas and thoughts permeated the air, in and out of the
minds and mouths of the hundreds of Astraeans trying
not to waste one second. They knew better than anyone
how little time they had, and somewhat frighteningly,
they knew how little time the multiverse might have.

While answering questions being posed to him by
a group of friends next to him, Mamdod couldn't help
but be distracted by a conversation growing in volume
on the other side of the table. A few members of Thyra's
and Siguren's group had become frustrated with each
other and were fanning the flames of an argument that
was attracting more and more attention. As the volume of
the debate grew, more and more stopped what they were
doing and focused on the argument.

"Look," a female Astraean named Reni clipped
sharply. She waved a handful of papers at a male Astraean
named Deneun, who had an opposing view. "There is no
precedent for anyone being able to control the ribbons,
or bend them to their will. Mamdod was only ever able to
show people which ones they can use, and even now," she
continued, while slinging her other, book-filled hand in
Mamdod's direction, "with all of his memory intact, he's
not aware of being able to abuse the power of the ribbons
in any way. Spending so much effort exploring that is a
waste of time!"

Deneun scratched his head, and spent a moment
biting his tongue, in an effort to not lose his temper with

Reni.

"Reni, we already know that there is more possible with the ribbons," he started out with, calmly. "Look at what we already know about Einar manipulating ribbon traffic. Stealing souls? Redirecting souls? Making weapons to extinguish all of an Astraean's past lives, all at once?"

The anger in his voice had quickly escalated as he listed his examples, wondering if she had already forgotten them.

"But that's all done artificially, or by methods he's come up with elsewhere," Remi volleyed back with force. "We have nothing to go on that would suggest he would be able to do anything more with the ribbons than Mamdod can do, which is virtually nothing!"

"We don't know what else he may have, Remi! He may just be waiting to become steward until he can use some other new contraption. Almost every day since we were attacked, we get blind-sided with some new revelation about what Einar can do, or has been able to do. He might just be waiting for the last leaves to fall to gain control of the island and unleash something else that we don't know about!"

"Remi! Deneun!" Mamdod shouted with only the intention of getting their attention.

"Please, stop," he asked respectfully once they were both looking at him. He then quickly looked around the table to try and gather the eyes of as many others as he could before continuing.

"Please don't let what has happened cause animosity between any of you, and please forgive me for the stress I have unintentionally burdened you all with. You all are doing phenomenal work. You have done exceptionally well with so many unknowns, and with trying to predict almost as many possibilities as there are stars. Now, I agree with Deneun in that we should continue researching what may be possible for Einar to do with the ribbons, if he gains control of the island, but I also agree with Reni that we should be careful and rule out anything that may not be possible, within the confines of physics, for example. For that, let's make sure your team is in contact with members of Elcyd's group."

Reni and Deneun both nodded appreciatively at Mamdod, and joined countless others around the table who had also been given a deferment on their stress, and a moment of clarity as he spoke. The two bickering Astraeans quickly looked back to each other and exchanged smirks of mutual embarrassment and recollected friendship.

The table quickly got back to work with a refreshed purpose and focus, though it was a fleeting rally. No matter how full the table was of hope and drive, it was a losing battle. Time was beating the Astraeans to the punch, and the chances of filling in the blanks of what might be possible if Einar succeeded Mamdod were slipping through their fingers like an emptying hour glass. As a group would cross one idea off their proverbial list, ten more would be spawned.

After Mamdod addressed the table, he watched Elcyd jog back and forth between members of his team, seemingly getting their input on a host of topics before darting away and making his way towards him. He approached with a face stretched out in excitement, and a mind full of thoughts to accompany the books under his arm and papers clenched in his hand.

"It's amazing," Elcyd began with a breathless whisper. "We pretty much have the sum total of all knowledge across the multiverse at our disposal and we still are at the mercy of mostly theoretical ideas when it comes to what we're trying to figure out."

Mamdod tilted his head and propped up his eyebrows in empathy. He was as aware and mentally fatigued as anyone.

"It's all uphill," Mamdod said in acknowledgment "What have you found?"

Elcyd came to Mamdod's side, flipped open a book on the table and framed the papers he had around it.

"Well, it's not so much what we've found," he started, "as what we think Einar might be able to do if he succeeds you."

Mamdod nodded as he peered over Elcyd's fingers that were pointing at portions of text. Mamdod skimmed, watched, and listened.

"We started our research by trying to put ourselves in Einar's head. So, he's had all this time. He's had all the time from when you came up with your game until now, so we started off with trying to figure out what his primary motivation might have been originally, and then we tried to extrapolate his original desires out to how they could have possibly evolved all this time later."

Mamdod rubbed his chin while Elcyd continued.

"Originally, we assumed that Einar simply didn't want to have to wait to succeed you, much less spend the time and effort to outlast Akal. He didn't want to wait out the natural progression of the game, so he began devising a way to prematurely get rid of Akal. But as we all know, it took a great deal of time for him to make that happen, so we think he came up with a whole host of things he wanted to do in the meantime, as well as things he wanted to do once Akal was dead. Akal's death was just the first, and we think, smallest piece. In a way, we think he might have tipped his hand on what he wants to do and what he might have planned. If he has been able to kill Akal, and route and manipulate ribbon traffic and information as we've suspected, he might have a way, or be working on a way, to somehow restart all of time. Hey may be able to reset all of existence, and have it all to start over with, as he wishes."

"That's unfathomable," Mamdod uttered with disgust. It was a disgust rooted not in doubt, but in the very real possibility Einar might attempt what Elcyd suggested.

"It would mean wiping out the existence of everything, and everyone," Mamdod started to imagine. "No universe, system, planet, life, person, or soul, will have existed. Nothing that has ever taken place, will have taken place," Mamdod whispered darkly. He then looked up to Elcyd with a stare of fear and fresh urgency.

"Before we get too far along in our plans to visit Earth, let's take our latest theories and ideas to Rigella," Mamdod suggested to Elcyd.

Chapter XV

U266

Mamdod, Elcyd, Thyra and Siguren took some time to speak with their individual teams, and the room as a whole. The result of their efforts didn't establish any hard evidence for specific actions Einar may take, but they were able to identify some definite concerns that had to be weighed against a possible trip to Earth, and must be brought up to Rigella. If anything, they were reminded of how little time they had to do whatever they could conceive.

After the group around the Grand Table had been disbanded, Mamdod and Elcyd made their way to Rigella. Before leaving the library, they reached out to a few senior engineers and asked them to meet them at Rigella's office.

Rigella's office was one of the busiest places in the Harbor, and it seemed to only grow busier by the hour. The flow of personnel was endless. Fabrication facilities staff, ADF subordinates, senior Sentinel leadership, ADF

Readiness Officers, Mamdod, Elcyd, and more cycled through, perpetually. Rigella had a large office, and it was more than justified. Every square inch of wall was taken up by monitors, charts, and diagrams. Almost every table surface held numerous projections of systems across the multiverse that the ADF was engaging the Einarians in. But for all of the warfare taking place, the intelligence being swapped between the Astraeans, and countless cultures, in addition to the defense, offensive and engineering data circulating all around, there was one piece of data prominently missing from everything. No one knew where Einar was.

Rigella lifted her head up in a quick break from a conversation taking place. She and other ADF leaders were deep within a large projection of the 9th universe, reviewing data. She saw Elcyd and Mamdod enter the room and held her hand up to those around her. She shouted across the room.

"Mamdod! How many leaves are left on the tree? How much time do we have left?"

The congested room, with almost a hundred people and creatures in it, came to a dead halt. Everyone turned and looked at Mamdod as he reluctantly answered after a taking a second to prepare.

"Not long," he said strongly so that there was no doubt or chance of misunderstanding. "There aren't that many leaves left," he added. "I'd say a week, at most."

"Did everyone hear that?" Rigella asked the room. "Each and every Astraean is proud of you, but we must locate Einar. We must find him! Keep working on it."

After her quick, but appreciated motivational

refresher, she gave the ADF leadership around her some instructions and closed the projection they were referencing. She weathered some interruptions as she made her way through her busy office, but eventually made her way to Elcyd and Mamdod.

"How is everything going down in the library?" Rigella asked with enthusiasm.

"Well, we just wrapped up down there," Elcyd replied. "I think we were getting to the point of diminishing returns, and given our priorities, we decided to let everyone get back to their regular duties after we collected our most important findings."

"Sure," Rigella provided quickly. "That makes sense to me. What do you have?"

Before Mamdod or Elcyd could begin outlining the work that had been done in the library, someone could be heard shouting for Rigella before he was even seen. Rigella, Mamdod and Elcyd ran out of the office into the corridor and looked down its extreme length to see an arm waving high in the air. The arm belonged to a rapidly approaching Astraean named Vas, who was screaming Rigella's name. The crowds in the corridor that were mostly made up of staff, intelligence officers, and engineers which had been circulating in and out of Rigella's office, parted to make way for the urgent messenger. Vas finally made his way through and slid to a stop and immediately bent to his knees in exhaustion.

"We know where he's at!" Vas wheezed through the shallow sliver of remaining breath he had. He took a few deep breaths to quickly restore his lung capacity and stood upright as he continued.

"We got the latest data back from Ontelbar and cross-referenced it with the gravitational lensing criteria we've been using. We know where he is!"

Rigella slapped Vas on the back and held onto his shoulder while steering him into her office.

"Come in here! Come here!" She ordered Vas with excitement. "Everyone! We may have him!" She announced to the room. "Everyone gather around! We need everyone to see this!"

As Rigella ordered the room to drop everything they were doing, Vas, who was known to many in the room as a prominent and respected ribbon cartographer, began cycling through universes on the primary projection table in Rigella's office. Very quickly, he realized they were cycling through in the order they were labeled by the Harbor, and to save time, manually tapped in *U266*. Universe 266 promptly popped up for everyone to see and when it appeared, the cartographer zoomed the display out slightly, to show the edges of the neighboring universes, as well as incoming and outgoing ribbon paths.

"Here we go," Vas said with wide eyes, excited to reveal what his team had learned. "It took some time to come up with an accurate search pattern, after spending even more time defining what we were looking for, but between our work here, and the work done at Ontelbar, we've been able to detect what we are very confident, is the Dark Artery."

Any other sound besides Vas' voice suffocated from the intensity of the moment. No one could hardly believe they were actually on the verge of reaching Einar. As Vas continued, the crowd condensed tightly around the projection. Each face stared intently, and the muscles for each ear in the room tightened so that not a single syllable was missed. Outside of the main projection of U266, Vas brought up a few additional, but smaller universes to outline the rest of his presentation.

"You see, we had to wait for some of our real-time data to come back in order to rule out some of these universes. The variations on gravitational lensing we were looking for were entirely dependent on natural objects, whether they were stars, planets, black holes, etc., and as more and more data came in, we could identify natural objects that were causing the lensing. It wasn't until we got our data back on U266 that we saw light bending around an object that not only wasn't there, but an object that seemed to be moving. Einar's ship is in U266."

The room broke its silence in a display of respect and appreciation. Some slapped Vas on his back, while others could be heard softly saying, "Wow!" Or, "Amazing!" The reactions were heavily restrained and cautiously optimistic because everyone knew how much more work there was ahead of them in not only engaging Einar, but defeating him. But this was a huge moment for the Astraeans. Until then, many had no expectation, only because of the scope of what needed to happen, that they would find Einar in time.

"Well done, Vas," Rigella praised with a firm pride. "Please tell the rest of your team, and relay to the Ontelbar, how grateful we are for their work."

Vas nodded humbly.

"So," Rigella continued. "Where have you tracked the Dark Artery to? Where has it settled?"

"Oh," Vas replied with an immediate uneasiness. The room's shuffling grew still again as they waited for the additional information.

"My apologies, Commander," Vas resumed reluctantly. "I'm not sure what you mean."

"Where in universe 266 did the Dark Artery settle?" Rigella clarified.

Vas licked his lips and swallowed. He was formulating his response very carefully.

"This," he started, turning back towards the projection, "is the most recent information we have."

Rigella leaned over the edge of the projection table and propped herself up as she gathered her thoughts. Her head dropped slowly, but quickly looked back up at Vas.

"So, just to confirm," Rigella resumed calmly, "the most we've narrowed his position down to, is U266. Correct?"

"Yes, commander," Vas replied professionally and quickly.

Rigella shot up from the table and shouted louder than anyone had heard her shout in recent memory.

"A WHOLE UNIVERSE?!"

The entire room froze. Even the Astraeans in the outermost perimeter of the group dared not continue their side conversations.

Rigella's chest heaved with the dark impatience of bloodlust. While she had been momentarily excited at the prospect of getting to Einar, the latest revelation of only having his position narrowed down to an entire universe infuriated her.

"Mamdod," Rigella blurted out, while quickly

trying to contain her anger, "would we have time to search an entire universe?"

The gathered Astraeans collectively looked over at Mamdod. He stroked his raised eyebrows slowly, and took in a deep breath to consider the futility of Rigella's proposition. Not wanting to delay the obvious answer for too long, Mamdod responded with the answer everyone expected.

"Even if we sent everything we had, I don't think there's enough time to comb an entire universe."

There was hardly any reaction from anyone in the room, including Rigella. They all knew it was too large a feat.

"Commander, I'm sorry for..." Vas attempted, feeling pressure to accept responsibility for not having more specific data.

"No, no," Rigella interrupted. She held her hand out as she spoke, assuring him that his apology wasn't necessary. Everyone in the room prepared to be overcome with an awkward discomfort from what they expected to be a stern reprimand.

"You and your team have nothing to apologize for," Rigella said sincerely, surprising the entire room. "Just minutes ago, we had no idea where he was. Now, we have some idea. This data is invaluable and has been arrived at under extreme pressure and time constraints. Well done."

The room breathed a collective sigh of relief from Rigella's note of appreciation. Friends and colleagues of Vas' slapped him on the back, and voices could be heard throughout the group echoing Rigella with their own comments of "Well done!" And similar sentiments.

"I think then," Rigella continued, having regained her composure, "that the time has come that we are out of time." Her voice dropped into a softer, and grave timbre. Her eyes danced back and forth to faces gathered around, to the projection of U266, and back to other faces. "I believe we need to recall most, if not all, of our deployed forces, and make an all-out push to U266, and spend whatever time we have left looking for Einar. There is no higher priority."

After giving the room a moment to soak in her announcement, she looked up from the projection and scanned the room for any blatant hesitance, or objection. She saw none, and continued.

"That's what we'll do," she continued. "If everyone could please leave the room to senior Harbor staff, ADF personnel, Sentinel leadership, and myself, we'll have a brief conference and make our plans known shortly. Thank you."

The room began to empty out, and quicker still when one of the ADF Secondary Commanders barked mildly at the departing crowd.

"Quickly now, quickly!"

Rigella began walking around the projection of U266 as Mamdod, Elcyd, and others spoke amongst themselves. The noise from the withdrawing personnel dwindled until there was no sound left but that from the conversations of those that Rigella requested to stay behind. She finished her lap around the projection table and stopped in front of her friends, colleagues and subordinates. She took a deep breath and shoved it out.

"Do we have any other options, or better approaches?" She asked with genuine concern. To make sure everyone was clear, she rephrased her question. "Do you all agree that we have no other choice but to go all in on a search for Einar in U266?"

The smaller group that had gathered around, looked between themselves and offered no sign of objection.

Elcyd looked to Mamdod, and then to Rigella.

"You said it yourself," he reminded. "We're out of time."

Rigella nodded at Elcyd, but scanned the rest of the group to be sure.

"Please everyone," Rigella offered. "More now than ever, if you have anything weighing on your mind, please feel free to share it. "The times when it looks like there are no other options are when it's most crucial to step back and make sure."

There were still no signs of objection from the group, or indication that anyone wanted to speak. And while there had been signs of Rigella's stress, and the effects of her responsibilities taking their toll on her, there was still, virtually no question of Rigella's desire to protect her people, or her ability to do so. A silent concern for her personal well-being had been alluded to in quiet conversations here and there, throughout the Harbor in recent time, but the concern had never had an opportunity to grow to any particular point, due to the pressures everyone was experiencing. The concern for the Astraean culture as a whole always took precedence over anything else. The Astraeans, and especially Rigella, were sacrificing themselves, in a host of ways, for the greater good. In that context, personally or collectively, the group gathered around Rigella saw no other possible course to pursue.

"We have to try," Elcyd replied, confident he spoke for the group. "Let's go get him."

"Good," Rigella snapped with a bright enthusiasm. She then turned and made her way around the projection once more. "Everyone, come in around the table."

The group fell in around the projection as requested.

"Alright everyone," Rigella started. "Listen sharply. We need to get this figured out as quickly as possible. How many Markarian-class Capital Stations do we have in service?"

One of the Secondary Commanders stepped closer to an ADF Readiness Officer and accepted the data tablet he had been offered.

"We have 24 active," answered the Secondary Commander.

"And the rest of the fleet. What do we have active and available?" Rigella prompted.

The Secondary Commander tapped his tablet and quickly brought up the rest of the figures.

"We have 823 Carina-Class Capital Carriers, with 3,703,500 fighter drones between them, as well as 1409 Scuti-Class Battleships, 1580 Cephei-Class Heavy Cruisers, 1733 Centauri-Class Cruisers, and 2004 Persei-Class Frigates. Not including the carrier drones, that's a total of 7,573 vessels, Commander."

As the figures were being read by one of the Secondary Commanders, a Sentinel started typing them into a terminal and added them to an empty corner of the projection. Rigella looked over at the Secondary Commander reading the figures, with a blooming awe over what the Astraeans had accomplished in such a short amount of time. The others in the room looked around at each other with a stoic respect, shared by Rigella, for the impressive amount of forces as they were being outlined. It was a respect forged from the fires of desperation and necessity. It was a respect for standing up in the face of hate and destruction and doing all that they could to answer the challenge of rightfully defending themselves and answering a call to war that had been thrust upon them without choice.

Rigella turned a dial on a command panel before her and spun the projection of U266 around slowly as she ruminated on deployment possibilities.

"Ok, Rigella began. "We've all agreed that this is pretty much our last shot at wrapping this up, so here's what we'll do." As she continued, she pressed various buttons and twisted the dial that spun the display around, to visualize her thoughts.

"Let's redeploy twenty percent of our forces, split evenly across divisions and classes, to the Harbor, for our defense, and keep them here through the end of the game, whenever that may be, when all of the leaves fall. Select our most battle-hardened and experienced forces to make up that twenty percent. In the hopes of overwhelming Einar with the other eighty percent, if we can find him, we'll sacrifice numbers for experience back here at the Harbor, should we need them."

The personnel around the table whipped into a

flurry of activity issuing commands to their subordinates through their tablets, updating the projection with relevant information, and punching various commands into the panels around the projection as well.

"From what I see here," Rigella continued, "there are seventeen universal intersections at various points around U266. I don't believe we will need to divide the remaining eighty percent of our forces into seventeen groups in order to cover all entries, but we do want to divide them into enough groups so that the majority of the outer reaches of U266 can be monitored, and then have them converge towards the center. Depending on where Einar is, the individual groups will eventually converge and quickly be able to leave no stone unturned. The question is if we have enough time to discover him."

Rigella took in a huge breath and let it out slowly while peering eternally into the projection.

"Everyone?"

The room quickly quieted and the activity around the table stopped. All eyes turned to Rigella.

"This is going to be our biggest and final push to defeat Einar. We have come a long way, and we have done ourselves, and the millions of species our souls represent, proud, regardless of the outcome. We have been presented with constant unknowns, and overcome them. An evil slaughter was shoved down our throats, but we did not choke. We rejected it. We fought it. We have countered it, and we will defeat it! We will encounter more unknowns before it is all over and we will overcome those as well. Stay calm, focused, and confident in our fight and our abilities. Keep me up to date, and keep your subordinates informed."

The room responded to Rigella's concise encouragement in the most professional of ways. There was no cheering, clapping or whooping. There were only calm, but strong responses throughout the room of, "Yes, Commander."

Chapter XVI

Narrowing it Down

It didn't take long for the state of things to trickle out of the room, through the corridors, up and down through the other floors, and then to the outer extremities of the rest of the Harbor. While the most sensitive of information was kept known to only a select few, such as the universe Einar was suspected of being in, as well as their approach strategy and tactical plan, the point that mattered the most to the majority of Astraeans spread quickly. *We think we found Einar!* The proverbial back of the Astraean culture straightened. The conversations became less frequent along the docks and in the lobby. And what was said, was concise and usually related to whatever someone was doing to help with the imminent mission. Any concerns about Earth, and their preliminary plan to visit, were shelved. They had no greater priority than Einar.

The lower sections of the new fabrication and

imaging facilities, that were responsible for creating the largest vessels of the ADF, went dark. The Astraeans, other staff, and resources dedicated to those levels were reassigned to the higher levels of the fabrication facilities, and elsewhere in the Harbor. The time leading up to lashing out for Einar was better spent on ensuring the ships that had already been fabricated were completely outfitted and that the ADF and other Astraeans had the smaller ships, vehicles, and equipment they needed. Whatever large vessels the Astraeans had were all they were going to have, until their engagement with Einar had come and gone.

As with any other culture or society, the Astraeans had busier times than others as far as commerce and trade, and the areas that were usually home to thousands of tents, tables, and towers of goods, were empty. Though at that moment, the vendors should have been plentiful and busy, the area had been effectively, and indefinitely, abandoned. Traders and merchants were needed elsewhere in the preparations to meet Einar, or they had left for their home worlds while the conflict was decided. There was no time left for the Astraeans to patiently plan, or time for anyone else to calmly wait for the end of Mamdod's game to arrive. The approaching finish was on the horizon.

The foot traffic in and around the main entrances to the Harbor lobby thinned considerably. The Helper staffing levels at the Helper Desk had been noticeably reduced. And while many of the areas of the Harbor became uncharacteristically quiet, cold, and empty, it wasn't for a drastically reduced population. It was a matter of the Astraeans being demanded or dedicated elsewhere.

The common areas, social centers, and general locations of fun and carefree interactions, had given up their children to the wardens of war, and their preparations.

The last few hours leading up to the ADF's departure to U266 would have been a poor indicator of the stress of the situation, however. Rigella's office only had a few of the senior Harbor leadership in it, who were providing Rigella with final updates on the status of the fleet, as well as Elcyd, Mamdod, Carthal and Heersan. Carthal and Heersan had been named Deputy Commanders for the sake of this mission, officially ranked just under the Secondary Commanders, but would be reporting to Rigella and commanding ships of their own.

Mamdod, who had not been given an official rank within the ADF, would be commanding a Carina-Class-RE Capital Carrier. He would be providing any and all ribbon energy support he could, and it was agreed upon unanimously between ADF leadership, that it made solid strategic sense to not only have him involved in the mission to U266, but to have him commanding a ship to make use of its various ribbon systems, and ability to provide ribbon energy support. The final few hours in Rigella's office were solemn, but motivated. The group of old friends, both in terms of their own spiritual age, and the age of their relationships, reinforced their resolve as they spoke with each other ahead of the operation.

As the Astraeans grew closer and closer to the end of Mamdod's game, and as the ADF prepared to leave for U266, Carthal's trademark playfulness had become increasingly absent. He kept a hope that a time would return that existence could be mostly full of joy and wonder again, but in the waning days leading up to whatever fight was waiting for them, the sparkle of that hope seemed to leave his eye. Those around him wished silently that he was merely burying it deeper and safer within himself, and that his hope wasn't diminishing entirely. The tone and dryness in his voice as he spoke, however, gave no indication as to which was the case.

"Mamdod's riding in to 266 from this intersection, along with this hunk of the fleet?" As he sought to confirm, Carthal reached out and pinched a virtual representation of the fleet from the projection, and moved it to the location of his assumption.

"Right," Rigella answered immediately. She then started to reach for various hunks of the ADF resting in the margins of the projection, as well.

"You'll enter from this intersection," she continued to Carthal. "Heersan from here, and as you can see, all of the others from these intersections."

The group watched intently as Rigella distributed the virtual groups of forces to numerous points around the projection. They had all gone over this countless times in the previous few hours, but recapped one last time for good measure.

Heersan looked over to Elcyd.

"I really wish you were going out there with us."

Elcyd didn't look at Heersan immediately, but stepped back and took a deep breath. He responded while still looking at the projection.

"I know," he said, shaking his head at the situation. "I need to be here for the few staying behind."

He turned and looked at Heersan.

"I want to be."

Heersan immediately nodded in complete understanding.

"There are so many unknowns, about what might happen if and when we find him," Rigella said with a soft concern. She looked up from the projection and around to the group. "I just wish we had more time."

"Well," Elcyd rapidly huffed out. "We don't."

He then pushed away from the projection table, turned around, and left the room. He didn't stomp out or sound angry. He simply left. He knew what everyone else in the room knew. There was no more planning to be done. No worthwhile discussion left. No more arrangements could be made and no new strategies could be considered. Like Elcyd, the rest of the room resented that the time had come, and that they had no choice but to take part in a battle, the outcome of which was nebulous, at best. The results of losing, or considering what a win might cost, was equally frightening.

"Ok, everyone," Rigella began. Something gnawed at her nerves, wanting to postpone the conclusion of their discussion. It was a conclusion she dreaded, not from fear, unwillingness or incompetence, but a fear of what might come to her people. Rigella looked down at the projection table control panel and let her vision go blurry as she continued.

"I am so grateful to each of you for so many things." She paused every few words, almost involuntarily, as if silently packing an extra paragraph of emotion, or twenty, into her comments.

"We know what to do," Rigella continued, pausing

again, "and we know how to do it. Begin your sweep of U266 as soon as you pass the universal membrane and proceed towards the center. Merge your sweep spheres with the others as soon as you're able. Keep in constant contact with each other, the rest of the fleet, and me. As soon as anyone locates the Dark Artery, and we can positively confirm, I'll evaluate how to proceed at that point, but we will more than likely make every attempt to board the ship, and capture or kill Einar. The preference of course, will be to capture him, to see if we can extract any information from him, depending on when he's captured, and what the status of the tree at the island is. The point is, keep the lines of communications open."

Rigella looked up from the table and saw that everyone was nodding, but not showing any signs of needing or wanting to add anything or reply. Rigella took that as her cue to swallow her fear for the future of the Astraeans. She did so literally and proverbially. She told herself that she would not allow fear, uncertainty, or mercy, to enter her mind from that point on. She had allowed too much, already. She was done with that. There was no more room for anything now but war, death, and victory.

"Let's get to our ships," she concluded.

***

The few remaining signs of life around the Harbor that hadn't already died were making the death rattle. The observation balconies were empty and the hundreds of archways embellishing the perimeter weren't shadowing over anyone. For the first time since it had been created, the fabrication and imaging facilities were dark. The sounds that accompanied the production had ceased, and the few Astraeans left straggling through the shallows and depths of the Harbor wore no smiles. Smiles had been pretty common among Astraeans, but not anymore. The corridors had grown dark, but a few engineers staying behind stood and quietly held sad conversations in the lobby. Some Helpers stood on the stairs talking, and looked out across at their Helper Desk with no one waiting to be helped. It was as foreign a sight to them as the unknowns of what the final fight with Einar, and the final moments of the ribbon island tree would bring.

The docks and piers were eerily empty and calm. Like a naval fleet leaving the safety of countless other harbors around the multiverse, to protect their ships from an impending storm, Astraean captains, owners, and pilots had either left for their homeworlds, or relocated to other areas of the Harbor to prepare to deploy with the ADF. The areas of the docks usually overflowing with cargo, food, tools, equipment, and everything else traded around the multiverse, were barren. The throats of Astraean life were constricting.

The command decks of the hundreds of ships preparing to deploy were also quieter than one might expect. Each movement was calculated. Each command and response was delivered with cold precision. Everyone was professional, and all checklists and final tasks were being accomplished with efficiency and accuracy.

Though each ship in the ADF, of any size, was more powerful than those of many cultures across the multiverse, each one was eclipsed. Though each ADF member was highly trained, beyond capable, and had the life experience from millions of lives each, there was still something more senior than any of them. And while there was no shortage of devastating weapons of all kinds, a more lethal arsenal waited for them. It was an eclipse from, the seniority of, and the lethality, of fear.

The force the Astraeans had created in the ADF was monumental by any standard. The armament contained within each ship could destroy anything the Astraeans could conceive of, and because of the ribbons, it was almost an infinite supply of obliteration. Each soul of every Astraean going to hunt down Einar had the knowledge to kill, destroy, and erase from existence, virtually anything the multiverse could throw at it. And while they remained calm and professional, and readied their fleet to depart, a cancerous tumor of fear grew and mutated throughout every ship. No matter what they had done, what they had learned, or what they had at their disposal, the mood was smothered by a parasitic imagination that forced upon them, all that might be possible.

But, and it was an important *but*, to the Astraeans, they continued to put one foot in front of the other, press the next command, or answer in the affirmative to their latest direction from their superiors. The fear not only lived and thrived alongside each Astraean, but it was welcomed. The fear had shoved its way in and made itself at home, but the Astraeans offered it a seat and a drink. It had monopolized a good portion of their thoughts, but what the Astraeans didn't do, was allow it to paralyze them. They didn't hide it or pretend it wasn't there. They took it, grabbed it, put it where they wanted it to be, and used it. It had brought the mood down, and stopped the smiles for a while, but such things are just side effects of the situation. In order to own their fear and use it against itself, they had to switch gears to a different side of themselves. They would change gears back to smiles and laughter when it was time, if there was time.

The final checks and orders started to taper off throughout the fleet. The time to head for U266 had come.

"Teams: Report your departure readiness status when you have interfaced with your respective ribbon," Rigella commanded. Her voice echoed throughout each ship, and bounced between the ships and all around the Harbor, under the Harbor's artificial atmosphere.

Most of the fleet was clustered together across only a few ribbons, but as the fleet grew closer to U266, they would begin branching off to other ribbons and intersections so that the independent groups could enter U266 from their designated entry point. Those that hadn't already positioned themselves properly did so quickly after Rigella issued her command. The fleet settled into their launching positions and the last echoes of Rigella's final commands shot out between the ships and across the Harbor, before landing and seeping into silence.

It was time at last. The Astraeans were about to decide their fate, or have it decided for them.

"Keep initial communications to a minimum", Rigella commanded, "until everyone has launched and until we reach our respective first intersections. Stay alert and stay focused. Relay all contacts and suspicious behavior of any unidentified vessels or entities. Fellow Astraeans, we are ready. We are ready to answer any challenge that Einar or anyone else in the multiverse can muster. We have the strength, the numbers, the experience, and the will of our people driving us. We fly now into a maelstrom of uncertainty, but we will fly straight and true to a destiny for ourselves that only we will decide! Primary team, announce your launch as you will. We are behind you."

There was almost no delay between Rigella's comments and the primary team leader's response.

"Primary team switching from standby to live engine mode. Confirmed that staggered launches with the rest of the fleet have been properly synchronized. Beacon departure checks overridden. Coordinates for first universal intersection have been locked. Primary team will launch in 5...4...3...2...1...Mark."

When the primary team leader finished her countdown, her ship, and those on the same ribbon launch point, jolted out from the Harbor and disappeared into the distance. Over the next few short moments, the rest of the departing ADF forces shot out from their respective ribbons and towards their own intersection destinations. The departures had been staggered slightly so that the entire fleet would arrive at their designated entrypoint to U266 at the same time.

The blackness of multispace lit up with the stimulated ribbons from hundreds of ADF ships shooting across the beauty of oblivion like a storm of slowly diverging comets. Many ADF crewmembers, without immediate duties while en route to U266, slipped over to various windows to gaze in awe at the staggering sight of their fleet. Some were able to temporarily forget about their uncertainty in the presence of such undeniable power and determination. The Astraeans were ready for a fight.

As the fleet began to approach their respective first intersections, Rigella's voice broke the silence of all ship communication systems.

"Approaching first intersection. Resynchronize approaches and prepare to confirm coordinates for your next intersection."

Soon after Rigella's comments, the fleet passed the outer Harbor beacon and continued on without disruption. Displays on all ships reflected the time counting down to the first intersection. Once each ship reached their respective intersection's threshold and changed course, the counters reset to reflect the time until their next course change. The communication channels were quiet, and everyone was proceeding to their next intersection as planned.

"There is a slight delay in team four's trajectory synchronization," Heersan announced over the fleet-wide communications channel, "but, as we anticipated, that should be remedied after they emerge from the Quidden Nebula."

"Understood," Rigella acknowledged.

The fingers of the speeding fleet continued to spread open ever so slightly with each passing second. Slowly but surely, the separate teams of the fleet began to put additional light years between themselves as they sailed closer to their various entrypoints into U266.

The third and fourth intersections came and went, and depending on where a team was entering U266 from, some teams would have no additional intersections, while some still did. After passing the fifth intersection, the relatively subdued communications channel began to stir with an anomaly.

"There seems to be a ribbon disturbance ahead on all team trajectories," announced Mamdod calmly. "Ah, looks like a time-space ripple."

Time-space ripples, as the Astraeans thought of them, were simply a registering of major space-time events throughout the ribbons. It was one of the ways major events get communicated, in a sense, to the rest of the multiverse. A harmless shockwave of data. They were natural and common, and while they had no immediate effect on the fleet or its approach to U266, it was worth noting as a simple matter of travel precautions for the fleet.

Mamdod wasn't expecting a reply, and indeed, his observation did not receive one. Such time-space ripples did not require anyone's attention in this situation. As some teams passed their last intersection and were on the final ribbon that would lead to their U266 entry point, others reached their next intersection. The fleet's shadow began to creep over the final approach to U266, and the Astraeans ached to unleash their web that they hoped would ensnare Einar.

In a hysterical scream of panic, one of the team leader's that was on final approach to their U266 entrypoint, ripped across the communications channels.

"The ripple is a deception! It's hiding enemy forces!"

Mamdod slung his body at his ship's command terminal and refreshed his ship's ribbon data sweeps. A cold shot of fear eroded the bottom of his stomach as he confirmed what the team leader advised.

"Confirmed!" Mamdod shouted in confirmation. "Be advised! The previously reported ripple is a false cover for a large number of ships!"

"Understood!" Rigella immediately answered. "Fleet. Prepare to engage the enemy!"

"Wait!" Mamdod shouted back. "Rigella, let me talk to them."

"Talk to them?" Rigella replied, barely containing a chuckle. "Why? We don't have time for that, Mamdod."

"I know," he admitted. "I just need to try."

"It's too late for talking, but if it will make you feel better," Rigella scoffed. "Go ahead. Fleet? Maintain course."

"Einarian fleet, this is Mamdod," he began, hoping to reach someone before the fighting escalated. "Before it's too late, please let us talk."

Mamdod watched his display as he spoke and saw no change in course or speed from the Einarians.

"Everything is all out in the open now," Mamdod continued. "The whole multiverse knows what Einar has done and how he has used the whole multiverse for his own amusement. Please don't keep fighting his fights. Don't kill or die to satisfy his ego."

Mamdod's eyes didn't leave his display as he spoke, and only after finishing his last plea did he see something change. The Einarian fleet was beginning to slow.

Mamdod tapped a screen and switched communications back to the Astraean fleet, only.

"Rigella. They're stopping. If we can get them to talk, we might save ourselves a fight. That will save lives, and time!"

Rigella rushed to mentally calculate dozens of scenarios and replied. She made sure she used a channel that not only the Astraean fleet could hear, but the Einarians as well.

"Everyone. Maintain current speed to the Einarian fleet, but take weapons offline."

After a breathless moment, the two fleets met. No weapons had yet been fired. The culmination of ancient planning on one side, and the ingenuity of desperate necessity on the other, stared down the lengths of their combined thousands of hulls, at each other.

As soon as the ships came to a rest across from the other, the Einarian fleet leader lit up the displays on the Astraean fleet, without warning, and without additional solicitation from Mamdod. It was Nununn. He was an infamous warlord and tactician, a Ferratine. A pompous race that found pleasure in conquering and domineering everyone else. The race was a rare one due to their constant in-fighting and battles to determine the more superior Ferratine. In addition to his involvement with Einar, Nununn stayed involved in his race's gladiatorial competitions. After over 700 fights, Nununn was undefeated.

Nununn's skin, like all other Ferratines, was made up of numerous discs of metal that resembled a dull gold, with small feathers sprouting from the extreme edges of each disc. These discs slightly overlapped and fell extremely flat against each other. Many Ferratines resembled large feral dogs, but with eight legs and a nose that hooked down sharply at the end. The discs at the end of their nose had no feathers, and made for a perfect stabbing implement.

Seeing Nununn flash up on their displays startled many. A Ferratine was a malicious, and perfect monster. When the video feed was established, Nununn's attention was dismissively focused on something off camera.

"It really angers me," Nununn said, with an ironically calm monotone, "that you assume we are too dense to know why we are fighting, or what we are fighting for."

Mamdod attempted to respond with respect.

"Nununn, I was only referring..." Mamdod attempted.

"I'm not finished speaking," Nununn said, stopping Mamdod in his tracks. He continued looking away from the camera. He held up one of his legs and gestured at his crew around him.

"I could leave right now, and anyone around me could leave to go where they wish. We were not forced to be here, nor were we forced to be anywhere before now. We have chosen to be here, and choose to fight."

"But Nununn," Mamdod finally jumped in with firmly, "he's deceived you into thinking what you're doing is a choice. He's using y..."

Nununn swung his stare towards the camera finally. Without saying a word, his imposing and dark beam of disgust interrupted Mamdod and caused him to freeze, mid-sentence.

"Mamdod," Nununn said softly. Each word was sprinkled with condescension and impatience. "Many of us have been with Einar from virtually, the very beginning. Have you not considered that the Astraean view might not be the best for the multiverse? Well, let me tell you...

Many have!"

Mamdod kept a resilient stance, but had no immediate reply. Rigella however, did.

"So, the Einarian view included the unprovoked attack on the Harbor, and waging countless wars across the multiverse?"

Nununn laughed at something he legitimately found funny.

"Means to an end, Rigella!" His laughter came to a close as he continued. "Look, you obviously don't understand, so let me help you so you'll quit wasting my time. The Astraeans have been imposing their will on the multiverse ever since Mamdod started his silly little game. The Astraeans have launched plenty of preemptive attacks through the eons in various forms across the multiverse because they felt their way was the best way. Well, that's all we're doing. Your objection to it is hypocrisy at its finest. No, no. It's time for something new."

"The only difference it seems," Mamdod replied calmly, "is that your preemptive efforts are only to serve yourselves, rather than for good or for pea..."

Nununn erupted in a percussive laugh once more, and started to say something but the first inaudible syllable was interrupted by Rigella.

"I've heard enough..." She said.

Nununn recovered from his laugh and could be seen gesturing to a member of his crew off-camera once more. He then terminated the video feed.

"Have our fighters and cruisers spread out," Rigella ordered. "Begin a full assault. Fire at will!"

Chapter XVII

Dark Matter Matters

Lannya and Azli choked down a few relieved breaths after making it back to Paige, but panic soon set back in. They had no clue what Einarian forces may be waiting for them in Rhombexian space or in any neighboring systems. All they knew is that they had to get as far away from Rhombex as soon as possible.

"Let's go!" Lannya shouted. "Set course for Salacia!"

Lannya raced up and down Paige's side deck rails to see if anything was following them up from the surface of Rhombex.

"Which one?" Azli shouted back while staring at one of Paige's command terminals. "There's more than one!"

Lannya spun around to Azli and threw her arms out.

"Are you kidding me?" She was disgusted at not having better information at their disposal, but not completely surprised. The multiverse almost defied the concept of size and while planets or systems with identical names could entirely be possible at random because of sheer numbers, many times cultures and species evolved with celestial bodies, races or events named in honor of any manner of thing from elsewhere in the multiverse.

"I don't know," Lannya angrily whined. "The closest one! Go!"

Azli punched in the coordinates and motioned at Lannya to get below deck as she cuffed her hands around her mouth. She wanted to make sure Lannya would hear her over the sound of Paige quickly coming to speed and over the machinations of Paige submerging into the ribbon.

"Max flow factor! Come on!"

They both quickly stepped through the main sail hatch and raced down the stairs. After reaching the common room, they both bent over and grabbed their knees in exhaustion. They hadn't really stopped since the pyramid on Rhombex exploded, and the subsequent chase from the Einarians. They gasped for breath and then collapsed onto nearby benches. Soft thuds and squeaks echoed throughout the boat as Paige's hull settled into its final preparations for submerged ribbon traveling.

"We've got a bit of time," Azli said to Lannya, through a final few catch-up breaths. "This Salacia is all the way in U1018."

Lannya rubbed her fatigued face and spoke into her hands.

"1018?" She dropped her hands and looked at Azli in surprise. "That was the closest one?"

"Honestly, I didn't look to see which one was where," Azli admitted, while confident she made the right decision for their safety. "I just picked one so we could get out of there."

Lannya acknowledged Azli's judgment call with an approving shrug and side tip of her head. She jumped up from the bench and joined Azli at the command terminal. She began to scroll through them out of curiosity.

"Let's take a look at the others." Lannya frantically looked through the list making quick judgment calls on which Salacias could be disregarded or not. "Before we spend too much time going to the one in U1018, do any of these look better than another?"

Azli stammered as the changing spheres of various Salacia projections reflected off of her face.

"I, uh.. I have no," Azli rambled.

"Come on!" Lannya screamed. She pounded the side of a cabinet before Azli could try to continue. "You were his pride and joy, Azli! He told you everything! Help us!"

"I've been helping you!" Azli screamed back angrily. "But I don't know which Salacia he went to! He moved it after I left. I don't know!"

"What an absolute joke!" Lannya punched the cabinet again. "You did so much for him, you killed so many for him, and you don't know where he might go?"

"No! He didn't need me to know! He didn't want me to know! I don't know!"

As Azli screamed, and continued to scream, in hopes of getting her mom to stop hammering her with questions, both their foreheads collapsed from the weight of their collective pain and their eyes filled up with water.

"I don't know! I don't know! I don't know the rest of his plans. All I knew I had to do was kill dad. All I had to do was stop you. Slow you all down. Get in your way. He just wanted to use me. He used me! I don't know where he's at. I don't know!"

Lannya slammed both of her fists into a sturdy shelf attached to cabinet, different from the one she had already punched, and used the momentum of her bouncing fists to shove herself away from Azli. She slid her hands over her head and grabbed handfuls of hair and pulled on them in frustration. She grunted from the pain. The stabbing spikes of the tension on her hair mutated her grunt into a stabbing growl. Once she was out of air, she stared at a wall of the common area through her tear-fogged eyes.

Azli stubbornly did everything she could to sniff as little as possible. Though she knew Lannya wasn't looking at her at the moment, she also swiped her eyes with her sleeve as fast as she was able. She wasn't worried about feeling shame, or being emotional in front of Lannya, but she felt as though she didn't deserve to feel the pain she felt at that moment. After what she had done to Akal and what she had brought upon the Harbor during that same fight, she didn't feel worthy of her remorse or grief.

Azli stared at the terminal and held her eyes open as long as possible, denying herself the trivial matter of blinking, just as she was trying to deny herself the release that her regretful tears would bring her. She leaned and loomed over the display, willing her tears to slow, and hoped the slight ambient light from the display would help dry up the few she had allowed to fall. And though she continued to expend all her energy on cramming her thoughts with the intention to abandon her emotions and feelings, a completely different thought began to wedge its way in. As the wedge wiggled further into her mind, she assumed the obviousness of its premise was the driving force behind its power to overwhelm her inner laments of disgust and compunction. She allowed herself a final sniff and looked at Lannya.

"We need to call the Harbor," Azli said softly. The logic in her proposition quieted her mind and steadied her voice.

Lannya turned around quickly, somewhat surprised either of them could speak so soon after their emotional outbursts. Azli's suggestion immediately started Lannya's mind racing towards a similar conclusion, but she stubbornly postponed her agreement.

"No, Azli," Lannya replied with a disarming tone. She spoke to her with a completely different demeanor than just moments before. "You and I, we have some serious things we need to talk about, and to keep talking about. We have issues, and we may always have issues, but what Rigella did back at the Harbor, was wrong. I don't want to have anything to do with her, now, and maybe ever. You came with me to the Harbor at my side. I brought you! You came willingly, and she wouldn't even let you leave the docks without beating you into a pulp?"

Lannya's voice grew loud again, this time, furious at Rigella.

"They could have talked about what to do with you all day and considered all kinds of options! But they didn't even talk. Rigella didn't give anyone a chance to talk! She just started beating you! In her position? With her responsibilities? With the trust she was given?"

Lannya had plenty more to say, but Azli stepped towards her mother with her palms out.

"Hey, you're not wrong," Azli affirmed softly. "I agree with you, but we can take that up with her later. I can't let myself go to that place of immediate hate and reaction that I went to for so long. Einar taught me to go there. He trained me to go there. I don't want to anymore. I understand why she did that. But right now, we need to talk to them. We need to see what they've learned and see if it can help us. We don't have the time to think about anything else."

Lannya gave no more quarter to her pride, and swallowed to dismiss any remaining qualms she had with reaching out. She felt unexpectedly pleased that Azli gave her the final push to make contact with someone back at the Harbor. She walked towards Azli and the command terminal, and as she passed Azli, she reached out, and squeezed her arm. A few taps and slight delay in waiting for an encrypted ribbon transmission later, an image of an engineer popped up on their display. A projection of Lannya's face glowed brightly back at the Harbor.

"Lannya?" The engineer exclaimed in surprise. "It's so great to see you! Where are you? Are you ok?" The engineer didn't need to ask where she was as Paige's location registered on an engineering terminal when the transmission was connected, but he was so happy to see her, he rambled out questions without thinking. He leaned over and checked the display for their location.

"I see you're in a ribbon, headed to U1018? Why are you going out there?" The engineer asked with a light-hearted confusion. Lannya was so focused on speaking with Elcyd, she didn't consider why someone would find their location odd, as if they should be anywhere else.

"Hello. I don't have time to talk. Can you please connect me with Elcyd?" Lannya sped through her request in a whoosh of blurred monotony.

"Uh, sure," the engineer replied as he looked around the room. He's..." The engineer looked over the monitor and camera he was using to communicate with Rigella and locked his eyes on who Lannya assumed was Elcyd. "He's way over there. He wouldn't hear me if I shouted. Let me patch you through to the terminal he's at."

Lannya looked at Azli and didn't say any final words to the engineer. She was already formulating which words to race through when Elcyd got patched in. After allowing a few seconds for the engineer sitting at the terminal to acknowledge the call, Lannya popped up on the next engineer's screen. Elcyd, who was absolutely taken by surprise at seeing Lannya, leaned over the engineer's shoulder and boomed at the display.

"Lannya!?"

Elcyd dropped to his knee alongside the engineer that manned the station.

"Elcyd!" Lannya shouted back with a warm smile, thankful she had reached him.

"Where are you? Where have you been?" Elcyd started rambling off questions of his own. "Is Azli still with you? I need to bring you up to spee..."

In her excitement to fill him in on what they had learned, she unintentionally interrupted him.

"You wouldn't believe how quickly we ran into trouble after leaving the Harbor. It's a really long story, but we think we know where Einar might be. We're headed for U1018, and to a planet there called Salacia. We got a tip that Einar's in or near a, Salacia, but there's a few different Salacias, so we just picked one to check out."

Elcyd looked with wild and wide eyes at the engineer.

"You said Salacia?" Elcyd sought to confirm.

"Yes, affirmed. Salacia. We were thinking the Harbor might be able to help us search them all quicker," Lannya responded, clueless as to why Elcyd would want to confirm.

Elcyd shoved out a quick, "Hold on," at Lannya's projection.

Elcyd leaned over to an astronomical cartography specialist nearby.

"Can you search U266 for anything named Salacia? S-A-L-A-C-I-A."

The cartographer had already begun searching before Elcyd finish spelling it out. When the results quickly appeared, he pointed at the relevant portion of the U266 projection he had queried.

"Yes sir," the cartographer responded nonchalantly. "In U266, there is a planet named Salacia right here near these coordinates. This quadrant."

The cartographer held his finger out at a point of the display casually. Elcyd leaned back to the display with Lannya on it.

"Lannya! Wait a minute!"

Elcyd leaned back over to the cartographer's desk to double-check his eyesight. He leaned back to Lannya.

"Lannya we already have the bulk of our fleet headed to U266," Elcyd advised. His speech sped up, and his voice raised with excitement. Lannya met his speech and voice with ever-growing eyes. They had put the last piece in each other's puzzle.

"They've engaged a fairly formidable Einarian force there," Elcyd continued. "They didn't know which planet to check, so they're splitting up to enter U266 from all over and sweep it from the outside, in, to try and find Einar. But you said he's on or near Salacia?"

"Yes!" Lannya shouted back in hysterical hope. "Salacia! U266 you said? We're on our way!"

"Wait! Lannya! You should meet up with the fleet..."

Elcyd couldn't get out any other comments. The hunt was on. Lannya closed the channel and punched the coordinates in for U266's Salacia.

Before the display had completely faded out, Elcyd had already begun sprinting over to the intelligence section of engineering. He blew by colleagues and friends in a frenzy that caused them to stop and stare with confusion. After a few weaves and dodges, he reached the intelligence section, in a frenzied whirlwind.

"Connect me with Rigella, Mamdod, someone with the fleet!" Elcyd shouted. His mouth hung open as he caught his breath.

The intelligence officer in charge at the moment didn't even look up from his terminal. He was intently focused on coordinates and projections of the battle the ADF was having with the Einarians.

"This is not a request," Elcyd blurted firmly. "I know which planet Einar is at!"

The intelligence officer jerked his head up.

"Are you sure? How did you find out?" The officer couldn't believe it.

Elcyd huffed at the officer's audacity. "You'll find out when I speak with someone with the fleet. Get me connected!"

An intelligence subordinate seated to the officer's side spoke up.

"Sir?"

The officer looked down.

"We've lost communications capabilities with the fleet for a moment. They're in a pretty heavy fire fight. We're working on restoring it as soon as possible."

"Look," Elcyd said calmly. "I don't care what any of you have to do, how you have to do it, or what means of communications we use, but I must speak with the fleet. Now. Get it fixed."

***

Lannya turned to Azli and roared with excitement while wearing a gigantic smile. "U266!" She ran over and slapped her hands down on Azli's shoulders. "We had the planet. They had the universe! Come on!"

Lannya shot over to the command terminal and changed their course for U266. Paige's hull popped a few times while she responded to their new path.

"Course change: Salacia, U266," confirmed Paige.

"Wait, wait," Azli asked of Lannya. "So, the

Harbor knows where to go, right? You got the universe info, and you told them which planet?"

"Yes, it was a great idea to contact them," Lannya admitted. "I can't believe I didn't want to. I wasn't thinking clearly."

"Who did you talk to?" Azli wondered.

"Elcyd," Lannya replied.

Azli looked around the common area as she processed everything.

"Do you think we should make sure Rigella or someone with the ADF knows? Maybe ask them to meet us?"

"Well," Lannya quickly began to propose. "I'm sure Elcyd will spread the word. They can meet us there if they want. I don't really want to wait for them, and I don't really have any desire to join back up with them right now."

Azli paced slowly in a few circles and continued contemplating all that had transpired. She had no immediate reply and decided that the best course of action at the moment was to consider checking into the lead on U266's Salacia they now had. Whatever the ADF was doing, Azli decided internally, might serve as a distraction for them to continue operating with some amount of stealth. She looked at the display and tapped it lightly, mentally signing off on Lannya's plan.

An unexpected calm settled throughout Paige's decks, and pulled the reigns on Lannya's and Azli's wild nerves. There would finally be no more uncertainty, and no more false starts to a resolution. There would be no additional waiting. They would finally be able to join the fight and reach a conclusion. The Astraeans were beyond fatigued from being dragged around by this war, and Lannya, or Azli for that matter, was no exception. Everyone was tired of it, and while the blame or justification was often blurred across sides, one thing was for sure. The breakneck speed and scale at which the war escalated wore everyone's soul down to a nub.

As the time ticked away towards the final leaves of the tree falling, each side was increasingly filling with sentiments of just wanting it to be over, and not caring who won. It was Mamdod's game, but Einar's war. It could actually be thought of as impressive, to some. The scale at which Einar could wage war over so vast an expanse of time and space, and especially the Astraeans' response, was nothing short of fantastic. In a fairly short time, Einar had effectively pulled the entire multiverse into a conflict that, except for a minuscule fraction, had no desire to be involved. Regardless, they were involved with it.

When Paige had gotten close enough to U266 to have it register on her sensors, her displays became blanketed by thick splatters of contacts. There were so many, the entire projection was taken up by them. They immediately caught Azli's attention as she shouted out at Lannya.

"Lannya!" Azli shouted while jumping up to lean over the display. "Look at this! The contact counter hasn't stopped growing since we came into range!"

Lannya rushed over and hovered over the display as well. She tapped a few commands and had the information in the margins of the display begin to categorize and classify the contacts.

"It's the ADF. Look," Lannya said as she pointed at the hundreds of ADF designations popping up. "The Einarians must have engaged them at the outskirts of U266 to slow them down. Well, that's good and bad I guess."

Azli looked to Lannya with a silent curiosity of whether or not they should stick with their plan. Lannya picked up on it immediately.

"We need to keep going. Someone needs to make it to Einar, and we have no idea who might make it or not. I think the ADF will be able to hold its own, but right now, we have no resistance of our own and we need to take advantage."

Azli looked back to the display to assimilate Lannya's comments and thought over whether or not to disagree or offer any comments. She couldn't think of anything and simply nodded in agreement.

As Paige zipped through the ribbons, passing planets, stars, galaxies, and various universes, Azli and Lannya watched as their changing position scrolled by, one set of coordinates after another, on the nearby display. They sat quietly and thought on the countless races and cultures in those locations, almost none of which escaped unaffected from the Einarian-Astraean war. In an almost catatonic state, they both simply sat motionless, and stared as the names, places, and memories flew by.

Lannya and Azli sat for a long time without speaking with each other. They didn't have much to say, and while it might not have been very strategic, they waited a long time before bringing up their plan. After the equivalent of trillions and trillions of light years,

Lannya finally licked her lips and spoke.

"So, I'm assuming we have a similar plan to what we were hoping to do in Rhombex?"

"Yeah," Azli obliged casually. She leaned over to a display and pulled up local Salacia space. "We can terminate Paige's ribbon travel here," she continued while pointing at the projection, "and then ride in to the Dark Artery on our own."

"And like I said before," Lannya started to recap, "I'm depending entirely on you to get us around on that thing."

"Yeah, I know," Azli said with a bristling confidence. "No one knows that ship better than me, except for maybe Einar himself."

Lannya started to humble her, but Azli anticipated her comments affectionately.

"And yes," Azli continued, "I am fully aware that any number of things could be different since I was here last, regardless of how little time has passed."

Azli turned and looked directly at Lannya with a cocked eyebrow of cautious optimism before finishing her thought.

"But we have some slight element of surprise," Azli felt compelled to add. "Even if it's just the unknown of when we or anyone else might get to the ship. But with so much of the Einarian fleet being tied up with the ADF, we need to take advantage of this moment."

"Understood," Lannya acknowledged. "When we get there, where are we entering from, and how do we get to Einar?"

Azli nodded again and leaned back over to the

display. After tapping a few commands, she inserted her hand into a ribbon scanner and had the projection form a representation of the Dark Artery. She then pulled her hand out and zoomed the display out some.

"Ok," Azli began. "This layout could have obviously changed since I was there last, like I said, and we should probably expect that to some degree, but the best point of entry for how we want to enter and what we want to do, is here, I'd say."

Azli gestured at the projection and tilted the display of the Dark Artery so that they could easily see the bottom of the ship.

"There are dozens of dark matter collection vents along this narrow area here," Azli began to explain. "And, if we make our final approach to the Dark Artery, in say, Zib form, then we'll get collected into the ship and can make our way from this collection processing chamber, here."

"Yeah, that will work," Lannya said with a lilt of confidence. "I have a few Zib skins."

"Good. Now, we'll need to be constantly on guard and think on our feet," Azli resumed as she returned the Dark Artery projection to its normal, upright position. "There weren't any security measures in those collection areas before, but there may be now. The vents may not even be there anymore for all I know. There are of course ports, doors, and hatches all over the exterior hull, but every one of those is monitored. I think this is our best shot at boarding undetected."

Lannya nodded while listening to Azli discuss their approach, and while watching the distance close between Paige and U266. She broke her concentration on the display and looked at Azli.

"And once we're on the ship?" Lannya's face showed no emotion. She was just making mental note of the plan.

Azli sucked in a deep breath and exhaled slowly while shaking her head. She knew there weren't many options, or much time to plan anything safer.

"I'll just try to access a ship console, see who's onboard, see where Einar is, and fight our way to him. I don't think it will take long for us to find a fight."

Paige vibrated and shook just enough to be noticed before her artificial voice came over the ship-wide speakers.

"U266 approaching. Disengaging maximum flow factor. ETA to Salacian moon, six minutes."

Lannya jumped up from her bench and walked to a command terminal and ordered Paige to surface from the ribbon. Azli joined her at the console as she finished, before they both walked to the stairs leading up to the top deck. Lannya recapped their plan as they ascended the stairs.

"We'll park Paige nearby, hop a ribbon in Zib form, and head for the dark matter collection vents. After that, we fight all the way to Einar."

"Yeah," Azli confirmed with a noticeable pinch of doubt. Lannya didn't say anything, though she caught her hesitation. They both just wished they had more time to develop a more tactical plan.

They stomped off the stairs onto the top deck just as Paige came to a rest in a ribbon right outside the Salacian moon's orbit.

"How do we know he doesn't know we're here?" Lannya asked as she tapped a terminal to secure Paige.

"We don't," Azli scoffed. "I guess we should assume he does."

Lannya's shoulders fell under the building weight of unknowns and uncertainty. Once again, she and Azli, just like the Astraeans as a whole, had few options, and little time.

"Well," Lannya said before laughing at the absurdity of the situation. "This is going to be a very interesting undertaking." She shook her head and laughed again. She saw little hope in what they were about to do, but found plenty of courage to try. "Ok," Lannya huffed as she changed subjects. "Paige is secure. She's ready for rapid departure if we get back."

Azli pulled up the projection of the Dark Artery a final time.

"So, with any luck, we'll be entering here at the collection vents," Azli reiterated. "If we get separated, let's try to meet here."

Azli tilted the projection down and continued.

"This is the command bridge. If Einar's not there, or if we haven't found him somewhere else by then, we can regroup and look somewhere else depending on whatever resistance we've encountered."

As Azli completed her suggestion, she tilted her head back to Lannya to gauge her feelings on her suggestion.

"Yeah, ok. And if something happens to the other," Lannya added, "Get back to Paige and get out of here. I made sure you have command access. Meet up with the fleet I guess."

Mother and daughter then continued to stare silently at the projection. Each of them raced down a checklist of things to consider, contemplate, discuss, plan for, or ask the other about. But nothing else came to mind. Even so, they continued to stare at the projection of the Dark Artery. They had just recently reunited, and the prospect of being separated, or losing the other, made them both feel less at ease than they already were.

Azli arbitrarily gestured to revert the ship's display to its normal position again. Hoping it would stimulate any additional concerns or thoughts, Lannya rotated the projection around and back a few times. Nothing came. Neither of them had anything else to say, nor was there time to say it.

"Let's go," Lannya whispered.

They both walked towards the starboard top deck rail. Lannya kicked a plate under a recessed cover on the deck, and made a portion of the hull slide back and down, revealing a direct path down to the ribbon they could jump into.

"See you over there," Lannya said. There was no emotion in her tone.

Azli nodded and jumped in. Lannya followed immediately behind. Almost instantaneously, they both assumed Zib form, traveled the distance from Salacia's moon to Salacia's upper atmosphere, and ejected themselves from the ribbon. There was no ability for them to communicate in this raw energy form, so they both could only proceed as planned. They made their way to the underside of the Dark Artery.

After slowly traversing the bit of remaining distance to the ship, both Azli and Lannya were sucked up by the collection vents that were, to their collective relief, still where Azli remembered them being.

The force of the vacuum that grabbed onto them both, startled Lannya's consciousness, but she remained calm. Their nebulous and smoky black blobs passed through the vents and rode the air currents through various tubes and ducts before falling into a collection tank. After realizing they had landed in the collection tank, Azli trickled her Zib form out through a bank of filters and then through an air intake vent to exit the tank. She then floated over to a panel in the wall and allowed part of her Zib form to come in contact with the ribbon stream flowing behind it. In a flash, she then assumed her usual Azli form and removed her hand from the ribbon.

She took in a huge gulp of air, as quietly as she could, to satisfy the need of her empty human lungs that had just regenerated, and backed herself up against a wall to avoid the windowed door and window next to it. When she had caught up on her breathing and after confirming there was no immediate threat, she bent over and ran to the back of the matter collection tank to signal Lannya that it was ok to exit and assume her human form as well. Azli watched as Lannya exited and went to the ribbon stream in the wall, also. Once Lannya had assumed her human shape, Azli waved her over to join her back behind the collection tank.

"I really didn't want to say," Azli whispered. "But I didn't think we would make it even this far."

Lannya jerked her head around from looking for

Einarians around the corner of the large collection tank, and shot Azli an angry look that quickly relented to an expression of understanding.

"I'm going to go back to the ribbon panel real quick," Azli whispered while joining Lannya in looking around for Einarians. "There's a terminal connected to it that I can use to see what we'll be dealing with."

Lannya stayed silent. She had nothing to add, yet.

Azli scampered back over to the panel, ducking under the window and past the door. Lannya kept her eye on what transpired while kneeling on one knee and just barely leaning past the corner of the collection tank.

Azli flipped down the terminal's screen and began to tap furiously. The first and most important thing she wanted to check for was for any current alarms or alerts. She found no sign that anyone was aware of, or alerted to their presence. She smiled and jutted her jaw out in Lannya's direction.

"I don't think anyone knows we're here," she whisper-shouted. "Not yet anyway."

Next, she checked the Dark Artery's current power, defensive, and weapons states. Current power levels were minimal, *probably because of the ship's recent move*, Azli assumed. The shields were down, which Azli also assumed, because of the matter collection systems being engaged, to replenish the ship's power. The weapon systems were offline. *We have a complete element of surprise*, Azli told herself. She pointed at her own eyes and the in the direction of the door and window, advising Lannya to keep an eye on them. She then waved Lannya over to join her at the panel. After a quick initial glance, Lannya shuffled over and joined Azli.

"I think we're in the clear," Azli said while scooping her head in slight disbelief. "Let me pull up the current schematic of the ship just to be safe."

Lannya kept her eyes on the window and door while Azli tapped the command to bring up the projection. *So far, still alive*, Lannya thought.

"Are there any bathrooms on this thing?" Lannya playfully but sincerely wondered.

Azli looked at Lannya to see how serious she was. Lannya grimaced, but reassured Azli.

"I'm mostly joking, but I should have gone before we left!" Lannya then motioned for Azli to continue. Azli responded with a disapproving, but silly smirk. She looked back to the ship projection.

"This looks completely unchanged." Azli's whisper flat-lined with a sprinkle of concern. She turned to Lannya.

"Look," she requested. She turned the projection and rotated it back and forth so Lannya could see it easily. Lannya tried to consider it a potentially good sign.

"If he was intending to change things around more, maybe he ran out of time because of how the Astraeans responded." Lannya took another quick glimpse through the door and window and then turned back to the projection. "What kind of numbers are we looking at?"

Azli tapped the screen again. The projection then became pitifully peppered in far fewer thermal and other personnel sensor readings than she was expecting.

"Well, whatever is going on out at the universe's edge with the Astraeans," Azli began with a slightly louder whisper, "it must have Einar's full attention." She was apparently feeling confident enough to stand slightly more upright and speak a bit louder. "There's hardly anyone here. Look. It's a skeleton crew."

"Then let's get moving," Lannya requested, still being cautious with her volume and movements. Lannya's hesitance brought Azli's confidence back down to a more reserved level. She bent back over and resumed whispering.

"Ok, then," Azli began to conclude. She looked back to the projection. "Let's just make our way to the command bridge then, like we had planned." She pointed at the projection and traced the path again that they had agreed on back on Paige. "Follow me closely. I'll take us a slightly round-about way so we don't have to walk in the wide-open corridors the whole way there."

"Right," Lannya agreed swiftly. They looked at each other with humorous hesitance. "Should we keep our usual skins for now, or what?"

"Yeah, might as well," Azli replied quietly. "I'm sure we'll have to change some, but it's just a matter of thinking on our feet, and we've done plenty of that before." She scooted up against the wall and peeked her eyesight out through the window a last time.

"You ready? Let's just go out here and hug the wall for a bit. Just stay with me. Hopefully this luck will stay with us for a while."

Lannya shrugged with a smile.

"We'll see soon, I guess."

Azli's chest bounced with a silent chuckle.

"Let's go."

Chapter XVIII

Old Stomping Grounds

Azli slid over to the collection room's door. It jerked open with an airy burst of compressed gas. She leaned out slightly to look down the length of the corridor.

Nope, Azli thought to herself, seeing no one to the right.

Clear, she then thought, after looking down the left side.

She waved Lannya over and they both ran through the door.

The corridor was extremely wide to accommodate various species or movement of vehicles and small transports from one area of the Dark Artery to another. And while many areas of the ship were frequently teaming with moving personnel, other areas, such as the section the collection mechanisms were in, were not. The section housed most of the ship's engineering, mechanical and propulsion systems. Most of the personnel in this section of the ship were largely sequestered and for the most part, sedentary in that they rarely left their post until their shift was over. The fact that the section was far removed from the more populated areas, was one of the primary reasons Azli suggested coming in through the collection system. Her thinking was that the collection chamber gave them the best chance at boarding undetected, and provided them with some time to check the ship's status, and assess their surroundings.

They scampered quickly to the other side of the corridor to put eyes on the entrances to the few hallways and rooms along the side of the corridor they had just been on. After taking only a moment to take in their complete, immediate surroundings, Azli looked back to Lannya. Her eyebrows vaulted in continued amazement that they had made it this far. She whispered to Lannya softer than she had spoken since they arrived.

"This way."

Azli took off in an occasionally skipping jog, hugging the wall of the impressively long hall. Nothing seemed out of place, and nothing seemed staged. To Azli, this area of the ship, as it was at that moment, seemed completely normal. The corridor of this area was as it she would expect it to be if they truly had an element of surprise. They both thought an element of surprise was entirely possible, but they didn't outright assume they had one. If anything, they assumed they didn't, and expected the worst at any moment. All they could do was continue on.

The sounds that bumped and clicked, or echoed from elsewhere in the ship, were moderate and typical. If the two stowaways were facing each other, they could still have heard each other whisper, but they took no chances and said little. The air was clear but saturated with the expected smells from the area, of oil, hydraulic fluid, warm plastics, bare metal, and various combustion processes.

The lights overhead were on and bright, as they normally would be in this area. And though the light wasn't assisting in their efforts to move stealthily, Azli wasn't too concerned because of the low population of the section. Still, she, with Lannya close behind her, pressed on to the service passage Azli wanted to get to, in order to get out of such a revealing location. It was the closest one to the collection area where they arrived. After a solid minute of jogging, ducking, waiting, popping into slight recesses to hide, and listening, they reached a very wide door, that was only approximately four feet in height. The service passages were usually reserved for use by remotely operated, low-profile vehicles, similar to those used in coal mines, to transport goods, supplies, and tools to other sections of the ship, without disrupting the flow of personnel. Azli reached it first and pointed to it. Lannya waited for her to open it.

Azli looked around quickly and winced as she reached into the recessed handle and spun it, hoping to deaden the sound of the unlatching door. Most doors in common areas and high-traffic sites were automated and activated by proximity, but the service passages were seldom used, and were opened manually. She waved Lannya in first, and then followed behind her. Azli closed the door behind them and took advantage of their first bit of privacy since the matter collection room. Both were bent over due to the low ceiling.

"Ok," Azli said, noticeably relieved to have made it into the passage. "We need to follow this to where it terminates, about the same distance that we've already covered."

She looked into the distance of the passage and pointed as she continued to explain the next stage of their route.

"There should be no chance of running into anyone down here, but if one of the supply transports comes by on these rails here," she advised, pointing at the floor, "just hug a wall and let it pass. There's enough room."

Lannya went down to one knee to give her back a quick rest.

"After that..." Azli said while slurping in a doubtful stream of air.

"We ride a small lift to the main level. That's where the command bridge is, and where we'll probably get shot by one of those perma-death things and die."

Lannya chuckled in futility and let her head drop before picking it back up with a slight smile. They both weren't completely out of hope, but they were continuing to try and find the humor in the overwhelming odds. Lannya bent back up.

"Ready when you are," she said. Azli nodded.

Off they went, bent over and walking as briskly as they could with bent knees. The light in the service passage was far less than in the corridor they had left, seeing that it was usually only used by automated supply transports, but the faint green light was enough to allow them to move quickly and safely.

Neither one said anything as they crept. Only occasionally would either of them allow a sniff or small grunt. While Lannya didn't have a memorized idea of where they were, Azli realized they were soon approaching the point of being closer to their objective, than not. After a long period of creeping quietly, Lannya stopped abruptly when the lights noticeably, and slowly, dimmed to absolute darkness, and then back up to their previous level.

"I think one of the transports is coming through," Azli said calmly.

As she and Lannya leaned up against opposite walls, there was no other sound at all, except for two soft, but high-pitched beeps. Lannya assumed it was the final signal of an incoming supply transport.

"I guess that's in case..."

Azli's additional comment was interrupted by a rapidly increasing light, and excruciating sound, approaching from far in the passage's distance. Before either Azli or Lannya could register what was happening or how to react, the light and sound passed them, disappearing into the distance they had already covered. With both of their backs sucked up against the walls across from each other, Azli and Lannya started at each other, frozen in recovering horror. The eyes of both women watered over slightly in the rush of fear and adrenaline, which was already dissipating, now that the unexpected danger had passed.

"...someone's working on the passage," Azli finally finished, through a dry and raspy throat.

Lannya's eyes, like Azli's were stuck open from the

surprise and shock. When her mind finally registered the supply transport had passed, Lannya peeled herself off the wall and collapsed to the floor on her knees and hands.

"You could've mentioned something," Lannya began through slightly labored breathing, "about how fast they come through."

Azli slid down the wall onto her butt and also allowed herself to recover. She silently laughed through a slowly growing smile.

"I didn't know they moved like that!"

Lannya let go of an audible chuckle and let her head hang as she grabbed a few breaths and sat back up against her own wall.

Mother and daughter rested. In whatever sense of resting they were able to take part in, they sat quiet and still, and collected their nerves. They knew they probably wouldn't have another opportunity to rest until their mission was over, for better or worse, so they took advantage. In the soft glow of the passage's green light, they were able to identify an expression on the other, that reflected a hint of an alternate reality, a different past and future. Wishes, hopes and regrets that for the first time, they both truly began to share.

No one needed to speak. Hearts can't speak. They looked at each other and considered all the laughs and adventures they might have shared if things had gone differently between them and their souls. There was an understood hope, that if they should survive, they might be able to remedy all they had missed out on so far. But, the *if* was almost too large, with too many variables, and too large a hurdle directly ahead of them. That hypothetical shared between them in the dim passage, however, was a bridge where one hadn't existed until then. They didn't care how beautiful the land was on the other side, how expansive or promising. It was simply a small victory for their relationship which came right then in the powerful fact that the gap between them had been bridged.

Azli took in a long deep breath and let it out slowly as if collecting the necessary energy to retain the quiet moment between them, forever. She also might have been trying to resist the urge to ask her mom to turn around and leave with her. The urge to go spend whatever time the multiverse as they knew it might have left, pulled and tugged on the sleeve of Azli's mind. They still said nothing, but both were distracted by the same thoughts. They wanted nothing more than to go and make some memories together, and to make up for lost time. Lannya recognized in Azli's face for the first time, the face of a loving and compassionate daughter, regretful, like all good souls, for their shortcomings and failures, especially those that hurt the ones she now loved. But also, like a good mother, Lannya saw the regret in Azli's face and sought to clear her mind of it.

"Come on," Lannya said as she leaned to the side and stood back up into a kneeling stance. She tapped Azli's foot. "Let's go cause some trouble."

Azli wasted no time and smiled as she stood up. They then set back off, shuffling and creeping down the supply passage.

After a few minutes of quick and constant walking down the passage, there was a sharp bend to the right, which Lannya remembered from the projection.

"We're close aren't we?" She correctly remembered.

"Yeah, just another hundred feet or so, and we'll be at the lift," Azli confirmed as they followed the bend around.

The green lights dimmed and brightened. Another few sharp beeps rang their ears. Azli and Lannya were both ready this time, and calmly watched as a supply transport raced into view. It passed by them, and then disappeared into the distant darkness. After it had passed, they walked a bit more and reached the lift's recess in the wall. They stepped into it and Azli reached to activate the lift, but purposefully delayed pressing the button. She wiped across her face with her hand and cracked her knuckles before starting to talk out the last few parts of their path.

"When I activate this, it will take us to the main level, flush with the floor of the primary corridor," she began. "Now, it's possible that we won't immediately run into anyone because of how low the crew numbers are right now, but if there's a chance of running into anyone at all while we're here, it will be now. Once we're discovered, everyone who is onboard will come. And I'm sure someone will let the Einarians out at U266's border know. We'll just have to do everything we can to keep moving forward, as quickly as possible, and get to Einar."

"I understand. I'm ready," Lannya said with a determined strength. "If you think of a form as we go that might suit us in a particular situation, just shout it out, or communicate it to me in whatever way we'll be communicating at that moment."

"Right, ok," Azli agreed. "Same goes for you. If you think of something, or have a better form suggestion, just shout it out. If we can't communicate, just go with whatever seems suitable at that moment or something that compliments the other, I guess. And if we get separated, we covered that."

Lannya nodded.

Azli took a final easy breath and reached for the lift's activation button. This time, she pressed it.

They both looked up as the lift started to move, and faced the exit that they saw approaching from above. As they reached the main level, the ceiling over the lift was at the same height of the main level corridor. They both stood up slightly, but not all the way to maintain a bit of their lower center of gravity in anticipation of any immediate combat. But after the lift docked at the top of the main level floor, there was no one in front of them. Lannya went to a side and peered down the hall. Azli flung herself up against the other corner and looked down her side. Both saw a few Einarians crossing the main corridor at various sections. Those on Azli's side of the corridor were walking away from them. One on Lannya's side was far down, but walking towards them.

"One over here," Lannya whispered at Azli.

Azli spun her head around and identified the Einarian walking towards them. She nodded.

"We're just going to have to sprint from here," Azli speedily whispered. "Down this side of the corridor, almost to the end. Then a left, and then a right onto the command bridge. The corridor is the longest distance. The bit after we turn left and then to the bridge isn't far at all."

Lannya stretched quickly and wiped her hands

on her pants as she psyched herself up. Azli turned from Lannya and whispered in the direction they were about to run.

"On 3... 2... 1... Go!"

Lannya and Azli shot out from the lift's recess in the wall, at a diagonal, to build up as much speed as they could by the time they crossed to the wall on the other side of the corridor. They were at a full-out sprint, making no effort to hide, stay unseen, or remain quiet. As with any traditional element of surprise, speed and efficiency were the focus.

Lannya did her best to listen out for anything or anyone alarmed at possibly seeing them, and surprisingly heard nothing to begin with. She assumed the Einarian that had been approaching them simply thought there was an emergency of some kind that didn't warrant alerting anyone. They continued to sprint without disruption.

They were covering a lot of ground quickly. They were both calm and focused as they ran. But, with the appearance of an Einarian emerging close-by from an adjacent hallway, the surprise was about to be ended, and the fight was about to begin.

The Einarian wasn't menacing or threatening at all. In human form, the Einarian simply had a few data tablets under one arm and began to point at the curious sprinters across from him.

"Hey! Azli!"

He shouted not in friendly recognition, but in surprised anger. The Einarian wasn't able to get anything else out, however. Using the force of her momentum, Azli crossed to his side of the corridor and slammed her stiff arms and open palms into the Einarian's chin. As he flew back slightly and threw his tablets into the air, Azli tried to retain as much of her energy as she could, and spun around him as he collapsed into an unconscious ball. Lannya had begun side-stepping once she saw Azli begin to cross, but resumed her sprint quickly once Azli had.

A different voice, initially faint and behind them, caught Lannya's ear. She didn't make the effort to turn, but she was fairly sure it was the Einarian that had been approaching them when they stepped off the lift. This one, was able to cause more alarm. The Einarian's voice, though far behind them, carried and echoed with significant weight.

"Hey! What are you doing? Who is that?"

"Azli?" Lannya shouted quickly.

"Yeah, I heard," Azli blurted out through heavy breaths. "Come on!"

They both continued to sprint, making no effort to stop and fight those who weren't forcing them to. The Einarians that appeared, seemed only to pop out through doors, or from side rooms with looks of confusion. None seemed to be armed from what Lannya could tell as they raced past them, and were not challenging them. Both Lannya and Azli had the same thought. The Einarian fighters must all be fighting the ADF.

While still sprinting, the end of the corridor ahead was now easily visible, but still a good distance away. Lannya and Azli continued to sprint, weaving in and out of slightly increasing groups of Einarians that had begun collecting in clumps in the corridor, outside their offices or areas of work. It was then, the ship's alarm finally began to sound.

The alarm started off with a low and sustained *blaaattt*, that finally gave in to a higher pitched and slightly shorter splat of sound. The pattern of higher, shorter, and quieter sounds continued in a similar manner, until the alarm reached a quick and high-pitched poke of sound. The alarm continued by repeating the pattern.

Slightly into the alarm's first cycle, Azli and Lannya saw what Azli recognized as traditional Einarian warriors emerge from a few rooms ahead of them. The end of the corridor, and the left turn they needed to make, was a still a few hundred feet ahead. With no other choice now but to fight, Azli slid to a stop in front of the Einarians. Lannya met her, shoulder to shoulder, a second later.

Azli looked out of her peripheral vision to confirm her mom was beside her. As soon as it registered that she was, she lunged at the grouped Einarians. Lannya was a fraction of a second behind her.

The fighting was thick, hard, and immediately complex. The Einarians were expertly trained, and like many of Einar's other plans, their training had probably been in the works for millennia. While the group of Einarians, Azli, and Lannya were getting a feel for the fight, the tactics and attacks evolved quickly.

The group of Einarians wasn't that large, but large enough to stall Azli and Lannya and demand their full attention. They were not going to be able to proceed any closer to the command bridge without working their way through the fight.

Initially, the fight consisted only of basic, and quick

kicks, punches and blocks, but soon started incorporating more advanced deflections, parries, and blocks. As Lannya and Azli started to improvise and step up their attacks as well, so too did the Einarians. The fight was extremely fluid and at times, appeared to hide its lethal intentions and violent foundation.

Lannya and Azli fought alongside each other in an impressive harmony. It was a harmony that one might expect to come from a pair of fighters that had traveled together for millions of years. And while they hadn't had the advantage of millions of years together, they had a jumpstart of a newly discovered bond. They were a mother and daughter with millions of previous, powerful lives.

The two of them changed styles and techniques by the second. Their peripheral vision was almost like a third fighting partner in that it gave the other clues as to how they would move or change styles next. In one engagement they would incorporate individual attacks from Kung Fu, Capoeira, and Muay Thai of Earth inspiration, and then in the next step would use adaptations of the Morg Jortu, a style of fighting from the planet of Trewe, in which fighting partners would use each other's momentum in combined attacks of joined throws and assaults. The Trewens had three legs, but Azli and Lannya were able to incorporate a lot from Morg Jortu. Every few seconds, there would be new techniques and methods, with an almost never-ending supply of martial arts to switch to next. As Lannya and Azli switched or adapted, the Einarians would as well.

The fight was mostly evenly matched. Even though Azli and Lannya were outnumbered by about three to one, only so many Einarians could engage them at one time. It would have been a matter of diminishing returns if there were any additional Einarians.

Like a chess match, the fight was a constant struggle to maintain the status quo until someone made a blunder that the opponent could take advantage of. But no one was making any mistakes. There were gambits and sacrifices. Azli would allow the Einarians to score a punch to the side and absorb it, if it meant opening her up to attempt a kick to her opponent's head. Lannya would turn her back to one Einarian on purpose, in hopes of inviting an attack, so that she could then spin and grab him to attempt a takedown. It was a constant stalemate. Each fighter was anticipating and pre-empting. No one was making any blunders. No one was falling for any gambits.

Stalemate, Azli thought. *That's exactly what he wants... to waste our time.*

Lannya was on the same page.

They're not fighting to win, she thought. *They're fighting to stall.*

Lannya and Azli knew they needed to change the parameters of the match if they hoped to progress towards Einar. Each moment of delay decreased their advantage, whatever amount it might have been. More blocks. Another knee. A roundhouse kick. The fight had become stagnant and predictable, but that had become a good thing. Once Azli and Lannya realized the Einarians were only fighting to stall, they could fight to satisfy that requirement and devote a bit of their thoughts towards changing their strategy. At one point in the fight, mother and daughter had a moment to catch each other's eyes. Without saying a word, they saw that they were in agreement.

After the two of them had landed their most recent attack, Lannya began a motion that appeared as if she were attempting an axe kick on an Einarian that was starting to roll over and stand up, after being knocked to the ground. She timed it slowly, and purposefully, so that she would miss her opponent. As she brought her leg down, she swept past the opponent who had just stood back up. She allowed the momentum of her leg to swing down as she normally would but didn't let her foot make contact with the ground of where her opponent had been. This caused her to sweep her footing out from beneath her, and crash to the ground. Almost simultaneously, Azli allowed an enemy to land a few hard shots to the face. She used a little bit of drama and exaggeration to make the hits seem more devastating than they actually were. To the Einarians, Azli and Lannya had been hurt or disoriented, and were on the ground, at their mercy. The fight had stopped.

The Einarians that had most recently attacked or defended came to a rest after seeing the two of them on the ground. Confident in their victory, and proud of capturing Lannya, and in their eyes, the traitor Azli, they quickly formed a tight and dominating circle around the two women. The Einarians and Astraeans alike, took a moment to catch their breath.

One of the Einarians stepped away from the circle to punch a flurry of commands into a nearby terminal. The remaining Einarians in the circle began to smile in various configurations of being pleased with themselves, as one of the senior officers stepped forward and knelt down close to Azli and Lannya.

"That was exciting!" The officer said to Lannya, through slightly labored breathing. He then turned to Azli.

"Azli!" He greeted with false enthusiasm. "Welcome back! We've missed you!"

Azli panted and slowly reached up to massage her jaw.

"For a moment..." The officer attempted.

Before he could finish, Azli reached up and whipped the Einarian's head around and snapped his neck. Lannya flipped over onto her stomach, and swung a leg around to sweep under the feet of the three Einarians nearest to her. After deflecting or stunning the majority of the group that was still standing, Azli and Lannya ran over and dispatched those that Lannya had swept, with lethal elbows, punches, and stomps.

By playing the role of wounded prey, Lannya and Azli were able to change the fight to once again seize an advantage of surprise. The few kills they had already made drastically improved their odds, and bolstered their ability to overpower the remainder of the group. With the floor littered with dead or incapacitated Einarians, Azli and Lannya did a final scan of the corridor. They confirmed they were clear for the moment, looked at each other and took off to dash through the last bit of corridor before the left turn. They had no idea what Einarians might be able to return in different forms, or how quickly. In the amount of time for just a few breaths, they reached it and rounded the corner. Almost immediately, they steered around the right corner to the command bridge.

But what they saw after the last turn was nothing they were expecting, and everything they didn't want to see. The ship configuration had indeed been changed. What should have been the threshold to the command bridge, only a few feet away, was a new, exhausting length of corridor, similar to the one they had just sprinted through and fought their way out of. While it wasn't as long, it wasn't just another hall they had to traverse to get to the command bridge. Between Lannya, Azli and Einar, were ranks and files of hundreds, this time, of Einarian fighters.

Azli's soul was slapped with shock. She stood, frozen, trying to register all that was before her. Not only had Einar apparently anticipated an attack on the Dark Artery, but he had changed the design of the ship, left an antiquated map for them to reference when they arrived, and obscured the number of Einarians on board.

Lannya was frozen in place as well, having had her emotions ripped from her, including most notably any hope she had of helping defeat Einar. But her and Azli's thoughts were all internal. They went by in a split second and gave way almost immediately to pride, self-sacrifice, anger, hate, and the notion of never giving up, despite whatever odds. They were going to fight and slaughter whoever or whatever they could before they fell.

Lannya looked to the ceiling, the floor, and to each side to establish her fighting environment. Spotting a ribbon scanner under a panel in the wall close to her, hope injected a fresh dose of itself into her soul. She had a plan and put it into action.

Jeramy Goble | 237

"Azli! Got a Wevvon?"

Lannya sprinted towards the ribbon scanner as she shouted her question at Azli, and by the time Lannya slipped her hand into the scanner, Azli was racing for the ribbon scanner as well, wearing a wicked grin.

The closest tiers of Einarians had already broken ranks and begun to charge at Lannya, but they had reacted too slowly. What had previously been Lannya's human hand disappeared into ribbon energy which then retracted away from the scanner and gave way to one of her Bisonine forms. Lannya's single Bisonine form took up most of the width of the corridor and startled many of the approaching Einarians. The Bisonines were a race of massive organisms, similar biologically to mammals with two primary segments to their body. They were dense, heavy, muscular, and powerful. Their primary method of locomotion was flipping one segment of their body over the other, and then repeating the motion. Each slam of a body segment into the ground ripped the air with gargantuan thunders of sound, and shook anything they moved on with the force that felt like continents scratching each other apart.

The approaching Einarians were taken by surprise by a perfect idea from Lannya. By the time Azli had reached the ribbon scanner, Lannya had already flipped her massive Bisonine body down the corridor a few times, slamming dozens of Einarians into the walls of the corridor, and knocking dozens more down behind them. They had a long way to go, but Lannya was merely clearing an initial path and disorienting all that she could.

Azli reached into the ribbon scanner, and as her

mother suggested, assumed a Wevvon form. A massive creature, menacing, threatening and devastating in any universe, Azli's Wevvon body swelled as it formed to take up most of the width of the corridor as well, and commanded a length that grew far up to where Lannya had already cleared a path.

The Wevvon body, long and bulbous, had hundreds of legs, similar to a millipede, that were mostly covered and protected by the Wevvon's leathery skin. At the front of its body, sprouted dozens of extremely long necks that whipped and slithered about, each one with a round, spherical head at the end. Every head had an orifice that sheltered a narrow beak, lined with rows of sharp teeth. These beaks could be extended out quickly from the orifice to chomp or bite, or, to regurgitate an electrically charged acid. The Wevvon was a monster, a nightmare, and a perfectly grotesque monstrosity.

There were a few other ribbon scanners throughout the corridor, but both Lannya in her Bisonine form, and Azli in her Wevvon form, were coordinating amazingly, and doing all they could to keep any Einarians from reaching them. They were working in beautiful tandem, and making quick and messy work of the poor creatures between them and Einar. Most had previous lives as well, and once killed, went somewhere, whether to the ribbon island or somewhere else at Einar's hand. Azli and Lannya didn't care. All they cared about at the moment, was that they were removing immediate obstacles from realizing their goal. Others in their way, were not so fortunate to have additional chances in the multiverse, and were merely single-lived creatures from various areas that had been recruited or swindled into service by Einar.

But the devastation was absolute, and they were progressing steadily towards the command bridge. Whether or not Einar had any additional surprises, wasn't known to them, but they were fighting well, and almost there.

It took a while, but as the number of Einarian fighters thinned out, some of them finally started to see the futility in fighting against a Bisonine and Wevvon and started to run backwards in the direction of the command bridge. Azli and Lannya were able to pick up speed. Before long, they saw him. They saw Einar.

The hundred or so Einarians that had retreated, lined the walls of the command bridge, scared and uncertain of what would happen next. Azli's mighty Wevvon form stopped at the command bridge threshold. Each of her necks bobbed slightly. Every beak in every head was poised to bite something, or spit its painful acid on someone. Lannya's Bisonine body throbbed with a building kinetic energy, ready to lurch and quake the ground once again. They stared Einar down, and waited for him to make a move.

He had summoned a ribbon and stood encompassed in it, ready to change forms, or shoot off into the surrounding space. The area immediately behind him was obscured from the huge, bright, and pulsating ribbon.

Einar stood with his feet planted firmly on the command bridge's deck. His body was slightly relaxed and lowered, ready to fight. His ribbon remained. With no apparent concern over their presence, Einar's vision had remained focused on the ground, but as the commotion came to a halt, he slowly panned his head up at them. The crack between his lips spread and crept into a sinister zigzag of a smile. He started to look over his shoulder, but stopped himself, and looked back to Lannya and Azli before looking up and laughing. With a bright flash, the ribbon silenced his hysterical sound and sucked him up into space. With Einar and the ribbon gone, Azli and Lannya could now see the entire command bridge. Just behind where Einar had been standing, they saw Akal.

Lannya flipped her body over to a nearby ribbon scanner and assumed her usual form. The center of her Bisonine form was a good bit higher than that of her usual human form, so as she changed, she fell to the ground and rolled onto her hands and knees.

"Akaaallll!!!!!" Her voice shredded through the ship with the painful surprise of having the pain of a million lives stirred and injected freshly into her soul, mixed with the emotion of seeing Akal only a foot from her. But it wasn't just the sight of Akal. It was his condition.

Akal was flat on his back, slightly reclined, in one of Einar's soul-torturing devices. He was seemingly unconscious and unaware of anything going on around him. His body, mind and soul were pierced by countless threads, holding every thought, emotion, experience and life of Akal's in total limbo. His soul knew nothing at the moment, except for disfigurement, manipulation, and pain.

Azli shot one of the beaks from one of her Wevvon's heads into the ribbon scanner, and also fell to the ground before quickly rolling and coming to her feet. Both Lannya and Azli started to sprint towards Akal.

The cowardly Einarians that had fled the fight previously, however, had other plans. Now that Lannya and Azli were back in human form, and possibly more manageable, they shot away from the walls and began to rush towards the Astraeans.

Azli and Lannya weren't paying attention. They couldn't. An endless kaleidoscope of emotion and confusion completely overwhelmed them as they reached the sides of Akal's torture device. Their hands and arms flailed wildly over the top of Akal, wanting to help him and rip the binding threads from him, but they were unsure if it would do more damage or not. They were at a complete loss of focus. They couldn't climb up from the pit of confusion they had fallen into. *I killed him!* Azli screamed angrily at herself over and over. *How is this possible?* Lannya was stuck on and stumbling over saying *I love you* to Akal internally, in as many languages as she could muster within her soul's core. This was a reality neither mother nor daughter ever expected an opportunity to face. They didn't know how to react. Everything they thought they knew about the multiverse, Mamdod, his game, what had happened to Akal, and what the situation was with the ribbon island, had all been dumped into a muddled puddle of chaos.

Neither Lannya nor Azli could take their eyes off Akal. Hoping their continued stare would jog something in their minds that made sense of how this was possible, they had become oblivious to the approaching throng of Einarians. All they had fought for, and were hoping to continue to fight for, was on the verge of being destroyed should they be captured or killed. Only when their concentration was broken by the sound of rapid-fire energy bolts were they able to look up.

Smeche had entered from a side chamber. He was not alone. Slung over his back was a large mechanical pack that dwarfed him in size. The pack, supporting itself with hydraulics, was anchored to a thick and stiff harness that Smeche wore. The pack started at the wearer's waist, curved a few feet to the back, up, around, and extended out over the head of the wearer, with four Gatling-style railguns, shooting hundreds of ribbon projectiles a second.

"Smeche!" Azli shouted in thankful surprise. He paused only a few seconds at a time to shout back, without looking to her to speak, so he wouldn't squander his strategy, or allow the Einarians to respond to his overpowering firepower.

"Go! Take him! Go!" He screamed between bursts of his weapons. "Jerk those lines out of him. It'll hurt, but he'll be ok!"

Azli continued to watch Smeche for a moment, trying to think if there was anything else she wanted or needed to say, but she didn't have the time. He was covering them handily, and was making quick work of the remaining Einarians, but neither she nor Lannya knew what might be coming. She thanked Smeche softly, knowing he wouldn't hear her, but also hoped she would be able to thank him properly in the future.

Azli looked back to Lannya.

"Rip those things out! Come on!"

Before Lannya could object or ask any clarifying questions, Azli jumped back over to the table and started grasping at clumps of the lines that painfully penetrated

Akal at almost every centimeter of his skin. Akal shot into some form of consciousness as they started to pull and rip the lines out of him. A tube of some kind that was inserted in his throat partially obstructed his screams of pain, but Lannya quickly jerked that out as well.

They didn't think they were ever going to finish separating him from it. They grabbed and grabbed, pulled and ripped. Clump after clump, the lines came out, with Akal convulsing, shaking and screaming at every turn. At last, they finally reached for the last grouping of soul-confining threads and jerked them out of Akal.

Azli scooped him up under both arms and slung him over her back. She looked at Lannya and waited for their eyes to meet. Azli pointed up and called a ribbon. Lannya summoned one as well.

Before Azli and Lannya shot off into space to make their way to Paige, Azli watched as Smeche ducked behind various points of cover, and then shot back out from the other side to resume his attack.

The last sound Azli heard on the command bridge, before she and her broken father were swallowed by a ribbon, was that of Smeche's weapon firing fiercely and constantly.

Chapter XIX

Stabilization

Lannya's feet stomped the deck of Paige's ribbon landing pad first, and was followed immediately by Azli. Azli bent her knees a bit as she landed, to soften the landing a bit for Akal's sake. Lannya began brushing Akal's hair back and frantically looked him over, not knowing what to look for and not knowing what Einar's contraption had done to him. Akal still looked unconscious as Azli held him in her arms.

"I'm going to set course for the Harbor," Lannya shouted at Azli, while racing over to a command terminal. She hastily shrugged and threw up her arms in a panic, not knowing where else to go. "Get him down to the stabilizing tube. I'll be right down!"

Azli nodded and shuffled quickly to the main sail hatch. She grimaced slightly from the weight of her father while stepping over the hatch's threshold. After disappearing down the stairs inside the sail, Lannya rushed through tapping the command to set sail for the Harbor at maximum flow factor. With a quick look around the deck, she watched to confirm the submerging process was initiating correctly, and then raced down the stairs inside the main sail to meet up with Azli.

The stabilizing tube Lannya told Azli to put Akal into, was a medical, but also a spiritual triage and stabilization device. It scanned the body, a bit at a time, for any wounds that could be quickly tended to by the device's automated medical implements, but also scanned the entire body using a non-invasive ribbon scanner for any spiritual trauma that needed attention. When the medical scanners completed their triage, they returned a flashing yellow message showing no medical issues that needed immediate attention. The ribbon scanner, however, began alarming immediately, returning a scrolling list of problems with Akal's soul. Lannya and Azli could only stare in pitiful silence at each other, and then back at Akal. They were at a complete loss for any hope that the stabilizing tube would do anything to help Akal.

After minutes of constant scrolling of Akal's issues, the stabilizing tube's display finished the list of findings, and then started back at the top of the list. This time, the device began popping up with "Stabilizing..." status bars, one each for every past life Akal had lived with related spiritual damage. Lannya and Azli weren't sure, but they assumed the device Einar had him connected to somehow ripped, tore, and otherwise damaged the integrity of Akal's soul to a critical state.

Azli paced around Paige's medical area with a

rough and furious stride. She was angry with herself, and still shocked at finding Akal. She was overwhelmed with a torrent of emotion, but was able to keep her hope that he would recover in the front of her mind. Lannya stayed practically glued to the stabilizing tube, and washed the clear top of it frequently with her tears. She could only wait while painfully and impatiently watching the countless status bars fill up from his soul being stabilized.

Lannya and Azli kept mostly silent as they approached their exit from U266, hoping they could make it out. Only Paige's occasional energy hums or mechanical thuds made any noise. But after time seemingly stopped for Lannya and smeared into a hellacious storm of uncertainty, she noticed movement underneath the stabilizing tube's tear-smudged top.

Her whole body jerked into a rigid stiffness. Her hands pressed on the glass with her fingers spread open.

"Azli! He's moving!"

Azli spun around from pacing and stared at the stabilizing tube with wide eyes. Her jaw dropped open. She wanted to race over to the tube, but one of her million thoughts while pacing was about how Akal would react if and when he saw her. Instead of racing over, she grabbed her face and dropped down and supported herself anxiously on the balls of her feet. Lannya turned quickly to see if Azli was coming over to join her at the tube and saw her keeping her distance. It took no time for Lannya to understand why. She whipped her head back around and stared down into the tube.

Lannya grabbed a nearby towel to scrub and wipe the top of the stabilizing tube. She didn't want her tears to get in the way of seeing her husband.

"Akal!" She moaned bittersweetly, through an increasingly achy throat. She looked over at the tube's display and saw that it read, *56% Stabilization*.

He's getting there, Lannya thought. *But even after he's stabilized, how bad off is he?* She wondered.

Akal rocked back and forth in the tube, only enough to be noticeable. His eyes were still closed. Lannya watched his knuckles start to twitch. His fingertips began to find themselves.

"Akal?" Lannya whimpered through a slight whisper. Her tears were in danger of smudging the top of the tube again.

His eyes opened as if from a long sleep. He was initially looking in the opposite direction and opened his mouth only enough to easily move and flex his jaw. He seemed to be disoriented and confused. But Lannya asking for him must have been echoing in his mind and soul, shooting a bit of reality into him from wherever he had just emerged from.

His neck spun around and his eyes flew open as wide as any human could open their eyes. He shot his arm out and slammed his open hand into the top of the tube in excitement.

"Lann!" He gruffly shouted. Before finishing the syllable of his wife's pet name, he let his voice crumble into joyous crying. His tears were falling, and the top was becoming blurry once more from Lannya's.

Azli wanted to join her mother. She was overcome with the desire to see her father, and stood up in preparation. She licked her lips to say something, thinking she should give some kind of warning that she was approaching, but that's as close to Akal as she made it.

Paige was suddenly struck by numerous objects in rapid succession. Each strike to the outer hull caused the boat to lurch violently. As Lannya and Azli were slung to the ground, Paige's damage alarms began to sound. Her voice came over the loud system.

"Multiple impacts sustained across all areas. Outer hull integrity down to 40%."

Lannya twisted around and crawled out from the corner of the room she had been slung into, and grasped for items bolted to the deck in an effort to reach a command terminal. The ship shook violently as the accumulating damage caused more and more of the ship's mass to lose control. The smoke and shaking blurred her vision to a point she couldn't make out objects ahead of her. She made her way by touch.

She couldn't make out where Azli was, or what state the stabilization tube was in. She put thoughts of Azli and Akal out of her mind as best she could as she slowly crept through the chaos towards the command terminal.

"Outer hull integrity down to 10%. Hull breach imminent. Repair of the outer hull is mandatory for sustai..." Paige attempted to advise her occupants, but her automated voice melted down into an incoherent ramble before fizzing out into a pop of static.

At last, Lannya finally found the base of what she felt to be the command terminal stand. Though she was not hurt, she was beyond disoriented, but put her all into climbing up the side of the command terminal and shoving her face into the display screen. With the state of the hull, she assumed she would only have one shot at entering her command.

Tap, tap, hull, shields, max flow bubble.

She pressed *Commit* on the command terminal display. As soon as she did, the violent shaking and slams from impacting projectiles didn't cease, but were rendered practically non-existent. A few more taps on the display and Lannya activated one of Paige's back-up vocal processors. The ship completed saying what it was attempting to say, and then announced Lannya's command.

"...ned life support. Submerged flow shield activated. Bubble strength at 90%."

Lannya thanked Hergie and the Imaging facility silently, for the new systems they had installed on Paige. They would not have survived without the new shield that provides additional protection to the ship while submerged. Lannya stretched her jaw in an effort to jar her hearing back to normal and looked around for Azli.

Azli was just beginning to crawl out of her own corner she had been slung into and staggered to her feet like a drunkard.

"How could we take so much damage while submerged?" Azli wondered out loud on her way to joining Lannya at the command terminal.

"I don't know," Lannya said on her way to check on Akal. "But once that bubble gets depleted, we're done."

Lannya stuck her head in the window of the stabilization tube and saw a substantial cut on Akal's forehead. His blood was on the inside of the clear top. Lannya's heart sank and her soul ran cold. She was however slightly relieved when she looked to the tube's status monitor. *Soul stabilization: 72%. Medical issue identified: Moderate laceration to forehead.* His life-signs were stable, and Lannya determined he had simply been knocked unconscious during the attack. *Stay with me sweet Akal*, she thought. *Stay with me.*

She looked at Azli.

"We need to make contact with the fleet. We have no other options."

Lannya jumped back over to the terminal and pulled up a map of their local space. She and Azli looked around quickly as the dull thuds of the continued assault outside could be heard.

"We just exited U266," observed Lannya. "It looks like part of the Einarian fleet broke off from fighting the ADF and decided to attack us. Let me confirm."

Lannya pinched, tapped and swiped the display. A few taps later, she confirmed her suspicion.

"Yeah, they're Einarians. I'm calling the ADF."

Azli looked up at her mother as Lannya attempted to establish communications. She knew Lannya didn't want to request Rigella's help, but they both knew they had no alternative.

Lannya tapped the command to signal the ADF into the terminal. Almost immediately, the call was answered. Mamdod popped up on Paige's display.

"Hey Lannya, we saw you go by. We're on our way to get those Einarians off you. That group was the farthest from us and had an opportunity to follow you. We're on our way. Hold on."

Lannya looked at Azli in excited disbelief, having had no inclination that they would get support so quickly.

"Thank you, Mamdod! Thank you!" Lannya shouted at the screen. "We're headed for the Harbor. We're just going to hold this course."

"Understood," confirmed Mamdod. "Hang in there."

Azli and Lannya continued to feel Paige being struck by the bombardment from the Einarians. Though the ribbon bubble was protecting them inside the ribbon, it was quickly diminishing in power. Paige reminded them.

"Bubble strength at 35%."

The attacks continued. The frequency remained steady.

"Bubble strength at 15%," announced Paige.

Lannya leaned over the stabilization tube and stared at her unconscious husband while waiting to see if they survived. Azli held tightly onto a support pole, looking up and around in the direction of the most recent explosion. Then with no immediate indication as to why, there was a sudden increase in attacks and intensity.

"Bubble strength at 5%."

Unexpectedly, Paige's shaking and jolts abruptly stopped, though Azli and Lannya could hear a muffled volley of traded attacks out in space. A part of the ADF had arrived just in time, and drawn the Einarians' fire. As the Einarians became distracted, Paige slipped away from the fight and rode the ribbon desperately towards the Harbor.

Chapter XX

The Old and the New

Just after Paige had broken free of the Einarian attack, Mamdod appeared again on her displays.

"I think you're in the clear now," Mamdod said through a quick sigh of relief. "The ADF is going to fall back and return back to the Harbor. We'll see you there."

"Thank you, Mamdod. That was perfect timing." Lannya leaned against the command terminal and huffed her own sigh of relief through her puffed cheeks. "What's your status? What's going on out there?"

"Well, it's been pretty pointless, actually," Mamdod explained. "The Einarians hardly did any damage to our ships. They just kept absorbing our attacks, distracting our plans, and making us confuse our tactics. Then, just before we saw you come into sensor range, some of them broke off to chase you, and the others just fled."

"Yeah, we were leaving the Dark Artery," Lannya began to clarify.

"Right, Elcyd had just let us know you had found it," Mamdod advised. "We were going to check it out, but, it's been destroyed."

"What? By the ADF?" Lannya questioned with a sharp curiosity.

"No, we thought you and Azli might have had something to do with that."

Lannya looked over at Akal in his stabilization tube.

"No, we didn't do it," she said softly, humbled at her growing realization. "I bet Einar set it to self-destruct."

She turned back to face Mamdod's projection.

"Mamdod," she continued after licking her lips. "We... picked up a passenger... It's Akal."

***

The returning fleet dripped down, and streaked across the area surrounding the Harbor for as far as any eyes on the docks could see. It was a triumphant and amazing sight, even by Astraean standards. The sounds of their engines spinning down reverberated like an ancient, cosmic choir inside the Harbor's artificial atmosphere. The overtones and harmonics filled the ears of the millions-of-years-old Astraeans and made their old jaws drop in innocent wonder.

But the gathering Astraeans on the docks, and the ship crews spilling out onto the decks of their respective ships, quickly became caught up in a whole different spectacle. The famous Paige was returning to the Harbor. Paige had become a legendary fixture in Astraean culture. She was almost mythical. She was Akal's ship. An original.

She had seen countless battles of remarkable significance and weathered some of the harshest storms and attacks. The sight of her condition now only added to her mystery and allure. The Astraeans looking at her hated to see her in such a disheveled state. With partially broken masts, and dents in her hull, they hoped she would bounce back soon and get back to helping their cause.

And while Paige had an anthropomorphic and affectionate place in the hearts of many Astraeans for simply being an interesting and quirky boat, the throngs of Astraeans on the docks and ships alike, were trying to get any and all possible glimpses they could of one of the rumored passengers. The news had spread almost as fast as the quickest ribbon speeds. Akal was alive, and he was coming home.

The individual ships in the ADF fleet began to stop and stack up as the Readiness Officers rushed to process, clear, and automate the fleet's docking procedures, into a newly assembled system of ADF-specific docks and piers. The hope was that having their own docking facility would speed up their deployment and return, and remove the impact on private and commercial arrivals and departures.

Astraeans of all forms and species began to clump and congest all perimeter areas of the Harbor as well. Everyone wanted to be able to slide up flush against outward-facing rails to watch Paige dock, and visiting traders and creatures from everywhere in the multiverse, pushed politely to get as close to the tall, arched windows as possible. No empty space could be seen on the main docks as they filled with excited friends and allies, or those curious about the state of one of the most famous beings in the multiverse.

Lannya weaved Paige, now surfaced, through the cluster of ADF ships. Azli stood solemnly at one of Paige's top deck rails and looked around with emotional humility at the enormous display of those looking at them. With each inch of their approach to the Harbor docks, Azli saw the fleet slow down to a crawl before stopping, in order to watch Paige and her passengers return. Lannya felt as if a new pair of eyes was landing on them with each second.

Though Azli and Lannya couldn't hear them, the entire area buzzed and rustled in flurries of jumbled conversations. All manners of questions were being asked amidst a hazy fog of confusion. While they had heard the rumors of Akal's return, the onlookers strained through the sea of their comrades to confirm that he was alive. They held hands and bounced up and down to look over shoulders. With giddy anticipation, they asked neighbors in the crowd, "Do you see anything?". And as Paige slid into place at the docks, directly in front of one of the Harbor's main entrances, the majority of the large conversations were snuffed, but those that survived broke off into smaller discussions of worry and concern about what this meant for the state of their war with Einar.

Elcyd had already emerged from engineering and jogged up to a nearby balcony overlooking the docks. While waiting for Paige's passengers to appear, he also became caught up in the power and majesty of the parked and waiting fleet. The sound of the crowd around him ebbed and flowed with varying pops and hums of shifting conversations. As he continued standing and waiting, Rigella appeared on one side, fresh off her ship, and parted the crowd with only a few ADF personnel in tow. Soon after, from the other side, Mamdod appeared from another crevasse in the crowd, and almost from directly behind Elcyd, came Carthal, and Heersan.

No one from the reunited group of friends said anything. They simply looked at each other and shook their heads at each other, in a combined look of disbelief, awe, and concern. The large portion of all of their emotions, by far, was excitement at the possibility of having their old friend returned to them, but a very present thought in each of their minds was a need for this event to happen quickly so that they can get back to figuring out what was happening with Einar. They needed to evaluate how much, or little, time they had left, and how to proceed. The group stood slightly near each other, and stared up at the top of the gangplank leading to Paige's top deck.

Azli and Lannya had gone below deck to the stabilization tube to retrieve Akal. He had regained consciousness, and the tube had sutured the laceration on his forehead. He was medically stable, and his soul was almost completely stabilized. He still needed an extreme amount of help, but he was strong enough to be helped off the boat. Finally, they appeared on the top deck. Everyone within hundreds of feet around, saw them. Azli was under one of Akal's arms with Lannya under the other. They started down the gangplank together.

The spectators made no sound. Whatever few sounds being made at the time they emerged were silenced. The whole area was blanketed in what felt like a dream, or an alternate reality the entire culture thought would never happen. For the longest time, every Astraean in the multiverse, as well as billions of creatures that knew about their situation, thought Akal was forever lost to the final ribbon's mysteries of death, never to be seen again.

Yet, there he was. Not only was he right up there at the top of the gangplank, but he was being helped down by his wife, and a previous sworn enemy of the Astraeans. It was an extraordinary moment. There was no one in the vicinity that didn't concentrate all they could on capturing the sights, smells, and sounds before them, and the wonder they felt in their memories, forever.

They moved slowly down the gangplank, but once they were roughly halfway from the docks, Rigella leaned over to a subordinate and ordered him to call a medical and soul health team. After her order was given, he unfolded a command tablet and processed the command. Rigella looked to Elcyd, Mamdod, Carthal and Heersan. They couldn't believe it. Their faces were expressionless like carved stone, caught between wanting to burst into tears, and scream at the top of their lungs with joy. They all wanted to jump the distance between them and the end of the gangplank, but their disbelief distracted them from trying. Rigella however, wasn't distracted. She took off, jogging to meet them as they reached the docks.

Rigella swallowed and watched with a hidden excitement at her friend coming home. Her old captain. Paige's old captain that she had shared so many adventures with, might yet be able to share in another adventure. Lannya kept her concentration centered on the gangplank, and her wounded cargo. Azli did the same, but as they reached the last few feet, Azli looked up, and burned a patient stare into Rigella, daring her to once again take issue with her being at the Harbor. Rigella said nothing, and returned no discernible expression or gesture. She let Akal, Lannya, and Azli pass her without issue. Carthal, Heersan and Elcyd rushed to their old friend's side.

Rigella wasn't the only one on good behavior. The majority of Astraeans knew about Azli's defection or surrender, they weren't sure which, and were not only incredibly skeptical of Azli, but justifiably hated her and wanted no part of her. And though many in the crowd wore their hate and anger on their faces, not a single shout or exclamation was sounded against Azli as she helped her father walk. It was the very definition of a solemn moment and everyone respected it.

Azli and Lannya, with Akal still draped over their shoulders, walked closer to the Harbor entrance and deeper into the crowd. Within moments, they assisted the medical and soul health (MSH) team that had approached, with placing Akal onto a gurney made of ribbon energy. Once he had been safely secured, Akal's friends fell in behind the team of doctors and ribbon energy specialists, and rushed to the Harbor's medical facility. Rigella didn't immediately follow. She forced herself to remain behind to direct the resumption of the returning fleet's docking procedures in their new facility. She was especially in no hurry to have to deal with Azli being at the Harbor.

Once Akal reached the Harbor's MSH facility, numerous doctors, nurses and ribbon specialists gently picked Akal up and moved him over to a flat table, topped with extremely firm, white rubber. The medical doctors and nurses used physical implements, imaging technology, as well as ribbon technology to check for any internal issues. Akal had none. The laceration on his head was rapidly cleaned and stitched with a fresh thread made of ribbon energy. Once it had been placed, the suture's temporary covering dissolved, leaving the ribbon energy inside to completely heal the wound within seconds. It was then time for the ribbon specialists to step in.

Once the medical team had completed their work, the ribbon team slid the table Akal was on into a much larger, and much more complex version of the stabilization tube Lannya had placed him in while on Paige. The chamber Akal was in now, was not just a stabilization unit, but via a connection directly to the ribbons, with access to any and all possible ribbon data, the chamber was able to analyze and repair a soul. The stabilization tube merely *maintained* the existence of a soul's connection with a past life. The ribbon chamber at the Harbor could actually examine a soul's past lives, and confirm that all memories, connections, emotions, experiences, and anything else existing between a soul and a particular life, were intact. In his current state, Akal more than likely only had something akin to drunken suggestions as to what his past lives were like. His soul was scrambled, jumbled, and incoherent.

Azli and Lannya shared all they could about what they had seen back on the Dark Artery. They explained in as much possible detail what the device Akal was in looked like, and how he reacted as they worked on removing him from it. Anything they could think of, that might assist those working on Akal, was shared. Ribbon specialists, onlooking medical staff, and Akal's friends exchanged quick thoughts and ideas as they worked on Akal and tried to figure out exactly what Einar had been doing with Akal's soul.

The chamber quickly completed the last bits of stabilization and then in a fraction of the time the stabilization tube had taken, did one more pass to confirm he was stable. After that, the machine scanned his soul's connection to his past lives.

Everyone in the room let their head drop.

Soul integrity, 17%, the chamber's display read.

Once the entire MSH team had stabilized Akal in all aspects, and the ribbon specialists had assembled all information possible on his current spiritual state, they stepped back and allowed the chamber to do what it needed to, in order to properly reassociate all past life data with Akal's soul. All anyone could do was wait. Rigella quietly crept in and looked over at the gathering of specialists, friends, and Azli. Heersan walked over to Lannya with a head full of questions.

"What did they do to him?" Heersan wondered in a confused whisper. A ribbon specialist nearby turned and looked at Heersan after hearing his question, but didn't want to interrupt. Lannya shrugged as she absentmindedly picked at her lips.

"I don't know Heersan. I don't know. But you should have heard and seen him as we ripped those threads out of him." She turned to Heersan with tears in her eyes. "It was horrible."

Heersan put his arm around Lannya and squeezed her to his side.

"I know, I know, Lannya. But you got him. You got him back," he whispered in affectionate praise. "They'll fix him."

Heersan looked over to the eavesdropping ribbon specialist.

"Right?"

The specialist inhaled slowly and put his hands on his hips while thinking.

"I'm fairly sure we can," the specialist replied while keeping his sight focused on Akal. "The biggest question I have, is how long it will take." The specialist looked back at Heersan. "There's no telling how long. We've never run into someone with this much disconnection before. And time is obviously not on our side."

Heersan turned his eyes back to Akal while still comforting Lannya. His mind raced through possibilities of what Einar had been trying to do.

"Was he trying to steal his past lives or something?" Heersan's forehead crunched together from a lack of ideas."

"I don't know," the specialist said, disappointed from having so little information. "It's actually like Einar was trying to... interrupt, or suppress the past lives. There's no sign that any of his soul's information was permanently damaged."

The specialist huffed out a puff of air in frustration at the situation, and patted Lannya on her shoulder before joining his colleagues back at the chamber.

The conversation caught Elcyd's attention, and while he hadn't been able to hear what was said, it caused him to turn to look at who was speaking. As he turned, he was surprised to see Rigella standing in the far back of the room. She stood alone, and leaned against the wall. He walked over to her.

"Hey, Rigella!" Elcyd greeted warmly. "Come on over," he beckoned innocently.

"No," Rigella said calmly. She shook her head as she took a deep breath. "I will later. And besides," she said, as she pushed off the wall, "I don't want to deal with *that* right now." She motioned gently in Azli's direction.

Elcyd looked at what she was pointing at, though he already knew. Looking back at Rigella, his face showed his mind searching for what to say, and how to say it.

"Rigella, we don't have time to worry about that right now," he said with a blunt honesty. "She's here. You're here. We're all here, but look, so is Akal! She helped bring him here. He's banged up, but he's here. We're not under attack this very second. We need to focus on our next move, and make it."

"Yeah, we're not under attack, and yes, Akal's here, and trust me," Rigella said, leaning in closer to Elcyd. "No one, outside of maybe Lannya is more excited to know Akal's alive than me, but that doesn't take away from the fact that thousands of others are still died at Azli's hands."

"Obsessing on that past moment will not help us win the future, Rigella!" Elcyd leaned in a bit further himself. "Work with what you have now, to solve the problem at hand. That's what we need you to do. That's what we need the leader of the ADF to do."

Rigella stepped back from Elcyd and squinted her eyes at him. She was surprised by Elcyd's stern lecture, and felt the rush of adrenaline compelling her to respond, but she couldn't think of what to say. She could only stare back. The silence forced her to start processing what he said. Elcyd started to walk backwards and return to the group surrounding Akal and with a confident authority, stared at Rigella for a few moments before turning around. He didn't speak with malice, and they both knew he spoke the truth. Rigella's eyes relaxed as he walked away from her.

I'm good at this, Rigella thought to herself, about how she was handling her leadership position in the ADF. *I love it. I'm good at it. I won the tournament, and I'm beyond experienced and qualified.* She wasn't so much responding internally to Elcyd's comments, but was trying to silence her own doubt, and her own fears that she may not get to Einar in time. She knew it wasn't only her responsibility, but should the Astraeans not stop Einar, or keep him from assuming control of the ribbon island, she knew that she would receive the majority of the blame, and assign the most, to herself.

But she was able to push past her pride and stubbornness. She was known for it, and had been known for it, for millennia. She was renowned around the multiverse, for, among other things, being selfless and for being able to step back and make as objective a decision as possible. For the first time since she had assumed leadership of the ADF, she admitted to herself that she may be failing. The thought had tried to break into her thoughts after she had assaulted Azli, but at the time, she was still able to ignore her doubts and shame from her loss of control.

As she looked at Azli, at Akal, at her group of friends, as well as the Astraean staff all over the room, she considered that she might be doing some harm. She wasn't doing more harm than good, but the harm she was doing, was a significant harm. It was a harm to herself. A harm to her peace of mind and emotional control. And that, as Elcyd proposed, was having a severe impact on her ability to keep her mind and conscious clear, and make the right decisions for the benefit of the Astraeans.

Rigella had to swallow as her eyes watered slightly. She was overcome with sadness at having failed herself, and as far as she was concerned, having failed the ADF and the Astraeans. She had passed through her constructive obsession, into a darker flavor of obsession that blends purpose and context with a self-serving consciousness. She had strived for some time not to cross the line, but the line had come and gone. She had slowly succumbed to the power of her emotions and become obedient to them. She was now a slave to destruction, darkness, death, and winning at all costs.

She was still standing by herself at the edge of the room. She looked on at the group ahead of her and started to panic over not knowing what to do or what to say. She wrenched her hands and felt her skin tingle with a clammy coldness that ushered in an overwhelming flush of regret and plummeting confidence. She started to ramble inside her mind. *I need to step down. I can't do this anymore.*

That didn't help much. Once she had made the decision to resign her role with the ADF, an entirely new web of questions began to weave around her mind. *How will I do it? Who will take my place? We don't have time for another tournament. They deserve for this to be quick and painless. The transition should be seamless.*

Her cold skin tingled faster. The beginnings of one

thought were interrupted by another, and then another, and then another. She was losing control. Her eyes jumped around chaotically from one face in the room to another. She was at the nauseous stage of panic, up until she saw Thyra walk in.

Thyra! Rigella thought. *We need Thyra.* Rigella's mind instantly drained all distractions and debilitating debris from her thoughts. The tingling in her skin stopped, and her mind's eye zoomed in on the clarity provided from the notion of having Thyra take over for her. *She's brilliant, quick, immensely knowledgeable, and capable. She's well liked, and respected. She would be perfect.* Rigella remained emotional, but her feelings of doubt and incompetence were replaced by a returning confidence and unbiased judgment She felt herself returning. She was getting over herself, and getting back to focusing on the right thing to do.

After entering the room, Thyra walked over to the group surrounding Akal's chamber and exchanged a few hugs and quick discussions. She placed her hands on her hips and took in the scene and situation. A few of the group came over to her, as well as a few doctors. After catching up with everyone and how Akal was doing, she caught Rigella out of the corner of her eye, turned and waved. Rigella returned a friendly bow of her head and waved Thyra over. She approached quickly, and with a smile.

"Hey, why are you over here by yourself?" Thyra asked with a kind curiosity.

"Oh, just taking some time and thinking." Rigella replied with a softness that had recently been absent from her conversations.

Thyra nodded quickly in complete understanding and returned to looking at Akal alongside Rigella.

Rigella started to waver. She wanted to procrastinate for a reason she couldn't identify. She wanted to start talking about the library, or how proud she was of the fleet's performance at U266, anything but giving up her position in the ADF. But, as quickly as the thoughts entered her mind, she wrestled them away from the hands of stress and doubt. She choked down a shot of her characteristic courage and went straight for what she needed to say.

"Honestly, Thyra," she started, after looking around for potential eavesdroppers. "I think I'm going to resign my position with the ADF."

A deep valley dug itself into the subtle wrinkles of Thyra's forehead. She spun around to look at Rigella. Her mouth sunk open as she stepped back from proverbial shock.

"What? What are you talking about? Why?" Thyra pleaded.

Rigella wanted to get it all out there first before explaining anything.

"And, I'd like you to step in for me," Rigella added. She hadn't looked at Thyra yet. She continued looking forward at the group. She spoke with wisdom and clarity.

Thyra looked at the group, and then aimlessly around the room as she tried to make sense of things.

"Wait, me? What? Wait, wait... Before we even get into the idea of me taking over for you, why are you wanting to step down?"

Rigella looked at Thyra with a shy honesty.

"The moment a leader starts acting on their feelings, ahead of what's best for the group, then it's time," Rigella explained. "Even if it's just one time, one time is too many. And I've done that a few times now, actually. It's time."

Rigella relaxed her posture a bit from the rigid topic and smiled at Thyra in sincere admiration.

"Is this because of what happened with Azli?" Thyra wondered fairly. "Look, there isn't a soul around here that takes issue with what happened. Even though most Astraeans agree with how you handled that, I can appreciate how you feel about it now. Everyone loses control sometimes."

"No, Thyra, no," Rigella politely corrected while shaking her head. "It isn't just that. I've been living in too dark of a place in my mind recently. I've been blurring the line, for far too long, between malicious hate, and strategic warfare. I was beginning to consider options and thoughts that no Astraean should consider in the name of defeating the enemy."

Thyra stretched her eyes and looked around the room again as she considered her statements. She looked back as Rigella continued.

"I think I've accomplished in my role, what needed to happen with the beginning of the ADF. For myself, and for the ADF, I think it's better that someone else take over and run with it. If you're willing to step in, I'd like to resign my position to you, to serve out the rest of my term. And, once that time is up, we can hold another tournament, as we've outlined in the rules."

268 | *Fates of Astraeus*

Thyra shook her head, not in rejection, but to help the proposal soak into her mind. She stepped back beside Rigella and resumed looking at the group.

"This isn't an answer just yet, but it would be an incredible honor, Rigella."

Rigella didn't say anything as Thyra continued to think out loud.

"I mean, I would be humbled to have that opportunity," Thyra added. "But I just don't know how I could improve on your leadership. If anything, isn't it a terrible time for a transition?"

Rigella's eyebrows twitched as she rolled her head back and forth quickly.

"Well, I've thought about that," Rigella replied with a quick understanding. "But, I really don't think it would be harmful at all. If anything, it would be an improvement in the day-to-day of the ADF. I've allowed too much baggage to build up between me and my duties. And yeah, from the assembly workers in the Imaging and Fabrication facilities, all the way up to my direct reports, ADF, Sentinel and civilian alike, we all know what to do. Everyone has their role and their job. Our people have their collective goal and determination. We need to locate Einar and stop him or this game."

Thyra continued to consider the implications of Rigella's departure from the ADF, and the prospect of becoming its leader. She had felt a little removed from the action lately, and while she normally would welcome the peace, Thyra was excited by the possibility. She was excited by the responsibilities and opportunity to apply her almost unmatched knowledge. She would never be more proud of any responsibility than that of being the steward of so much knowledge in her role at the library, but she had been yearning to lend to the efforts against Einar in a more concrete and tangible way. *What better way than to lead the ADF against him?* She thought. But like Rigella, or at least how Rigella had been up until recently, Thyra was not one prone to make irrational or quick decisions without whatever amount of thought a particular decision warranted, and this was no different.

Thyra sidestepped closer to Rigella and tilted her head towards her.

"What will you do if you step down?" Thyra wondered softly.

"Oh," Rigella replied immediately, having already answered that for herself. "I'll still be part of the fight, and will help defeat Einar. I just need to fight my own fight."

Thyra continued looking at the side of Rigella's face. Rigella hadn't taken her eyes off her friends, or the glimpses of Akal she was able to get through the occasionally shifting group. She needed to train her focus on something other than Thyra while they had this discussion. Too much intimacy in the conversation between them would knock too many supports out from under Rigella's emotions. She was doing well, and slowly but surely starting to rebuild the foundation of what made Rigella, *Rigella*.

Thyra finally gave Rigella's peripheral vision back to her and stepped back to rub her face, ending with massaging circles on her eyelids.

"I'd like to take a bit of time to think about it,"

Thyra requested. "If you think we have the time." She looked back at Rigella. Rigella was already nodding.

"Sure, of course. I'm glad you don't have an immediate answer actually. You can turn it down if you want, and I'll press on and work to keep my emotions and things in check, but, while the largest motive for me stepping down is the immediate future of the ADF, part of this is just for me."

Rigella turned her head enough to make eye contact with Thyra. Thyra easily understood in that moment's silence between them.

"Do you care if I talk with anyone about it?" Thyra wondered and asked out of respect.

Rigella hadn't thought about that. She found it a fair question, but stumbled mentally for how she felt about it.

"Uhh," Rigella mumbled, looking surprised. "No, uh, maybe keep it to just a few right now?"

Rigella initially felt hesitant to allow it, but she couldn't produce any good reasons.

"It does make sense," she continued to Thyra. "It's a big decision and obviously has a huge impact on the ADF, so yeah, of course."

Thyra looked at the group and back to Rigella. She knew why Rigella was initially reluctant.

"I was only thinking of, you know, just a few people," Thyra said reassuringly, gesturing only at Elcyd and Mamdod who were standing off slightly separated from the rest of the group.

Rigella shut her eyes and nodded to signal Thyra that she was more than fine with it.

"Ok then," Thyra said. "I'll just think on it some and discuss it a bit and let you know."

"Thanks for hearing me out and considering it," Rigella said after a calming sigh. "I'm going to head to my office. Let me know once you've decided?"

"Of course," Thyra obliged. She then stepped and hugged Rigella like a sister would. She hugged her for an extremely long and needed time. After rubbing and tapping Rigella's back a few times, they parted.

"Talk with you soon," Rigella ended with a slight smile. Thyra nodded and watched as she backed out of the room.

Chapter XXI

His Last Hurdle

Thyra wore a smile but it quickly departed along with Rigella. Her smile wasn't a facade or forced. She simply devoted all of her mind's energy on the decision ahead of her. It was a massive decision. She turned to face the group and stood for a moment.

I need to talk to Elcyd, she thought, but remained in place. She wanted to get her thoughts in order, anticipate some questions and think of some answers. Most importantly, before the ideas of Rigella stepping down and taking her place got into anyone else's mind, she wanted to take a few moments to confirm how she felt about it, or at least at that moment.

I'm up for it, she thought. *I can do it. Just, the timing... The timing.*

Thyra walked towards the group surrounding Akal's chamber. She saw Lannya and Heersan speaking with Carthal ahead and to the side of Azli. Azli was noticeably keeping her distance from everyone for now. Elcyd and Mamdod were further separated still from everyone else, rubbing their chins and discussing various plans of action. As Thyra approached Elcyd and Mamdod, Thyra thought to herself, we all need to come together. She approached them from behind and let them finish their current conversation. She looked between their shoulders at Akal. She wasn't able to make out any improvements with Akal's situation.

Elcyd turned soon after Thyra approached and greeted her.

"Hi Thyra, how are you?"

"Pretty well," she replied after a hefty sigh.

"What?" Elcyd inquired with a slight smile. "What's troubling you?"

Mamdod continued looking on at Akal.

"Oh, no," Thyra said in a lilt of reassurance. "It's nothing troubling me. It's um, just a decision I need to make. I was actually hoping to talk with you both about it."

Mamdod slowly turned and gave Thyra his undivided attention. Both Mamdod's and Elcyd's curiosity spiked as Thyra noticeably put the final touches on her impending comments. She delayed broaching the subject for a moment, if only to give her mind time to finish organizing her thoughts about Rigella's proposal.

"How's Akal doing?" Thyra asked respectfully. Her eyes showed her genuine sincerity before getting into her own issues.

Mamdod turned towards the chamber. His reply was deep and flat. He was worried.

"No change," he said, before turning back to Thyra. "But at least he's here," he continued. "At least he's back."

The degree of regret Mamdod still felt over the results of his game dripped from each syllable as he spoke. Regardless of fault and what his game had brought to the multiverse, the Astraeans, and most visibly at the moment, to Akal, dug into his soul's peace deeply and wore on him heavily.

Thyra nodded and rubbed Mamdod's shoulder. She rolled her head to the side and replied through an empathetic glance.

"And it's so great to have him back," she said. Mamdod nodded quickly and did his best to return a smile. He looked back to Akal.

"What were you wanting to talk about?" Elcyd asked gently. Thyra sucked in a deep breath and jumped right into it.

"I was just speaking with Rigella," she began. Elcyd and Mamdod both looked around quickly for her.

"No, she's.. She left," Thyra clarified.

"Why?" Mamdod asked curiously. Thyra shrugged, not from not knowing why, but because it was a simple answer.

"I think she uh, needs a break."

Mamdod and Elcyd looked at each other in a silence loaded with meaning. Thyra immediately inferred what they had probably discussed about Rigella. Mamdod turned back to Akal, having no expectation that the conversation would go where it did, next.

"She's asked me to take over for her as Central

Commander of the ADF," Thyra revealed firmly.

Mamdod spun back around.

"What?" He said, completely shocked.

"What?" Elcyd said, for the same reason. Even though Thyra deduced they had been discussing her recently, she saw that they weren't expecting this at all.

"She..." continued Thyra, being careful to respectfully explain Rigella's reasoning. "She believes her professional motivations and," Thyra paused, as she carefully chose the right words, "her decisions, are being too," she paused again, while selecting words, "blended with her personal motivations and decisions. She's afraid it will lead to endangering the ADF, the Harbor, the Astraeans as a whole."

As Thyra explained what had caused Rigella's proposal, Mamdod and Elcyd both relaxed their concerned and confused faces. Thyra could see that the justification made sense, and that Rigella's request for someone to take her place, wasn't all that much of a surprise.

Elcyd scratched his face, looked to Mamdod and back to Thyra. Mamdod looked at the ground and quickly evaluated his own thoughts.

"Well, we," Elcyd began, gesturing towards himself and Mamdod, "have no reason to hide anything from you. We've been talking recently about how we were worried. There isn't really a better word for it. We've heard things she's said, and watched as she's done things," Elcyd continued as he turned in Azli's direction. "And we were worried for her."

Mamdod looked up and picked up where Elcyd left off.

"I don't think we were ever worried about her judgment, the performance of the ADF, or the safety of our people, because, whether we knew it or not, we were pretty sure she would do something like this. She seems to have identified a problem, and is working to stay ahead of it."

Elcyd agreed succinctly.

"Exactly."

The three of them bounced their eyes back and forth from each other, wondering what came next. Mamdod's curiosity did.

"Have you already thought about whether or not you'd want to do it?" He looked at Elcyd as he continued. "I obviously see no reason why she wouldn't be perfect for it." He shrugged, not really having any argument or objection.

"No, I agree," Elcyd replied to both Mamdod and Thyra. "Thyra, I think you would do a magnificent job, I just honestly wasn't expecting a leadership change right now."

"Yes... Right," Thyra immediately responded, almost with enthusiasm. She was glad her desire to remain objective was rewarded, and that they shared her reservations over the timing. "I had exactly that same thought and concern. I even said as much to Rigella."

"Really?" Elcyd inquired gently. "What did she say?"

"Uh, she just said," Thyra stumbled, working to recollect, "that she wasn't worried about us or the ADF being under different leadership... that we all knew our jobs, and what had to be done."

Elcyd and Mamdod looked at each other as Thyra expanded on her own thoughts.

"And to make it clear from the start, I would be proud and beyond motivated to do right by that position. But, if the consensus is that something else needs to happen, then I will not challenge that. I want the best for the ADF and our people."

Mamdod smiled with affection at Thyra, and held his hands up and open at Elcyd, deferring to him, and others, for any continued discussion or decision. Mamdod had been largely uninvolved in most Astraean and ADF decisions, and he didn't want this to be an exception. Ever since his arrival, he had given no indication of wanting to step on the toes of those that had made decisions for the Astraeans over the ages, and had no desire to impose his will. Much like he had done through space and time on the ribbon island, he was predominantly a guide, an adviser, and a listener.

Elcyd smiled at Mamdod in acknowledgment of his deference.

"Well, we can of course bring it up to others if you want and discuss it," Elcyd said to Thyra. "I can't see why anyone would have any issues with you, personally. As far as how we would handle it, I assume we would announce you as Rigella's replacement for the remainder of her term, and at the term's end, a tournament would be held to choose a new leader. But, I think whatever decision is made should be made quickly so we can move forward with as little distraction as possible. And to make sure, you would be willing to accept the position?"

"Yes, by all means," Thyra confirmed.

"Then let's move forward with this," Elcyd said decisively. "Let's reach out to Rigella and let her know your decision, and to get her involved with the transition. Then, speak with anyone else you might want to, and we'll need to review the rules to make sure everything takes place officially, and correctly."

Before Thyra or Mamdod could add anything else, a series of stinging and scraping blasts began roaring through the room. A startling storm of accompanying lights began strobing and alternating between a dense amber and bright yellow. The chamber Akal was in was beginning to fail, and the dozens of staff nearby raced to surround it, scrambling to determine the issue.

Those not working to address the immediate problem with the chamber covered their ears. The sound was just on the side of painful. It was a rarely heard sound. It was an alarm of catastrophic failure.

Lannya shot over to the side of one the ribbon specialists.

"What is it?" She shouted, as loudly as she could over the alarm.

The ribbon specialist was frantic, looking back and forth between Lannya, the panel in front of him, and Akal. As he tried to answer Lannya, he cut himself off to hear what members of his team were saying.

"It's... the chamber... it's getting some kind of feedback... resistance or something!"

Lannya didn't understand. She shouted her follow-up questions.

"What? What does that mean? What's happening to him?"

"There's something that's preventing the chamber from repairing the link between his soul and past lives. The energy's getting kicked back and building up. We need to figure out what's going on before the energy builds up to a critical level!"

Elcyd, Mamdod, Thyra, Azli, Carthal and Heersan had quickly joined Lannya, in an attempt to hear for themselves what was going on.

"This shouldn't be happening," the ribbon specialist belted. "Someone's manipulated his energy to make this happen."

Mamdod leaned in and shouted.

"Can you shut it off, or stop the process?"

"Yes," the specialist yelled back, "but if we do it abruptly like that, it will kill him. Everything he is. It would be like closing up the chest cavity in his soul, in the middle of performing billions of heart bypasses."

Azli stared at her father in helpless horror. She suspected Einar had sabotaged Akal somehow.

Without saying anything to anyone, Carthal darted around the back of the group and hurled himself into the chamber's door. Physicians, specialists, Heersan and others, shot over to the chamber windows. The staff fumbled feverishly to get in the room to wrestle Carthal out of it. The amount of energy involved inside was enormous, and terribly dangerous. He was hoping to disrupt the energy build-up or get Akal out somehow. He approached the bank of machinery connected to millions of tiny ribbon threads behind Akal.

"Carthal!" Heersan screamed while pounding on the glass. "Get out of there! What are you doing?"

"You can't do anything, Carthal!" One of the ribbon specialists shouted. "You can't decipher another soul's information on your own! Get out!"

Not only was trying to disrupt the energy buildup pointless, and fatal, on a scale that would destroy all of the lives associated with all the souls within the immediate vicinity, but it was futile to even try to make the sacrifice. No one had the capacity to interact with the energy, much less correct whatever was preventing the chamber from repairing the links between Akal's souls and his past lives. No one could do anything about the impending disaster. Except for one person.

In the commotion of Carthal's selfless attempt to do something to save his struggling friend's soul, no one had noticed what was going on behind them.

Almost immediately after Carthal ran and busted into the chamber, Mamdod had summoned a ribbon that had uncharacteristically shot through the entirety of the Harbor to where he was at, not harming the building at all. The ribbon Mamdod called was brighter and wider than any had seen before. The biggest portion of the ribbon coursed up and down like a vertical river with separate bands of energy circling around it.

Only after the ribbon specialist had shouted at Carthal that there was nothing he could do, was anyone distracted by the escalating light behind them. The ribbon swelled to about double its already impressive size before collapsing to a sphere that radiated a blinding white with rippling currents of bright blue striking around it like lightning.

Just as those in the room had turned to see what

was happening, and registered that Mamdod had been encompassed by what was now a never-before-seen ball of ribbon energy, the ball shot off from where Mamdod had been standing, through the chamber window without damaging it and stopped, hovering just above the machinery Carthal was trying to disrupt.

Carthal squinted and flinched from the startling ball of energy. Finally, being distracted from his intentions, he covered his ears from the alarm. And though the chamber was becoming increasingly unstable, and the materials in the room began to shake violently from the accumulating energy, Carthal could hear Mamdod's voice clearly in his mind, without distortion, coming from the sphere.

Go, Carthal. I'll take care of this. There's nothing you can do.

Carthal was unable to move as he asked himself if he had really heard what he had just heard. He wasn't completely sure who had said it, or what they might actually be able to do, to help Akal. But something gave him peace. Something reassured him. Carthal crept over to the door and using his elbow from his bent arm as he held his ears, punched the metal beam he had used to keep the door from opening on the outside, out of the way. Specialists and doctors grabbed his arm the moment the door cracked and dragged him away from the chamber.

Once Carthal was safe, everyone locked their eyes on the sphere inside the chamber. Heersan helped Carthal to his feet. Everyone knew they could do nothing, but they had even less of an idea of what Mamdod was doing, or thought he could do. Having no idea if anyone would survive, they couldn't help but find calm in the wonder and intrigue of what was happening inside the chamber. They looked on, hoping that if they survived, that they wouldn't have to lose their friend, again.

Mamdod's sphere of ribbon energy slowly descended into the primary collection of ribbon streams that linked all the machinery, which was, in turn, connected to Akal via subsequent streams. As the sphere dissolved into the ribbon strands, every visible and exposed strand of any length, anywhere in the chamber, shifted from the typical bright blue, to a pitch black. The ribbon strands remained black as the shaking continued to intensify. The screaming and flashing alarm continued.

The violent jerking of the room, and the materials in it, continued to increase. No one knew what was happening, and the staff inside the room started to shout at people to get out. Outside the room, ribbon scanners, ribbon devices, machinery, terminals and anything else connected with the ribbons also began to turn black. A general security alarm began to screech everywhere. The entire Harbor was in danger from the violence happening inside the Harbor's ribbons.

Mamdod was inside the ribbons, fighting the millions of tainted and malicious bits of ribbon energy Einar had injected into all of the links between Akal's soul and his past lives. The countless barriers between Akal and his past lives were not only preventing the links from being repaired, but were slowly causing him to forever lose his tie to a particular life. Somehow, Mamdod realized as he fought, that Akal did in fact still have all of his past lives, but not for long.

At great cost, Mamdod was able to decipher not only the information from Akal's soul, but also exactly how and where Einar had attached his malicious data. For each of the millions of parasitic leeches, Mamdod was able to project a past life's soul fragment of his own onto the corrupt portion of Akal's soul information, encase it, and purify it. As the majority of Mamdod's past lives were spent to clean Akal's, that life of Mamdod's was not lost, but absorbed forever back into the ribbons. As each one was purified, it returned from the infected and disputed black color, to the bright and healthy blue. The ribbon strand associated with that particular link between one of Akal's past life and his soul, was fully repaired.

Over the course of only a few minutes, this happened millions of times. As the collection of individual ribbon strands returned predominantly to their healthy blue, the violent shaking subsided. The Harbor-wide alarm ceased. Soon after that, the chamber's alarm also stopped. The chamber had become still and quiet. Mamdod was nowhere to be seen, but all of the ribbon strands were blue once again. Lannya shoved a table that had slid into her out of the way, and sprinted over to the chamber's status monitor. She read its readings aloud to the room.

"Soul stability, 100%. Soul integrity, 100%. Soul-to-past-life linkage, 100%. Medical health of current form, 100%. Chamber functionality, 100%. Chamber stability, 100%"

She spun around 360 degrees, grinning ear to ear at the doctors, ribbon specialists, her friends, her daughter, and then back to Akal. His open eyes locked onto hers.

Chapter XXII

A Decision is Made

Lannya latched onto the chamber's window and broke into tears. Her smile held, however, as her tears plummeted down her cheeks. She made no sound. Her immensely ecstatic heart had shoved her well past the point of audible crying.

Akal rolled to a side and sat up on an elbow. He squeezed his forehead and pinched the inside corners of his eyes. He was absolutely exhausted, but he was complete, whole, and healthy.

Lannya finally made a sound. It was a chuckle wrapped in rapturous disbelief. And though she was glued to watching her husband adjust to his newly conscious and repaired state, Lannya was distracted by Mamdod's absence, or at least the absence of the ribbon sphere he had just condensed into. After thoroughly scanning the chamber, Lannya spun around again to check behind her. No Mamdod. She looked specifically at Elcyd and

284

then back to Akal. No Mamdod. It firmly registered that Mamdod had somehow given himself to the defense of Akal's soul and life. Mamdod was gone.

Lannya coughed out a heartier sound of overwhelming joy as a flurry of emotions clamoring for space in Lannya's heart beat down every door of her senses. That which was being the loudest at the moment, was the realization of absolute selflessness Mamdod had exhibited in saving her husband. He had saved him, and because of that, Lannya could look through the chamber window at her recovering husband.

Her damp hands slid down the window and left a foggy path as she began moving towards the chamber door. Her eyes remained on Akal with each step. She wanted to smell him. That's all she could think of. She wanted to smell his hair or the back of his hand as she kissed it. She didn't care if there was anything unpleasant to smell after having been trapped, restrained and tortured. He didn't deserve for her to care about that. She didn't think about any of that. She just wanted to begin smothering her senses in everything that was him.

Akal had sat up and crawled his legs around with the heels of his feet and slowly let his legs drape off the table, being careful to respect gravity a bit. He wasn't sure what his muscle strength would be like. It wasn't bad. His legs dangled loosely as he rolled his neck and shoulders. He just wanted to be sure of his state so he could run. He wanted to run to Lannya.

Well, he at least did his best to run. As Lannya reached the threshold of the chamber door, Akal pushed himself off the table and onto his feet before falling down to his knees. He immediately pushed up with his hands, however, and stood up. As he grimaced from a startling twinge in his back, he rushed for Lannya. In a mixture of hopping, hobbling, and skipping he made it within arms-length to her before starting to fall again. But Lannya had met him. She caught him under his arms and squeezed a hug like she had never hugged before. She didn't care if she hurt him. She needed to hold him as tightly as she could.

The two of them turned and twisted in an embrace they never wanted to end. They both erupted in an unabashed torrent of crying, sobbing, rough gulps of air, and laughing. Their bodies were as tightly compacted against each other as possible as they continued holding each other for minutes. Everyone outside watched and relished their reunion with the bittersweet backdrop of losing Mamdod. After even more circling, twirling and rocking in their embrace, the two soulmates finally parted, if only slightly, enough to grab on to each other's faces. An almost equal amount time that they had spent hugging, was spent staring, loving, wiping the other's tears, and kissing.

All those on the outside waited their turn to welcome Akal back and give him their own hugs, but they were in no hurry. They simply lined the outside of the chamber, and smiled in at the blissful couple.

Azli didn't join the group along the chamber windows, however. It wasn't for not wanting to see Akal, or not wanting to take in their love, but because of the guilt she felt. She was the reason they had to go through the pain they did. She knew Einar orchestrated everything, but she also knew she was the one that pulled the trigger on that weapon that killed Akal. But that was something else on her mind. *If I killed Akal*, she ran through her mind. *How was he standing right over there in that chamber?* With the guilt and the questions, she decided to slide down a support column to the floor, and wait her turn to greet, ask, and to answer.

It wasn't long after Azli slid down to the floor that Akal saw her. While still locked in an embrace with Lannya, he had to strain harshly to place the face he saw through the chamber window. He absolutely could not remember who she was, but that didn't last long. His mind must have chosen not to recognize her for a moment. It must have tried to prevent him from recognizing her. But he did.

In a split second, Akal pushed away from Lannya, and summoned a ribbon that, like Mamdod's, caused no harm to the room. As soon as Akal was encompassed by the ribbon, he changed forms into that of a Deun, with a clap of thunder. His body grew and began rippling and rapidly rolling around on itself. The countless sections, made entirely of sloshy sand that could be manipulated and moved as the creature wished, began to rearrange themselves at two long extremities that began to take shape. As the configuration completed, the ends resembled barrels, or cannons.

As soon as they formed, they discharged and shot two massive shockwaves of energy through the chamber wall. By the time Akal's Deun arms recoiled, the still present ribbon shifted him back to his usual human form. His ribbon turned blood red as its energy pulsated and streamed around him. Akal was furious. He was livid, enraged and hateful, after spotting Azli. He began to march towards her.

Akal passed through the hole in the chamber wall he had shot out. The force of the energy had slammed through the wall slinging the rest of its energy, and the resulting debris, into Azli, knocking her onto her side. She quickly started to sit up and shake it off as Akal approached. He only wanted to stun her, initially. The last thing he had known about Azli up until that point, was that she was with Einar, who was still called Daebaugh as far as he knew right then, and that she thought she was killing him. He wasn't done yet.

Akal seethed inside his ribbon. His chest heaved up and down and his eyes were caught in blinders of rage. He wasn't exactly sure what else had happened after he was struck by the weapon on the roof the Harbor, but he did know that Azli's face was synonymous with the attack. He wasn't conscious for anything that had transpired since then, so he was ready to resume the fight. He was ready to kill Azli.

He stomped one foot forward and paused to check the stability of his stance. He was perfectly solid. The ribbon he called had seemed to replenish his last remaining bits of deficient health and spiritual will, and revived his overall power. Akal was back, with no exception. The only thing lacking now, was his knowledge of what had transpired between the attack on the Harbor, and that moment. He would worry about that later, however. The farthest thing from his mind was the possibility that Azli had defected.

He continued to march forward towards Azli with

a severe and exposed glare. His rare and odd ribbon of ruby red followed him as he walked. It kept up with his pace. He marched methodically towards Azli but slowly picked up speed. Within a few steps he was jogging. A few steps later, sprinting. The ribbon circled, streamed and throbbed around him as he started to think of the form he would take to end at least one of Azli's forms.

Before he could lash out, just before changing forms, he heard something that broke his attention. He slid to a halt within feet of Azli.

"Akal! Wait, wait!" He heard from behind him. Various voices mixed in intensity and volume blended together to break him out of his lethal trance. Elcyd, Heersan, doctors and ribbon specialists, everyone in the room screamed in hopes of breaking Akal away from his intentions. It worked. He heard them.

As soon as he stopped, Lannya caught up to him and tripped, after being too panicked to restrain her momentum in time. She stumbled down to her knees and slid around to the front of Akal.

"Stop! Akal! Don't do it," Lannya begged. "Don't hurt her! She's come back to us! She's on our side now! Please! Look!"

Azli had plastered her back against the column once again and forced herself to remain in place as Akal approached. She fought a thousand urges of as many flavors, to scamper, scatter, run and flee. But, her guilt, her shame, her hate and disgust for herself, made her stay. She deserved whatever pain Akal was about to deal her.

Both Lannya and Azli radiated in the red, ancient and stupefying sight of Akal's ribbon. They stared up at him from the floor with entirely different shades of uncertainty. Akal stood in his enormous ribbon, throbbing from anger and adrenaline. His dark memories and painful confusion kept the coal shoveled into the stove of his hate and anger. His focus had stayed on Azli ever since he saw her, but at last, it finally broke. He looked down at Lannya and registered her pleas.

"Akal. Everything is ok now. She's our daughter again. She's with us," Lannya reiterated through tears. A smile formed on Lannya's face, masterfully painted into existence from a nurtured realization that she finally, truly felt that way, and that Azli had indeed given up her twisted Einarian path, and returned to them.

Akal's ribbon pulsated while the room waited to see what Akal would do. For a time that no one could define, Akal just stood, seethed, and thought.

But something finally changed. Signs that Akal was calming down slowly started to present themselves. The speed at which his ribbon's energy streamed up, down, and around, began to slow. The column of bright red slowly began to fade to the usual bright blue of all ribbon energy. His face loosened. He was starting to let himself believe Lannya's words. Then in a snuffed whisper, Akal's ribbon branch retracted back up through the ceiling and out into space. The disheveled room and its mentally trampled occupants fell quiet.

Akal continued staring at Azli, but his face had no more signs of anger or hate. He looked down to Lannya, reached for her hands and helped her to her feet. He then looked back to his friends, doctors, and ribbon specialists, and nodded at them. It was ok. They were ok.

What to do with or say to Azli didn't come quickly to Akal. He grabbed Lannya's hand and began walking with her back to the group. They both looked over their shoulder at Azli for a bit as they turned. Azli stood up and brushed the altercation off. As Lannya and Akal joined their friends, Azli stayed in place and looked on.

The collection of old friends and faces of those dearest to Akal swarmed him as he and Lannya approached. Tears fell everywhere and decorated the exclamations of joy and love. Akal's arms flailed in slow motion as he reached to hug one friend after another. He squeezed his arms around Elcyd, held Carthal's face, and then latched onto Heersan. His fate lit up after seeing Thyra and thought how long ago it seemed that he ran into her on the docks of the Harbor when he first arrived. With each embrace, smile, and sniff, however, something prevented him from attaining his joy's full potential. He slipped back over to Lannya and grabbed her hands. He looked at her softly, with a potent sadness. He squeezed her hands and approached the broken window of the chamber. His wife and friends followed closely behind.

Akal didn't have all the answers or understanding, but at some point between being shot by Azli's weapon, and now, his memories and total awareness had returned. The knowledge temporarily blocked because of Mamdod's game, were no longer restrained. He knew, and remembered all that his soul had to know and remember. He knew Mamdod. He remembered who Mamdod was to him. He remembered Daebaugh, as he still thought he was called, everything. His soul crumbled as he looked into the chamber.

"Mamdod..." Akal said gently, almost calling to him. "What did he do? It's all," Akal continued while stopping to swallow. "It's all kind of hazy."

"You were dying," Elcyd returned sadly. "He saved you somehow."

Akal kept his eyes focused on where he vaguely remembered Mamdod's energy shooting into the room before merging with the ribbon threads. He was completely lost in his sorrow. He had lost the closest thing he had to a father. They hadn't spoken with their full mental capacities since before Mamdod started his game. The last time they spoke on the island, Mamdod was only some curious guide to Akal. And to Mamdod, Akal was just another soul needing direction. It hurt Akal even more, knowing they were ignorant of each other's connection the last time they met.

The flood of memories and input into his mind caused Akal to block out everything around him as he caught up with his thoughts. He absentmindedly leaned onto the windowsill that he had knocked out shortly before. The splinters and small shards of glass left in the pane cut into one of his hands. Blood began to seep out across the ledge, and drip down the edge of the wall. He didn't notice. He wasn't hurting from the glass. He hurt from losing Mamdod.

It hit him like a slug to the gut that he had no opportunity to prepare for. It was a hollow hurt. He couldn't escape it or do anything to avoid it. It was pure loss and sorrow. It made him think of everything else that had happened. It made him panic over everything he missed while he was a prisoner. It made him think of who else was missing. He spun around and looked at the group again. He scanned their faces and took an inventory. He ran through whatever chronology he had to reference and who might be where, or what might have happened to them. But for one person, he kept coming up empty. For one person, he had no information. Akal struggled to find the answer in his mind, but it was no use. He kept waiting to see some faces that never appeared. After scanning the group multiple times and confirming she wasn't there, he had to ask.

"Where's Rigella?"

Thyra shot a glance at Elcyd, and everyone saw it. They saw that Thyra knew something, and that Elcyd probably had an idea, but wondered what the problem was. Thyra wasn't sure how to reply, or if she even should. Elcyd came to the rescue.

"I believe she's in her office," Elcyd replied between a few flicks of his eyes at Thyra. Carthal helped out with the conversation as well.

"You see, Akal, after the attack on the Harbor that we thought you died in, the Astraeans formed the Astraean Defense Force to fight back against Einar. Einar is the name that Daebaugh goes by now. Rigella is the leader of the ADF."

Thyra looked at Elcyd again. She still didn't know how the possible transition from Rigella to her should be brought up to the group, or when.

Akal floated his focus to a random area of the room as he processed what Carthal had said. He nodded just enough to approvingly signify that the information made sense to him.

In a sudden rush of clarity, Thyra felt the urge to get it all out in the open. No one had the luxury of treating anything delicately.

"She's actually asked me to take her place as leader of the ADF," Thyra stated strongly. Everyone swung their heads towards Thyra with looks of surprise. "She's wanting to step down and stay in the fight on a more personal level."

Elcyd's face was the only one unchanged as the others reacted. Akal, having been out of action for the past few months, looked around at the others, trying to decipher their surprise.

"What's wrong?" Akal asked to anyone that wanted to answer.

Heersan spoke up first. His eyebrows jumped from not having a concrete answer.

"Uh," he began with a mumble. "I don't think that there's anything wrong. I just don't think any of us had any idea she was wanting to do that." Heersan looked directly at Thyra, at Elcyd, and then back to Thyra. "Is she ok? It seems like an odd time to..."

Thyra anticipated the question.

"Yeah, she's fine," Thyra reassured everyone. "She's just expended a lot of energy leading the ADF and getting it to where it is, overseeing the creation of the fleet, and all that. She's putting the ADF and the Astraeans first. She thinks the ADF would be better served right now with a fresh set of eyes, and a fresh mind."

Everyone looked at Thyra, mostly with expressions of satisfaction with her answers and information. They all had follow-up questions, and assumed there was more to the story, but no one had any desire to press Thyra for further details. No one would have been served by forcing the issue right then. And though he had been in the dark for months, Akal, along with Heersan and Carthal, had a fairly good idea of the overall issue.

"Are you going to take her place?" Carthal asked innocently. "How will that happen?"

"Well, the rules for ADF leadership transitions, outside of the tournament held at the end of each leader's term, outline a simple process for the leader to appoint a replacement. The appointee is then voted on by the Secondary Commanders, as well as a few senior civilian Harbor leaders."

The group stood quietly as they waited for Thyra to answer Carthal's other question.

"And," she said through a humble hesitation, "I will step in for her if I'm voted through."

Her friends nodded, and some smiled slightly. They had every confidence in their friend, and were encouraged by her enthusiasm. She was a great friend, a great person, and a great Astraean. Once they each finished taking in all that Thyra had said, they allowed their minds to drift to other topics.

Akal rubbed his head. He felt a bit out of place. He had no desire to feel out of place, and surely didn't want to be a burden to his friends, his people, or their efforts to destroy Einar, so he spoke up.

"I'm remembering some of what Mamdod's game outlined," Akal said softly, in the shadow of his mentor's passing, "but, it's been a long time. How far along are we? What's happened while I was out, and how much time do we have?"

Elcyd and each of the group spent the next few minutes catching Akal up. It didn't take long. Akal remembered that he and Einar had been challenged long ago by Mamdod, to do good for others in the multiverse, and that whoever survived the other would take his place. The group mostly caught him up on details of the ADF, battles that had taken place, some of the answers they had learned, and some of the questions they had. As the discussion unfolded, Akal recalled what he thought at the time was being killed, but at that point in the conversation, it was he that had to catch the rest of the group up. Lannya looked back at Azli, and gently tilted her head, beckoning her to come closer and listen. Azli started to approach, even though she had already been close enough to hear the majority of the conversation. She approached within a few feet of the group and stopped with folded arms. She listened, and came no closer.

"It was one of the strangest things I've ever seen, anywhere in the multiverse, or from any of my past lives," Akal continued with a mood of sustained confusion. "When I got struck by that weapon Azli had, I went to the ribbon island thinking I had lost all of my lives. I spoke with Mamdod a bit and stepped into the final ribbon. But after that, it's hard to explain."

The group was extremely intrigued, and Azli felt outright stupid. Not only for, as far as she knew then, killing her father, but because Einar had apparently kept her in the dark about some things.

"The flow of the ribbon in our faces," Akal continued, "after we lose a life and head to the island, it wasn't the same. It was thicker and rougher. It felt like the ribbon energy was infected with something, or influenced by something."

"Well, that would make sense," Thyra offered. "We've slowly discovered that Einar has been manipulating ribbon traffic, data, and circumventing movement of souls throughout the entire multiverse."

Everyone was crunching data in their heads, calculating, and beginning to put a few pieces together.

"Einar made the ribbons think you were dead!" Elcyd suggested with enlightened excitement. Akal started to nod as he picked up Elcyd's train of thought.

"He couldn't or," Akal paused while constantly re-evaluating his assumptions, "didn't know how to truly kill all of my lives, but he figured out a way to trick the ribbons into thinking he had!"

"Those weapons never extinguished souls, they just redirected them to wherever he wished," Heersan surmised. "That means, all of the Astraeans they killed on the Harbor roof that day, might be alive somewhere!"

Lannya grabbed her head in anguish.

"If that's true, I hope they all didn't go to the Dark Artery like Akal did. Einar self-destructed it!"

"Oh," Akal spoke up. "I have no idea where I went initially after I was hit. I could have gone straight to his ship, or somewhere else, and then got moved. All I know is that once I emerged from that contaminated ribbon, I landed in that device, or whatever it was, almost immediately, as far as I remember. Other than a few foggy blurs and muffled sounds, the next thing I remember was seeing Lannya through the stabilization tube window on

Paige."

An excited silence fell upon the group. Realizations that Einar might not be as powerful as previously thought, or that his tools couldn't do what they previously assumed, gave everyone a fresh jolt of hope.

Azli then spoke, surprising everyone and startling some. All turned to look at her, except for Akal. She muttered flatly, in shame and humiliation.

"He never told me what those weapons actually did. He didn't trust me."

No one said anything through the awkward silence. There was nothing to say to Azli at the moment. Lannya's heart hollowed slightly at being torn between the pity she felt for her daughter, and the hate she felt for Azli and all the pain she had caused everyone.

Elcyd pinched his lip while continuing to assimilate all the information that had been shared. He then huffed out a determined sigh and followed it with their most pressing issues.

"Well," he started, as he looked at Akal with an odd smirk. "The ribbons think you're dead, so that doesn't change anything yet, at least with how the tree at the island is shedding its leaves, and how the ribbons are ready to crown their new steward. And then there are the leads we had on where Einar might be manipulating data traffic from. We have a pretty good inclination that he might be doing it somehow from Earth."

Akal dropped and tilted his head as if struck with a painful epiphany. He slung his hands into his hair and paced a slow circle. He turned back to the group.

"Earth? Now that you mention it, I remember part

of my strange ribbon travel being really bright, really sharp and familiar. Painful, sterile..."

Akal spoke quicker and quicker. He raced towards a realization he didn't want to realize. His speech became rougher as he voiced his conclusion.

"I think it was the walls of the Habitats!"

"The Habitats?" Lannya blurted in a hateful surprise. She hated almost nothing more. She looked at Thyra and then Elcyd with wide and rabid eyes. "If Einar is hijacking the ribbons from Earth, then this," she shouted pointedly at the situation, while gesturing at Akal, "is just another piece of evidence!"

Elcyd scanned the group for reactions. Akal wanted to add to his thoughts, and add a suggestion, but didn't want to start giving orders or begin dictating to anyone.

"So, how do we proceed, and what is our priority?" He wondered.

Thyra offered a suggestion on something they could take care of fairly quickly.

"Before we decide how to act next or set out for somewhere, maybe we should meet with Rigella and get that taken care of?"

Lannya agreed.

"Yeah, it wouldn't take long to gather the Secondary Commanders and the required Harbor personnel for a vote," she offered.

"Right," Elcyd supplied. "Let's go talk with Rigella. After that, we'll decide what comes next."

Everyone agreed silently and started to leave, but Akal made a request first.

"Would anyone mind if I had a few minutes head

start? I'd just like to talk with her a bit."

No one voiced any objections. As the room started to empty from the doctors and ribbon specialists, Akal reached for Lannya and hugged her. He kissed her cheek and then whispered.

"I just want to check on her," he explained in a whisper. Lannya hummed a quick, but approving mumble as she squeezed his hand. He let go of her hand gently and turned to leave, and came face-to-face with Azli. There was no chance for either to avoid locking eyes.

Akal stopped and let his eyes dig into Azli's. His face was stern and hard, but the numerous things that came to his mind that he wanted to say, were not. Still, he didn't speak to her. He didn't want to yet. There wasn't enough time for all the things he wanted to say. Azli stared back at him. She wasn't challenging him, nor was she angered or offended by Akal's glare. She welcomed his stare and was prepared to be admonished. But no admonishing came. Akal held his tongue and stepped away. After he resumed making his way towards the door, Azli looked to her mother. Lannya raised her shoulders to take in as much air as possible. She sighed with a patient understanding of how difficult it would be for Akal and Azli to come to any form of understanding.

By the time the door to the MSH facility shut behind Akal, his mind was already full of things he wanted to say to Rigella. He stared at the ground and briskly stomped through the corridor. He kept coming back to similar thoughts of being surprised that Rigella would have ever been interested in a leadership role like the one she was in to begin with. He had always known her to be the quiet and methodical one of the original Trio. It wasn't a case of being introverted, or awkward. She just liked to work alone, and maybe, he thought, not bother others with her thoughts, from her point of view. Akal had no doubt that she had been and was currently doing extremely well in her role, he was just surprised. And while the notion of her wanting to step aside now that everything had been established and was working well didn't surprise him, he still just wanted to make sure his old friend was all right.

Akal finished traversing the lengthy and curved secure corridor that the MSH was attached to, and landed at an open, and beautifully ornate stairwell with a circular staircase. It was a staircase used mainly for day-to-day Harbor personnel, staff, and engineers. And even though it was largely unseen from the public eye, it featured wide marble steps which reflected the dark and star-sprinkled light of space from the open ceiling. Akal grinned as he shuffled quickly down the stairs. He had missed the joy the Harbor gave him, and was grateful to still be in existence after being completely unaware for the past few months. Upon reaching the bottom of the circular staircase, Akal's close proximity automated the opening of another door that led to a small corridor, another door, and then the main lobby.

Akal stepped on the plate that activated the last door before the lobby, and was stunned by what he saw. The sight was unexpected and caused him to shoot back a few steps before quickly settling. Through the door, into the lobby, Akal saw only faces. He couldn't see the opposite wall of the lobby, the floor, the Helper Desk in the middle, nothing. Only faces. His fellow Astraeans had packed themselves into the lobby to wait on word of his condition.

He stepped forward to reclaim the steps he lost from being startled. There was no spare room except for the few inches at a time those around him politely provided him with as he inched further into the lobby. Almost immediately, a voice shouted out from a few feet deeper into the crowd.

"It's Akal! He's ok!" The voice exclaimed.

The resulting noise was deafening. The explosion of sound from the crowd cheering him on, instantly caused Akal to flinch from the shock of sound. His heart bubbled over from what he saw, felt, and heard. His eyes became immediately sore under the weight of his accumulating tears.

He pressed forward through the crowd, albeit slowly. Rigella's office was on the opposite side of the Harbor, and he needed to get to her sooner, rather than later. As he continued creeping through the crowd, he dabbed his eyes on his shoulder while reaching out to touch faces, grab hugs, and receive them. While in reality, he moved through fairly quickly, to him, it seemed like time stopped as he made his way. Akal cherished every embrace, every squeeze of a handshake, kiss on the cheek, and slap on the back. And though he had only been gone for a few months, there was an odd ambiguity that accompanied his emotions. It was a combination of feeling like he had just seen some of his friends, and at the same time, felt as if it had been eons.

The sea of fellow Astraeans, as well as non-Astraean friends and allies, seemed to only grow thicker as Akal approached the other side of the vast lobby. He had finally crossed the distance, but was still as joyfully worn and emotional as he was when he first stepped through the door. Akal wasn't aware, but Elcyd, Lannya, Carthal, Heersan, Thyra and Azli had entered the lobby as well after thinking Akal had enough of a head start. But like Akal, they were surprised by the huge crowd. They had arrived just in time to hear the growing demands for a speech from Akal.

"Speech! Speech!" Countless voices shouted from all over the lobby. Thousands of pairs of arms shot into the air, with many of them clapping and encouraging him. Akal thought initially that there wasn't enough time to oblige them, but selfishly, yet innocently, wanted to talk to the huge gathering of old friends.

Akal waved both hands in acknowledgment of the crowd's demand, and pointed at a staircase he was headed for so he could be heard better. This wasn't the large, main staircase, but a smaller staircase that led to some administrative areas of the Harbor.

Akal weaved his way through the crowd, and made various faces of playful displeasure at being urged to speak. But, he quickly made his way to the small staircase and took a few steps up. Once the entire crowd of thousands had noticed him and identified him, the crowd erupted once more in ecstatic applause. He held up his hands, begging his fellow Astraeans to quiet down so that he could speak. Time was not a luxury. The crowd obliged him, and simmered down quickly to only a few whistles and straggling claps.

"I have never been so humbled than I have been

today. It is so good to be home!"

Another roar of approval erupted from the crowd, before quieting down once more.

"I don't have a lot of time to talk," he continued. "And the truth is, none of us have a lot of time, do we?"

Akal looked away due to a distracting epiphany before turning his attention back to the crowd.

"It's almost funny. Our people, with millions of lives and an almost endless supply of recyclable time, is running out of it. But the great part about that, is that the future is unknown. And unknowns are exciting. They're a good thing! When something is unknown, that means that the worst possibility isn't a forgone conclusion. I'm about to meet with the ADF and Harbor leadership, my friends, and we will have a plan to you soon, to extend our final welcome to the unknown future!"

Akal waved quickly again before hopping off the stairs, and resumed his path to Rigella's. The massive sea of Astraeans and allies, across the huge lobby floor, began to howl and screech in inspiration and determination. No one was afraid of the dwindling timeframe, nor was anyone afraid of the unknown future. Each and every Astraean heard Akal's comments and screamed fear into submission. They would not give up until there was no chance of doing anything else.

***

Rigella's office was quiet, which was rare. Normally, anyone approaching her office could hear the sound bellowing out her door the moment they entered the corridor far up from her office, but that wasn't the case as Akal made his way to see his old friend. He walked in slowly and respectfully, never having seen the room before, or at least in its current form as Rigella's ADF office. The room was scattered with projection units, maps, weapon prototypes, and the main display table in the center. Akal saw a stack of paper on a desk that looked as if it had recently been straightened. Perhaps, Akal thought, Rigella was already preparing to leave, but was distracted by a round of doubt and second guesses. Any doubts of Rigella's looked to have forced a premature break from her preparations. She sat in the chair at her desk, with her back to the door. Her elbow was on the edge of her desk, as she supported her mind's dead weight of sadness on the outside of her knuckles.

"Ri?" Akal offered the silent room.

Rigella dropped her arm and spun around. She hadn't been crying, but her face was defeated and flattened from disappointment. But Akal only saw that face for a moment. As soon as Rigella spun around and saw him, her face stretched with excitement, and conveyed a rarely expressed love for her old friend. She threw herself out of her seat and ran over to him with outstretched arms. She seemed to have forgotten to slow down as she sprinted at him. Akal caught her, but was almost knocked down from her momentum. They both busted out in hysterical laughter as Rigella hugged him with a strength that jabbed a pleasurable pain into each other where they made contact.

They continued to hug while spinning in circles and rocking side to side. After a few more chuckles, Akal finally leaned back from Rigella and grabbed her shoulders.

"Rigella..." Akal sighed with a smile. His smile was a broad one that made the muscles in his face begin to strain. Millions of memories, saves, fights, and past laughs kept his smile strong and wide. "I can't believe I'm looking at you right now!"

Rigella shook her head in shared disbelief. She cupped Akal's face and let her hands fall to his shoulders.

"Are you ok?" She asked with a feigned concern. She playfully spun him around and checked him for injuries and wounds. "Are you all in one piece? Missing anything?"

Akal couldn't answer through his laughter and nodded as he took her teasing.

"Yes, yes," he finally allowed. "I think I'm back to normal."

Rigella shot up sarcastically.

"Well that's not good!"

They swapped another round of laughter and, for a moment, the two old friends forgot the pain, the loss, the pressure, and the veiled future. It wasn't long before the chuckling subsided, and reality set back in.

Akal looked away and stepped further into the room. He looked over the projection of the multiverse, which was still displaying the most recent deployment in U266. He wasn't really looking at it. He used it simply as a visual anchor while trying to figure out what to say next. Rigella crossed her arms and waited for her old friend. But she wasn't able to wait too long. She was too concerned about Akal.

"Joking aside, are you really ok? What happened? What did he do to you?"

Just as he had done with the others, Akal took the next few minutes and caught her up on the few details he remembered after Azli shot him, as well as what the others had brought him up to speed on. Between the facts regarding what Einar had done to trick the ribbons into thinking Akal had been killed, the suspicions over Einar doing something on Earth, and the fact that Einar still needed to be taken care of, everyone was now on the same page.

"And there's one last thing, Rigella," Akal said with a soft sadness.

"What?"

"Mamdod's dead," he said as quickly as he could, working to maintain his composure.

Rigella's eyebrows slanted in. Her cheekbones jumped as her jaw plummeted in surprise.

"Dead? When? How?!"

"The machine or whatever that Einar had me in..." Akal said, through welling eyes. "It corrupted all of the links between my soul and past lives. When they tried to repair them, I started to slip away. Mamdod summoned a ribbon, merged with the MHS systems and cleared the infections somehow. He never showed back up."

Rigella didn't understand as she looked aimlessly around the room for ideas.

"Well is he still in the ribbons in some form or something? Did he take the final ribbon?"

"I don't know," Akal said through a hollow hardness.

"I'm so sorry, Akal," Rigella offered sincerely. She wasn't one to often let others see the warmth of her soul, but Akal was one of the few that had that honor. "It's been so good to have him here. He's been great for me, for Elcyd, for everyone. There isn't an Astraean anywhere that doesn't love Mamdod, you know that. Sure, some people were upset over the result of his game for a while when he first showed up, but, that animosity didn't last. They didn't hold Einar's actions against him. Everyone knows there's nothing but goodness in him. He helped us a lot."

Rigella's voice faded out as her shared sorrow for losing Mamdod smoldered brightly in the steady breeze of Einar's influence.

Akal forced himself to change the subject. Mamdod would have been the first one to suggest they keep moving forward.

"So, are you really wanting to go through with this? Leave the ADF?"

Rigella walked behind her desk and fell back into her chair. Her face flattened once again and her eyes froze on a random spot on the top of her desk. She was in no hurry to answer, but wanted to get talking about it out of the way.

"Yeah," she answered. Her voice was dry, and dark. She looked possessed as if suffocating from another soul's plastic bag and couldn't do anything about it. "I don't want to lead anymore. I don't want to make others do what my mind comes up with."

Rigella's eyes drifted to Akal. Something in her wanted to make sure he understood her words as she said them. Akal hadn't seen Rigella like this before.

She swallowed before continuing, but she still

sounded like a ghost caught in someone's grotesque shadow.

"In all our fights through the ages, I could live with what I thought, what I did, and what I had to do, but the scale of this... I can't take it anymore. I need to step away."

Akal walked around to the side of his friend's chair and knelt down, looking up at her as he rested an arm on her desk.

"Ok," he said reassuringly, trying to comfort her by matching her raspy whispers. "I know you know what needs to be done, and I know you know what's best for you. I've never doubted you or your decisions, and I'm not going to start now. I just wanted to check on you."

Rigella gritted her teeth and looked at Akal.

"You didn't see what I did to Azli, Akal."

The others had told Akal about the incident, but hearing Rigella's voice as she brought it up, and seeing her eyes as she mentioned it, gave Akal's mind a drastically more vivid set of brushes for his imagination to paint with. He recoiled from Rigella, if only slightly, and slowly. His absence during recent events confused his heart, mind, and soul. He frustrated himself by not knowing how to feel about Rigella's attack on Azli.

He took a step back while still kneeling, and began to stand up. He was preparing to say something to Rigella, only so the discussion between them wouldn't be left where it was currently hanging. But, before he could reply, a few knocks landed on Rigella's door. Elcyd's head leaned into view before stepping a foot in.

"Hey. Can we come in?"

Rigella beckoned them in with a quick whip of

her head. In stepped Elcyd. Following behind him were Carthal, Lannya, Heersan, and after a noticeable delay, Azli.

"That was some crowd out there," Carthal said with a reserved praise.

Everyone walked deep into the room and approached Rigella's desk, alongside Akal. All, but Azli. She initially stayed near the door. Lannya scooted up close to her husband and leaned in for a whisper.

"Are you two ok? Did we give you enough time?" She wondered considerately.

Akal looked at Rigella as he pondered how to respond to Lannya. Their earlier conversation made his mind itch with unresolved blisters, and his concern for his friend was far from alleviated.

"I don't know," Akal started. He looked at Lannya with concerned eyes and looked back to Rigella as he continued. "She's in a bad place. I think Thyra stepping in for her is a good idea."
Lannya nodded gently before taking Akal's hand and kissing it.

Carthal and Heersan tried awkwardly to talk amongst themselves while everyone else figured out what to say or do next. Lannya and Akal did the same. Elcyd walked around behind Rigella's desk and patted her on the back. Azli was still by the door and Thyra stood by the main projection table. Being ready to get on with it and keep things moving, Rigella broke the uncomfortable silence and jumped up from her seat just as Elcyd patted her.

"Ok, well, as you all probably know by now,"

Rigella blurted officially. "I'm resigning my position with the ADF, and have asked Thyra to take my place and serve out the remainder of my term."

Rigella gestured at Thyra as she spoke, causing everyone to look at her.

"Have you decided?" Rigella asked of Thyra.

"Yes, I have," Thyra immediately replied. "I would be proud to step in and do what I can for the ADF, and the Astraeans."

Rigella gently slapped her hands together and held them together while letting a slight smile show. She was equally excited for Thyra, but also relieved.

"Outstanding. There are a lot of reasons why I'm stepping down, and why I'm stepping down now," Rigella continued. "But, I just think for the good of the ADF, and for the best chance of success in whatever coming engagements with Einar we have, that it's best for me to step away. I think I've done what needed to be done for the establishment of the ADF, but I believe we need a different type of leadership now. I'll still be involved in the fight, but more on the scale of the types of work I used to do before all of this."

She looked to Akal, and then Elcyd, before ending her comments with a question.

"Do we need to get the Secondary Commanders and Harbor leadership in here?" She asked, signaling that she had no more to say. She was ready to be relieved.

Elcyd's eyebrows jumped from the abrupt pace with which the conversation was moving, but couldn't think of a good reason to postpone, nor could he think of any questions or concerns. Everyone was on the same page.

"Uhh, sure," Elcyd stuttered only from trying to keep up. "I'll reach out to them right now."

As Elcyd made his way over to a terminal to assemble the required personnel for the vote, Rigella approached Thyra.

"Thank you, Thyra" Rigella offered. She looked away, and then back again, as she switched mental modes from personal, to professional. "You will be an amazing leader."

Azli peered into the group and listened as the conversation unfolded. She had nothing to add, and nothing to say, and there sure wasn't anyone asking for her input. If anything, she was glad to see Rigella step down from her position of power, especially after what she had done to her on the docks. But, having recently returned from the darkness herself, Azli appreciated and respected the fact that Rigella had begun making an effort to address her own demons.

Thyra bowed subtly in recognition of Rigella's praise, and made a request of her.

"Assuming the vote goes through, and the transition does indeed take place," Thyra began. "Can I still seek your counsel from time to time, especially early on?"

"Oh, I would be glad to, of course," Rigella sincerely provided. "I'll be there for anyone, any time," she added. "I just need to get away from the title... the role..."

Thyra saw that Rigella wanted to expand on what she wanted to get away from, but she stopped herself, and simply smiled at Thyra.

"Well," Thyra replied, in an attempt to bring the conversation back to a happier and lighter place, "I'm just thankful I'll be able to lean on you."

Rigella gave Thyra another smile. This one however, seemed forced, as though she were running out of energy to maintain a guise of strength. Before Thyra could put too much thought into it, Elcyd tapped a few closing commands on the terminal and walked briskly back to the group.

"Ok, everyone. Both Secondary Commanders are on their way, as well as a senior member from each of the Sentinel, engineering, intelligence, and fabrication units. Between those six, and me, it will take a majority vote of at least four to approve Thyra's appointment."

Heersan spoke up respectfully.

"Well, I don't think there will be any voting issues, or delay. Everyone's wanting to get this taken care of quickly," he said.

"Right," Thyra agreed. "While we wait for them to get here, do you," she began to ask while looking at Rigella, "have any thoughts on how we should proceed?"

Thyra truly had no desire to run Rigella out, and wanted to let her know that she was sincere in hoping she could depend on her counsel. But, she wanted to include everyone else as well. She addressed the rest of her concerns to the entire group.

"We really only have enough time to pursue one course of action, and I don't know what that should be," she admitted.

A silence followed as everyone considered their options. Carthal stared at the floor as he thought out loud.

"We're about out of time. Einar knows this. We're getting desperate. Einar knows that, too. He also knows that a lot of his secrets are no longer secret. His smoke and mirrors are dwindling. I would think that he might be desperate as well, to keep us in the shadow of a final bit of ignorance. If he's never been able to manipulate the ribbons to the extent that we thought he could, then there has to be a weakness, or a disadvantage to his tricks, that he's hoping we don't find or take advantage of."

"Well, this kind of goes back to the rumors we've heard about Earth," Heersan added to his husband's thoughts. He began to stick his fingers out as he counted through various points of information.

"Between what Mamdod said he heard from souls passing through the ribbon island recently, what Azli's shared about what she knows, and what Akal told us about thinking he might have seen the Habitats as he was captured, then maybe checking out Earth should be our next move. We were headed there anyway until we were distracted by U266."

Elcyd shuffled his feet and began to rub his forehead.

"I would agree," he said. "I *want* to agree. It just seems too easy. I hate to ask 'what if?' all day, but who's to say that these little clues or hints getting through to us wasn't part of Einar's plan? What if throwing our last chunk of available time at investigating Earth doesn't turn anything up? The last leaf falls. The ribbons still think Akal's dead. Boom! Einar is the new Mamdod, and we still have nothing but horrible ideas of what that would mean."

There was no immediate reply. The only sounds heard were those of repositioning shoes, people shifting the way they were leaning, a creak or two from the involved furniture, and a few frustrated sighs.

For the sake of argument, Lannya considered throwing out the idea of heading to Earth all together.

"If we take Earth off the list of possibilities," she proposed, "then there's nothing else left on the list." Her shared frustration caused her to chuckle. "And Elcyd, you suggest it may be too easy, but, again, like Heersan said, we were distracted by U266. Going to Earth may seem easy, but the difficulty of the task doesn't matter if we run out of time to even try it."

Azli hadn't moved from her spot. She kept one ear on the conversation, but had started to stew more and more over being used by Einar, and by being kept in the dark. She had been fooled and wasn't smart enough to realize she was being used. She had only brought pain to others. She had contributed nothing to anyone. Her internal self-deprecation was relentless.

Then, without warning, a humongous epiphany slammed itself into her mind. She leaped away from the wall and towards the group.

"Wait! Wait!" Azli began. Her hands flared out and her eyes danced around as she gathered her thoughts.

"Smeche!" She shouted while looking at her mother. "He, he was like, Einar's number two while I was still with them. But, something must have happened because he helped us escape. He might be able to confirm some things for us!"

"Azli, the Dark Artery blew up," Lannya reminded

her. "It self-destructed. I doubt he..." Azli knew that, but was desperate to help.

"Let me try to contact him. He may have escaped. I've got to try," she pleaded.

Lannya couldn't find any harm in the idea, but deferred silently with a look to Rigella and Thyra. Thyra was open to the idea, but the glare from under Rigella's brow signaled that she had little faith in Azli, or her idea. Still, Rigella said nothing. After a painful few seconds, Rigella slowly turned her head and looked at Thyra before offering a barely noticeable shrug. It was Thyra's decision to make.

Thyra looked around the room. Everyone, including Azli, waited for Thyra to give the go ahead or not.

"Well, we're waiting for the vote anyway." Thyra then looked directly at Azli, and spoke with a stern superiority.

"Use encryption. Send it from a dummy ribbon. Destroy the transfer wave logs once you send the communication. Use the same methods in your instructions to him on how to reach us, if he even can."

Azli nodded anxiously, yet excitedly. There was nothing else in her mind, except for hoping Smeche was still alive. She jogged over to the nearby terminal, and was followed by Carthal. With a flick of her head, Rigella silently suggested he assist her, or probably more likely, make sure what she was doing was legitimate.

He looked around the room to silently spread his doubt and to signal he would keep an eye on her.

"I'll give you a hand, Azli."

Chapter XXIII

Relieved

Azli stepped up to the terminal and glanced at Carthal for a little guidance. He pointed and explained as she tapped.

"Yeah, just tap that Communications button," Carthal began. "Then choose Ribbon as the method, Artificial as the type, and Finite for the lifespan. Slide that over to how long you want it to exist. Choose your encryption level and tap that box that says Retain Transfer Wave Logs to disable it."

Azli quickly tapped through the steps and followed instructions, showing no sign of trying to deceive anyone.

"After that, it's just a matter of putting in the destination. You have that info?" Carthal inquired curiously.

"Yeah," Azli replied with a twist of doubt. "But, I have no idea if he'll be able to receive this. I don't even know if he's alive. But, I've got to try. I've got to do something."

Carthal looked on with a level of suspicion that was beginning to level off. If he didn't know any better, he would have thought she was actually trying to help. He watched her supply the terminal with her best estimate of the time, space, universe, and spirit data needed to track down Smeche. The speed at which he might receive the message decreased exponentially, the farther away he was from where she estimated his position might be. And of course, if he had been killed or somehow obscured or detained by Einar again, he would never respond. It was a waiting game at this point.

Azli looked at Carthal as she tapped *Send*. He nodded at her in approval, and motioned for her to return to the group, or at least return a little closer to everyone than she had been before.

They walked back over and Carthal shrugged quickly at Rigella, relaying subtly that he didn't seem to have any issues with what Azli had done and communicated. As they returned from the terminal, members of the summoned voting group began trickling into the room. The Secondary Commanders entered, followed by the Sentinel, engineering, intelligence, and fabrication unit leaders. Akal's face popped with excitement and admiration when he saw that Hergie was the fabrication representative. He jogged over to him and squeezed the tall and lanky Oreis as firmly as he could.

"Hergie!" Akal bellowed. "My old friend! You are a sight for sore eyes!"

"MR. AKAL, IT IS WONDERFULLY great to see you too. SO GLAD TO LEARN NOT DEAD."

Azli, the only one new to the Hergie experience, was the only person in the room to grab their ears. Akal laughed and slapped Hergie playfully on what would best resemble his back, and steered him further into the room. Everyone was ready to get down to business.

"Thank you all for coming," Elcyd began with an official tone. "And for coming on such short notice. As you all know, we have the first occurrence of a current ADF leader wanting to resign their position and simultaneously appoint a replacement to serve out the rest of the current leader's term. This requires a vote that we are prepared to witness and record today. Do any of you have any questions or concerns? If not, we can proceed directly to the vote."

Neither of the Secondary Commanders had anything to say as they looked at each other, and then to their soon-to-be former Supreme Commander. Rigella's face was stiff and her body was at attention as the discussion took place. No one from the group of Sentinel, engineering, intelligence and fabrication leaders had anything to say either. Everyone was aware of the situation, the need to act swiftly, and the dwindling amount of time they had to act.

"Very well," Elcyd continued. He looked over to the others and made a request. "Will one of you please act as the official scribe for this vote at the terminal over there, and two others act as witnesses?"

Heersan looked to Lannya and Carthal and waved them over. Heersan began to type and tap the display as the event unfolded. Elcyd began to dictate the official notes for the vote.

"Rigella, the current Supreme Commander of the

ADF is resigning, effective immediately. As a result, she has appointed as her replacement, for the remainder of her term, Thyra. We have assembled the required voting group of the two ADF Secondary Commanders, as well as a leader from the Sentinel, engineering, intelligence and fabrication units."

Elcyd scanned the room quickly and looked to the Secondary Commanders, to begin recording votes.

"Secondary Commander. As to the matter of accepting Rigella's resignation and acceptance of her term's replacement of Thyra, do you vote yes, or no?"

"Yes," the first Secondary Commander returned quickly.

With no hesitation, Elcyd looked to the other Secondary Commander, and then to each of the rest of the voters.

"Yes," voted the final Secondary Commander.

The Sentinel, engineering, and intelligence representatives each voted "Yes" as well. Finally, it was time for Hergie to vote. Elcyd addressed him.

"Though we already have a majority vote, Hergie, what is your vote?"

"YES," Hergie shouted.

Elcyd placed his hands on his hips and took in a deep breath before whooshing it out. He walked over to Thyra and stuck his hand out. Akal comforted Rigella slightly by rubbing her back.

"By a unanimous vote, Thyra," Elcyd offered. "You have been approved as the new Central Commander of the ADF. Please place your hand in the nearby ribbon scanner so all rights, privileges, and security protocols can be transferred seamlessly to reflect your ascension."

Elcyd tapped in a command to instruct the terminal to process the change in command. Thyra did as instructed and let the ribbon scanner read her data and switch over all official ADF references from Rigella to her. After a moment, line by line, a display zipped through an updated list that included such things as who the Secondary Commanders' superior now was, what the chain of command now reflected, as well as things that were transferred to Thyra, such as commands, controls, and codes, which could only be accessed, activated, initiated or changed, by Thyra.

In just a few seconds, the ribbon scan had completed, and the display read, *Complete*. Elcyd turned to Rigella.

"Rigella, you are hereby relieved as Central Commander of the Astraean Defense Force." Elcyd walked closer to her as he continued. "I know everyone here joins me in thanking you for the wisdom and strength you displayed during the creation and organization of the ADF as well as its numerous, successful deployments."

No longer acting in an official capacity to an ADF official, Elcyd reached out and warmly hugged her. The entire group of old friends clapped warmly, and sincerely, save one. Though Azli had enough intelligence to internally recognize Rigella's achievements, how she had treated her on the docks simply did not allow her to clap for her. The applause died down quickly.

"Thank you, Elcyd, and everyone," Rigella said with meek gratitude. Looking at Thyra, she continued.

"We all know that Thyra is one of the finest

Astraeans we know, with an incredibly brilliant mind, and enormous heart. I'm grateful, and thankful, to have her take my place."

With a fresh burst of applause, Rigella made her way over to Thyra and shook her hand. Rigella then quietly made her way to the back of the group, and already felt the burden of power lighten. The demons she was forced to keep by her mind's side began to look around for something else to do. She started to zone out, and truly relax for the first time since she won the tournament. She only needed to think about her own actions. She was once again responsible only for herself.

The group drew in closer to Thyra to congratulate her, offer their congratulations, and shake her hand, and even Azli came closer, but still kept a distance. And since she had already offered her initial, and legitimate appreciation and accolades, Rigella remained far removed from the group. She was the first to hear the terminal begin to hiss and scratch.

"...have recei... your messa... Azli. This is Sme... Pleas... confir... you ar.. receiving. I have received your message. I repeat. Azli, this is Smeche. Please confirm you are receiving. I have received your message."

"Thyra!" Rigella shouted, wanting to bring someone's attention to it, if not Azli's.

Thyra tilted her head around Elcyd's side and looked over at her. Rigella pointed at the terminal.

"Azli's message!"

The group had all been distracted by that point and silenced their conversation in order to hear. They didn't understand initially why the communication quality was so poor. Azli beat everyone to the terminal, either from having been the one that sent it, or more likely, being the most excited to hear his voice.

Azli tapped the command to accept the secure transmission.

"Smeche, I'm here! I'm receiving you! Thank you for helping us on the Dark Artery! I'm here at the Harbor with the Astraeans. What is your status? How did you get out?"

Thyra, Akal, Lannya, Carthal, and Heersan drew in behind Azli and looked over her shoulder. Elcyd, and the engineering representative that had come to vote, worked to tighten up and strengthen the transmission ribbon. Rigella didn't move, but she listened.

"Azli! Good!" Smeche replied with elated exasperation. He stuttered as he started compiling the answers to her questions. His reply was also delayed by the sound and shock of a moderate impact.

"I... I had been planning on leaving for a while. Seeing you and Lannya inspired me to speed up the time-table. I had a ship ready to go." Smeche looked away from the camera on his end and appeared to furiously tap on a command terminal of sorts. He looked back to the camera.

"I've had enough of him."

Azli grabbed the frame of the terminal display and squeezed it tightly. Additional sounds of muffled explosions and impacts could be heard, but Azli didn't register that it was an immediate threat to Smeche.

"Do you know anything about Earth, or if Einar's doing anything there? The Astraeans are running out of time and ideas."

"Earth?" Smeche posed, not out of confusion, but out of surprise that what he knew wasn't already common knowledge. "Yeah, that's where he's controlling the ribbons from."

"What?" Azli shouted, surprised to have it so easily confirmed, with no previous knowledge of her own. She looked up in astonishment to the ADF's new, and then old, leader.

"Yeah, that's been a fairly secret initiative of the Dark Team for ages. He's groomed and molded Earth, and its people, to be less inclined to ask questions or challenge authority. He's been hiding his ribbon controlling systems there almost since the planet formed."

Azli looked away for a moment and felt herself slipping into a deeper pit of hate for Einar and further shame from the swelling realization of how much she had been lied to, and how much Einar had hidden from her. She knew of Einar's Dark Team, the team of Einarians tasked with handling highly sensitive missions, but she never had any inclination that they were involved with any specific operation on Earth. Suddenly, Azli's seething was interrupted by an extremely powerful explosion that came from Smeche's end.

Rigella had slowly but steadily begun approaching the group and the terminal, curious about, and attracted to the state of whatever combat Smeche seemed to be in.

"Smeche? What was that? Are you under attack?"

"Yeah," he said, half chuckling. "They found me. I didn't expect to make it too far, but I had to try."

"Where are you?" Azli asked while looking at

Thyra and making a rushed assumption. "We can come to you!"

Thyra stepped around to Azli's side, ready to admonish her for making such an assumption, and for speaking for the Astraeans, but before she could, a grotesque and horrifying scream shot out from the terminal. It was Smeche.

"Azli!"

His agonizing voice quickly grinded into a gritty gargle. Then, after a huge fireball swelled into the video feed's frame, the transmission signal was severed catastrophically.

"Smeche!" Azli screamed at the display, gripping the unyielding metal as tightly as she could.

The room became the very definition of silent. There was no static. No scratching. No one spoke.

Rigella felt something bubbling up within her. She didn't know what the emotion or feeling was until it spilled over, and out of her mouth. She had no control over it.

"Now you know how we felt," she said to Azli, as maliciously as she could.

Azli took as long as possible to turn her head to look at Rigella. She may have been trying to change her mind about her next action. Using her grip on the terminal as an anchor, Azli pushed off, twisted her body, and came around in 280 degrees with a punch that was taken completely by Rigella's cheekbone.

The room was stunned by an unexpected fear. Each person in the room grappled with mixed emotions of feeling that Rigella was out of line, but that Azli deserved her pain, also. No one knew what to do or say. They could only stand, wide-eyed, and see how Rigella responded.

Azli's fist had sent Rigella spinning almost entirely around, and to the ground on one knee. Rigella had initially grabbed her jaw in a reflex, but as she went to her knee, let her hand drop. She simultaneously turned back around, and stood up. Her face displayed a sickening, yet extremely satisfied grin.

"Hurts, doesn't it?" Rigella asked Thyra about her pain for Smeche.

"Enough!" Akal shouted. He got in between his old friend, and his daughter.

"I will not allow either of you to waste our peoples' time any more than you have," he scolded fervently. He then looked to Thyra for their next cue.

"Ok," Thyra said, quickly picking up on his glance. "For better or worse, good or bad, trap or not, we have no other choice than to go to Earth. If anything, Smeche seems to have confirmed our suspicions. We need to uncover all that we can, and investigate any and every lead. With any luck, we might be able to stop his means of manipulating the ribbons, and maybe even draw him out for a fight before the last leaves fall, if he's not a coward. Elcyd and Rigella, would you follow me to the Readiness Office?"

Thyra took a few steps towards the door, with Elcyd right behind her. Rigella didn't move. Her eyes remained locked on Azli over Akal's shoulder. Her smile faded to a cold flatline of death, ready for Azli to make another move.

"Rigella!" Akal shouted. She was distracted enough

to let only her eyes move. She whipped her eyes to him, and then back to Azli. Still looking at her, she slowly sidestepped away from the stalemate and joined up with Thyra and Elcyd.

After they had left the room, Akal turned to Azli, feeling as if he needed to say something to her. He looked over at Lannya and found a reciprocal expression of being lost for words. There was a hypocrisy in Rigella's comments and her enjoyment of Smeche's death that Akal felt he needed to apologize for, despite what Azli had done in the past. Astraeans didn't, and shouldn't, rejoice in the pain of others. This was a perfect example of why Rigella needed to step down, and why everyone welcomed her decision. Regardless, Akal said nothing, only because he didn't know exactly how to express what he felt, or how to say it, especially considering who he was talking to and who else was in the room. Azli recognized Akal's desire to say something, but she shook her head slightly and waved him off.

"She was right," Azli said just above a whisper. She looked up from the floor, having surprised herself by what she said. "I shouldn't have hit her."

Azli backed away and left the room. Concerned about her daughter, Lannya looked at Akal, and then followed her.

Chapter XXIV

Readiness Check

Thyra, Rigella and Elcyd walked briskly through the corridors. They then flew down the stairs, threaded themselves through the still-packed lobby, and jogged over one of the bridges extending from the docks to the ADF Readiness Office. Earth was the Astraean's next destination, and they needed to get underway as soon as possible. While the ADF and Harbor leadership were fairly confident they would encounter Einar's ribbon manipulation system, whatever it was, the prospect of engaging Einar and stopping him from taking over control of the ribbon island was still a complete unknown. But, the time for considering other plans was over.

As they walked up the ramp to the ADF Readiness Office entryway, Thyra looked back over her shoulder at Rigella.

"Like I said, Rigella, I'd be grateful for any input and advice you have as we make this leadership transition.

Please let me know if you have any thoughts or concerns."

"Of course," Rigella obliged quickly.

"So, the plan is definitely to check out Earth, then?" Elcyd sought to clarify. Thyra looked over her other shoulder.

"Right, if we can't stop Einar in time, hopefully we can at least destroy whatever he's using to manipulate the ribbons. If we don't destroy him, we'll at least be able to slow him down for a while. We just need to see how much of the ADF we can get mobilized for Earth and how quickly."

The door to the Readiness Office whooshed open as Thyra, Elcyd and Rigella approached. Revealed behind the door were ranks of various ADF personnel, standing at attention, and creating an appropriately ceremonious path for their new leader to travel. Word spread quickly that the ADF leadership had changed, due in no small part to the innocent gossip from the engineers that were monitoring the secure ribbon traffic while ADF leadership authority was being transferred to Thyra. The room was crisp and quiet, full of ADF members of all ranks, proud of their organization, their people, and their new leader. With a respect and professionalism that rivaled much older organizations throughout the multiverse, the subordinates throughout the room proudly showed their respect and solidarity for their new leader. Rigella scanned the room from behind Thyra and beamed. She was grateful to have been relieved from the stresses of leadership, but absolutely loved the ADF and what it had become. Seeing her former comrades do right by their new leader in such a respectful and impressive fashion, helped scrub some of the cloudy demons away from the windows of her mind.

Thyra couldn't help but suck in a rush of air from what she saw. The respect shown her so quickly after accepting the position twinged her emotions with a wave of warmth. But she showed no signs of her emotion, save a humble smile. Thyra looked around her immediate vicinity and inspected those nearest to her. She resumed walking, making her way towards the end of the aisle, to speak with the ADF Readiness Officer they had come to meet. With each step, she inspected another few ADF personnel. As Thyra passed, along with Elcyd and Rigella behind her, each ADF officer raised their chin another millimeter.

"We're with you Commander!" An officer shouted from the back. The room erupted in a combined show of support.

"ADF! ADF! ADF!" The room roared.

Thyra allowed her grin to grow. Elcyd's chuckles, swamped by the cheering, accompanied an unrestrained smile from Rigella. After the end of the third cheer, Thyra stopped, feeling compelled to speak.

"It is such an honor to be received and welcomed as I have been," projected Thyra. "Thank you, truly, for this. I am fortunate in knowing that you will continue doing the same honorable and meaningful work that you have been doing, and that you will show me the same level of competency, strength, and respect that you have shown Rigella, and will continue to show her as our former leader."

A warm round of applause quickly rose to the roof of the chamber. Rigella stepped up quickly to wave and look around the room in appreciation for the recognition. Thyra continued.

"It is no secret that time is running out. Rigella has never shied away from that fact, and neither has the ADF. The Harbor leadership, and the Astraeans as a whole have not avoided that fact. We will not concede to time or anything else now. We have kept time at the forefront of our minds from the beginning, and we will not begin entertaining fear now. We will welcome the dwindling clock, and grab it, and clutch it with a deathgrip as we take it with us into the abyss if we must, but we will not give up until choice is no longer an option. Let us go to Earth and eliminate Einar's twisted time toys and traps of torture, and maybe, even Einar himself!"

The ADF personnel shouted another exclamation of approval to the rafters, as Thyra resumed her march through the chamber. Ready to meet them at the entrance to his office, was Barliman, the primary Readiness Officer. With his hands on his hips, he looked out admiringly at his gathered colleagues, and savored their enthusiasm for their new leader.

"Supreme Commander, Thyra! Welcome!" He said after a snappy salute. "Elcyd, it's great to see you. And Comman... uh, Rigella, thank you for your wisdom and leadership."

Rigella grinned playfully at Barliman, recognizing his innocent reflex in calling her Commander.

Thyra smiled at Elcyd, partly for Barliman's harmless mistake, and partly from not being used to being referred to as Supreme Commander. She returned Barliman's salute and shook his hand.

"Do I have you to thank for that welcome?" Thyra asked warmly.

"I wish I could say yes, Commander, but they came up with that on their own."

Thyra laughed and looked back through the assembled personnel.

"Well, that was most appreciated," she said. Thyra then took a deep breath and let some of the levity fall from her face.

"Tell me Barliman," she asked gravely. "How long before we can have part of the fleet ready for a trip to Earth?"

Barliman looked at Thyra with a hint of confusion.

"Um, as soon as you wish, Commander," Barliman replied.

It was Thyra's turn to be confused. She looked to Elcyd and Rigella for a clue as to what she was missing. If Elcyd knew, he was hiding it perfectly behind his expressionless face. Rigella however, let one corner of her mouth slide up into a proud grin.

"Ok," Thyra replied slowly. "What kind of numbers do we have available?"

Barliman's confused glance remained.

"Everything, Commander. The entire ADF is at your disposal," he advised. "Everything that we deployed to U266 has returned, as you know. And everything that didn't go to U266, has since been recalled.

The mystery and humor in the situation was due only to the fact that very few outside of the ADF knew that the entire force had returned. Thyra, having just replaced Rigella minutes prior, wasn't aware of current numbers of available forces. Rigella's smile was born from the relished prospect of having the entire ADF available to wage a final stand, to whatever end. It was going to be a good fight.

"Oh! Well, fantastic, then," Thyra acknowledged.

She took a moment, and let her eyes float past Barliman, and then to the walls behind him. Her eyes were open, but her mind closed to everything but her passion for her people. She felt an overwhelming presence of awareness. It was an awareness that her decisions on how to deploy the ADF may be her first and last as Supreme Commander. Indeed, she considered that it might be the final decision made by any Astraean. The possible finality in her awareness made her heart hurt from the fear of billions of years of Astraean life being ended. She initially considered, but then expelled, the possibility that their entire culture's knowledge, love, stories, experiences, history and relationships might all end. She was able to expel the thought with help from her conscience, and by the use of logic.

"Well, we're about out of time, and since we're practically emptying out the Harbor anyway, we might as well give this all we've got," Thyra decided. She did however look to Elcyd, and then longer, at Rigella. Neither gave any sign of disagreement.

"Barliman," Thyra began. "Please ready the entire fleet, and all ADF personnel, for deployment to Earth as soon as possible. We will need the fleet to prepare for any level of combat in local Earth space, and we will need every infantry element to prepare for a landing. Notify me when preparations are complete. How long do you anticipate that taking?"

"I don't believe it will take any longer than a few hours, Commander. Protocol is to begin resupplying all ships after each deployment, and we've already been at that for a while. Outfitting infantry and other support personnel doesn't even take that long."

"Perfect. Let's get to it, Barliman," ordered Thyra. Barliman initially complied with a firm and professional salute.

"Yes, Commander. Right away."

Barliman about-faced and jogged back into his office, and over to a command terminal. He began flying through commands in a blurry tangle while leaning over slightly and announcing their orders to the entire Readiness group. As he spoke, sections of the accumulated Readiness personnel began to fall out to begin tending to their orders, to the point that the room emptied. Across the Harbor, other elements of the ADF began to scramble to coincide with the preparations to deploy.

Thyra then turned to Elcyd.

"Elcyd, please don't consider this an order. Out of respect, and considering you're not an official ADF member, I wonder though, if you might consider announcing and organizing a civilian compliment to the ADF."

Elcyd started to respond, but it was unclear what his initial thoughts were. He stopped himself and looked at Rigella who seemed to have shared the gravity of what Thyra was getting at. Thyra elaborated.

"How this fight will end for the Astraeans, is unknown to each of us. I think anyone that wants to be involved, should be allowed. If you would consider leading it, I think our people would be an immense resource on the ground."

Elcyd nodded slowly with a solemn understanding.

"Yes," he replied solidly. "I would be happy to."

"Great," Thyra acknowledged. "Speak with the Secondary Commanders to let them know, and to coordinate with them. You have the final say over the civilian element, and if they have any concerns or questions, have them contact me."

"Of course," Elcyd complied with another nod. He reached for Rigella's shoulder and squeezed it before dashing away to take care of his new duties.

The last matter for Thyra to attend to before concentrating fully on her new role, was seeing how Rigella cared to be involved. Thyra wondered aloud.

"Did you want to continue working with me, join up with the fleet somewhere? Or..."

Rigella thought quickly, but she had already made up her mind.

"I think I'll check with Akal. It'd be nice to fight with him again after so long, not to mention Carthal and Heersan."

Thyra replied with a warm but contained smile. The idea of Akal and the original Trio fighting again made Thyra happy, but she also knew that getting their old group back together may be easier said than done. Rigella knew that as well.

"I know," Rigella huffed through a quick sigh. "If they'll have me."

Thyra let her smile grow, pleased that Rigella

recognized the coming challenge.

"Good luck, Rigella," Thyra offered her warmly. "Please reach out to me if you have any thoughts or ideas at any time. I hope to do you proud!"

"I have absolutely no doubt you'll do us all proud," Rigella returned honestly. She grabbed Thyra and gave her a few solid and slow taps to the back. She then pushed away and after a quick silent glance, turned and headed for the main Harbor complex.

***

Never before had each and every Astraean come together in a single attack force. The closest they had come previously was during the defense of the Harbor during Einar's initial attack, but even then, a large portion of the Astraeans were away from the Harbor at the time, scattered across the multiverse. Nor was there a fleet, an ADF, or anything remotely close to the scale of power and experience they now had at their disposal.

This was an entirely unprecedented effort being made, but it was an extremely organized and powerful one. Virtually every Astraean was preparing for war. Each Astraean, with millions of previous lives and knowledge of combat and warfare, across an immeasurable sea of species and cultures, were assembling and preparing to unleash their ancient and collective wisdom. A battle-hardened fleet, of various disciplines and configurations performed last-minute system checks. Newly created and advanced ribbon tools, weapons, devices, and ship enhancements, added to the list of things that helped even the odds between Einar's almost infinite head start on them. But regardless of any advances they had made, or technologies they wielded, it was still unknown how far they had bridged the indeterminate gap.

The bulk of the ADF had gone to U266 recently, but now, every Astraean was preparing for war. Engineers, Sentinels, and even vendors, secured sensitive areas of the Harbor, and packed up their wares. Doors were locked. Ribbon terminals were disconnected and powered down. Displays were shut off, and countless docking systems, kiosks and terminals were put offline. Physical displays and artifacts inside the library were stored and locked away. Library data, as well as a wealth of ribbon data found throughout all Harbor systems, was purged, erased, or transferred to various systems and ships across the ADF. It was a dark and morbid assumption being tended to, but it was necessary. Should the Astraeans be entirely or largely defeated during the upcoming fight, then they had every intention of leaving as few spoils of war for Einar as possible.

Due to the nature of having almost endless past lives with access to their knowledge and experiences, no Astraean was unqualified to meet Einar in battle, nor would anyone be left behind. Everyone wanted to contribute and take part. At Thyra's request, and with Elcyd's guidance, everyone would have a say in their fate.

Chapter XXV

Occupancy

Rigella felt the tips of her nerves tingle with short jolts of adrenaline. She was excited. She hadn't been able to keep to the shadows and fight a good fight of her own, in a very long time. Not until her fairly recent revelation that she didn't want to lead the ADF anymore did she realize how much she missed it. The intimacy of personal combat.

She approached the first terminal she came across, in hopes of quickly locating Akal and the others, but discovered it had been turned off along with the rest of the Harbor's systems. She scoffed and dismissed it with a wave before jogging to her old office to see who may still be left there. With each step, she suddenly became more and more aware of how foreign the Harbor felt to her. It had never been so quiet, empty and so cold. Never before had the entire Astraean culture prepared to abandon the Harbor with the possibility of never returning. It was a precedent that no one felt good about, though it was prudent. There were still so many unknowns about what Einar could or couldn't do with his ribbon manipulation systems, or if he did in fact now have a way of permanently killing an Astraean's entire existence. In turn, they had to assume the worst possibilities. The Astraeans had developed an unfortunate propensity for assuming the worst recently, and this was just another morbid expression of that. It had become common, and they had become numb to it.

Rigella's return trip to her old office didn't take long. She didn't expect Thyra to be there as she had just left her, but she assumed someone would still be there. She was wrong. With the encouragement from a bit of panic, she doubled back through the corridor, back down through the Harbor and out to the docks. She wanted to be in the fight, and wasn't worried about being involved, but she wanted to join the fight from the decks of Paige, like she had done before, alongside Akal, Carthal, and Heersan, like old times.

Her discomfort with the empty and eerie Harbor drifted to the back of her mind. It had been replaced with worry from missing her old crew's departure. Her quick walking evolved to jogging, which quickly became sprinting with a peculiar desperation. She didn't care about being alone, and she didn't care about fighting alone. But she also wanted to get back to the routine that she had missed for so long. She wanted to get back to feeling like she did before she thought she lost her friend. Before she lost herself. Before she lost control. The periphery became a superfluous blur as she ran. She just had to get to Paige. She remembered where she was moored from when

Lannya and Azli returned. She was almost there. *Last turn,* Rigella thought as she rounded a corner. A splash of relief shocked her system. There was Paige.

"Hey!" Rigella shouted up to the top deck. She cupped one hand around her mouth. Her voice was high and friendly. She slowed her run down as she reached the base of the gangplank, when Akal and Heersan stepped to the edge of the top deck rail. In Heersan's hands was a long length of rope. In Akal's, a moderate stack of small arms ribbon capacitors. Having been distracted from their departure preparations, they both looked down at Rigella. Their faces were surprised, yet preoccupied.

"Hey!" Rigella repeated, not as loudly. "Mind if I tag along?"

She posed her question lightly, but rhetorically, having no doubt she would be welcome. Carthal stepped to the rail. Lannya and Azli appeared at the rail right after.

Akal looked at Lannya and Azli only because they had entered his peripheral vision. He looked back to Lannya, trying to figure out how to answer her. Heersan looked to Akal, wanting no part in making the tense decision. In fact, everyone was waiting on Akal to answer. He was more or less the ringleader between himself and the original Trio, but having Azli and Lannya in attendance brought an entirely new set of awkward considerations, mostly because of Rigella's behavior recently.

Rigella's smile, which had grown wide from having reached Paige, and from seeing her old friends, quickly fell. Somewhere in a portion of her mind that she was trying to silence temporarily, Rigella was fairly confident that Lannya and Azli would be there. But, her mind succeeded at blocking out the possibility. She stared up at them, trying to signal silently to everyone that she knew she was the reason for this stagnant encounter.

Azli almost immediately turned away from the rail and disappeared out of Rigella's view. She didn't really hold any grudge against Rigella for how she attacked her on the docks, but Azli decided it would be best that she not play a role in the decision to have Rigella join them or not. Lannya, however, was still angry with Rigella. But, she also practiced some extreme willpower and bit her tongue. There were more important issues to worry about. She followed Azli's example and also went back to work out of Rigella's view. Left at the rail was Akal, Carthal, and Heersan.

Carthal and Heersan continued to shift their eyes between Akal and Rigella. They both wanted their old friend to join them, but they also felt uneasy with how she had reacted to Azli. It wasn't so much a disagreement with her actions, but a concern for Rigella's loss of control.

"Akal?" Rigella asked with a whimper. The real possibility that she would be turned away entered her mind.

"I don't have all the details about what happened while I was gone," Akal began. "But what I have heard doesn't sound like you."

Rigella whipped her head away and bit her lip, unable to hide from her recent behavior.

"We don't need that, Rigella. Not now."

"Akal," Rigella started. That's as far as she got for a moment. She had to look away and chuckle. "I can't believe I'm even able to address you right now," she said out loud to herself.

"I thought you were dead," Rigella began calmly. "We all thought you were dead, because of her."

Rigella pointed in the direction Azli had disappeared to as she continued.

"We thought thousands of others died with you on the roof, and we all thought she had a part in that. We don't even know where those other people are!"

Rigella forced her complaint to a halt as she sensed her anger building. She huffed forcefully to calm herself down and ended her speech.

"I'll apologize for losing control, but I'll never apologize for the hate I felt for her."

"Felt?" Akal prompted, wondering if she meant to refer to her hate for Azli in the past tense.

Rigella shrugged and flicked her hands gently. She couldn't adequately define how she felt about Azli right then or not. But she did know she didn't show up to fight with Azli again.

"I just want to fight Einar, and I want to fight beside my old friends again," Rigella concluded.

Akal rolled his head down and grabbed his face to massage it. He wasn't sure what to do. He still felt slightly uncomfortable from being so far removed from recent events, and frequently second-guessed himself on what to say or suggest. But, it was obvious Paige's crew was deferring to him on this decision. If anyone doubted his judgment due to his absence, it wasn't any of the people on Paige.

Akal swung his head around and lost himself for a moment in the web of ships in all directions and quickly came to a conclusion. *If we can look past Azli's past and have her on board*, he thought, *we can surely have Rigella*. He swung his head back to Rigella.

"Get up here," he lightly ordered.

Rigella's soul surged with relief. Her circulation raced with anticipation. She slapped the round metal top at the end of the gangplank's rail and swallowed up the ramp in huge, leaping strides. The sound of her rocketing up the gangplank caused Lannya and Azli to reappear from a storage hold near the tactical fighter bay. Lannya let a data tablet droop to her side while Azli put down the ribbon consistency calibrator she had been using. Similar to Carthal and Heersan only a minute earlier, they wore looks of confusion as to why Rigella had been allowed on board, but deferred silently to Akal for clarification.

"Look, everyone," Akal quickly began, wanting to snuff the fire before it flared up. "We don't have enough time to address our individual problems. We need to set those aside, and focus on our fight with Einar. Understood?"

Carthal and Heersan showed no signs of having an opinion on the matter. They were thankful they were relatively free of distraction and able to focus on the upcoming fight. Akal's comments were primarily for Lannya, Azli, and Rigella, who each reacted to Akal's statement with obliging silence or nods of acknowledgment Akal had no desire to press the issue or make a scene, he just wanted to make it clear what the priority was. After he felt they had reached an understanding, he pressed on.

"Ok, Rigella, since you're here, go ahead and check up on the fighter. Carthal and Heersan, if you two will make sure the capacitor systems are charged up, including the shields, I'll make sure the fabrication modules and pads are good to go. Lannya, would you and Azli do a diagnostic pass on the sails and propulsion interface?"

Lannya nodded and waved at Azli to join her at the main mast for their first check as everyone else darted off to tend to their respective work. Akal stepped towards a ribbon pad to begin his chore, but was briefly interrupted by the dense shockwave of a capital carrier spinning up and priming its engine. He quickly recovered from the surprising sound and lovingly slapped one of Paige's support columns. He was thankful to be onboard, and thankful Paige had once again been fully repaired.

***

The artificial atmosphere around the Harbor continued to weather additional, but harmless, eruptions of engine sounds from the rest of the fleet as it prepared to depart. One by one, each of Paige's crew finished their work and returned to the top deck, staring up in a lethargic awe at the fleet moving into a departure formation. Carthal and Heersan kept to themselves, as did Lannya and Azli. Rigella stood off by herself as a communication came across Paige's primary command display. Akal was already standing nearby and tapped a command to have the message broadcast across the entire ship. It was Elcyd.

"Hello, everyone," he began. His voice was weighted and deliberate. "We will be leaving soon, to chase our fate, to challenge our fate, to make what will quite possibly be our last decisions in our existence. We don't know what we will encounter, but I have no doubt that we have given ourselves every possible chance we could have imagined. There is nothing else we can do, friends. We are out of time. But this is not a dark time for me. We are only out of time for planning. Now it is time to act. I have no fear, and I will not waste however many seconds I may have left, giving any thought but hope and excitement, to the unknown. If by some chance there is something beautiful and triumphant waiting for us at the end of the final ribbon, or nothing at all, I welcome either outcome with a smile. We don't know what awaits, and until that result is realized, there will be no crater in my heart. I am going into battle proudly, with you, with each of you, my friends. My family. Where we end up is of no consequence. All that matters to me in this moment is that we are standing up for our destiny, together."

Elcyd's attention was beckoned just after reaching the end of his statements. A member of his crew signaled that the ADF fleet was ready for departure. They were checking in with Elcyd and the civilian ships he was responsible for. He turned back to his ship's camera.

"I will signal Thyra and the ADF that our civilian squadrons are ready once I receive the last few confirmations from those ships still preparing. After that, we will all make way for Earth."

Elcyd sat back and relaxed his voice.

"We all have our orders and plan of attack. Stay focused. Stay vigilant. Fight hard and well. Stay in communication with your captains and your ADF contacts if you make it planet-side. I'm sure I'll see many of you out there, but for those that I don't," he said, before pausing and smiling. "I'll meet you back here at the docks."

His final comment was accompanied with a wink.

It was half playful, and half serious. Even in the face of the unknowns awaiting them, and an unspoken doubt shared across the entire combined fleet, his hope was another example of everything Elcyd was. He was reassuring, hopeful, and positive. His video feed ended.

Akal turned around slowly, and dragged a thoughtful stare between each person on the ship.

"You know, standing here, on Paige, with all of you, is something I can't properly process. The last time I fought beside any of you, feels like a different reality, something different than a different reality. Even as an Astraean that has experienced millions of lives across hundreds of universes, this feels strange. But here I am. Next to me are my best and oldest friends, my wife, and my daughter. I never thought this would happen. I never thought this group would be together."

Akal reached for the command terminal and began tapping in the confirmation sequence to signal that Paige was ready.

"I'm like Elcyd. I don't even really care what happens from here on out," Akal resumed delicately. "I've got everything dearest to me right here, in one spot. Nothing could be better for me than this. I've already been stuck in a blurry limbo, not being able to live, not being able to die, so I don't see how anything could be worse than that. Between that and having you all here with me now, I can sail happily into any nightmare."

Lannya crossed the deck towards Akal with a slow grace, allowing herself time to cherish the sight of her husband after the words he had just shared. She held her hands and brought them up to her nose as if contemplating how to verbalize a thought. But as she slid up next to him, any thought of speaking gave way to a superior idea. She wrapped one arm around his waist, and cupped a cheek with the other, bringing his face close, and kissed him. She had never been more proud to be his wife. She had never been so thankful and grateful for him.

Her kiss was proof. Her lips were softer than cotton, but as hers enveloped his, Akal felt a density from her lips that felt much deeper and fuller than their deceptive size. She pressed in slowly, and as she did, Akal could feel the tremble from each muscle used to deliver her kiss. It was a blend and style of kiss that no soul would soon forget. It was a kiss of true love and regard, from a shared pool of passion. Lannya knew she had made the right decision. No words would have come close to what they had just said to each other, without uttering a syllable.

Chapter XXVI

Decoys

Within minutes of the bright and spiritual kiss coming to an end, the inspired mood of Paige's crew was tarnished by the ADF's massive battle fleet being ready to sail off to war, and to death. The civilian fleet, consisting of ships of all configurations from across the multiverse, and only slightly smaller in number, was also poised to strike. Unruly shadows from one set of ships draped over another, like a phantasmal master manipulating an enslaved marionette. Occasionally, the ships would burp bursts of propulsion spikes as they sat idle, prior to launch. The common thuds and elephantine sounds of the massive ships sang through the air in a prelude to combat. What were normally thought of as benign sounds and not given a second thought, became a dissonant drone to those that knew it would not end until the fight began.

Thyra had confirmed with all subordinates that the ADF was ready to make way for Earth, as Elcyd also communicated the civilian fleet's readiness. Once ship times across the combined fleet were synchronized, all ships plotted their course, confirmed their plan, and launched. They were off to Universe 9, and to Earth.

The journey to Earth was a familiar one, a common one, an old one, to almost every Astraean. It was as familiar a planet to them as possible. Countless eons had been spent across millions of different souls on Earth. The journey itself brought with it no concern or confusion. What did accompany this trip, however, was a sense of dread. Though there was an abundant supply of hope and a feeling of right being on their side, the majority of Astraeans still found themselves doubtful of their chances. The amount of time Einar had to plan and prepare for these last few hours was simply too large an advantage, they thought. Regardless, they would give Einar the absolute hardest time they could, until the last leaf fell. The leadership had done their job. They had given their people the tools, courage and fortitude to fight.

The initial departure from the Harbor was smooth, quiet, and predictable. The path through Harbor space, and past the beacons was ordinary. The bit of communications taking place between ships was sparse and routine. Occasionally there would be a confirmation of trajectories, or updates on estimated arrivals at certain points in their flight plan. Sonar and radar operatives monitoring areas in and out of the ribbons provided updates from time to time. There were no contacts, and the ribbon paths were clear. Ribbon integrity on all ribbons, was optimal.

But once the leading edge of the gargantuan, combined fleet passed by the Harbor's outermost beacon, chaos erupted.

The ADF led the combined fleet, with all civilian elements to the rear. Countless ships toward the front began taking massive damage from numerous flux charges set in the ribbon. Outside of the Harbor's reach, Einar's forces were able to drop them and obscure them from the ADF's sensors. As soon as they passed the last beacon, they sailed straight into them.

Thyra was flooded with damage reports and additional flux charge contacts, but she quickly took action.

"ADF and civilian element," Thyra began calmly. "Slow to flow factor five. ADF, make a path for the ribbon sweepers and let them take the lead. Once we've regained control of the ribbon paths, we'll resume our original speed."

A large display near Thyra with thousands of small symbols representing the fleet began lighting up as their captains confirmed Thyra's orders. Any that didn't light up were followed up with by subordinates.

As instructed, the civilian element slowed, in coordination with the ADF slowing down, except for the ADF's ribbon sweepers. The fleet shifted and slid around to allow them to rapidly reach the front of the fleet at which point the sweepers deployed an extended hull made of ribbon energy, far out in front of them. These hundreds of sweepers, spread throughout the various ribbons the fleet was traveling in, shoved the flux charges out into regular space, rendering them harmless, or exploded them far out in front of the extended ribbon hulls. The fleet was safe again, for now.

"Commander," one of Thyra's lieutenant's beckoned. "We have severe damage to many of the ships from the original leading wave, but no ship losses."

"Understood, thank you," she acknowledged before addressing the fleet again.

"Those ships that have sustained damage, fall to the rear of the ADF formation and begin repairs," she instructed. "All ships, resume original course and speed."

With the sweepers leading the way, the Astraeans were able to quickly resume their course with only a negligible delay. The sweepers were a new Astraean design and recently added to the ADF fleet, and must have been unknown to Einar. They continued to expel the flux charges from the ribbon without issue.

The fleet continued to make their way well into deep multispace without issue, though the number of flux charges in their path ahead of them remained steady. Thyra opened up a channel to Elcyd's ship. The channel opened quickly, but Thyra made an extra request of her communications officer.

"Patch Paige in also, I want to know what they think," she ordered professionally.

The communications officer swiped through a few screens on the display and tapped the symbol representing Paige.

"I have Thyra standing by," the officer advised to Paige's crew. They quickly huddled around the screen as Thyra began speaking with Elcyd.

"I think we must assume that Einar is monitoring us, and the status of these flux charges, as well as our position," she proposed. "Elcyd? Rigella? Thoughts?"

Elcyd tended to an itch under his lips as he considered how he felt about it. On Paige's display, the crew could be seen turning to Rigella to see what she had to say. Elcyd spoke up first.

"As long as we're not taking damage or casualties, I think we should maintain course."

Rigella, not being in a hurry to step on toes or assume the role she had just given up, waited until Elcyd finished.

"I agree with Elcyd. Regardless of their motive, if they're going to let us advance without challenge or casualties, for however long, I think we should take advantage of that as long as we can. Of course," Rigella added, "we should always be cognizant of a possible trap."

"Ok, thank you both," Thyra offered sincerely. "I was of the same mind, but wanted to see how you felt. Thyra out."

The transmission ended. Rigella continued to stare at the terminal, exploring possibilities on how a potential trap may present itself. Without realizing she was, Lannya added to Rigella's internal dialogue as she began to speak.

"I wouldn't be surprised at all by a trap," she said. "He likes surprises too much. He likes to trick, and overwhelm. He likes to deceive and give people the illusion of having options. I don't like this."

Referring to the current ease of their travels, Carthal agreed with Lannya.

"Yeah," she's right, Carthal added. "I'm sure he's anticipated this."

"I don't think it's a secret that he's anticipated this," Akal snipped, only in an effort to get to a strategy.

"The question is, how do we give ourselves the best chance possible when there's no element of surprise?"

Azli, who had been mostly keeping to herself since she and her mother returned, cleared her throat and asked a question of the crew.

"What about Thyra's imaging system, or whatever it is?"

Heersan prodded dryly for elaboration.

"What about it?"

"Hasn't she been working on extending that technology? What if the fleet suddenly tripled or quadrupled? And approached from various directions?"

Azli proposed her idea with confidence. Lannya knew where she was headed.

"We could swarm the approach to Earth with waves of phantom ships! We could divide his defenses and confuse them!"

"If he wants to play games," Azli concluded. "Let's give him a game."

Akal was already tapping a command to establish a new connection with Thyra's ship. His fingers flew as his grin widened. Thyra popped up on Paige's display. She was focused on a ribbon engineer's display, but acknowledged the incoming transmission.

"Hey Akal," she said quickly.

Akal wanted to waste no time and launched right into their idea.

"Thyra, how far along have you and Siguren gotten with the imaging system?"

She was immediately distracted from the ribbon engineer's display and began to turn slowly towards her command terminal's camera. Her eyes darted back and forth as she extrapolated possibilities from Akal's question. Before she replied, he asked another.

"Is it possible to use it this far out in the ribbons?"

She looked directly at the camera before attempting to confirm.

"Decoys?"

Akal's grin turned into a smile, revealing crisp teeth relishing in the ingenuity.

"That might work!" Thyra added excitedly. "We're far too exposed and that would help. Let me talk with Siguren. If we can come up with something, I'll announce an update soon."

"Sounds good," Akal obliged. Once the channel had closed, Akal spun around to Azli. He was still smiling.

Aboard Thyra's ship, she reached over and opened a channel with a different ship, before reaching out to Siguren. Her display lit up as it was accepted.

"COMMANDERTHYRA SO GOOD TO SEE, what can I do for?" Hergie wondered helpfully.

"Hello, Hergie! If we were to get you access to the imaging system Siguren and I have been working on, how quickly could you import the schematics and designs for all ADF vessels?"

Hergie stared at the camera on his ship's command terminal in silence. While no distinguishable expression could be seen on his face, Thyra assumed he was either confused, or thinking about her question.

"I DO NOT KNOWWHY this is need.What were YOU HOPING..."

Hergie stopped mid-sentence when the reason

struck him.

"OH ISEEWHAT HAVE planned.I could take care of THIS IN A FEW MINUTES ONLY."

"Perfect!" Thyra shouted. "Stand by. I'll have Siguren contact you shortly."

"AFFIRMASTOOD," Hergie oddly confirmed.

Thyra closed the channel and finally opened up a channel to Siguren's ship.

"Well, hello there, Commander!" Siguren affectionately opened, along with a wink.

Thyra's mind was too busy to allow her to register a cute response. She continued right on with business.

"Hey. Do you think we could adapt our ribbon chaffs to interface with our imaging system?"

Siguren's playful dimples fell to a serious face as he considered her question. Chaffs were a defensive mechanism deployed during a battle to throw off the targeting systems of any ribbon weapons that were pursuing an Astraean ship. The group's thinking was that they could be altered in a number of ways, to include possibly representing realistic representations of ADF ships. Siguren looked away as he considered Thyra's question, and then turned back to the video feed.

"You're wanting to turn the chaffs into decoys!" He inferred. A grin returned, but this time, from his excitement at the idea.

"Precisely," Thyra confirmed quickly.

"I don't see why not. The biggest challenge would be maintaining the energy needed to sustain such a huge amount of visual data per ship image, but if they're going to be within the ribbon the whole time, that shouldn't technically be an issue."

"Great! Can you get started on that right away? I've already spoken with Hergie. He's preparing to send you ship designs and schematic information to put into the imaging system. We're going to need a few different decoy copies of the entire fleet. When they're ready, we'll send them ahead of us, and from a few other locations to confuse Einar on exactly what is approaching, and how many."

"We'll make it happen!" Siguren complied.

Thyra responded with a quick kiss to her fingertips and then placed them on the camera on her end. She closed the channel with Siguren and opened one with Elcyd once more. She also connected feeds to the Secondary Commanders' ships.

"Everyone, Siguren and Hergie are working on a plan to alter our fleet's chaff systems so that we can deploy them across a wide spectrum of approaches to Earth. Instead of serving as chaffs, they will be altered to interface with our imaging system and create fleets of ADF ghosts that we hope will distract and confuse Einar's forces."

The faces of all three recipients of Thyra's video lit up with pleased excitement.

"Stand by for more details and information on how they will be deployed."

After closing the channel, Thyra wanted to start setting the stage for their deception. She addressed a nearby fighter drone officer.

"They're probably monitoring us," she whispered devilishly. "Send out a few dozen unmanned drones to attack some of those charges in front of the sweepers, and slow the combined fleet by half again. Let's play along for a bit longer."

"Yes, Commander."

With a few taps on a display, the drone officer opened the fighter bay and sent two dozen drones ahead to overtake the sweepers and begin attacking the flux charges. They were able to destroy a few, but the defensive measures on the charges quickly returned fire and destroyed the drones.

"Ok, good," Thyra said with a nod. "They'll think we're still trying to figure out how to overcome these charges."

The next few minutes consisted of similar drama and deception. A series of fake transmissions, erroneous coordinates, and displays of futile attempts to bypass the charges added to a building facade of difficulty. Thyra was just buying time for Hergie and Siguren.

"Make sure to include messages referencing other areas of the multiverse and possible approaches," she directed to her communications officers. "And mention something about primary, secondary, tertiary fleets, and cloaking procedures. When these fake fleets show up out of nowhere, we want them to think they've been hidden somehow."

"Right away Commander," her communications team responded. She had another idea, and contacted Siguren again.

"Siguren, we want to make sure Einar thinks these are all different fleet segments. Can you alter the appearance of the decoys a bit so that everything isn't an exact duplicate of us? Different heat signatures, crew levels, hull colors, armaments, and so on?"

"Yeah, I think we can do that," Siguren replied quickly, obviously busy with his work. "We should have the first batch available for deployment in a few minutes. Stand by."

"Understood."

While Siguren and Hergie finished up their work, Thyra took the opportunity to bring the fleet up to speed.

"Everyone, this is Thyra. In just a few minutes, we will be implementing our plan to deploy a massive amount of decoys along alternate paths to Earth. We are hoping this will adequately disrupt and confuse whatever Einarian forces are undoubtedly waiting to intercept us. Once we deploy these decoys, we will make every opportunity to monitor them and any reaction to them. As long as there seems to be a reasonable success in confusing any Einarian forces, we will maintain course, resume maximum flow factor, and invade Earth as rapidly as possible with hopes of finding Einar's ribbon devices. Stand by for decoy deployment."

While waiting for an update from Hergie and Siguren, Thyra ordered the combined fleet to do a final systems check, to include a check on offensive and defensive systems. The fleet diagram on her nearby display lit up quickly as ships checked in. All ships were in order. Finally, Siguren's voice piped up.

"Ok, Thyra. I believe we're all set here. We have two batches of modified chaffs ready, and can have a few more ready in just a few minutes. Did you want to wait until those are ready, too?"

"No," she said, not concerned with having to wait.

"It would actually be good if we staggered them anyway. I think it would appear more realistic that way."

"Mmm, right," Siguren softly agreed.

"When we deploy these chaffs," Thyra wondered, "will he be able to see them traveling to where we want the decoys to appear?"

Hergie had the answer to that question.

"Negative, Thyra. Initial SIZE OF CHAFFTOO SMALL TO TRACK.will not show up on their systems UNTIL CHAFFTAKES SHAPE OFDECOY."

"Outstanding," Thyra replied, to both Hergie and Siguren. "This might just work."

"When you're ready, Commander," Siguren acknowledged respectfully.

"Ok, then," she replied with a quick huff of nerves. "I've notified the fleet, so everyone should be prepared."

She reviewed the final strategy by bringing up a projection of the area surrounding the 9th Universe.

"Deploy the first set of decoys, directly across from us, on the opposite side of U9. A minute later, deploy the second set at 90 degrees, either side. When the next set is available, deploy it opposite the second set. Continue in a similar pattern, halving the angle, and then across from the other, until about four or five decoy sets have been deployed. If we need to reassess whether or not the decoys are still needed, or if we need more, we'll decide that, then."

"Understood," Siguren complied as he began to tap and program deployment instructions.

"Fleet, this is Thyra," she announced to all ships. "The first set of decoy ships is about to be deployed." She closed the fleet-wide communications and returned to Siguren, only.

"Go ahead and deploy the first set. You have control. I'm opening your comm to the fleet."

"Understood," Siguren bellowed professionally. "Deploying first set of decoys on my mark. 5. 4. 3. 2. 1. Mark."

At the end of the countdown, an explosion of bright flashes could be seen erupting from the bow of most of the ADF ships. The brilliant balls of energy quickly caught a current within the ribbons and disappeared at an immeasurable speed into the ribbons ahead of them. The first set of decoys were on their way.

"First decoy set, deployed," Siguren finalized. "Time until detonation: 42 seconds." Though the chaffs were eventually going to change into ship decoys, *detonation* was still an accurate term. When they reached their designated spot in the ribbons, they would explode, and their energy would be translated by the imaging system into decoys.

"Fleet, synchronize secondary clocks to 34 seconds on 5. 4. 3. 2. 1. Set," commanded Thyra. "When the chaffs detonate, resume maximum flow factor, and resume course for Earth."

She swapped communications channels once more, and spoke only to her direct subordinates, as well as Hergie, Siguren, and Elcyd.

"Well done, everyone, well done. Deploy the additional decoy sets at our previously agreed intervals."

***

During the time spent discussing, configuring

and deploying the initial decoy set, the combined fleet traversed the majority of the distance between the Harbor and U9. Additional faked attempts were made to clear the flux charges, beyond the sweepers brushing most out of the way in the hopes of continuing to give anyone monitoring them the idea that they were still having problems.

All sorts of odd behavior for Einar's benefit were presented. Some ships would eject themselves out of the ribbons just to rejoin haphazardly. Other ships would branch off and take detours as if trying to plot a new course to Earth, in hopes of avoiding the flux charges. A whole host of similar behavior almost gave the entire Astraean culture cause to laugh at their tricks, but the gravity of the situation didn't allow it.

The fleet pressed on, growing ever closer, and the last 34 seconds before the detonation of the first decoy set came and went. As the seconds ticked down, Thyra shot out an order to her radar and sonar specialists.

"Ok. Identify all contacts."

The radar and sonar techs flinched as their previously empty displays flashed with text, colors and alerts. They immediately began flying through tapped commands, identifying the newly appearing contacts as friendlies. The specifications of the decoys' classes, weapons, shields, and crew began scrolling rapidly down on display's margin. It was too distracting. A tech tapped and slid it out of the way.

"It looks like a successful detonation, Commander!" Another tech exclaimed innocently. "I'm scanning for hull resistance, mass, temperature, anything that might give them away as decoys, and I'm getting good readings.

They look good."

A minute since the first set's detonation and the second set's deployment came and went. Siguren came over Thyra's open communication channel.

"Second decoy set detonating in 5. 4. 3. 2. 1. Mark."

"Contacts?" Thyra requested.

"One moment, Commander. Registering and organizing," a technician replied. Again, the radar and sonar technician displays were flooded with info.

"Identifying, Commander."

Thyra stood by patiently, but intently.

"Ok, yes Commander. This set looks good, too!" He turned to look at Thyra as he reported the status of the second set of decoys, but almost immediately whipped his head back. Something new was alerting on his display.

It was the Einarians. Almost immediately after the detonation of the second set of decoys, a massive swarm of Einarian ships struck out from Earth and began making their way to decoy set two.

"Ok, it looks like they're biting!" Thyra shouted. She sat down in her chair, and tapped a display to issue a General Quarters command. Whether it was in space, or after reaching earth, or both, combat was imminent.

"Siguren, keep deploying additional decoy sets as we discussed. However many you can get out before we reach Earth."

"Will do!" He shouted back quickly.

"How long until the Einarians reach decoy set 2?" She asked of her technicians. The tech that had announced the Einarian contacts tapped through a quick calculation.

"At their present speed? 87 seconds, Commander."

"Ok, good. We'll have another decoy set out by then. Maintain course and heading."

Thyra, her crew, and the entire ADF went quiet. Every eye was on a display, their weapon, their fighter, or their superior. Consoles, rooms, fighter cabins, and control rooms glowed in the slowly oscillating red of general quarters. Though they were the ones charging headlong into war, a scale of engagement never seen before by the Astraeans was charging back at them. As they grew closer to Earth, the inevitability of the final struggle against Einar made its grand entrance. The thin rope supporting the last bit of safety, of being removed from the conflict, was cut.

"Commander, the third chaff set has detonated. The decoys are in place and are en route to Earth as well," a technician announced.

"Very well," Thyra acknowledged. She tapped over to her channel with Siguren.

"When the Einarians reach decoy set two, how long before find out they're fake?" Thyra wondered.

Siguren hesitated.

"Ehh, it depends on their tactics and what their sensors are set up for, I guess. The decoys don't have any real mass, so if an Einarian ship collides with one, that would give it away. They would just fly right through. But, the decoys are programmed to avoid collisions, so I don't know how long before that might happen. They're emitting fake data of all kinds, so as far as physics go, they should appear to be legitimate. The only other thing that might tip them off is the strength of the decoy weapons. They're not lethal at all. They only have enough power to present themselves visually, so that might just confuse the Einarians. I don't know, Thyra. I don't know how long it will take for them to figure it out."

"Ok, I understand," Thyra acknowledged. Her tone was approving and grateful. He and Hergie had done great work, and she wasn't disappointed in any way. "Even when they do figure out they're decoys, it will take them some time to figure out which set is real!"

"Exactly," Siguren affirmed.

"We're just hoping to buy some time and open a window to get to Earth. Ok," Thyra began to wrap up. "The Einarians are about to engage decoy set 2."

For a moment, Thyra and the rest of the ADF felt safe in the quiet red glow. Battle hadn't come to them just yet. The darkest dip between the repetitive red pulses felt the best. A comforting swaddling that whispered a lullaby lie of safety. But that moment extended to another, and then another. It was starting to feel too easy. They breached the ninth universe's outer barrier. Only two more intersections, and then it would be straight on to the Milky Way. The trip was smooth. They were advancing without disruption. The Einarians were tied up with the decoys. The deception was working.

Paige, in the rear half of the combined fleet, was sailing along with the other segments of the civilian fleet. Like everyone else, her crew was waiting, and sailing anxiously, desperate for the fight to begin. The icy glow of the streaming ribbons clashed like opposing elements against the red of general quarters. The color conflict shined through windows across the fleet, and reflected off the faces of Paige's crew as everyone awaited the title bout.

With no initial indication as to why, the leading radar technician suddenly screamed out.

"Commander! The Einarian force engaging the decoys has completely disappeared from my radar. I have zero enemy contacts."

Thyra's breathing sped up dramatically. She turned her head slowly to the radar tech, with a depressed shock. She had no idea what was coming. Her communications channels started to crack and sizzle.

"We're getting some odd readings back here."

It was Elcyd. The civilian fleet was starting to register anomalies in the space outside the ribbons near the rear.

"Thyra?" Akal asked through his own transmission, hoping for clarification on what he had heard Elcyd say.

It was too late.

With a series of explosions, the power of which could not easily be quantified, portions of all ribbons being used by the Astraeans on their way to earth, were obliterated. The segments that were destroyed were just behind the last few ships of the civilian section, confining the fleet to their current ribbons. Their only other choice was to leave the ribbons and enter the local space of U9, which would have to be traveled at less than the slowest ribbon speeds. That wasn't an option.

After the Astraeans were cut off from the rest of the surrounding ribbon system, and had their course options robbed from them, the anomalies previously identified began to reveal themselves. At the rate of dozens a second, ships from the Einarian fleet began to spring up from the darkness. The Einarian fleet had countered the Astraean deception with their own duplicity. The Astraean decoys had been fighting Einarian decoys all along.

The real battle had now begun. The combined Astraean fleet had no legitimate choice but to hold its course to Earth, as orders flew across the fleet to reconfigure their formation to address the threat to the rear.

The threat was more than a threat. It was a menacing wall of power and intimidation. Ships of the Einarian fleet littered the ribbons, but also, the space outside the ribbons. Somehow, the Einarians had harnessed the ability to have fully independent propulsion systems that could travel at ribbon flow speeds, but did not require connection to the ribbons to do so. The Astraeans were being pursued from the rear at all heights and angles. From inside and outside the ribbons, the Einarians were beginning to wrap their forces around the rear of the Astraean ships.

As long as they remained inside the ribbons, combined with the power and capabilities of their ships, the Astraeans were relatively safe. Their defensive and shield systems were able to withstand the assault from the Einarians. With a constant connection to the ribbons, the Astraeans could sustain the relentless storm of attacks from the Einarians, from all manners of weapons. But they would eventually need to exit the ribbon. Whether to make their landing on Earth, or to attempt an escape, the relative safety of the ribbons would not last.

Thyra's quick thinking to reconfigure the fleet also aided their safety. She ordered the largest and most defensively capable ships to the rear, as an added precaution to protect the smaller ships. Beyond that, Thyra and the rest of the Astraean leadership scrambled for thoughts on how to act next, but before the next, coherent plan could be made, a fresh wave of contacts flooded radar displays across the ADF.

"Commander," a technician announced with surprising calm. "We're registering a new, massive array of contacts." His display scrolled rapidly with another list of Einarian ship data.

"Where?" Thyra shouted angrily.

"Directly ahead, Commander," he replied darkly. His answer dripped with a morbid understanding. The Einarians had begun their assault from the rear, and were awaiting the Astraeans to the front. Their plan was obvious. They were going to encompass, contain, and destroy the Astraeans.

From the moment the Astraeans deployed their first set of decoys, Thyra's mind raced along, as fast it could, just on the edge of catastrophe. Much like Rigella would have done, Thyra constantly referenced her knowledge and experience, and applied that to countless hypothetical scenarios, feverishly evaluating the best course of action. This point in the encounter was no different. She suddenly remembered a conversation she'd had with Mamdod. While everyone was huddled over the Grand Table, hypothesizing, and researching, Mamdod had shared some of his ribbon wisdom that she now might be able to apply.

The Astraean ships shook from the rear Einarian assault, just enough to measurably wear on the Astraeans nerves and morale. Accompanying the shaking and dull thuds from the absorbed impacts were the hollow pounds and pops, allowing no Astraean soul a moment of peace.

But even so, Thyra's mind was clear as she formulated her idea.

She raced over to her massive command display, after a few unsteady stumbles, and grabbed onto its frame to stand steady. Letting go of the stand for a moment, and with a rhythmic rap of knuckle taps, she shot open a comm channel with Elcyd and the Engineering team.

"Elcyd! Is there a way you can swap the fleet with our second decoy set?"

"What?" His question was glazed partially in confusion, and partly with trouble hearing her.

The engineers leaned in towards their terminal to better hear the conversation.

"Mamdod mentioned something to me about the possibility of items in a ribbon jumping great distances automatically, or having two things swap places. Do any of you know anything about that? Can we do that?"

Elcyd flinched and instinctively ducked from the increasingly loud and violent blasts pummeling his ship. One of the engineers responded first, occasionally startled and interrupted by his own ship being bombarded.

"I...," he attempted. A sharp, ripping sound came from just outside the hull, forcing him to cut himself off. "I've never heard of that," he rushed out, not knowing when he'd be interrupted again. "Even if it were possible, you can't dedicate the ribbons to something like that while you're inside them. It would be disastrous. If you were to somehow force a ribbon to do that, the surrounding stream we're traveling in would be siphoned into the new action. It would be like ripping the fleet out of time and space temporarily."

"If we had the fleet exit the ribbons into local space," another engineer added, "we might be able to figure it out."

"Local space isn't an option with the amount of Einarians out there," Thyra shot back. "We need an idea, now!"

"Would it be possible for a secondary ribbon?" Elcyd wondered. Thyra's face twisted, having no idea such a concept or theory existed.

"A secondary ribbon?" She repeated, hoping for elaboration.

"Yeah," Elcyd returned quickly. "A ribbon within the ribbons. It wouldn't need to be as substantial as the natural ribbons. Only separate. Something to provide a path for the swap between our fleet and the second decoy set.

"One second!" The lead engineer shouted back. He could be seen tapping calculations into a display off to his side. His ship's feed shook and rocked, but he flew through the calculations as quickly as he could.

"I think it might be possible! If we use the artificial ribbon emitters from all ships of the combined fleet, I think we might be able to generate an adequate ribbon of a different energy signature, and then use it to slingshot us to the spot the decoys are at, and have them, sent here! As long as we can have our ships maintain a connection between the natural and artificial ribbons so the ribbons know where we want to end up, we should be ok!"

Thyra hollered into her command terminal to compensate for the sound from the Einarian barrage which was plaguing the entire Astraean fleet.

370 | *Fates of Astraeus*

"Can you make the swap seamless? Can we make the Einarians think they're still pursuing our real fleet after the swap?"

"Uhhh," the lead engineer grunted, as he turned away to do a different calculation. "We can swap the data attributed to us and to the decoys easy enough, but I don't know if the flashes from initiating the secondary ribbon will give us away or not. If we can contain the secondary ribbon completely within the primary ribbons, I think we can pull it off."

Thyra shouted back quickly in hopes of maintaining some focus for her crew, amidst the deafening chaos.

"Well, seamless or not, make the swap happen! Our current course is compromised! Let me know the second you're ready to activate the secondary ribbon. Roughly how long until it's ready?"

The engineers swung down out of view as their ships were struck by another volley, but came quickly back into frame.

"It should only take a few minutes, Commander. We need to confirm the figures."

"Understood. Get to it!"

The engineers shot out of view to work through the math needed to program the individual ribbon emitters properly. Thyra then had a final request for Elcyd. She swiped his channel onto her primary display.

"Elcyd, announce our plan to the entire fleet and then check in with the engineers. If the swap is successful, we'll end up on the opposite side of the Milky Way, away from the Einarians. And then we'll make a sprint for Earth."

"Will do!" He complied with a belting grimace.

"I'll be watching our defenses until the swap. Let me know if you need anything from me."

Elcyd nodded quickly and closed the channel.

Chapter XXVII

A Plunger Hunt

The Astraean fleet passed through the last intersection on their current path before reaching the Milky Way. There were only seconds left before they reached the new group of Einarians in front of them, and Thyra was starting to get nervous. She reached for her terminal to check with the engineers, but before she could input any commands, Elcyd's voice shout out through the fleet.

"Everyone, this is Elcyd. We're going to try something. In a few seconds, we're going to initiate a series of secondary ribbons that will allow us to swap places with decoy set two, getting us out of this trap, and clearing what will be our new approach to Earth. We will have the fleet's course and heading changed automatically. Stand by!"

Elcyd left his fleet-wide communications channel open as he addressed Thyra personally.

"Thyra! The engineers are ready!"

"Ok! Now!" She ordered adamantly.

The lead engineer spoke up.

"Yes, Commander! Ok. All fleet-wide engineering teams, activate your individual ship's ribbon emitters with the data we provided on my mark. 5. 4. 3. 2. 1. Mark!"

Blinding blazes of bright lightning radiated through every window across the Astraean fleet. Sensors across most ships momentarily reported errors from having lost their discernible position. Something was happening, but it took a moment for anyone to register what, and if their attempts were successful.

Only a few seconds after the ribbon emitter flashes had begun, they stopped. Thyra and the rest of the fleet quickly scanned displays and terminals for fleet status, and for individual ship damage and anomalies. Like the rest of the fleet, Thyra took a quiet second to find some relieved joy in the possibility of their experiment working. She felt her face start to smile in amazement. She whispered to her crew.

"Report our position and all contacts."

The slightly stunned crew reset their sensors and tapped through displays.

"Commander! We have successfully swapped locations with decoy set two! The Einarians have not changed course to pursue us. No immediate, local hostile contacts!"

The maneuver was successful, but it was only one step in an incredibly daunting plan. Thyra let her smile form completely, before quickly letting it recede. She shouted to her crew and the rest of the fleet.

"Go, go, go!"

The sprint was on. The Astraeans wanted to take advantage of every second they had made for themselves and get to Earth with as little conflict as possible. After the swap with the decoys, the Astraean fleet emerged just outside the second quadrant of the Milky Way. They quickly passed through the outer arm, the Perseus arm, and then entered the Orion Spur. Earth's solar system was on the horizon. Thyra started to outline her instructions.

"Fleet, I want the civilian element to prepare to arrive at Earth and for an immediate ground invasion. Our absolute, top priority is to find Einar's systems and destroy them. The ADF and I will accompany you until we reach Earth, but continue on and re-engage the Einarians to give you as much time planet-side as possible. Their surprise advantage has been nullified. Elcyd will have complete and final authority over the civilian fleet's actions. Keep your chain of command in the loop, and Elcyd will keep me updated. Good luck."

Elcyd flew through a series of commands on his ship, to instruct the others of their final approach, and then reached out to Paige.

"Akal?" He started, with a tense calm.

"Yes! Elcyd!" He almost immediately replied.

"Will you and your crew take the lead on the ground efforts once we make our landing? Yours and Lannya's recent lives on Earth will benefit us greatly."

"Sure, of course," Akal quickly obliged, looking up and around to Lannya and the others.

"Ok," Elcyd confirmed. "I'll be sending instructions for our final approach in a moment and will advise everyone on your role."

"Understood," Akal replied before closing the channel. He spun around and stared a thousand words into Lannya's eyes.

"Ready to pay the Habitats a visit?" He asked her.

Lannya grinded her teeth and nodded.

"Which Habitat?" Heersan asked, slightly annoyed from the lack of details. "Where in the Habitats?"

Rigella pointed out another valid concern.

"What are we looking for? And how do we know it's even inside a Habitat?"

Akal huffed with frustration as he steered Paige into position to be one of the lead landing ships.

"Guys, we don't have those specifics. We've never had them. We're going to have to do some digging."

"Wait! Wait!" Azli shouted. She flung her arms out as she pieced together bits and slivers of memories that had floated to the top of her mind. Her eyes danced and darted as she processed her thoughts.

"I remember him saying..."

Thyra licked her lips as she almost had it.

"No, I remember him laughing... He was laughing with someone... and talking about having to move the relays, and when he did, he put them on the roofs. I had no idea what he was talking about at the time. He was laughing that no one knew they were there because the atmosphere was toxic!"

"That's it!" Akal shouted. "Carthal, tell Elcyd that we think Einar's system is made up of devices on the Habitat roofs. Have him get teams to each Habitat. We'll head for NAM2. And ask him to update Thyra."

Lannya ran over to one of Paige's tactical terminals, quickly followed by Akal, and tapped in a command to bring up a projection of Earth.

"Ok, everyone!" She began. "Here are the current Habitat locations. This network of Einar's, as Azli suggests, must be made up of relays that connect to each other, one each per Habitat roof, I guess. We need to get down there and knock them out."

Azli was confused over a critical piece of their plan.

"How are we going to combat the atmosphere?" She asked in a panic. "Which form should we use?"

"Oh, we've got something for that," Carthal replied enigmatically.

Rigella offered additional conjecture on how Einar's relays might work.

"He must be generating some kind of artificial ribbon network, similar to what we have at the Harbor. The relays probably speed up the energy more and more at each point, so that it can be powerful enough by the end of the loop to process whatever instruction he wants to carry out."

The crew was silent as Jupiter rapidly grew in size on the horizon, before quickly shrinking behind them. Their arrival at Earth was imminent.

"Ok, everyone," Elcyd boomed over the civilian communication channels. "I'm launching some local atmosphere stabilization pods at each of the Habitat sites. We all know what to do, so let's get down there and destroy these things. Talk with you soon, and be safe!"

The seconds ticked down on Paige's arrival counter. Just before the civilian fleet ejected itself safely from the ribbons into local Earth space, Azli caught a glimpse of Rigella. Rigella slowly spun her head and met her with a warrior's grin. It was a grin of dark pleasure and simultaneous innocence. At that moment, Rigella felt no animosity or hate for Azli. Azli had just helped them with a key piece of information on the location of the relays, and on top of that, they were riding into battle. Together.

The time had come. With a thunderous boom inside the ribbon, the civilian fleet shot out of it, and into the vacuum of regular space. Almost immediately, the hundreds of ships were harmlessly enveloped in gargantuan flames as they sliced into Earth's atmosphere. The Astraeans had arrived.

Each Astraean ship suffered no damage as they ripped through the skies, and all ship sensors showed completely clear radar. There were no hostile contacts. The impressive site of the civilian fleet began to branch out to make their way to their assigned Habitat locations. Paige led the group headed for NAM2.

The ships made their final push through the atmosphere which allowed Paige's crew to begin making out features surrounding NAM2's immediate vicinity. Lannya and Akal leaned over the rail as Lannya placed her hand over the top of Akal's. They stared down through the occasional breaks in the weather, at the features they knew well and had seen over the course of many human lifetimes. But, they never knew they existed in their last regular lives before becoming Astraeans. Einar had orchestrated it all, and denied so many things, to so many.

"Well, what's the plan boss?" Rigella asked of Akal, playfully, as she had so many times before. Akal nodded at her in acknowledgment of needing to communicate their team's plan. He opened up a comm a channel.

"Alright, NAM2 team," Akal began. "Let's get our support ships to assume an escort posture and protect our attack ships in an approach straight for the roof. Let's get in, get out, and then help out the other teams."

The NAM2 group complied quickly and accurately. Though the civilian fleet weren't official ADF personnel, Astraeans were Astraeans, and had a wealth of militaristic and combat training in countless forms, across countless cultures. Discipline, coordination, and execution were not a problem.

The descent towards the roof was quick and uneventful. There were no interruptions. The crews were geared up, prepared, coordinated, and motivated. The attack ships slung open their doors, hatches, ramps, and gates. The Astraeans that would be taking part in the roof attack stood by, ready for the command.

They waited too long. In the haze of the congested skies, the Astraeans had failed to see a building energy, or anything else on the roof.

When the NAM2 group couldn't practically get any closer, a rounded square of energy shot out from the edges of the NAM2 Habitat roof. Depending on the position of the ships, some ships were immediately destroyed, or severely damaged, with most ships escaping with minimal or no damage. These attack pulses came once every half second, rendering the air space surrounding the Habitat virtually worthless from a safety and strategic point of view. Akal shouted at the NAM2 team.

"Land! All NAM2 ships, land at the base of the

Habitat, at its entrance. We'll go in through the front and work our way up."

The number of damaged ships was fairly small, but the ones that had been hit the hardest contributed to the already-polluted area, and made the scene tactically unusable. Between the smoke and massive flames being whipped and expanded by the wind, visibility was virtually null. One of the largest ships that had been hit belched and flung large, flaming chunks of its outer hull across the whole area. As instructed, after the blast from the roof, Paige and the rest of the NAM2 group commenced a controlled dive and dropped out of the sky. Akal and the rest of the crew slipped their feet into the scooped recesses on the top deck to allow for the almost vertical dive Paige was in. Grabbing on to nearby supports and posts, they all looked back up to make sure none of the raining debris was following them down.

As they raced downward, inches from and parallel to the outer Habitat wall, Carthal barked an astute question to anyone that cared to answer.

"How do we know it's any safer down there?"

Through the scraping wind and dusty air, most turned and squinted at Akal, displaying expressions of variations on Carthal's concern. He raised his eyebrows slowly, trying to come up with an answer.

"We don't!" Akal shouted back. There was no playfulness or amusement in Akal's response. They were doing something each of them had done countless times. Adapting. Winging it.

Paige's altitude alert sounded. Without even looking at the alert to confirm the numbers, Akal waited two seconds and then shouted a command at her. He knew his boat.

"Paige, level off! Emergency stop! Hold on everyone!"

As instructed, Paige quickly, but smoothly leveled out. The drastic shift caused Paige's crew to experience a severe amount of G-forces, but they were the maximum possible without causing injury to their human forms. Many ships, including Paige, deafened the immediate area by the sounds of their hulls fighting against the friction of their rapid descent and landings. By the time Paige had reached a 45-degree angle in relation to the ground, she had fired her ribbon thrusters which formed a cushion with their combined puffs of ribbon energy.

Paige had landed safely. Akal stretched his face and forced a few deep breaths to recover from the extreme G-forces they had experienced. He reached up to check the display and looked out to the rest of the crew. They, too, were beginning to peel themselves off the deck and step out of the deck recesses.

"Is everyone ok?" He asked.

Some answered his question with a few mumbles, and others answered with a less than ecstatic, "Yeah..."

He helped Lannya up as Carthal and Rigella came to Azli's and Heersan's assistance, respectively. Akal looked everyone over quickly and raced back to the command terminal.

"NAM2 team. Secure your ships and make your way to me at Paige. We need to get to the Habitat!"

Elcyd had fired the atmospheric stabilization pods at the Habitat locations earlier, but that only meant that the area was *survivable*. Most of the Astraeans could now simply breathe in their regular forms as they carried out their mission. The temperature, wind, dust, noise, and practically everything else about the surface of Earth, was as unforgiving as it was when Lannya had been banished so long ago.

Akal, Lannya, Azli, Carthal, Heersan and Rigella slid down the sail ladders, shot down the main stairs, and jumped out an aft hatch, before plopping their feet into the dead sand of Earth's scorched surface.

Crews from other ships quickly began accumulating around page. As they waited for more ships to land, those that had congregated so far took shelter under Paige's rounded bow. The air was thick, and unforgiving. As more Astraeans gathered, the harder it was to see where the edge of the group was.

Akal started to shout out to the group, to have the captains report to him so he could determine how many ships had landed, but his plan was interrupted. A young officer from another ship raced towards the group with his back to them. Following closely behind him was first, the sound, then the shadow, and then the hull, of a massive attack cruiser.

The young and obviously inexperienced officer turned quickly to locate Akal, and sprinted to him.

"Our captain's going to shoot out the door!" The officer shouted proudly through cupped hands. Akal recoiled with a disgusted quickness.

"With what? That cruiser? It'll bring down the whole Habitat! Get back in there and tell him he does not have permission to fire!"

The officer looked at Akal with confusion and stumbled backwards before darting back over to the cruiser.

Akal followed his order up with a command to the rest of the civilian fleet.

"Everyone, this is Akal. Do not fire on the habitats with your ships. They are more than likely still populated, and firing on them with our ships will cause massive casualties. As previously instructed, secure your ships and report to me!"

"What about Paige's fighter?" Rigella asked.

Akal shook his head.

"Maybe, but it would take too long to spin up."

Akal had an idea and roared it out to the crowd.

"Does anyone have a plunger?"

The bulk of the group looked at Akal, and each other, in confusion. There were no immediate answers. But the storm bestowed a surprise on Akal. From deep within the outer ring of the group, emerged one of the more well-known captains of a science vessel.

"Hey Akal, you mean a BHS? I'm pretty sure I do," he offered with a holler.

"Good! Go get it!" He implored.

A BHS, or black hole simulator, was made of flexible segments of machinery that could be placed in a variety of ways, and when activated, would create conditions similar to a black hole. They were also colloquially referred to as plungers, and for a reason.

The science vessel captain returned fairly quickly, along with two of his crew. Together, they were carrying the lengthy bundle of a simulator

"Let's wrap it around the door frame," Akal ordered as he ran to meet the group. He scooped up two arm-fulls of the tangled mess and led them over to the Harbor entrance.

"Why haven't we run into anyone down here," one of the science vessel crew wondered.

"Probably because they counted on the atmosphere being enough of a ground deterrent," Akal wisely surmised. "Ok," he said as they reached the door. "Activate the magnets and throw it up there!

With a few taps on the final link in the simulator string, they then started heaving sections of it up, onto, and around the Habitat entrance. It was a heavy contraption, but mainly time-consuming from having to hurl each link into place. But at last, they finished, and the simulated black hole was ready to be activated. They raced a few hundred feet back to rejoin the group under Paige.

"Most everyone that's landed is here now, Akal!" Heersan shouted.

Akal nodded at Heersan, and scanned the group quickly before turning his attention back to the Habitat door. "Alright, let's get it turned on!" Akal yelled with enthusiasm.

The science vessel captain nodded at Akal and tapped the simulator's remote activation pad. Immediately after, the group noticed a quickly-growing hum emanating from the string of fluxomagnetic modules framing the Habitat entrance. As the hum grew, the space in the center of the simulator started to darken, before quickly turning into black nothingness with no discernible depth or form.

Next, a portion of each module detached and floated away from the door to a pre-programmed distance, before sliding towards the center of the newly formed, secondary ring, creating a sideways cone, or, plunger, of sorts. In only a few seconds, the plunger, or simulated black hole, sucked away the outer Habitat entrance, into itself, into nothing. The science vessel captain deactivated the BHS and turned to Akal with a look of disbelief. He hadn't seen one in action before, and even if he had, it was an impressive sight to witness.

"Come on," Akal beckoned gently.

As they and the rest of the group under Paige's bow started off towards the entrance to the Harbor, Akal stopped soon after and took stock of the area.

Virtually every available square foot of ground that Akal could see was taken up by a ship. The remaining Astraean stragglers streamed through the narrow lanes created by them and rushed into view. The NAM2 group had grown quickly.

"Everyone gather to my voice!" Akal rallied, as he turned back and forth so as many as possible could hear him. "We need to push into the Habitat!"

He waited a few more moments to monitor the stream of Astraeans making their way towards him, but then turned and tried to jog, to return to the front of the group. He was barely able to. It was in reality, more like hobbling, shuffling and stumbling. Everyone was being deliberate with each step as they shielded their eyes and mouth from the particulate and wind. The air, while not poisonous or toxic at the moment, was still one of the more challenging environments in Astraean memory.

As Akal struggled to reach the front of the group, the crowd grew thicker and slower. Just as he was about to stop due to the proximity of those around him, he looked up and saw a windy wall of dust move by and reveal once more, the gaping hole in the wall of the Habitat. Everyone had stopped to wait for Akal. He stepped through the last edge of the group and examined the damage done by the BHS more closely.

The area of the wall inside the BHS' outline was gone. The bulk of the airlock was gone as well. There was a direct, and for the most part, unobstructed path straight into the interior of the Habitat. The Astraean raiders on the outside, inched closer and closer towards the breach in the wall, with deliberate caution, as well as with a healthy dose of confusion. Even while still outside, Akal and the others expected to see at least a few residents of the Habitat from where they were.

But, there weren't any. They saw no one. The group outside inched closer.

Akal was in the lead. He slid his feet slowly through the sand, and only a small distance at a time. He was looking, listening, smelling, and touching for anything that seemed out of place. His feet continued to shuffle and slide. The large group of Astraeans behind him followed similarly, and closely. Finally, Akal's foot slid not into more sand, but onto a piece of the Habitat wall outside of the BHS outline that had been affected, but not destroyed. It was bent out and down into the sand, almost like a welcome mat. Akal felt the metal slide up under his foot. He looked down and tapped it. After looking back at the group, then to Lannya and Rigella, he took another step. They had reached where the center of the airlock had been. There was more Habitat floor under them than sand, now. They had entered the Habitat.

Still paranoid about traps, or at the very least, still being careful and concerned about the safety of his people behind him, Akal continued to walk slowly as they inched further into the ground floor of the Habitat. There were still no residents in sight.

The sense of urgency to begin climbing up through the Habitat to the roof was palpable, but was hampered by the caution caused by the eerie silence and desolation.

Lannya leaned towards Akal.

"They are still populated, aren't they?" Lannya whispered. "It hasn't been *that* long since our last regular lives were here."

Akal's eyes whipped back and forth from one side of the Habitat to the other.

"I would think so," Akal replied softly. "We've never heard that they've been aband..."

Akal stopped. His head was bent up towards the upper levels of the Habitat.

"I saw someone up there!" He huffed through a loud breath. "Split up. One half take that staircase, and another take this one. If we run into trouble, just keep pushing forward and up to the roof."

One half of the group began to split away, with most members looking up to see if they could spot whatever it was that Akal saw. They scampered quickly across the ground floor and started up the stairs. Akal's half of the group began ascending their staircase. Still, there were no sounds, or further possible hints of occupants.

The two groups of Astraeans quickly climbed the first, second, and third floor stairs. They then started for the fourth floor, but before they took another step, a loud and violent mechanical crunch came from high above them. Immediately following, an unidentified voice shouted.

"Now!" The stranger signaled. His voice reverberated and echoed ominously throughout the Habitat's cavernous atrium.

Akal wasn't surprised, and was ready for it. He screamed over to the other half of the group.

"Here we go! Push!"

A flood of pitiful humans started to pour out onto the ground floor, armed with various ribbon weapons. They began shooting at the Astraeans from in front of the hole the BHS had created, blocking that potential exit. Another group of Habitat residents emerged from recesses and previously closed rooms on the first and second floors. The Astraeans began receiving fire from them as well.

Lannya's initial glimpses of those firing on them revealed what looked to be the expected Habitat residents. But, she was also struck with a wave of fear over a sickening possibility.

"Akal!" She screamed over the thunderous attack. "I think some of these are our people!"

Akal strained to hear her, but was able to make out what she said. He ducked and crawled to quickly get a better look for himself. He confirmed Lannya's fear. Einar was somehow using the Astraeans that he had intercepted from the ribbons against them.

"Hey!" Akal shouted across the atrium to the other half of his team. "Some of these are our people!"

He repeated his observation to his side and issued an order. "Do everything you can to avoid killing shots! Disarm or incapacitate!" He looked back quickly at the Astraeans being controlled below and was overcome with a cancerous sadness, but quickly expelled it from his soul. *The quicker we focus and get this done,* he thought, *the quicker we might be able to save them.*

Above the Astraeans, an even more dire situation confronted them. Residents of the Habitat, as well as Einarians and controlled Astraeans, aimed ribbon rifles and weapons of more exotic flavors at Akal's people and suppressed their movements even more. The fight was expected, but having their expectation realized didn't make the situation any easier.

Backtracking wasn't an option. Fleeing wasn't an option, either, if it was even possible. The suppression fire was constant, and the Einarians were ready to combat any potential form changing the Astraeans may have in store. And then, there was the issue with the atrium.

Normally, the Habitat atriums were unobstructed, straight shots directly to the top-most floor. A person could stand at the railing of any floor and see all others, but that wasn't the case now.

While the Einarian and other Habitat defenders continued firing at the Astraeans, a cover slid back, high at the top of the atrium, and revealed a thin disc. It was quickly encompassed by a pop of some form of artificial, malicious energy, the Astraeans assumed, judging from its unusual, black color, and then dropped from itself, dozens of stringy ribbon segments that extended down to the ground floor. Akal and other Astraeans assumed these were to prevent them from using that space to their advantage, and to minimize their use of legitimate ribbons.

The Astraeans had initially slid up against the walls of the atrium corridors for cover, but the longer they stayed there, the more fortified in their positions the Einarians and Habitat defenders became. Akal repeated his command, though it was only barely heard through the gunfire.

"Push!"

The Astraeans on both sides of the Habitat stripped themselves quickly off the wall and pushed single-file in their respective halves, up the stairs to the fourth floor.

They had taken advantage of their ability to still maneuver somewhat, and came bursting up onto the open fourth floor corridor. No longer did they have to move in single-file. They were in columns of three or four, in varying positions of cover and attack posture. Their tactics, efficiency, and success were all something only an ancient culture such as the Astraeans could attain, after spending eons fighting alongside each other.

Only some of the Astraeans had brought weapons with them. The others took weapons from the Habitat residents and kidnapped Astraeans as they were subdued. Akal's people continued to push up, floor after floor. Soon, the resistance was purely Einarian, and the fighting became much more challenging, and improvisational.

The Astraeans became bogged down about two-thirds of the way up the Habitat. There were very few losses, on either side of the fighting. It was another stalemate. The Astraeans, and for that matter, the Einarians, could only occasionally sneak in a quick ribbon strike between the dangling branches from the ribbon energy prohibitor in the atrium, and even then, it was only a one-off form change, or some kind of weapon or tactical tool spawn. It was never anything significant.

Heersan ran to a door entryway Akal had taken cover in, and was shooting from, to coordinate their next move.

"Akal!" He shouted, to get his attention. "We can't stay here. We have to move."

"I know!" Akal shouted back over his shoulder. "Got any ideas?"

"Yeah, I do, actually! Let me and Carthal try to do something with that thing in the atrium."

Akal took a break from shooting and fell back further into the doorway.

"We have no idea what that thing is or how dangerous it is. What were you wanting to try?"

Heersan smiled and let out a playfully hysterical chuckle.

"I don't know!" He laughed. "But we have to try something!"

Akal didn't know what to say or how to respond. Nothing was coming easily to him on how to overcome the ribbon inhibitor.

Heersan saw Akal's loss for words and turned towards Carthal.

"Come here!" He shouted to him, beckoning him over.

Carthal started to run over, skipping crazily over rifle bolts landing near his feet. Heersan leaned into his ear.

"We need to do something about that thing!" Heersan suggested to Carthal. Carthal looked at Akal with a smile, and then back to Heersan.

"Sounds good to me!" Carthal responded with a jester's grin.

"Ok," Heersan said, beginning to strategize. "I think there's a pattern to the way those branches flail around. If we can catch a window when there's an opening, we can call a ribbon and change into something that will help."

"Let's time it just right and sprint out towards the rail when the window opens up," Carthal started to suggest, "and then, you can grab a form to cover me while I take a form to shut that thing down."

"Once you've gained control of the atrium," Akal added, "we can go on a full offensive all the way to the roof."

Carthal and Heersan looked at each other and nodded at Akal.

"Ok," he said. "We'll all help with covering fire until you two have it under control."

Akal turned to Rigella, Lannya, and Azli to relay the plan and have it passed along in-between exchanging gunfire with the Einarians. Heersan leaned over to Carthal and pointed.

"I think that's the beginning of whatever cycle that thing has. Look."

The disc's branches swung and flailed independently but never struck each other which might suggest a pre-programmed pattern, Heersan considered.

They also seemed to spin and twist with a consistent speed. As the branches turned and whipped, one could rarely see any of the actual Habitat roof through the disc that the branches dangled from. Only when each branch seemed to complete a rolled and whipped helix, from its top to its bottom, did the disc wobble slightly, and reveal a path to the roof, and view of the sky. The wobble appeared to be caused by a fresh pulse of energy to restart the cycle of spinning branches. There were approximately seven seconds between cycles.

"Yeah, I see it, I see it," Carthal said excitedly, having their plan validated. Heersan considered which form to assume first while Carthal counted to confirm the length of each cycle.

"If you want to catch the first window and grab a skin that can cover me," Carthal proposed, "I'll follow right behind you, dive over the rail and use a Genspo skin."

Heersan's eyes shot wide open.

"What? Yeah," Carthal replied confidently. "I'll transform just before I hit and eat this thing up."

"Yeah, but what if your timing is off?" Heersan shouted over the nearby fire-fight.

"You'll just have to get used to another face I guess!"

Heersan shook his head with loving disapproval.

"Seven seconds between windows," Heersan scolded quickly. "Don't splat before then!"

Carthal could only wink and chuckle.

"Ok, Akal!" Heersan started. Akal ran over.

"There looks to be seven seconds between this thing's cycles. I'm going to run out, call a ribbon, change into something to give us all some cover. Carthal will then catch the next window and change into a Genspo and destroy that disc and its branches. After that, like you said, it's on to the roof."

"Alright, we're ready!" Akal shouted.

Heersan leaned into Carthal and stole a forehead kiss.

"See you in a bit" Carthal shouted.

Heersan pointed at him.

"You better!"

Heersan turned back to face the atrium and looked up.

"I'm going to wait a few cycles to confirm the timing again," he shouted over his shoulder, "and then I'll go."

Most of the group took turns exchanging fire with the Einarians while being pinned. The stalemate had gotten old. Heersan, Carthal and Akal waited.

One cycle went by, and another. The seven second timing seemed to hold. Heersan bent at his knees slightly and shot off.

Almost immediately, he had attracted a large increase in fire from the Einarians, but Akal and the others helped offset that some. The Einarians couldn't sustain their attention on Heersan for long. As soon as Heersan was in an adequate position in relation to the gap in the disc, Heersan attempted to summon a ribbon. A millisecond of fear and doubt shot through Akal's and Carthal's veins, but it wasn't justified.

A ribbon shot down through the skylights in the roof, through the opening at the edge of the disc, and swallowed Heersan up. The ribbon wasn't artificial, fabricated, malicious, or otherwise manipulated by Einar. It was a healthy and legitimate ribbon. Heersan had done it.

The ribbon quickly receded and revealed Heersan's new form. He had transformed into one of his past Lizeer lives. Almost as soon as his ribbon receded, his Lizeer body went on the offensive.

Lizeers were tall creatures, about the height of a Habitat floor, sometimes taller. Heersan's form was just shy of touching the ceiling of the floor he was on. His tall body was made up of numerous small chambers, each with numerous types of energy that could be rotated inside the chamber, and selected. The bulk of the chambers that a Lizeer was made of were completely internal in that they were the main source of Lizeer life. They could not be altered or used for any other purpose but to metabolize energy and sustain the Lizeer. Their energies were refilled by absorbing energy in a variety of forms, from the numerous locations they traveled to and from. There were however, chambers of this energy that a Lizeer could do with as they wished.

The Lizeer's main body was a lanky trunk, similar to that of an Oreis, but it was wider and metallic. The numerous energy chamber appendages of a Lizeer spun and circled around their body, to serve as a form of circulation. Aside from the main Lizeer trunk and their primary, life-supporting chambers, they had some hundred that circulated around them, eligible for a variety of uses.

Heersan went to work. His hundred or so available energy chambers went into full attack mode. As they spun and twisted around his body, they unleashed large, lethal spreads of constantly changing energy in all directions. He was essentially a sphere, made up entirely of rifle barrels, firing suffocating flurries of energy bolts of too many kinds for the Einarians to adapt to. Before Carthal had even done his part, some Einarians had already begun to fall back.

But, the time *did* come for Carthal to do his part. Once he saw that Heersan's ribbon had worked and that he was easily holding his own, he counted the cycle once more, just to be safe, and then sprinted for the rail.

His path to the rail was clear, and except for one or two bolts he had to zig-zag around and hop over, he approached it without issue. He dug into an all-out sprint, and after looking at Heersan to confirm he was still ok, Carthal smiled, vaulted, and jumped over the rail.

Seven seconds.

The married Astraeans each kept the count in their heads. One of the pair was desperate to help his mate, and the other was desperate to keep his mate covered long enough. The result of an Astraean death at this point was a complete mystery. Never before was death such a negative thought for an Astraean or imminent possibility. Whether or not one life died, all lives died, or if they got ushered away to some limbo of an Einarian hell, and with Mamdod gone, the fact of death had been grotesquely mutated from a calm doorway to a soul's plethora of options, to an unknown. A very mortal unknown. While death was ambiguous, and while no Astraean knew what Einar could or couldn't do with souls, no one wanted to risk a death, and Heersan most assuredly didn't want to lose his Carthal.

Four seconds.

Heersan's Lizeer body was formidable and relentless. The vast majority of the Einarians firing down from the high floors were forced to back away from the rails and regroup. Many were killed. And though the ultimate fate of a killed Einarian was also unknown to the Astraeans, Akal and the others didn't care. They had to get to the roof.

Heersan and Carthal continued to count down. It went by fast, but each second was packed with a lifetime of anxiety. Three. Two. One.

Carthal's soul pleaded for a beacon. Zero.

No ribbon.

Carthal continued screaming internally for a ribbon. His face was stone cold, bleached in white fear from the rapidly approaching floor where Akal's last regular life had met its end.

But, instead of slamming into the floor and into a lifeless puddle, Carthal had accounted for the distance he had to travel after jumping and given himself an extra few seconds. His count was off just slightly from when the disc's cycle restarted. Down shot his ribbon.

Heersan continued to overwhelm the Einarians, as well as the remaining Habitat defenders that hadn't retreated. He saw the flash of what he felt confident was Carthal's ribbon out of the corner of his eye, but that's as much as he could tell right now about whether or not Carthal had made it. He needed to see him, or at least Carthal's Genspo form. He was about to.

Carthal's ribbon struck, and immediately

transformed him into his Genspo form. Form wasn't an entirely accurate way to describe the Genspos, however. The Genspo form Carthal had assumed more closely resembled that of a large lake of goo, but a very unique type of goo. Genspos were entirely parasitic. They were intelligent parasites. They lived by consuming energy, and anything emitted that may be harmful, from whatever the Genspo was feeding on, was absorbed by the Genspo and dispersed throughout its large mass. As the Genspo fed, it would quickly grow in size for a time as it ate, making Genspos extremely dangerous and difficult to destroy. *Here we go*, Carthal laughed to himself. *The Astraeans have a Genspo on their side.*

A few seconds after Carthal's countdown had finished, his huge Genspo mass had already landed, or splashed onto the floor and had begun moving towards the center. Carthal strained his newly formed Genspo mass to reach the lowest hanging branch from the atrium disc, and latched onto it with a bit of room to spare. After that, the disc branches never stood a chance.

The Genspo climbed and grabbed, swallowed and extended to the other branches. One by one, foot by foot, Carthal climbed up the branches and consumed them and absorbed their energy. Though these branches were made of artificial and malicious energy, Carthal was unaffected as Genspos only metabolized raw energy. The malicious spiritual encoding Einar had placed inside his artificial ribbon system was of no consequence to Carthal.

Higher and higher Carthal climbed up the atrium. Finally, he reached the level Heersan, Akal and the others were. His friends and husband screamed and barked with approval. Heersan's Lizeer body stopped firing just before summoning a ribbon to return to his normal human form. He then ran over to the rail and looked up admiringly at his husband's sickening Genspo form and smiled from ear to ear. Between Heersan's inexorable assault and Carthal's consumption of the branches, and soon, the disc, the Einarians had no choice but to fall back, or up, towards the roof. The Astraeans were now free to move and advance as they wished. Most importantly, they also had the ribbons at their disposal for the first time since the fight had begun.

"Ok, everyone!" Akal shouted. "Let's go!"

Heersan looked back to Akal as he was shouting his orders, but stayed by the rail and waited for Carthal. Looking up, Heersan saw Carthal's messy mass wash over the last bit of the atrium disc. As the disc and branches were consumed, Carthal ran out of anything to grasp onto. Once he had destroyed the disc and final bits of the branches, he flung his Genspo form out to the nearest corridor railing and attached to it. He started to slide down it, and summoned another ribbon and returned to being Carthal. Heersan grabbed onto him tightly as if he hadn't seen him in a lifetime.

When Heersan let go of him, Carthal met him with a disgusted and bent face.

"What is it?" Heersan blurted with quick concern.

Carthal fluffed out his cheeks and exhaled.

"Whew, I think I ate something..."

Heersan didn't even finish rolling his eyes before grabbing him and pulling him back towards the rest of the group.

Chapter XXVIII

Bonds

The Astraeans were finally able to move. They pushed forward and up, and found a fresh dose of motivation and will in their successful strategy. It wasn't over yet, but the fight was not as one-sided as they had anticipated.

They raced up the remaining stairs and floors, pausing only to repel isolated resistance from small groups of Einarians that hadn't made it to the roof. There were sporadic flashes of ribbons, being summoned by Astraeans and Einarians alike, but the Astraeans had the advantage. They were more coordinated, responded with superior firepower, and anticipated the form changes by the Einarians. With their suppression fire being eliminated, and without their ribbon containment disc in the atrium, the Einarians were being pushed to the roof easily and quickly. But the Astraeans knew better than to dismiss the Einarians so carelessly. They were well aware that the Einarians were simply delaying and stalling as much as they could. The Astraeans weren't having any of it. They moved up through the floors as rapidly as possible, regardless of how dirty or messy the fighting had to be.

When they reached the top floor, Akal waited for his half of the group to tighten back up before stepping to the rail. Whatever Einarian element was left had retreated through the old but familiar door with a sign on it that read, "Off-limits to residents." Akal took advantage of the pause in fighting and whistled over to the other half of the Astraean group who had reached the top from their side of the Habitat.

"Hey! Everyone ok over there?" He shouted quickly. He watched as their half tightened up as well. A few at the front of their group shot out a thumbs-up at him.

"Ok! See you up there!"

Akal retreated from the rail and headed for the door and waved for his group to meet up and follow him. He slung it open and led his group up the dozen steps to the roof.

Both halves of the Astraean group launched out onto the roof from their respective sides of the Habitat, and blanketed the ground quickly as they joined back up with each other. As the two groups reassembled, each Astraean could just make out the retreating Einarians and their ships through the blinding light coming from Einar's NAM2 ribbon relay.

The Astraeans hadn't quite known what to expect as they ascended the Habitat towards the roof. And now that they saw it, they still couldn't quite believe it. The base of the relay took up almost the entire expanse of the roof.

The majority of the weight of the relay was distributed towards the outside of the base and was packed with panels of controls, circuits, lights, buttons, and switches. There were occasional doors, as well, that led to the interior of the base. None of it appeared haphazardly assembled, nor was anything cluttered. It was a gargantuan and beautiful display of technology. It was a technology that seemed to have been well thought out, over the course of perhaps, eons.

Sitting atop the enormous base was a simply, yet firmly supported ring. The ring was approximately twenty feet thick and a few thousand feet wide. Pulsing through the center of the ring, was a horrifyingly dark stream of Einar's fabricated ribbon energy. It approached from far out at one angle on the horizon, passed through the ring, and then disappeared at another angle on the horizon, on to the next relay. Frequently, small lightning strikes would pop at various points in the stream, corresponding with when the artificial ribbon would intercept and change something in a natural ribbon.

"Thyra?" Akal shouted into a communications module. "We've located the NAM2 relay. We'll notify you once it's been destroyed.

"Understood. We've got our hands full up here, but some of the Einarians are starting to pull back. Keep us updated."

"Will do."

Akal closed the channel and waved the group over closer to him. The ambient sound from the relay and artificial ribbon was practically deafening, not to mention, almost blinding.

"Ok, let's do a *very* quick analysis of this thing and come up with a way to destroy it as quickly as possible, or at least deactivate it, safely, if possible. Spread out around the base and see what you find."

The group began to disperse immediately, but stopped when they were distracted by a different voice behind them. One Einarian hadn't departed just yet.

"Akal!" Einar greeted with a sadistic pleasure.

Akal and the other Astraeans turned around slowly, to meet him. Akal opened his hand with his palm facing his friends behind him, ordering them silently to hold.

"Before anything else is done or said," Einar continued glibly, "I just want to make sure we all understand that no matter what any of you do to my relay, or me, for that matter, that nothing will change the fact that I'm minutes away from taking over the ribbon island. Your crusade has failed."

"We don't really care about that, Daebaugh, or, Einar, or whatever you go by," Akal replied calmly. "At least when we destroy this thing, you won't be able to alter the ribbons like you have been."

Einar let the weight of his arms fall to his side as he clinched his fists. His face became warped with ferocious hate.

"I'll just build another one!"

Akal stared blankly at his angry adversary, but found a smile to offer him.

"Well, it will probably take you a while, right? And maybe by then, we or someone else may have figured out a way to end you."

Einar laughed at what he thought of as the pitiful Astraean mindset.

"Who cares if you destroy it?" He dismissively offered through hearty guffaws. "It will just be a setback. A delay. The point is that you only have minutes before I own the island, and the ribbons. It may take a bit of extra time, but I'll eventually own your souls, too."

"That's fine," Akal answered. "We'll gladly take that extra time."

Akal slung a shout over his shoulder.

"Go!" He shouted at his friends.

The Astraeans sprinted around the relay's base to determine how to destroy it as Akal summoned a ribbon. From high in the sky, out in Earth's local space, the ribbon stream shot down an extension and struck him. He shouted at Einar as he waited to choose a new form to fight Einar with.

"What have you got to lose?" Akal challenged.

Einar smiled. He just didn't need to fight. He summoned his own ribbon and was gone.

Akal turned around quickly to see who was still nearby. Rigella and Lannya had remained to see what happened and were closest.

"Stay here and get that relay down! Once you do, make sure the others know how to get theirs down. I'm going after him!"

"Akal!" Lannya shouted in vain.

"Make sure these are destroyed!" He repeated lovingly. The obvious urgency was understood by both Rigella and Lannya.

He maintained his eye contact with Lannya. They

made no gestures, and shared no words, but they knew they loved each other. Akal, still surrounded by the ribbon he had called to threaten Einar with, rocketed away in pursuit.

Akal had lost track of Einar. The few seconds it took for Akal to launch up after him was plenty of a head start, but Akal wasn't worried. He knew where to go. Whether he was headed there immediately or at a later time, Einar would eventually make it to the ribbon island. That's where Akal would meet him, or wait for him.

Akal's spirit ripped through the ribbons. In just seconds, Earth seemed as far behind him as his blissful and ignorant single human life before becoming an Astraean. Before discovering the Harbor. Before learning of his daughter. Before traveling the multiverse with his friends and fighting through millions of lifetimes in an effort to help others. Before now. Before the end.

His mind and soul went limp in the bittersweet beauty of the ribbons. They comforted him and protected him. Their timeless energies nestled him within their streams and assured him everything would be ok, that he would be safe, and that no harm would come to him. But, just as the most well-meaning parent, such promises could never be guaranteed. That awareness stuck in the shadow of Akal's mind, and he didn't ignore it. He embraced it and mentally welcomed it.

Peace and safety were of no concern to him anymore. They had nothing to do with what needed to be done. His future as an Astraean was of no consequence. Being able to enjoy his wife, daughter and friends, wasn't even in top ten of his priorities at that moment. The natural progression of the countless worlds across the multiverse didn't matter. The Harbor, Paige, and a wealth of other things, were all pointless. That is, if Einar won.

If Einar won, everyone would be subject to his rule, his will, and his contortion of the ribbons. No longer would the Astraeans or multiverse's residents enjoy free will within the context of a naturally occurring, and morally ignorant existence. They instead would be pawns, slaves, and drones under the malevolent thumb of an anarchistic, and egomaniacal immortal. The Astraeans knew that Einar rationalized his motives and actions by wanting to free the multiverse from the Astraeans, but that was too ambiguous, too vague, and most of the multiverse now knew the truth. Einar didn't want to live in a multiverse where he could be held accountable for anything, by anyone.

With his priorities straight, his soul calm, and his mind sharp, Akal closed his thoughts to everything else but the ribbon path ahead of him. True and straight Akal glided, until at last, he landed on the ribbon island.

It was his first trip back to the island since Mamdod died. He initially felt a rush of affectionate nostalgia, but his heart soon dropped. The globs of backed up soul traffic on various ribbons, waiting to be received onto the island after Mamdod's death, made Akal angry. He couldn't stand the thought of Einar being the one that would soon guide, or use, their future. The superfluous darkness he had just expelled from his thoughts and soul tried to beat their way back in.

The grass on the island had thinned slightly. The tree looked old, rotten, and diseased. All but three dead leaves had fallen from it. Akal had never seen the tree in such a state. And out by the old stone bench with his back to him, was Einar.

Akal stepped slowly, but solidly, closer to Einar. He stopped soon after however, and summoned a ribbon. As soon as it struck him, he directed a wide wake of energy at Einar. He had to fight him. He had to do something.

Einar spun around and beckoned his own ribbon to deflect Akal's initial blitz. He was in no mood to entertain Akal.

"If you leave, right now," Einar began through disgusted contempt, "I'll allow your people to exist."

A leaf blew off the tree. There were two left.

"For a little while, anyway," Einar added.

"Do you remember when Mamdod explained his game to us?" Akal asked, unimpressed with Einar's cocky proposition.

Einar plopped down on the bench and looked up at the remaining leaves. He could not care less about Akal's presence.

"How did you channel your bond to the rules into that leaf, or whatever it was you did? I'm honestly curious."

The next to last leaf popped off the tree.

Einar pointed up to the last leaf and smiled. He then offered an answer with little concern for actually considering the reason.

"I guess I just have a special bond with the ribbons,' he said with a shrug.

Down came the last leaf.

Einar shot up off the bench. His head cranked up at the naked tree as his body stretched as tall is it could before beginning to jump up and down. He was excited. His demented face widened as he danced in circles, wider and wider, he spun. He had spent something more than his whole life, his whole awareness, and something outside of time preparing for this. He was about to become the master of the ribbons, the master of the island, the master of existence.

Each ribbon started to raise up, out from its path through the island and then pierced through Einar. One by one, and faster than the quickest ribbon speed, thousands by thousands they struck him. Within a few seconds, Einar was overtaken by an enormous ball of energy, created by the ribbons intersecting at his one point. The ribbons were registering their new, selfish guardian. His selfish act which had begun so many ages ago was paying off.

Akal stood by, helpless, hopeless and watched the multiverse's nightmare crawl into reality. He breathed faster and more erratically as the sickening sight before him slapped his soul and stabbed his heart. He had failed. His people had failed. After all the platitudes, efforts, fights and speeches, they had lost. His body radiated with waves of cold fear in the realization that he had been wrong. Akal knew they would overcome Einar somehow. But, no. Everything that was anything, time, space, life, death, and all that was in between, allowed Einar to win.

To win...

Einar wanted to cheat, and to win, and to steal the stewardship of the ribbons. He was selfish, and wanted to continue being selfish.

With almost no warning, Akal's soul and thoughts resurrected his hope. He had an idea.

He took off in a sprint and headed straight for Einar. Within seconds, he dived at the humongous ball of ribbon energy encircling Einar and rolled into the landing. He jumped to his feet and spoke to Einar.

"I've got a special bond with the ribbons, too."

Einar looked at Akal, having absolutely no clue what he was talking about, and he didn't care. He smiled at Akal with disdain as the ribbons began to lower back into their usual spot after completing their guardian reassignment.

But suddenly, being encompassed in the ball of ribbon energy as well, Akal quickly cycled through a few hundred of his past lives, and paused on one. He had somehow condensed the energy attributed to that group of lives into a single point within himself. In a violent strike of power, the energy from those lives lashed out and destroyed one of the links between a ribbon and the island, and in turn, Einar's connection to it. After unleashing the first pulse of energy, he returned to his form as Akal. The destiny and fate associated with the location attributed to that ribbon was no longer at the mercy of the island, or its steward, whoever it was.

Akal whipped his head in the direction of the broken ribbon link, after having startled himself with the success of his idea. He slowly looked back to Einar, and smiled.

He did it again. Akal cycled through another batch of previous lives and harnessed the energy associated with them. After launching the next batch out from him, the wealth of energy destroyed another link between the ribbons and the island.

He cycled through more and more lives. Countless other ribbon links with the island were destroyed. Faster and faster Akal severed Einar's selfish grasp on the multiverse, by being selfless. In sacrificing his past lives and their energy, he was removing the need for the island, for a ribbon guardian, for Einar. The fate and destiny of each universe, planet, race, culture and their associated ribbon, would forever be uninterrupted, and seamless, free to set their own course.

Einar flew into a rage, bucking and flailing all over the island. He screamed and wailed in countless languages while desperately scratching for ideas on how to stop Akal. He changed forms hundreds of times. He switched to creatures and beasts of various sizes and capabilities. No effort, attack, or ribbon energy variation could help Einar stop, interrupt, or prevent Akal from what he was doing.

Faster and faster the connections fell. Akal was fully focused and in tune with his sacrifice. As his millions of previous lives dwindled, so too did the ribbon-island intersections. Though the whole of his soul's energy was being slowly expended, he had never felt more complete. He closed his eyes. He had never felt such a presence of purpose.

Einar finally gave up on trying to stop Akal. He had exhausted himself, his mind, and spirit. After a while, he just walked up as close as he could to Akal and stared at him with a childish frown and pitiful slouch. Einar had wasted all that he had ever known, and all that he ever would be.

Akal opened his eyes as his last few thousand lives compressed and shot out to take care of the last remaining connections between the ribbons and the island. He saw Einar, but didn't consider him or regard him. He smiled at him, but through him. He had found joy, and claimed it, rightfully, and deservedly.

The last batch of energy, from his last cluster of past lives, struck the final blow to the final ribbon that passed through the island. With the destruction of the ribbon's connections to the island, Einar, having become one with the ribbons as its newest guardian, was also obliterated. All that remained was Akal's last, single form, the island, the bench, and a newly verdant tree.

There was technically still one ribbon that remained, but it was the only one that didn't pass through the island. Still connected, the ribbon that had no origination and an unknown destination, was the final ribbon. As the almost completely solitary island drifted off into space, Akal watched the newly freed web of uninterrupted ribbons grow fainter and fainter into the distance. Among them, sped bulbs of ribbon energy, flashing crisply and flowing freely throughout the web as souls came and went along their way.

There was nowhere for Akal to go, and no means for him to do so. His only option was to take the final ribbon. His chest bounced with a silent chuckle as he hoped the relays had been destroyed so that his trip on the final ribbon wouldn't be intercepted this time. His faith and confidence in his wife, daughter, close friends, and fellow Astraeans, gave him no doubt that he would have safe passage.

But he wasn't in a hurry. He didn't need to be. He walked delicately over to the stone bench and took a seat under the thick but warm shadow of the ancient tree. He kicked off his shoes and swung one foot back and forth just over the tops of the grass.

He looked up as his foot played, and peered out into the dark dawn. His delight in the unknown had returned. Enigmatic mysteries and ambiguous outcomes were once more exciting things to ponder over. The final ribbon looked as beautiful to him in that moment as any other ribbon that he had ever had the fortune of traveling on.

He stood up and put his full weight on his foot, before picking it back up and tickling the grass a few more times. He wondered if Lannya, or Rigella or anyone else would be coming by soon to check on what had happened, and he had trouble deciding if he wanted to wait for them or not. It wasn't a question of wanting to see them, but for him, it was a matter of simply doing what came next, what was inevitable. He had no doubt what came next, because Einar was gone. His wife and daughter were together. He didn't question if there was anything else to do, because those two things were all that he needed to ensure.

He began to walk over to the final ribbon, dragging his feet softly, to get as much grass caught between his toes as possible. He unashamedly walked fairly slowly, in a bit of indulgent procrastination. But the procrastination wasn't from fear or hesitance. He just wanted to play in the grass a little longer.

But, the distance to the edge of the island just in front of the final ribbon was eventually reached. Akal stopped and looked around a final time for any signs of incoming ships. He didn't see anything, and he was perfectly fine with that. He turned back to the final ribbon with a content smirk, and hopped in.

Epilogue

Had Akal waited just a few seconds longer, he would've been faced with the agonizing process of saying goodbye. And, those he loved would have faced that same agony. Paige, the rest of the civilian fleet, and the ADF flew into the area surrounding the ribbon island just after the flash of Akal's departure into the final ribbon, and the final ribbon, as it existed up until then, had dissipated. They had defeated, or sent fleeing, the remaining Einarian forces, and destroyed Einar's entire ribbon relay system. Some Astraeans remained behind on Earth to begin attempts to restore the kidnapped Astraeans' souls and memories now that the relay system had been destroyed. The view before everyone else after racing to support their husband, father, friend, and fellow Astraean, was one they did not expect to see.

No Einar. No Akal. And after Akal had stepped into it, no final ribbon. Its link with the island disappeared with Akal. All that was left was a simple chunk of land, floating in space, with a bench and lavishly leaved tree about it.

The ribbons intersected with themselves and floated brilliantly nearby, no longer attached to the island.

There would never again be a gate on the ribbons or a master of them, as Einar had tried to become. And though Mamdod had been a tremendous guide with nothing but the best of intentions for those that passed through, the need for guidance had come and gone. It wasn't that Mamdod was no longer needed, but that he had helped accomplish what needed to be done. Akal, Mamdod and the Astraeans, had stopped Einar, or anyone else, from ever again corrupting the multiverse's natural flow.

Each soul would now be free to experience life and death, and all things in between, without interference or influence. They would come and go about the ribbons freely, having no need to pass through the island anymore, with only the secrets of life steering their destiny. And, should the day come when their soul had spent its lives, whether in a flurry of selflessness or a torment of selfishness, the final ribbon would await them, in whatever new form it may take, and the unknowns surrounding their ultimate fate would be revealed. Whether or not those unknowns would be feared, was the ultimate choice, and the ultimate power that all were now free to wield.

Paige's crew bunched up along the top deck rail facing the intersecting ribbon web and the separate, empty island. Bursts of hectic communications from all over the ADF and civilian fleets crammed themselves harshly through Paige's speakers. The confusion across all ships on exactly what had happened was rampant, but the picture was quickly becoming clear to Lannya and the others aboard Paige. Heersan reached over quickly to a terminal and muted the speakers.

Carthal collapsed onto a bench and held his head, heartbroken over truly losing his friend, while Heersan consoled him as best he could through his own pain. Rigella, not wanting to believe the unspoken truth, scanned the sea of space, over and over, looking for any sign of Akal. She slid back and forth along the rail to examine various areas of space, not wanting to let go of the rail, or her hope.

Lannya cried freely. She felt a pain familiar to what she had felt when the Harbor was first attacked, and when she thought she had lost Akal to Azli's weapon. But as she turned her head to look at her daughter, with tears of her own falling onto Paige's rail, Lannya's pain took on an entirely different meaning.

This wasn't a pain of darkness created by evil and hate stealing something from Lannya. It was a pain of love and need. It was a pain born in the realization that Akal valued nothing more than the opportunity for her to have a relationship with their daughter. It was a pain caused for all the right reasons, and by Akal's sacrifice. It was created by Lannya's immediate need to see, hold and touch her husband, and not being able to. In a very worthy consolation, Lannya reached out and grabbed their daughter, squeezing her with the strength of two parents, and kissed an eternity of love onto her cheek.

Thank you for buying *Fates of Astraeus*! I truly do hope you were able to find something to enjoy.